Praise for
Bitter Water Blues

"There ain't much quaint and cuddly about Patrick Shawn Bagley's Maine, where the only folks more dangerous than the thugs and gangsters From Away are the locals. Bagley sandblasts the chipped veneer of small-town charm to expose the rot beneath. *Bitter Water Blues* is a vivid, unflinching portrait of desperate people struggling at the margins of society to survive."

—Chris F. Holm, author of
Red Right Hand

"Bagley's debut novel is pitch perfect crime fiction, as dark and raw as it gets with a rich tapestry of intersecting characters who bring a beleaguered blue collar New England community to life with the style and powerful punch of a seasoned veteran...a story of redemption and revenge, second chances gone awry, double-crosses and finding loyalty where it counts, even if a little too late...a refreshingly masterful new voice in noir, and highly recommended."

—Ed Kurtz, author of
Nothing You Can Do

"A glorious boilermaker of noir and East Coast gothic. The action is as taut as a sprung snare and Bagley tightens the screws with every page."

—Laird Barron, author of
Blood Standard

BITTER WATER BLUES

PATRICK SHAWN BAGLEY

BITTER WATER BLUES

Down & Out Books
3959 Van Dyke Rd, Ste. 265
Lutz, FL 33558
www.DownAndOutBooks.com

Cover design by Eric Beetner

ISBN: 1-946502-68-5
ISBN-13: 978-1-946502-68-1

For Tonia, Rowan, and Sarah.
They know why.

Author's Note

Although there is an actual Wesserunsett Lake in central Maine, the lake and town of that name depicted in this novel are imaginary. Likewise, my use of surnames common to the region is not intended to reflect upon any real persons living or dead. Honest.

PROLOGUE
JULY 20, 2005

Deke's Music was in a half-vacant strip mall down on the ass end of Staten Island, not far from Wolfe's Pond Park. It was five minutes to nine, almost closing time. The lights in the parking lot came on as darkness slid across the sky.

Joey Connolly sat in his car, a white Crown Vic, listening to a mix CD he'd burned that morning. Carey Bell played "Low-Down Dirty Shame." Some serious harp blowing on that track. Joey kept the volume low. He watched the music shop, tapped the steering wheel, whistling along with Bell's harmonica licks.

Deke's last customer had left twenty minutes earlier, carrying a little bag that couldn't have held more than a set of strings, maybe a few picks. In the two hours Joey had been sitting there, only three people had gone into the store. Only the one with the small bag bought anything.

When the song ended, Joey switched off the ignition and got out, checking that his shirttail covered the piece holstered at the small of his back. He didn't wear suits; with his crooked nose, wide shoulders, big hands and broad Irish face, a nice suit just screamed *Hey, I'm a thug trying to look respectable.* Unless he had to go in to the office or meet Mr. Petucci someplace, Joey dressed in jeans, T-shirts and work boots. A fitted Yankees cap covered his short blond hair. If you're going to whack guys for a living, you might as well dress comfortably.

He walked inside and locked the door behind him, turning the lock between the knuckles of his index and middle fingers. The metallic click was covered up by Sonny Boy Williamson wailing on "One Way Out" from the wall-mounted speakers. Joey grinned. He had expected to hear some hard rock or the lame shit that passed for it these days. At least this Deke guy had good taste.

Steve "Deke" Deacon stood behind a glass counter going over the day's receipts.

"I'm closing," Deke said without even looking up. He was in his late forties, with long gray hair pulled back into a ponytail. A faded Humble Pie T-shirt hung off his scrawny frame. "Was there something special you wanted?"

The store was like the music shops Joey had haunted as a teenager, back when he believed he could be the next Eddie Van Halen: a small space, the floor so crowded with drums, amps, PA speakers, mixing boards, keyboards, guitars, basses, mike stands, stools, racks of sheet music and self-instruction books that there was barely enough room for a path from the door to the register. The walls held more guitars, suspended by their headstocks, and an array of straps, cables, strings.

Deke still didn't look up, probably figuring his customer would just take the hint and leave.

Joey was pulling a pair of latex gloves out of his jeans pocket when he spotted the sign above the counter: NO SMOKE ON THE WATER. THIS MEANS YOU.

Funny guy.

Joey shoved the gloves back into his pocket. He took a sunburst Telecaster from the wall and plugged it into a Marshall stack. He cranked up the volume and reverb, played the main riff to "Smoke on the Water." *Nah nah nah, nah nah nah-nah, nah nah nah, nah-nah.* It had been years since Joey last held a guitar. He remembered the right power chords, but his fingers were clumsy. The frets buzzed. Without a pick, the fingers of his right hand flailed the strings. Not that it mattered. Most of the clowns who came in here to dick around with the axes probably butchered it, too. That was why Deke had the sign. Joey crunched through the riff again, sounding shitty without even trying. *Nah nah nah, nah nah nah-nah, nah nah nah, nah-nah.*

Deke came out from behind the counter, waving his hands and pointing at the sign. He yelled something Joey couldn't hear over his own racket. When Deke reached to shut off the amp, Joey flipped the guitar around, grabbed it by its neck just above the headstock and swung it like a baseball bat. He hit Deke hard, right across the upper arm. The Telecaster shuddered but held. Deke screamed, dropped to his knees clutching the injured arm.

Joey said, "Pete Townshend wasn't lying when he said Fenders are hard to break." He returned the guitar to its place on the wall and put on the latex gloves.

"You broke my fuckin' arm," Deke said. Red-faced, with tears glimmering in the corners of his eyes, he looked up at his attacker.

Joey grabbed Deke by the ponytail, dragged him screaming to the back room. He kicked Deke's feet out from under him. Opened the breaker box and flipped three and four switches at a time until he had killed all the lights at the front of the store. Deke rolled on the floor, groaning. The stereo kept playing. "One Way Out" ended, replaced by Albert Collins doing "I Ain't Drunk."

Joey listened for a moment, looked down at Deke and said, "You got thirty-three large for me?"

"What the fuck're you talking about, man? I don't know you."

Joey squatted next to him. He jabbed his finger against the broken arm. "I'm not big on introducing myself. Only reason I asked about the money is, I was told to. You were loaned money in good faith, and you haven't paid it back."

"That's what you want? Jesus. Did Ferrari send you?"

"Ferrarro. Not Ferrari. And no, he didn't send me. I don't work for Teddy Ferrarro. When Teddy's dipshits came to collect and you flashed that .45 you keep under the counter? That was stupid. Teddy had to tell his boss, who happens to be my boss, that you were causing problems. You see where I'm going here?"

Deke tried to sit up. "I should've pulled the gun on you, you son of a bitch."

Joey rolled his eyes. "Now, I'm asking you one last time: Do you have that money for me?"

Deke shook his head, biting his lip against the pain in his arm.

"That's what I figured." Joey stood, pulling his .22 Ruger and thumbing off the safety.

Deke held up his good hand. "Wait. Jesus, man. I can get you some of it."

"How much?"

"I don't know. Maybe five grand tomorrow and five more next week."

Joey pointed the automatic at Deke's forehead. "Not good enough."

"C'mon, man. We can work something out, some kind of payment plan, right?"

"I'm not one of those consumer credit counselors, Deke. I don't get paid to negotiate. If you handed me half the money right now, that would be something. I'd be authorized to give you a couple more weeks, but the vig would keep piling on."

"Where am I supposed to come up with that kind of money?"

"Not my problem. You knew the rules when you took the money. That's what I don't get. You own this place, get to be your own boss and be surrounded by music for a living. If I had a gig like this, I'd be happy with it. What kind of moron fucks all that up by going to a shylock?"

"You don't understand. I was…"

Joey cuffed Deke upside the head. "Rhetorical question."

"So what makes you better than me, huh? All I did was borrow money. You? You fucking kill people."

Joey stood up. He held the pistol loosely at his side. "Not better. Smarter."

"Please, man. I'm begging here. You don't have to do this."

"I know," Joey said. "That's why I'm quitting."

"What?"

"Quitting. I'm sick of this whole fucking business. The goombahs I work for are on their way out. They won't admit it, but that's because they're like you: too dumb to face facts. The real players now are Ukrainians, Russians, Vietnamese. Crazy fucks. So I'm walking away."

Deke wiped his eyes, sat up a little. "Yeah?"

"Soon as I'm finished here." Joey grabbed Deke by the shirt, hauled him into a kneeling position.

"What? Wait. Jesus Christ, man, you said you quit."

Joey shook his head. "If I don't do you, somebody else will."

Stepping around Deke, Joey aimed the pistol at a spot just behind the guy's left ear. Squeezed the trigger. There was a small pop. The spent casing *tinked* against the cinderblock wall before hitting the floor. Deke's whole body shuddered, then sagged. Joey kicked the corpse onto its belly and parked another round right next to the first hole.

Joey liked revolvers, especially the .38. John Florio had once told him that using the same kind of gun again and again was like signing a confession because it helped the cops establish an MO, but Joey placed too much value on the dependability of his favorite revolvers to jump around. He only used the Ruger this time because the boss insisted.

A pair of .22 slugs in the back of the head meant a mob hit, and Mr. Petucci wanted a clear message sent to anyone else who might get ideas about trying to play hardball when a shylock came to collect. The automatic was the only .22 that Joey's gun source had on hand. Joey had to admit the damn thing did make for a nice, tidy kill. The slugs would bounce around inside Deke's skull until they used up their kinetic energy, pureeing his brains in the meantime. Deke was just as dead as if Joey had shot him with a bigger, flashier pistol like all the TV tough guys used.

Joey policed his brass, sliding the empty casings into the pocket of his jeans and taking care not to step in the pool of blood spreading outward from Deke's head. He took a penlight from the other pocket and made his way through the darkened store. With a handkerchief, he wiped down the Telecaster he'd held, as well as the Marshall's knobs. Got the lock on the front door, too, in case he'd left a partial print there.

Shining the light around to make sure everything looked cool, he spotted half a dozen Lee Oskar harmonicas in a plastic display case on top of the counter. He'd always wanted to play harmonica. There was never enough time to learn and the wise-guys would've given him a ration of shit about it. Bad enough they still called him Joey Kotex after so many years.

Well, fuck those assholes.

Joey slid open the case and grabbed a harp, turned it over in his hands. The harmonicas were all in different keys and he didn't know which ones would be best for a beginner. Joey grabbed C major, an A minor and a G minor. He could buy any others he needed later.

Joey stopped at a McDonald's a few miles up the road. He ditched the latex gloves in the men's room, took a leak and washed his hands. On the way out, he stopped at the counter to order a Filet O'Fish meal with a medium Sprite. He ate in a booth by a window that looked out onto the parking lot, reading a day-old *USA Today* someone had left behind.

When he was finished, Joey wiped tartar sauce from the corner of his mouth and dropped the napkin on his seat. He slid the empty shell casings from his pocket, wrapped them in the dirty napkin. That went into the bag along with the rest of his garbage. Joey dropped the whole mess into the trash receptacle by the exit.

He headed back to the city. The pistol would get tossed into the river. The stolen car would be stripped, sold as spare parts by Shelly Kowalski's crew. After that, Joey needed to see the boss, let him know the job was done and get paid. Then Joey would pack a few things at his apartment and go. He had enough cash to get by for a while. Just in case, he still had five bank accounts, each under a different name and each with about eight thousand dollars. Best to leave that money alone for now.

The end of Joey Connolly.

The end of Joey Kotex.

Nice and clean.

The CD changer clicked and hummed. Magic Sam's jangling guitar licks filled the car. Singing along to "Sweet Home Chicago," Joey drove north.

1

TUESDAY, JUNE 8, 2009

Joey used his key to let himself into the club at 8:30 in the morning. Whitey's Blues wouldn't open until eleven, but Joey saw Grace Turner's purse on the bar. No sign of Grace herself, though. She was probably in the office. Joey locked the door, headed for the bar. The tables were bunched against one wall, the chairs upturned on top of them.

When Joey had first bought the club, he'd wanted it to feel like a real down home juke joint. They had thrown sawdust on the floor every night for authenticity. Then a woman slipped in the sawdust and sprained her ankle. She threatened to sue. Joey settled out of court. It wasn't cheap. In the old days, he would've given her a couple of hundred bucks, made sure that she and her husband both understood what would happen to them if they refused to let the matter drop.

Joey went behind the bar to mix himself a screwdriver with vodka from the top shelf. He stood there sipping his drink, looking around the room. The red brick walls were covered with framed posters advertising old shows all around Chicago's West and Near North sides, joints like the 708 Club, Silvio's on Lake and Kedzie, the Gatewood Tavern, the Flame Club, Mother Blues, Club Alex. The performers were a who's who of the blues: Howlin' Wolf, Etta James, Otis Rush, Little Walter, Muddy

Waters, Robert "Jr." Lockwood, Magic Sam, Sonny Boy Williamson, Koko Taylor. Whitey's wasn't big and trendy like Buddy Guy's Legends over on Wabash or B.B. King's club or the House of Blues. But it was his place.

There was a matted and framed copy of Dave Hoekstra's *Sun-Times* article about Koko Taylor's death lying next to Grace's bag. Koko had sung four tunes with the Whitey's house band the previous summer. It was a surprise for Joey's fortieth birthday, arranged by Sam Turner, Grace's dad. Joey owned a copy of Koko's old Chess single, "Insane Asylum." She'd autographed the sleeve for him. It was almost a week since she'd passed away. Joey only met her that one time, but the world seemed like an emptier place without Koko Taylor in it.

Fuck, he was getting soft.

Since cracking the big four-oh, he'd begun thinking about all the death he'd seen. Begun thinking about the deaths he'd caused. They didn't haunt him, those murdered people. It wasn't as though Joey saw their faces every time he closed his eyes. But there was regret, a feeling that he'd wasted half his life being someone else's weapon.

Joey sipped his screwdriver. This was no way to start the day. He put "Queen of the Blues," his favorite of Koko's albums, on the stereo and let it play low.

Grace Turner came out of the hallway. She spotted Joey drinking, said, "You're going to account for half our liquor order if you don't leave that stuff alone." Grace was thin and wiry, with high cheekbones and a slender nose. She had coffee-and-cream skin and hair that showed just a touch of gray in the short curls. She wore a men's denim work shirt with the sleeves rolled up to her elbows, khakis and running shoes. It was her usual outfit. Because she was divorced and dressed butch, some people took her for a dyke. Joey had never known her to date men *or* women. He didn't give a damn either way. Grace was Grace. That was good enough.

Joey rinsed the glass, left it upside down in the sink. "It has orange juice in it, so it's nutritious." Some water had splashed on his Blind Pig Records T-shirt and he reached for a bar towel.

"God, I can't stand health nuts. Pour me one, too." Grace slapped a folder on the bar and climbed onto a stool.

Joey said, "What's in the folder?"

Grace smiled. "Applications for the wait staff opening. Want to look them over before I start setting up interviews?"

"Hey, you're the manager." Joey slid Grace's drink across the bar.

She took a sip. "There's no vodka in this."

"It's too early for liquor," Joey said. "Besides, you'd set a bad example by drinking on the job."

"Funny. A lot of the guys my dad used to play with were drunks or junkies," Grace said. "I'm not saying there's a problem here, but you've been hitting that stuff pretty hard lately. You want to keep learning what Dad knows about blowing harp, I'd tone it down some. He sees it and he'll drop you like a bag of rocks."

Slammin' Sam Turner was a local living legend. At one time or another, whether on a stage or in a studio, Sam had played with practically everyone from T-Bone Walker to Susan Tedeschi. He had retired from performing in 2007, at the age of seventy-one. Even then, he'd only been playing local clubs.

The old man was withered and tough as rawhide, but fires of joy danced in his eyes when he played music. He'd been trying to teach Joey harmonica on and off for the past four years. Joey's plan was to front Whitey's house band himself. He could sing okay, but the harp was still a struggle. At the end of Joey's most recent lesson, Sam had said, "Boy, you couldn't play a tune right if I put a damn gun to your head. At least you can sing halfway decent."

It didn't keep Joey from going back to learn what he could.

It didn't keep Sam from doing his best to teach him.

Joey looked at Grace. "He dumps me, he loses his supply of Krispy Kremes. Anyway, I seem to remember a time when you wanted Sam to stay away from me."

"Well, you grew on me." Grace started thumbing through her stack of applications.

Someone knocked on the door. Joey looked up. Two guys in the brown uniforms of deliverymen stood there trying to see into the darkened club. The one cradling a cardboard box in the crook of his arm knocked again.

Grace groaned and slid off her stool. She crossed the room and leaned close to the door. "No deliveries before noon," she said, pointing at a sign taped to the glass. "And you have to go around the back anyway."

Joey was about to head down the hall for the office when he heard the click of the door being unlocked. He stopped and turned to look.

The door was open. Grace walked backwards across the room with her hands raised. The two deliverymen stepped inside. One paused to lock the door. They both carried pistols that looked like 9mm Glocks. Empty now, the cardboard box lay on the floor.

Joey said, "There's no cash here, guys. We made our deposit last night."

"Shut up," one of the men said. He was a big guy, six-two or six-three, looked like he went about two-fifty or so, shoulders wider than Joey's. The guy behind him was almost as tall, but scrawny as hell, with a face like a weasel's. Weasel Face waved his pistol slowly back and forth, his glance darting from Joey to Grace and back again.

Nerves?

Weasel Face said, "Keep your hands flat on the bar, Joey."

No. Not nerves.

The big guy ushered Grace back to the row of stools. She sat down and folded her arms across her chest, glaring at him. "You know these assholes, Joe?"

"No."

Grinning, Weasel Face stepped closer. He looked at the big

guy and said, "Check the back rooms, Nick. I'll keep Mr. Connolly and his friend occupied."

Grace said, "See? You're making a mistake. Joe's last name is Collins, not Connolly."

Nick came back a few moments later, shaking his head. "We're good," he said.

Weasel Face's grin widened. "Okay, you're to come with us, Joey. You and Miss Turner."

"The fuck we will," Grace said.

Weasel Face aimed his pistol at Grace's forehead, thumbed back the hammer.

Joey leaned slightly forward. "Look, guys. Nobody has to get hurt here. Just put away the guns and we'll talk."

Weasel Face snorted.

Grace stared at the muzzle of the pistol, said, "Maybe you don't know them, but they sure as hell seem to know you. What's going on, Joe?"

Weasel Face said, "Nick, put Miss Turner in the van and wait for me. I'm going to have a little talk with Joey here, make sure he's with the program. We don't want any ugliness."

The big bastard shoved his gun into his waistband before grabbing Grace by the left elbow and clamping his free hand over her mouth. She kicked and punched him, for all the good it did. Nick dragged her outside without breaking a sweat.

When they were gone, Weasel Face stepped closer to the bar but stayed out of Joey's reach. He aimed the pistol at Joey's heart. "She's a fighter," he said. "You been getting some of that black pussy or is she a carpet-muncher?"

Joey stared at him.

Weasel Face shrugged. "Now then, are we going to do this like professionals, or are you going to give me a hard time?"

"Who sent you?"

"Who the fuck you think?"

Joey's answer was silence.

Weasel Face nodded, said, "That's right. This is a great big wake-up call from Carl Petucci."

"Why take Grace if you're just going to whack me?"

"I appreciate the fact you didn't try pretending not to know Mr. Petucci. Saves us a lot of time, and time is definitely a factor for you. Nick and me are going to take you two for a ride. Then we're all going to get on a private plane and take a nice trip home to New York. If you want her to live, you'll play along."

"Chicago's a closed city," Joey said. "Word of this gets out to the right people and Carl's fucked. These guys in the Outfit, they'll kill you for pissing on their turf, too."

"That's what you think, smart guy. Somebody here owed Mr. Petucci a favor, made sure we got a free pass for the day."

Joey scowled. "Okay, I'll go with you. No problem. You're the man with the gun. But there's no reason to drag Grace into this. She doesn't know anything about my old life. Why complicate things?"

Weasel Face shrugged again. "I said I don't know, man. If it was up to me, I'd give you a couple in the back of the head right now and call it a day. But this is business, and I'm only the delivery guy. You understand me? You're a pro, or you used to be. Hell, I ain't been around that long and even I've heard of Joey Kotex. Mr. Petucci wants me to come get you, so here I am. He says bring Grace Turner, too. So..."

Joey sighed, rolled his shoulders to loosen the muscles. He straightened up and rubbed his hands together. He should have known the Petuccis would find him sooner or later. The question now was what to do about it.

Weasel Face watched Joey and nodded, said, "Now you've got the right attitude about the whole thing. It's just business, and we're professionals, right?"

"If you say so." Joey kept his expression neutral.

"It's not personal. I mean, I got a lot of respect for you." Weasel Face snickered, said, "Joey Kotex. Fuck. Did you really take a bullet in the arm and patch yourself up with duct tape and a maxi pad 'cause you couldn't find any bandages? Your balls gotta be like coconuts. I'm building up a rep myself, you know?"

Joey said, "How about a drink?"

Weasel Face chuckled and shook his head. "You're not going to try and pull a shotgun out from under the bar are you?"

The Ketel One bottle still stood on the bar. Joey poured two shots and slid one across. Weasel Face stepped forward. He took off his brown trucker's cap and dropped it on the bar. Laid his pistol on the mahogany, but kept his hand on it with his finger in the trigger guard. He hoisted the glass with his left hand.

Joey picked up his own drink. Each man raised his glass to the other. Weasel Face tossed back the vodka. Joey dropped his and brought his left hand down on top of Weasel Face's gun hand, pinning it to the bar. When the prick tried to yank free, Joey grabbed him by the hair, slammed his face down onto the wood. The Glock went off. Glass exploded behind Joey.

From somewhere outside, Joey heard the sound of an engine turning over. *Don't run, Nick. Wait to see if your buddy had to shoot me. Don't you fucking drive away.*

"Son of a bitch!" Weasel Face's nose and mouth ran with blood. Joey yanked his head up and smashed it into the bar again. This time, the fingers went limp, releasing the pistol.

Picking it up, Joey kept a good grip on Weasel Face's hair. He made his way along and around the bar, dragged the guy to the middle of the room. Joey said, "We're going outside now. You're going to tell your boyfriend to let Grace go."

Weasel Face spat blood onto the floor. Then he spat out a tooth. "Are you out of your fucking mind? All Nick's going to do now is leave without us. Even if you could kill us both and grab the nigger, they'll just send somebody else after you."

"Good point," Joey said, forcing him to his knees. He let go of Weasel Face's hair, stepped back. Weasel Face looked up just in time to take a bullet through his left eye. Joey made it to the front door before the body hit the floor.

Nick sat behind the wheel of a brown van parked at the curb just east of Whitey's front door. Its engine was running. Joey raised the pistol, but the big bastard stomped on the gas and yanked the wheel hard to the left. The van tore out into traffic, sideswiping a taxi. Horns blared. The cabbie screamed Cuban-accented obscenities. Nick ran a red light at the corner and was gone.

Lowering the Glock to keep it hidden against his leg, Joey went back inside and locked the door. He walked past the dead man, careful not to step in the widening pool of blood. There was a phone book behind the bar. Joey started to put away the Ketel One, then changed his mind and took a long pull from the bottle. Flipping through the yellow pages, Joey dialed the number of the first airline to catch his eye.

2

WEDNESDAY, JUNE 9

Last time Joey saw the Old World Café, there hadn't been any customers, just a couple of low-rung wiseguys nursing cup after cup of decaf while they played cards at a rickety table and watched the door for Carl. This afternoon, the place was jammed. It was fixed up like a Starbuck's knockoff, with wireless internet access and something that sounded like Dave Matthews piped out through overhead speakers. They didn't call it the Old World Café anymore, either.

Now it was Java 'n' Juice.

For a second, Joey thought the Petuccis must have packed up and moved their operation somewhere else. Then he spotted Sal Manfredo standing at the back, near the door to the stairwell. There was no mistaking Sally for anything but a goombah. He wore a maroon suit over a navy shirt that was unbuttoned halfway down his chest. With his slicked-back hair and shiny black shoes, he must have seemed like a sideshow freak to the neo-hippies, students and business types lined up for overpriced coffee. Even Joey, dressed in faded jeans, black Doc Martens and a *Whitey's Blues* T-shirt, looked less out of place.

Joey walked up to him, said, "That you, Sally?"

"Long time no see, Joey. When they told me to keep an eye out for you today, I thought *holy shit*. Where you been?" He held out his hand but Joey didn't shake it.

"Wow, doorman for the Petuccis. Looks like you're moving up in the world. This mean you've stopped beating up old ladies for their Social Security?"

Manfredo's eyes narrowed. He opened the door and made room for Joey to go through. "I gotta frisk you," he said when the door banged shut behind them.

Joey stopped, held his arms out at his sides while Sally patted him down. There was nothing to find but Joey's wallet, the Leatherman tool clipped to his belt and a C major harmonica in his front pocket. The harp was one of the three Lee Oskars Joey had swiped from Deke's Music his final night on the job.

Sal returned the wallet and harmonica, but held onto the Leatherman. He cocked a thumb at the stairs and said, "You can go on up." There was an old elevator that opened directly onto Carl Petucci's office, but it was kept locked, and the boss had the only key.

When Joey turned on the first landing, he looked down and saw Sal talking on a cell phone. Probably telling the boss that Joey Kotex was coming up. Sal always liked to act the big shot, but it was clear that no one had told him why Joey was here.

The smell of espresso and pastries followed Joey all the way up the stairs to Carl Petucci's fourth-floor office. A big guy in what looked like a Perry Ellis suit met Joey on the final landing. His gray suit jacket barely contained his biceps and shoulders.

"Didn't think you'd have the balls to show up," the guy said. "I told Mr. Petucci you was probably on your way to Mexico right now."

Hearing the voice, Joey pictured the hulking bastard dragging Grace out of Whitey's. He said, "Nice to see you, Nick. I hardly recognize you without the brown shorts and knee socks. Sorry your buddy couldn't make the trip with me."

Nick's jaw muscles rippled like he was chewing a tough piece of meat. He said, "You know the drill."

Joey stood still as he was frisked a second time. Nick slid the

Lee Oskar out of Joey's pocket.

"Don't worry," Joey said. "That harp isn't loaded."

Nick held the harmonica between two fingers and stared at it like it was some kind of alien artifact.

Joey said, "You blow through it and it makes music."

"Yeah, I figured you for the kind of guy that likes to blow things. You a cocksucker, Joey?" Nick gave him a tough-guy stare like he had been practicing it in a mirror, just waiting for the chance to use it on someone.

Joey stared, holding out his hand until Nick blinked and returned the harmonica. The muscle-head opened the door, leading Joey past the secretary's desk. The woman behind the desk was busy typing something on an old PC. She didn't even look up as they walked past her and into the office. Nick closed the door behind them before crossing the room to stand next to his boss.

Sitting behind a huge wooden desk, Carl Petucci grinned. He was even fatter now than Joey remembered. When Carl smiled like that, his eyes almost disappeared.

Joey said, "Nick must be new. The new ones always act like hard-ons."

"Same old Joey," Carl said. "You ain't changed a fucking bit, have you? I wish you hadn't whacked Paul, though."

"Who said I killed anybody? You got witnesses? Anyone find a body? Big Nick here was hiding in the van when the shooting started, and he burned rubber soon as I stepped outside. Maybe Paul decided to find another line of work."

"You're here and Paul ain't. I can do the math, Joey. Killing the man seems unnecessary to me, is all."

"Kidnapping my friend was unnecessary."

"Would you have come otherwise?"

Joey shook his head.

Carl laughed. "See?" he said. "There's my point. You killed Paul and ended up standing here anyway. It was a waste."

"Where's Grace?"

"We'll get to that, Joey. Keep your fucking pants on and we'll talk business."

"I don't have any business with you, Carl."

"You used to call me Mr. Petucci. What's with this first-name-basis shit?"

Joey said, "I called you Mr. Petucci when I worked for you. I quit four years ago. Now you're just a guy named Carl to me."

Carl's face reddened. "You don't quit me, fucko. Nobody quits." Spit flew from his mouth as he spoke.

Joey smiled, didn't say anything. Maybe the fat bastard would have a heart attack and die right here. Save Joey a lot of work.

Nick took a step forward. "You want me to teach this prick some respect, Mr. Petucci?"

"Shut up. Just shut up." Shifting in his chair, Carl loosened his tie. His color returned to normal and he nodded at Joey. "We're getting off on the wrong foot here. Sit down and we'll talk. We've got a lot to discuss."

Joey sat down on a leather couch almost as big as the Dodge Charger he'd left behind in Chicago.

Carl said, "Joey and me need to talk about some things in private, Nick. Go on out and get yourself a Powerbar or something."

Nick lowered his arms and shook his head like he had water in his ears. "But Mr. Petucci…"

"But Mr. Petucci *what?*"

"I shouldn't oughta leave you alone with this guy."

Carl said, "He doesn't have a piece and you'll be right outside. Besides, Joey wants to find out where his lady friend is."

"I still think…"

"You ain't paid to fucking think. Do what you're told."

Nick stalked past Joey, giving him the stare treatment again.

Joey yawned.

The bodyguard slammed the door.

"When my older brother James ran the show, he'd have broken the legs of a guy who got all pissy like that," Carl said. "But I guess Nick's grieving or some shit. Paul was engaged to Nick's sister."

Joey stayed silent.

Carl steepled his fingers against his lips and blew out a breath. "Forget all that yelling you and me just did. Appearances, right? This is just us now. I don't get why you took off on me like you did, Joey. I just don't fucking get it. You want to try explaining it to me?"

"No."

"Hey, you own a bar in a spook section of Chicago. You hang around with spooks and you play spook music. And you got the stones to give me attitude? You think you're better than me, is that it?"

"It was nothing personal," Joey said. "I wanted out of the life. So I quit. End of story."

"Joey, you could have come to me. We could've talked about it, worked something out."

Joey laughed. "Yeah, sure. I tell you I quit, and then a few weeks later, they find me in the trunk of a car. Look, Carl. Can we cut through the bullshit and get to whatever it is you want from me?"

"I got a job for you."

"Of course you do."

Carl sat there, mouth shut tight and jaw working slowly. Then he smacked his lips and said, "You ever met my wife?" He leaned back in his chair.

"I met her one Christmas," Joey said. "It must have been in '96 or '97. She seemed like a nice lady."

"Thanks for saying so, but the woman drives me fucking apeshit, Joey. She gets these obsessions, and suddenly we have to rearrange our whole fucking lives. Like last October, Gloria's waiting for a cleaning at the dentist and she starts flipping through the goddamn magazines. She sees pictures of this old farmhouse in Maine, all fixed up nice and jammed full of antiques and these huge fucking maple trees out in the yard. Now she's got to have one. A summer place in Maine. She's been on my ass about it for months. Like I got nothing better to do than drive out to the middle of nowhere and look at houses, right? So I find a whole bunch of real estate websites for Maine. They got pictures of the houses and all the details like how many square feet and what the taxes cost and shit like that. But you know what else they got? Pictures of their sales guys."

Grinning, Carl leaned forward. He handed Joey a web page he had printed out, from a company called Wesserunsett Realty. Joey looked it over. A series of thumbnail photos ran down the left side of the page: real estate agents smiling for their customers. The fourth picture from the top was circled in red ink. According to Wesserunsett Realty, the man's name was Evan Barker and he lived right there in Wesserunsett, Maine.

Joey said, "So what? You want me to kill him so the people that own the house knock a few thousand off the price, something like that? Jesus Christ, Carl."

"No. Look closer," Carl said. "Just picture him with longer hair, blond instead of brown, and a big bushy mustache like he was one of the fucking Village People. It's Todd Evans."

"Evans? Wasn't he that porn director, the one who ratted out your brother?" Joey stared at the picture, trying to recall Evans' face. This guy could be him. Maybe.

Carl nodded and sat back, folded his hands across the bulge of his belly. "I called his number and pretended to be interested in one of their listings. I recognized his voice right away. How could I ever forget it, the things he said to me?"

Carl and Jimmy Petucci had been looking for Todd Evans since 1996, when Evans turned rat and got their youngest brother, Michael, sent down on a murder beef. Something like that had only been a matter of time—Mikey being unable to hold his temper and never caring who saw—but a rat was a fucking rat. For most people the sight of Mikey P. beating a hooker with a chair until there was nothing left but a pile of stinking meat and splinters of bloody oak would have been enough to ensure silence. Problem was, Mikey had picked up the hooker in Brooklyn and taken her against her will over to Newark, where he killed her. Kidnapping and crossing state lines to commit murder put the case under federal jurisdiction.

The feds had had a hard-on over the Petuccis for years. For them, nailing the youngest brother on a murder rap was a wet dream come true. They were happy to supply Todd Evans with a new identity in exchange for his eyewitness testimony. Before Mikey's arrest, Evans had called Carl, demanding three hundred thousand bucks to forget what he'd seen in that Jersey warehouse. Carl told him to go fuck himself, so Evans testified and Mikey P. got hauled off for a twenty-five year jolt.

"It's a trap, Carl."

"What makes you say that?"

"Evans went into witness protection. The feds would never set him up with a job that requires his picture and address to be on a fucking website. This Evan Barker thing's a goddamn trap. Or it's not him at all."

Carl laughed. "I got a source says Evans slipped his leash a couple years ago. Had some kind of falling out with his minders and took off. The feds don't know where the fuck he is."

"If your source is so good, how come he didn't hand you Evans when he was still in the program?"

"Took us a while to make this guy roll."

"I still say so what? You went through all this trouble because you want me to hit Todd Evans?" Joey stood up, tossed the print-out onto Carl's desk. "You got plenty of guys to do that shit. I'm not a mechanic anymore."

Carl laughed. "No? You took out Paul easy enough, and I figure Nick's lucky to be breathing right now. Face it, Joey. It's like a riding a bike: Whack a few guys, and you never forget how."

"Get John Florio to do it. He's better than me."

"Florio's dead. Six months now."

"No shit?"

"No shit."

Florio had been a mentor of sorts to Joey, later becoming the closest thing he had to a friend in the Petucci organization. "I'd wondered why you sent those two pinheads after me instead of John. I don't suppose he died of natural causes?"

Carl frowned. "It was a hit. We still don't know who or why, but we will."

Joey said, "All right, say I kill Evans. Then what? You let Grace and me go?"

"That's the idea. All your past sins forgiven. You can go back to your niggers in the Windy City if you want, I don't give a shit."

"I'll say it again. You went to a lot of trouble to get me in on this, Carl. What's the real story here?"

Carl laughed so hard he started coughing. Wiped a tear from his eye, said, "You still got it. That makes me happy. I heard from a guy, almost a year ago, that you were hanging with a bunch of moolies in Chicago. He brought me pictures to prove it. I didn't know what to do with you right then so I had the guy keep an eye on you. Then this thing with Evans fell into my lap. I knew it was tailor-made for Joey Kotex. See, I know why you whacked Paul even when you didn't have to. It's because you love killing, Joey. Tell me I'm wrong."

"Quit jerking me off and just get to it," Joey said.

"All right." Carl waved his pudgy hands and smiled. "There's more to it, yeah. A lot more."

Joey sat back down.

Carl said, "I need you to get something from Evans before you do him. I ain't real thrilled about telling you this, Joey. But you were always a guy who could keep his mouth shut, and that's another reason I need you for this."

Joey sat there, waiting for the story to unfold now that Carl had gotten started.

"I ain't got any kids of my own, Joey," Carl said. "Mrs. Petucci, she's got some problems. You know, with her female parts. So we never was able to have children. My brothers? They were blessed with more fertile wives. But families can be trouble for a man, too. I mean, look at my brother Michael, for example. James and me, we tried for years to calm him down, but it never worked. Something in the blood, the recessed genetics or whatever you call it, something that makes him behave like that. Michael has five children, and they're all good kids but one. You know the one I'm talking about?"

Joey said, "Angie."

"Yeah, Angela. I hate drugs, you know that, Joey. Extortion, numbers, whores, loan sharking, having a guy whacked, I got no problem with any of that. Anybody does business with me, they made a conscious decision and know ahead of time the benefits of coming to me and the price they pay if they fuck up. It's consensual. Drugs aren't like that. You lose your fucking mind, so I don't have nothing to do with them."

Joey forced down a laugh at Carl getting self-righteous about drugs. Carl had drunk a cup of coffee and eaten an entire box of donuts while watching Joey bury a guy alive for fucking the family out of some money. But Carl Petucci insisted drug dealers were the real lowlifes. Never mind that Carl had his porn operations, and drugs were practically mandatory for that business.

Carl said, "But my beloved niece Angela got into drugs. Crack. I don't know how she got started, and I guess it don't matter, but we kept trying to get her clean. Finally, I put the word out: Anybody who supplied our Angela with drugs would end up getting sold to the school district as cheap hamburger. It worked for a while, then we found out Angie was using again. But nobody knew who was selling her the shit. Remember I sent you out to ask a few questions? People always give you what you want."

A few questions. Right. That was one way to put it. He'd

never inflicted so much pain on so many people without killing any of them; it was that kind of work that eventually led him to quit. Straight-out killing wasn't so bad, especially when it was quick and more or less clean, but the beatings and the torture? During his final few months with the Petuccis, the thing that most worried Joey was that he'd started to get a rush from the agony of others. He knew some guys for whom inflicting such pain was better than sex. The last thing he wanted was to become one of those psychos. But did the fact that he'd taken so long to quit mean it was already too late?

"But nobody knew," Joey said.

"Not so much as a fucking whisper. Then this little bastard Todd Evans calls me up, says to check my mail for his latest video. I tell him, I don't watch your movies, and I don't care what's in them so long as they're making me money. Evans giggles like a girl and says I'll want to see this one. So I pop it in the VCR in my office, just me and Ronnie, my bodyguard at the time, in here to see it."

Back when Evan Barker was still Todd Evans, he worked for the Petuccis, directing porn flicks. There was a lot of money to be made, even if most of the big porno outfits were out on the west coast—and this was before the internet allowed every schmuck with a webcam to crank out product. The hooker that Mikey Petucci beat to death had been in some of Barker's videos. Rumor had it that Mikey had wanted Barker to make a special, private edition movie for him starring the hooker and a pony. She refused. Mikey P. beat her to death.

Carl wiped sweat from his forehead. "It was Angela, our little Angela, doing things you wouldn't even see in a Times Square peep show, Joey. She was smiling, but you could tell it was because she was high as a fucking kite."

"So Evans was her supplier," Joey said. "Giving her the rock so she'd be in his movie?"

"He was going to blackmail me. Said I was to give him three hundred grand for the tape or he'd make copies and deliver them free to everyone I did business with. He tried to blackmail me over Angela, not her father. Evans didn't give a shit about the dead hooker, not until I sent some guys out to get him. He found out they were coming, ran to the feds. That's really why he rat-fucked my brother Michael." Carl's face blanched. "You bring me that tape, Joey. I want to burn it right here, but first you make sure it's the original and there ain't no copies. I don't want to find out he's turned it into a DVD or put it on the fucking internet. Then you kill that little prick. When he's dead and I've got the tape, you get your friend back, and we never have to see each other again."

It was all bullshit. Back when Joey worked for the Petuccis, he'd almost never been told the reason for a hit. Carl or Jimmy just said go kill so-and-so. That was it. All this information about Angela and Evans meant one thing: As soon as Joey did the job and handed over the videotape, he and Grace were dead.

Joey said, "How do I know Grace is still alive? Let me see her."

Carl glared at Joey for a long moment before buzzing his secretary and telling her to send Nick back in.

"Nick, bring up our guest." Carl fished around in his pants pocket, came out with a key ring. He flipped through them until he found the one he wanted and handed it to Nick. "I don't want to wait all day, so use the elevator."

That meant Grace was probably stashed in the basement. The knowledge did Joey no good, since he was unarmed and Grace was—maybe—being kept five floors down with at least a couple of guards. He filed it away for later.

After a couple of minutes, Nick came in with Grace. Her clothes were rumpled and her hands were cuffed behind her. A strip of duct tape covered her mouth, but she wasn't blindfolded. A bruise showed under her right eye. She saw Joey and tried to shout through the tape.

Joey jumped up. He looked at Grace but spoke to Carl. "Who hit her?"

Carl said, "She kicked Nick in the balls, so he maybe had to knock her down. You can see it didn't hurt her none."

Nick gave Joey a *c'mon-and-do-something-about-it* sneer. Joey stared back until the steroid freak looked away. His attention seemed drawn by the print-out on Carl's desk.

"Get her outta here," Carl said.

Nick yanked Grace's arm, hauled her backwards toward the door.

When they were gone, Carl slapped the top of his desk. "So now you've seen her. I want this shit over and done with fast."

Joey said, "Might take some time. I'll have to make sure this guy really is Todd Evans. I'm not popping some fucker just because you think you recognized his voice after all these years. If it turns out he is our boy, I have to convince him to give up the tape before he dies."

"That'll be the easy part," Carl said. "You got until Saturday to kill the little shit and get back here with the tape. And I don't need to tell you what's going to happen to your girlfriend if you fuck this up."

Carl opened a desk drawer, came out with a Beretta. Said, "So, we got a deal or what?"

If the whole thing really was a set-up, he wouldn't dare give Carl to the feds because Grace would be killed. If he refused the job, Carl would kill Grace anyway. Probably make Joey watch before he got whacked, too. So what choice did he have? It was Grace or a jerkoff-movie scumbag like Todd Evans. Joey said, "All right. I'll do it. You supply me with a clean car and a .38 revolver, a Smith & Wesson, a Colt or a Taurus. No fucking automatics. I also want five grand in expense money."

"Five grand? I look like a cash machine to you?"

"I'm going to pop a guy who tried to shake you down for three hundred large, and you're busting my balls over a lousy five grand? The Russians must be cutting deep into your territory if you gotta tighten the budget like that."

"Who told you that? The Russkies are for shit." A vein

throbbed above Carl's right eye. "Another couple years and those cocksuckers will be scurrying back to Moscow. I'll still be right here."

Joey shrugged. "I just figured times must be tough if you're putting on fuckups like Sally Manfredo."

"Okay, enough," Carl said. He pointed the Beretta at Joey. "Five grand plus the car and guns, but keep your fucking smart-ass remarks to yourself from now on."

"Just tell Mr. Universe out there to give me back my Leatherman." He would do this thing. By the time he came back with the tape, he might even come up with some way to make sure that he and Grace could get out of here alive.

Yeah, no problem.

3

A Pakistani cabbie drove Joey to the Target on Flatbush Ave. and kept the meter running while Joey went in to buy a disposable cell phone. When Joey came out and slid into the backseat of the cab, he asked the driver, "You know the Westin over in Midtown? On West Forty-Third?"

"Hell yes."

"Good. Get me there before I fall asleep on you. I've been awake for a day and a half."

Joey went upstairs to the room he'd reserved right after booking a flight out of Chicago. His bag and laptop were on the bed, where he'd left them before meeting with Carl. Joey could see the corner of 8th Avenue and West 43rd from the single window. No view of Times Square, not that it would have looked any better from fifteen floors up anyway. He closed the curtains, moved his bag to the floor and his computer to the coffee table. He kicked off his sneakers and lay down on the bed, figuring to catch an hour or two of sleep. He had to meet with an old friend tonight. Tomorrow morning he planned to close out the five bank accounts he still had under false identities before leaving for Maine.

He woke in darkness, chilled with sweat and feeling more tired than when he had gone to sleep. The sheets were in a heap at the foot of the bed. Joey rolled over, looked at the clock on the nightstand. Eight-thirty. Jesus, he'd slept more than five hours. His eyes burned. Another five hours' sleep might do him some good. He rolled out of bed.

After a quick shower, Joey put on a clean black T-shirt and the jeans he'd been wearing all day. Then he caught a cab back into Brooklyn. Morris Spielman and his son Philip ran a kosher deli up in Midwood. Joey went in, ordered corned beef on rye with onions and mustard and a cream soda. Phil, working the register, did a double take when he saw Joey. Kept his mouth shut, though.

The place was busy, even near closing time. Joey sat at a small table in the back corner and waited for Phil or one of the kids making the sandwiches to call his number. The smell of fresh bread and mounds of sliced corned beef, turkey, pastrami, those fat dill pickles made Joey's stomach growl. Spielman's had always been one of his favorite places to eat.

They called his number after about twenty minutes. Joey got his food and returned to the table. There was a slip of paper beneath his sandwich. It read *around the back*. Joey ate slowly, savoring the salty beef and thick rye. He washed it down with cream soda and left.

An alley ran between Spielman's and the coin-op laundry next door. Joey walked past a Dumpster, felt hot air against his legs from the laundry's exhaust fans. A light above the deli's back door shined down on Phil Spielman. He sat on an upturned milk crate, smoking a cigarette.

"Heard a rumor you were dead," Phil said. He was a short, chubby guy in his mid-forties with a shaved head and a goatee.

Joey stopped in front of him and leaned against the brick wall. He said, "I am."

Phil blew smoke out of his nostrils. "You get around pretty good considering most people think you ended up as chum out in Raritan Bay."

"Not yet. I need a piece."

"I'm outta that business, Joe. Ever since Pop died."

"Morris passed away?"

Phil nodded. "Three years ago. Lung cancer. I decided it was time to go straight. Make sure my boys grow up right, you know?"

"Sorry for your loss. Morris was a good guy," Joey said. "Those are your kids working in there tonight?"

"Yeah. I gotta get back in there soon, too." Phil took one last drag off his cigarette, flicked his butt against the laundry's wall. "Sorry I can't help you, man. You always treated Pop and me right."

Joey said, "I came here because I know I can trust you. I got one last job to do, and it stinks. Bad. But I have to do it. The guy's supplying me with a piece, but I don't trust him to give me a clean one. Can't take any chances."

Phil muttered something in Yiddish, stood up and adjusted his pants. "I still got a couple things left. Been meaning to get rid of them, but never got around to it." He turned to go inside.

"A .38," Joey said.

"I remember."

Joey waited in the alley. In the old days, he would come to Spielman's, order a number three to go and feel the reassuring weight of a revolver at the bottom of the bag when Morris handed it across the counter. If Joey was just there to eat, he sat at a table. Morris and Phil took good care of him either way.

Phil came back out carrying a brown paper bag with the top rolled down tight. He handed it to Joey, said, "It's a.38, clean as a whistle. I got it through a straw buy four years ago. Never even been fired. I threw in a box of cartridges."

"How much?" Joey slid a roll of bills from the pocket of his jeans.

"It's on the house."

"Come on, Phil. How much?"

"You're doing me a favor, taking it off my hands."

Joey said, "I have to give to you something."

"Do this for me, then. Stay alive and watch your ass, but don't come around here anymore. I got a feeling your boss wouldn't be happy to find out about our little transaction. Plus there's the kids, you know…"

"All right," Joey said. Phil wanted a clean break, a chance for his kids to lead normal lives. Joey could relate.

Phil held out his hand and Joey shook it.

Before returning to the hotel, Joey got rid of the gun Carl had given him. He removed the cylinder, dropped it in a garbage can three blocks from Spielman's. The frame went down a storm drain back in Manhattan. Joey kept the cartridges. He'd need those.

4
THURSDAY, JUNE 10

First thing in the morning, a couple of detectives stuffed Hag in the backseat of a patrol car. Handcuffed but back in his own clothes for the first time in six months, Hag looked over his shoulder at the prison. The fucking hellhole. At least he could tell people he had lived in a foreign country for a while, even it was only Canada.

"I thought you Mounties all dressed like that Dudley Do-Right," Hag said. "You two must be on the elite team, the ones that don't fuck their horses."

The Mounties didn't answer. They drove him in silence from Quebec to St. George, then on down to Maine and the border station north of Jackman. Some Canadian border agents took custody of him there. The Mountie who handed over Hag's paperwork said, "He thinks we're all into bestiality up here."

The border guys scowled, dragged Hag into a small room. There they strip-searched him, reminding him all the while that he could never return to the land of the Great White North. After they let him dress and told him he could go, Hag went out and crossed the lobby to the Maine side. He turned around, flipped those Canadians the bird, hit them with, "Celine Dion sucks moose cocks, eh."

The American Border Patrol guys watched all this. They

shook their heads. One, smiling like his whole week had just been made, said, "Charles Hagopian. Welcome home, sir. Come this way, please." They ushered Hag into another small room. No big deal, Hag played it cool.

Then they ordered him to strip.

Shit.

By the time he was allowed to leave the building to look for Earl's Jeep, Hag felt like a whole herd of horny bull moose had mistaken his asshole for Celine Dion's mouth. Worse, he didn't see the Jeep anywhere, goddamn that numbnut Earl.

Some lardass in a beat-to-hell old pickup honked his horn. Hag gave him the finger. The horn beeped again. This time Hag looked close and saw that the guy behind the wheel was Earl. Shirt untucked and only half-buttoned, boots untied, Hag limped over. He opened the door, climbed into the truck.

Earl said, "Hag, you look like crap warmed over." He turned the old Ford around and drove out of the parking lot, onto Route 201.

"Me? Check out a mirror, you fat fuck. Those are the same filthy sweatpants you were wearing last time I saw you. How about you get this thing moving?"

Theirs was the only vehicle in the southbound lane. Hag kicked at a pile of empty beer cans on the floor. "The hell happened to your Grand Cherokee anyway?"

"Credit union had it repo'ed," Earl said. "I needed something in a hurry, and this truck was cheap."

The inside of the truck stank of stale cigarettes and old motor oil. Hag said, "Cheap? You telling me you paid money for this wreck? Man. They saw you coming, didn't they?"

Hag leaned forward, picked up the empty beer cans, chucked them out the window.

They rode quietly for a couple of miles. Hag listened to the tires rolling over pavement and looked out at the green-brown blur of the trees that crowded the roadside. He turned to Earl and said, "How many payments you miss before they took away your Jeep?"

Earl shrugged. "Seven or eight, something like that. I didn't make it easy on them, either. I'd hide it in my mother's barn and drive her car around town, 'til she got mad and told me to quit running up her mileage. I got laid off from New Balance, and Stony ain't had no work for me since you got busted. Not that he ever paid us much anyway."

Hag and Earl had been friends since they were both thirteen years old. It was long enough to know when Earl said "laid off," he really meant "fired."

A Playmate cooler sat between them on the bench seat and Hag opened it, fished around in the ice water and came out with a can of Coors Light. He drank it down so fast he didn't even taste it until after he'd finished swallowing. The first alcohol he'd drunk in six months that wasn't distilled beneath another con's bunk. He burped, said, "Speaking of money, we need to make some."

Earl spotted a fox crossing the road and swerved to hit it. Missed. "We can talk to Stony, now that you're back. Maybe he'll have something for us."

Hag opened another beer, sipped at the foam instead of chugging it. "Fuck Stony. I ain't working for him. I'm almost thirty years old and I'll be goddamned if I'm going to waste any more time running shit into Canada for that little prick. He pays peon wages and leaves me out in the fucking cold when I get busted. I'm just lucky I didn't have any of that shit on me when the Mounties got me."

"But Stony..."

"But Stony my ass. I'm sick of it, Earl. We're going into business for ourselves now."

Earl shifted in his seat, looking like he might wet himself. "I don't know, Hag. Stony's got a wicked bad temper and he ain't going to like anybody trying to compete with him. Plus you still owe him all that money."

Hag snorted. "What fucking money?"

"What you got busted with. The money them Canadian cops took off you."

"Stony can lick my balls. I ain't paying him what I don't owe him in the first frigging place, and I ain't talking about selling drugs anyway. That shit's for morons. It's time you and me made us some real money. I did a lot of thinking up there in jail, and I know just what we're going to do."

Earl looked over at him. "So what's this bright idea, professor?"

Hag finished his second beer. He burped again and grinned, his face flushed. He said, "I met a guy there, was in jail waiting for trial 'cause they said he'd hired a hitman to kill his wife."

"So?"

"So that's what we're going to be, bud. Hitmen."

"You ain't just yanking my chain, are you? You really mean it. Seriously?"

"Dead serious." Hag laughed, thinking he was funny. "We're going to be hitmen, just like I said. This Canadian guy? He was my cellmate, and I got him all fucked up on pruno one night so he told me the cops were right. He really did hire a guy to blow his wife's brains out. Cost him ten thousand bucks, but then the hitman got caught and ratted on him."

Earl said, "Ten grand. Man. Hey, was it Canadian money or American?"

"They live in Canada, retard. What do you think? But that ain't the point anyway. We can be our own boss, keep all the money ourselves."

"C'mon Hag, get real. What do we know about that stuff?"

Hag cocked his index finger and thumb like a pistol, pointed it at Earl. "Killing some guy? For that much money? Pop pop. Man, how frigging tough can it be?"

5

Heron Lane didn't have any herons. What it did have was twenty single- and double-wide trailers all lined up next to each other like shotgun shacks on narrow lots. Their front windows looked out onto the Catholic cemetery across the street, while those in the rear gave a good view of the backside of Wesserunsett's strip mall: Dumpsters behind Hong Kong Palace, the loading dock of the vacant Sherwin Williams store, the Dollar Queen, stacks of plastic milk crates and some broken carts near the back doors of the Wesserunsett IGA.

Bob Rowell didn't mind babysitting his father-in-law so long as there were beers to drink. They sat out on the front lawn, watching the sparse traffic go by. The old man sat rigid in his plastic chair, holding a can of beer on his knee. Armand LeBlanc was always tight-lipped, but today he wasn't saying a damn thing. That was fine with Bob.

A red Grand Am full of high school girls went past. Bob said, "You see that, Armand? The titties on them young girls? I think the schools put growth hormones in the water fountains. Them tight little tank tops they wear don't help none either, so you know damn well they want to give you a good eyeful."

Armand didn't answer, kept staring at the cemetery across the street.

Bob shook his head and said, "I hope I don't ever get so old I'd rather stare off into space than look at a nice set of jugs."

He tipped his head back, took a long swig off his can. "All them young girls get their nipples pierced, you know. Nipples, belly buttons."

Armand slumped over to his left and fell out of the chair. He let out a sort of gurgle. A string of drool trickled out the corner of his mouth.

Bob set down his beer, said, "You don't care about tits and you can't hold your liquor. Jesus, but it sure must suck to be old." After hoisting him back into the chair, Bob picked up Armand's beer and shook it gently. Still a little in there, so he put the can in the old guy's hand. No sense in wasting it. Bob brushed some of the dirt and grass blades from his father-in-law's clothes so Joyce wouldn't see it and have a shit-fit.

Two lots down, Larry Nichols, the neighborhood queer, was slapping a new coat of stain on his front deck. Larry gave Bob the stink-eye. Bob ignored it. The guy wasn't bad for a homo. And he kept his place up nice. Not like the shithole that stood between his lot and Bob's. That Earl Coro was a goddamn pig, his trailer rusted and filthy, the yard overgrown. Even his pickup truck looked like something that had been pulled out of the lake.

A breeze carried the smell of grilling meat from the backyard. Bob glanced at Armand, said, "Them steaks must be just about ready. I hope Joyce don't burn them this time."

Still no answer from Armand. Bob drained his beer, bent down to grab another one from the box, and said, "You better not have any more. You're hammered already. Look at that faggot, pretending he didn't see you fall but watching all the same." Bob gave Larry a big fruity wave.

Armand slid down on his scrawny butt, ended up sitting on the ground with his legs splayed out in front of him.

Bob stood up so fast he knocked his own chair over backwards. "That's it. I'm hauling you back to the home. Let them CNAs deal with you." When Bob grabbed Armand this time, he noticed the left side of the old man's body was stiff as morning wood while the other side was limp. Bob leaned over his father-in-law, gave his face a gentle slap.

"Hey, Armand, you hear me?" He slapped Armand again, harder this time, trying to get a response. He gave him another one. Goddamn it. Bob reached into his pocket for his cell phone, remembered he'd left it on the kitchen table. Better get his ass in the house and call nine-one-one.

The he heard a scream.

Bob looked up, saw Joyce running across the lawn toward him. She was short and round. Everything on her jiggled and bounced as she ran.

Joyce said, "My daddy! What did you do to him, you son of a bitch?"

She had a long grilling fork in one hand.

6

When Wanda Philbrick turned onto Heron Lane, she saw half a dozen people gathered on the Rowells' lawn and in the driveway. The pair at the end of the driveway jumped up and down, waving their arms over their heads to make sure she stopped at the right place. They got out of the way when she pulled in, only to swarm her as soon as she got out of the cruiser.

"We think he's had a stroke," an older lady said.

"What?"

"A stroke. You know…" The old woman crossed her eyes, stuck her tongue out the side of her mouth and held her right arm close to her body, flapping it against her bony chest. "A stroke. Larry did some first aid on him."

Then Wanda spotted an old man lying on the ground, surrounded by empty beer cans. A skinny, gray-haired guy in stained running shorts and a T-shirt crouched over him. He had placed the old man's feet up on a lawn chair to keep the blood near the body core. What the hell was going on here? "You're Larry?"

The man nodded. "Larry Nichols. Where's the ambulance?"

"If you called for an ambulance, it should be here any time," Wanda said. "I'm here because somebody reported a domestic assault."

The old lady laughed. "That'd be Bob and Joyce. She got mad at Bob and chased him into the house with a pitchfork or something."

When Wanda first responded to the call, the county dispatcher told her Bob Rowell was the one who had called nine-one-one. He said he was trapped in the bathroom and his wife was trying to hack through the locked door with a butcher knife. Then he either hung up or got disconnected. Wanda thumbed her shoulder mike and called back in to make sure the ambulance was on its way. She told Larry to stay with the stroke victim and the rubberneckers to stay clear.

The trailer was a double-wide with a small deck facing the street. Wanda heard faint country music. She banged her fist against the screen door. No answer. Wanda pulled her Beretta.

"Wesserunsett police! Come on out here and let's get this sorted."

Hearing someone groan, Wanda opened the door and slipped inside. A grilling fork lay on the carpet, its tines covered in something that could've been barbecue sauce or human blood.

The living room opened onto the kitchen. The table had been overturned. The floor was covered with broken glasses and plates, silverware, a ceramic sugar bowl. Two pots stood on the stove. The larger one had boiled over, leaving a foamy streak down the front of the stove. The room smelled like burnt potatoes.

Wanda turned off the stove before crossing the living room to a short hall with three more doors. They were closed, but the one at the end was chewed up. Splinters hung from deep gashes and the handle of a big knife stuck out about five feet up. Wanda shook her head. Cheap hollow-core door; even the old lady out front could've kicked a hole through it.

"Mr. Rowell, are you in there? This is Officer Philbrick of the Wesserunsett police."

His voice muffled by the ruined door, a man said, "You're that woman cop?"

"Good guess. You can unlock the door now."

She heard grunting in reply, shoes sliding on tile. The ambulance siren sounded close.

"Mr. Rowell? Unlock the door."

"I think my ankle's broke."

"What happened here, sir?"

"I was trying to climb out the window and I fell, hit the toilet then the floor. Jesus, but it hurts."

"You made your nine-one-one call from in there?"

"Yeah, but I dropped the phone out the window when I slipped."

Wanda sighed, took a step back and kicked. The door flew off its upper hinge and stood propped against the shower curtain rod with the knife still sticking out of it.

Bob Rowell lay on his side in front of the toilet. He said "I need to get up."

"Hold still or you'll make that leg worse," Wanda said. "The EMTs will take care of you. Where's Mrs. Rowell?"

"But I got to take a wicked piss."

Wanda holstered her sidearm and clicked on her radio to report the injured man to dispatch. She wadded up a couple of towels for a pillow, laid them under Rowell's head. "You stay put for a minute, like I said. I have to find your wife."

"She's in Eric's bedroom."

"Which door?"

"Um...the right one. No wait, it'd be on your left," Bob Rowell said. "Fuck. I can't tell. I'm all turned around. You're going to get me out of here, ain't you?"

Wanda drew her pistol, moved to the door on the left. "Mrs. Rowell, I'm sure you heard me talking to your husband. We need to put an end to this right now, ma'am. Come on out and we can talk."

Outside, the sirens stopped. Wanda heard the old lady shouting at the EMTs. Bob Rowell said, "Hey come on, get me up. I'm gonna piss myself any second."

Wanda knocked on the bedroom door. "Mrs. Rowell, I need to make sure that you're okay. I don't want to break down another one of your doors."

Joyce Rowell opened the door a crack and looked out. Her face was a mottled red, her cheeks slick from crying. Wanda stepped back, raising her pistol. "Open that door all the way and put your hands where I can see them, Mrs. Rowell."

"My knife got stuck," Joyce said. She opened the door and stepped into the hall, empty hands out in front of her. "I guess you got to take me to jail now."

"That's up to your husband, ma'am, if he wants to press charges. But he's going to need to go to the hospital first. Then you're both going to have to give statements."

Bob said, "I ain't pressing charges. Just get me up to the damn toilet."

With the back of her hand, Joyce wiped snot from her lip. "He beat up my father. Had him down on the ground, hit him in the face."

"That's a lie," Bob said. "I was just trying to wake him up. He looked passed out to me."

Wanda led Joyce back into the bedroom and sat her on the bed. The curtains were drawn, the room gloomy. Wanda stepped on a toy truck. "You have a son?"

Joyce nodded. "Eric. He's over to his cousin's house. Gonna spend the night there."

Wanda said, "It looks like your father had a stroke. He's going to Skowhegan in an ambulance."

Joyce Rowell blew her nose into a wad of tissues the size of a baseball mitt.

Bob sat up as much as he could. His face glistened with sweat. "I can't hold it no longer."

Did the guy expect Wanda to pick him up and let him lean on her shoulder so he could pee? "You'll have to hold it, Mr. Rowell. Help's on the way."

Bob lay back on the towels and said, "Too late. Hey, if you're going out to the dooryard, grab me another beer."

7

Grace Turner sat cross-legged on her cot, with her back resting against the closet wall. Except for trips to the bathroom every few hours, her captors kept her locked in here. Whatever clothing had hung in the closet was gone, even the rod. All that remained was the lingering smell of mothballs. A thin, frayed carpet covered the cement floor. A basement? It was damp enough.

With the cot squeezed in there, Grace had just enough room to stand up and shuffle from left to right with her calves brushing the edge of the cot while her chest grazed the door and wall. The only light came through an old-fashioned keyhole and the crack beneath the door. What little fresh air she got trickled in the same way.

The swelling under her eye had gone down some, but it was tender to the touch, would probably stay that way for a couple of more days.

It was Nick, that big gorilla-looking son of a bitch, who had punched her. Yeah, she'd tried to kick him in the crotch when they were dragging her off the little private plane. What the hell did they expect?

Thanks?

A smile?

A blow job?

Another big guy, this one wearing a green-and-yellow nylon windbreaker with matching pants, said, "I ain't banged a black chick in a while. Let's pass her around."

His buddies laughed.

Grace said, "Try it and I'll make sure you never fuck again." Her hands were cuffed behind her back, but she could still bite. And kick.

So Nick grabbed her by the arm and yanked her close. Looking at the moron in the track suit, he said, "Gino, you'll fuck anything if it holds still long enough." Nick's free hand shot up to Grace's left breast, pinched the nipple, twisted it.

Grace screamed. Instead of trying to pull away, she brought her knee up between his legs. Nick let go and turned aside. Grace was thrown off-balance, landed on her ass. Gino hauled her up by the shirt collar and held her there. That was when Nick punched her in the face. Then they'd blindfolded her, stuffed her into the back of a van she'd seen when the plane landed, and brought her here.

Wherever the hell "here" was. The building was old; that much was clear. Grace vaguely remembered being shoved onto the plane back in Chicago. After putting her in the phony delivery van, Nick had jabbed her with a needle. The entire flight was a blank until she felt a bump and heard the squeal of rubber on tarmac. She thought Nick and his crew had Brooklyn accents. But so what? Joe had one, too.

Joe. This whole mess was about Joe. Grace thought she knew him well. But who was he really and what had he done to piss these people off? They'd dragged Grace out of the closet yesterday, slapped duct tape over her mouth and handcuffed her before taking her up in a rickety elevator. Then they stepped out into an office. There were windows in this room, but the heavy brocade drapes had been pulled tight.

A fat man sat behind a big desk. Joe was on a leather sofa with a beer in his hand. *Beer?* The son of a bitch was drinking beer while these animals had her locked in a fucking closet? Grace tried to yell at him through the tape. Joe had stood up and asked about her black eye. That gave Nick and the fat guy a big laugh. Then Nick had dragged her back into the elevator and down to her cell. No, it wasn't a cell. If it were, it would have more space and light and a toilet of its own. There might even be someone she could talk to. Being in this stinking, stuffy closet...this was more like psychological torture.

Grace leaned forward to bang on the door. She said, "Hey." Pounded the door again and again until the heel of her hand burned. "Let me out. I have to pee." She sat back, waited for Nick or one of the other assholes to walk her down the hall to the bathroom. The door opened. Grace squinted against the light, saw a big man silhouetted there.

"Come on. You're in such a hurry, let's move before you piss your pants." It was Nick. His cell phone rang then, and Nick gestured for Grace to sit still. He flipped open the phone, said, "Yeah? Yeah, that's right."

Nick took a piece of paper from the pocket of his sport coat. Grace craned her neck to see what it was; something printed off a website, but she couldn't get a decent look. Nick nodded a couple of times at whoever was on the other end of the call before saying, "Wesserunsett, Maine. 538 Sirois Road. Yeah, both of 'em. You can e-mail me the pics like before."

When Nick ended the call and told her to hurry up, Grace slid off the cot. She said, "If that was your buddy Joe Collins, call him back and tell him the next time I see him, he's dead meat."

Nick snorted and grabbed her by the elbow. He said, "You'll have to get in line."

8

Joey drove into Westbrook, Connecticut, a little after noon. It was time to get rid of the gray Lincoln Carl Petucci's guys had given him that morning.

He stopped for lunch at the Denny's just off I-95. Parking close to the door, Joey made sure the car was locked up—his laptop and the duffel bag with his clothes, CDs and close to fifty grand in cash lay on the backseat—before going inside.

The restaurant was packed. Conversations and laughter competed with noises from the kitchen. The hostess told him there was a twenty-minute wait. Joey spotted Shelly Kowalski in a booth across the room, said, "I'm meeting someone. She's right over there."

Shelly sat hunched over a paperback book—*Money Shot* by Christa Faust. She toyed with the straw in her iced tea while she read.

Joey slid onto the seat across from her. "Good book?"

"Mmm." She did not look up. "Full of bad people. You'd feel right at home with them."

"Order yet?"

Shelly shook her head. She was in her late thirties, short brown hair, big brown eyes. Her blue work shirt had *Shelly* stitched over the left breast in yellow thread, a patch reading *Kowalski's Garage & Towing* over the right. She said, "Waiting for you, stud."

Joey saw a waitress standing near the counter, motioned for her to come over. She ignored him. "Can't beat the service here," he said.

"It's your own fault." Shelly used the paper from her straw to mark her place in the book before laying it on the table. "You don't call me for, like, four years, and where do you decide to take me? Fucking Denny's."

"Hey, this is your town, not mine. I was in a hurry and didn't have time to check the Michelin Guide for five-star restaurants."

She snickered. "This is fine. I'm not exactly dressed for a romantic rendezvous."

A different waitress came over to take their orders.

"Chicken tenders with onion rings and a garden salad. Ranch dressing," Shelly said. "Regular dressing, not that fat-free stuff."

Joey ordered a turkey club and fries. When the waitress left, Joey sat back. "So how you been, Shell?"

"Are we doing small talk?"

"I guess not. I need a car."

"What's wrong with the Lincoln you came in?"

Joey scratched his chin. He said, "Looked like you were too deep into your book to notice that. I'm impressed."

"Joey fucking Kotex calls me out of the blue and asks for a meeting. You think I don't come prepared?" Shelly set a cell phone on the table next to her book. "Lee's out in the parking lot. He told me when you pulled in. Oh, and he says you ought to wear a longer shirt to cover that piece."

"I didn't come here looking for trouble. It's why I wanted to meet in a busy public place, so you'd feel comfortable. I didn't want to just show up at the garage and freak you out."

"You've been gone a long time," Shelly said. "Petucci know you're back from the dead?"

"I'm working for him."

"So you say. Where you been, Joey? Maybe you're with the

feds now, wearing a wire."

"I don't need this shit." Joey stood, tossed a couple of twenties on the table, said, "Enjoy your lunch."

Shelly laughed. "Get over yourself, will you? I was just busting your balls."

Joey sat.

The waitress brought Shelly's salad and a coffee for Joey. She'd forgotten the ranch dressing, even got pissy when Shelly mentioned it. When she walked away, Shelly said, "I'll give you a car for free if you whack that bitch before we leave."

Joey relaxed, sipped from his mug. He said, "I'm out of the life now."

"You just said you're working for Carl."

"One last job."

"Right. I didn't know Carl understood the concept of *one last job*. Listen, back when there was still a British Empire, if some poor dumbass joined the army—taking the King's shilling, they called it—he signed up for life. That's how guys like Petucci operate. You know the fucking rules, so don't kid yourself." Shelly had gone to college to make her mother and father happy. She earned a B.A. in history at Brown before coming home to take over the family business. Shelly once told Joey that working with cars was more satisfying than the study of history because engines could be fixed while people refused to learn anything from the mistakes of the past.

"Carl can go to hell for all I care. If I got the chance, I'd help him on his way. But I'm doing this one thing for him, then I vanish again. For good this time."

"One way or another, huh?"

"Something like that."

Their meals arrived. This time the waitress remembered Shelly's salad dressing. "You're welcome," she said.

Shelly ignored her. She dumped ranch all over her salad, squirted ketchup on her onion rings and chicken. Shelly had always been able to eat like a trucker and keep herself in shape.

After a bite of chicken, she said, "I take it you want something reliable that doesn't stand out."

Joey had a mouthful of turkey, lettuce and bread. He nodded.

"I can take care of you, no problem. Always did, right? I'm curious as hell, though. Where you been all this time?"

Joey swallowed, used a paper napkin to wipe mayo from the corner of his mouth. "Chicago. I own a club there. Whitey's Blues. Nothing fancy, but it's mine."

"Cool. So that's your life now? You're not in with the Outfit or anything like that?"

"I'm straight. Coming back into this now wasn't my idea."

"I'll bet," Shelly said. She finished her salad, pushed the bowl aside. "You meet anybody out there? Is there is a Mrs. Kotex and a bunch of little Kotexes?"

"That's funny. No, there's nobody like that. But I've got a family, though. A guy named Sam and his daughter Grace. They're the best people I've ever known."

Shelly clapped a hand to her breast, said, "You wound me."

"I was pretty fucked up when I got out there," Joey said. "That first year, I figured every guy I saw on the street was some asshole looking to take me out for Carl. Got kind of paranoid, you know? Grace and Sam brought me back to life."

"Yeah, that's fascinating. You're not going to start talking about Jesus now, are you?"

Joey laughed. "No, I didn't get religion."

"Well, thank Christ for that."

9

"A sheriff's deputy was on the way. You should've waited for backup." Chief Ed Gauthier paced around his office while Wanda sat in a straight-backed wooden chair in front of his desk.

"I know," she said. "I know it would've been proper procedure, but I didn't think there was time."

"Dispatch told you Deputy Barnes was five minutes away, so don't try bullshitting me," Ed said. He was a thirty-three year veteran, with nine of those years spent as Wesserunsett's police chief.

"This time last year, Kyle Barnes was a security guard at Walmart. And besides, he's a midget."

"He is not a midget," Ed said.

"Come on, Ed. What is he, five-six, five-seven? He doesn't even come up to my shoulders. How'd he get to be a cop anyway? Barnes is the kind of little man who struts around with a chip on his shoulder because he feels he's got to prove something."

Ed stopped behind the desk and sat down. "It's not his fault you're an Amazon, and we sure as hell aren't here to discuss Sheriff DeLong's hiring policies, Wanda. We're talking about your conduct. Anything could've happened in that house. Five minutes might seem like a long time to wait outside when you don't know what's going on in there, but it's a helluva lot more of a wait when you're in trouble and need the help."

"I had it all under control," Wanda said.

"This time you did. But I'm telling you right now, there better not be any other times." Ed unwrapped a piece of nicotine gum, popped it in his mouth. "I know you're bored here, but from now on you wait for backup. That or you start looking for an opening in some other department. You'd do well with the staties. They'll teach you how to play by the damn rules. I don't know why I can't."

"I never said I was bored."

Ed picked up the phone. He paused with his hand over the buttons and looked at Wanda. "You don't have to say it. You show it, which is just as bad. Maybe worse. So you take your head out of your ass and get back to work now. I have to call Barry DeLong and explain why you didn't leave anything for his deputy to do except direct traffic."

Wanda went out, closing the door behind her. Margie Kennard worked the reception desk. She looked like Tammy Faye Bakker's long-lost twin, except for the cheap Avon jewelry. Since all nine-one-one calls were now routed to a county call center in Skowhegan, Margie only worked part-time. She did a little typing for the chief, filed paperwork, made coffee if she felt like it. Mostly she read romance novels and did Sudoku puzzles.

Margie looked up from a Bertrice Small paperback. "He chew you out?"

"Oh, like you didn't have your ear pressed against the door the whole time." Wanda picked up the coffee pot, sniffed at it, sloshed it around a little and put it back on the warmer. It had most likely been sitting there for hours.

The receptionist laughed, her makeup cracking slightly. "I've got to eavesdrop. There's not much else for me to do around here," she said. "Ed was almost right, you know."

"Jesus, Margie. Not you, too."

"He thinks you're bored because it's easier than talking to you about the baby."

Wanda said, "It's not about the baby. That's not the problem."

Margie raised her penciled-on eyebrows. "Okay, fine. Maybe I've got an ulterior motive for wanting you to join the troopers. With you out of the picture, I'll have to chase the men off with a stick."

"I can't picture you chasing away any man, with or without a stick."

Margie shrugged. "So I don't like playing hard to get."

"Looking for another husband? You can have mine."

"Oh hell no, honey. I've worn out three husbands already. One man can't handle this much woman. I just want to have me a little fun."

Wanda grabbed her hat. "You do that. I need to go out and catch some bad guys."

"I'll tell you what you ought to do." Margie stood up, leaned over the desk, shaking a pudgy finger at Wanda. "Take off an hour or so, tell Jim to let somebody else fill the pill bottles, and meet you at home. Or just call that guy you've got going on the side. It's never too late in the day for a nooner."

But Wanda didn't go home for a quickie. She finished out her shift parked by the elementary school with her radar gun pointed down the street. By three o'clock she had issued six speeding tickets and busted a seventeen year-old girl for driving without a license.

She stopped by the station to turn in the cruiser. Bill McKinney, his belly straining the buttons on his uniform, came out the door as Wanda was going in. He stepped aside to let her through, a smirk on his broad face.

Wanda took off her hat and sighed. "What now?"

Big Bill shook his head, walked out laughing.

Margie had gone for the day. The door to Ed's office stood open. The chief was on the phone with someone. That was fine. Wanda didn't want to see Ed anyway. When she checked her mailbox, she found a note on department stationery. Someone had drawn a lousy imitation of Calvin, the little boy from the "Calvin and Hobbes" comic strip, grinning over his shoulder and urinating on the ground. It was like the decal some morons put on the rear windows of their trucks. A message in shaky block letters ran beneath the cartoon figure: HELP! I GOT TO PEE! Wanda grabbed a pen. She drew an arrow pointing at Calvin's crotch and wrote: TRY TWEEZERS, NEEDLEDICK. She folded up the paper, slid it into McKinney's mailbox. See if that would make the idiot laugh.

10

Hag and Earl stopped at the Northland Hotel in Jackman for lunch and a few more beers. The Northland was a big red building that looked more like an auction barn than a hotel from the outside, but the place was clean and cheap and did great business during the fishing and snowmobile seasons. You could get a room for fifteen bucks a night, so long as you didn't mind sharing a bathroom with a bunch of other people. Hag liked to stop here to get warm after making winter drug runs into Canada along the ITS snowmobile trail. Middle of the day in June, he and Earl had the place to themselves except for a couple of guys at the bar.

Hag told the waitress to bring a pitcher of beer. When she left, he turned to Earl, said, "So you with me on this, or what? Buds? Partners? Compadres? Me and you against all the assholes in the world, just like always."

"I just don't see how you're going to do it," Earl said. "How do you get hired to do the thing, the job? It ain't like you can put an ad in the paper, you know."

"First of all, retard, it's called a *contract*. You get a *contract* to kill a guy. We just got to let it get around that we're guys who can take care of things for people."

Earl looked away, said, "I bet you'll be glad to get back home."

Hag snorted, digging at a deep gouge in the tabletop with his fork. The last person he wanted to see was his wife.

Earl said, "Roxanne told me to make sure you went to see her when you got back. She moved to Skowhegan a couple months ago. They finally got to the top of the waiting list for Indian Ridge."

Hag said "So the Rock got into a welfare apartment. Whooptie-shit for her."

"She wants to see you, Hag. The kids do, too."

"My kids don't hardly know me, and I got doubts that a couple of them are mine anyway. I mean, you ever seen two white people have a black baby? Know why the Rock wants to see me? Money. I bet she thinks I still have that eighty grand the fuckin' Mounties confiscated. Only time she ever wants me around is when she thinks my wallet's too fat."

"She's working at that new Chinese place in Skowhegan. Know what Roxanne did last week?"

"Brought you a pu-pu platter? Licked your balls? How the fuck should I know?"

"No," Earl said. "She gave me some money to pay a speeding ticket."

"Who popped you?"

"Wanda Philbrick."

Hag grinned. "Man, I've wanted to put the boots to her since high school."

The waitress returned with the pitcher and two pilsner glasses. Hag checked her out when she leaned over to set the beer on the table. She caught him trying to stare down her blouse and straightened up, scowling.

Hag grinned, said, "No harm in looking."

She snorted and walked away.

"I bet we'll make so much money, pretty soon we can buy our own fucking bar," Hag said as he poured beers for both of them. "Private. Just us and a bunch of strippers."

Earl glanced away and sipped at his beer. Every time Hag tried to look him in the eye, Earl stared off to the side.

Hag said, "You don't want to do it, do you?"

"I've never had any reason to kill nobody."

"No? How about a shitload of money? That's reason enough for me."

Hag downed another beer. He said, "I need you in with me on this. You do the driving, keep a lookout for cops and witnesses. It's all you got to do. I'll be the shooter. Deal?"

"I guess so."

Hag laughed and slapped the table. All he needed now was a gun and a client.

11

Shelly sold Joey a white 2004 Toyota Corolla for seven grand, cash. "They're dependable and they're everywhere," she said. "You won't stand out." She wouldn't accept Petucci's Lincoln as part of the deal, though she did have her head mechanic, Lee, drive it to the bus terminal and leave it there. Joey had made sure to wipe it down good after transferring his things to his new car. The Toyota had new Pirelli tires, a new battery and brake pads. One of Shelly's other guys changed the oil and plugs, checked the transmission fluid.

Shelly took Joey into her office to wait while one of Shelly's guys changed the oil and plugs. Lighting up a menthol cigarette, she said, "I missed you. I kept expecting to hear from you. For a little while."

"I had to make a clean break."

"Hey, it's not like we were engaged or anything, right? We already knew the long distance thing wasn't working."

Joey nodded. "We had a lot of fun."

"Yeah, we did," Shelly said. "You ever think about me?"

"Sometimes. You?"

She shook her head. "Not for a long time."

"Saying I'm sorry won't change anything."

"It'd be nice to hear anyway."

"Sorry."

Shelly laughed, put her feet up on the desk, knocking a pile of invoices to the floor. "Wow. That was quite a moment," she said.

"What do you want from me?"

"Nothing, Joey. Not a goddamn thing." She went out to check on the mechanic's progress.

Joey slid into her chair, opened her desk drawers. He didn't know what he was looking for other than assurance Shelly wasn't setting him up. She was too calm about his sudden reappearance. There was a loaded .25 automatic in the middle drawer. The thing was barely the length of Joey's hand. A chick gun, not Shelly's style at all. Maybe she'd won it in a poker game. Joey took out the pistol, pocketed it.

Feeling around under the desk, he discovered Shelly's real piece. A holster fixed to the underside of the lap drawer held a Dan Wesson .357, aimed at the center of the chair Joey had been sitting in. If she'd wanted to, Shelly could have leaned forward, grabbed the thing and blown Joey back through the doorway.

It was probably for emergencies only, nothing to do with Joey. But he couldn't take the chance. Joey removed the cartridges from the cylinder, dropped them and the .25 into the wastebasket where he covered them over with some greasy, crumpled invoices. Not finding anything else, Joey slid the .357 back into its hiding place and returned to his own chair.

Shelly returned to tell him the car was ready. "Don't be a stranger," she said when Joey got behind the wheel.

12

By six o'clock, Joey was across the Kittery Bridge and heading northeast along the Maine Turnpike with Son House moaning on the CD player. According to the map, it would take him another two hours to reach Wesserunsett. Traffic wasn't bad, even for rush hour. The Corolla handled well. It had New York tags, registered to a rental franchise owned by one of the numerous Kowalski cousins. The guy owed Shelly a favor and would claim Joey as a legitimate customer should the question ever be asked.

Joey planned on keeping such questions from coming up at all. He would get the tape from Evans—now Barker—and try to make the switch for Grace. Carl intended to fuck him over; Joey felt sure of that. There was nothing to be gained by letting Joey and Grace live. So Joey had to come up with some kind of rescue plan. It was funny, really, the idea of rescuing Grace Turner. She and Sam had saved his life. He'd repaid them with lies.

It was a Sunday afternoon in the spring of 2006. They sat at opposite ends of the couch in Joey's apartment in Beverly. Grace had a beer in her hand. Joey stuck with RC Cola because he was on the wagon. Whitey's Blues had been open a couple of months. Business was starting to pick up, but Joey's stockpile of cash kept getting smaller.

"I wanted to talk to you about the club," he said.

Grace arched one eyebrow. "I already know what you're going to say, Joe. Just like you already know the answer."

Joey snorted, said, "So we're a couple of mind readers, huh? You don't have the slightest idea what I'm going to ask you."

"No?"

"No."

She turned toward Joey, leaning back against the arm of the overstuffed sofa. "You're going to tell me money's tight and you're worried about your bar."

"Well..."

"Don't you interrupt me," Grace said, waving a finger at him. "Money's tight, and you see a way to draw in the crowds. You want me to convince Dad to come out of retirement and front your house band."

"What? You think I want to take advantage of Sam, cash in on his name?"

"Wouldn't be the first time somebody tried it." She took a long pull on her beer, eyeballing Joey over the bottle.

"Hey, fuck you. All I want from Sam is to learn harp. That's it. He's my friend, the only real friend I've had in a long time. I'd kill anybody who tried to use him like that."

Grace said, "Big talk."

Joey got up, started pacing. He was barefoot and the coolness of the floorboards helped calm him. "Look, I want you to manage Whitey's," he said. "I'm doing okay, but I know you could do it better."

Grace stared at the place where Joey had been sitting. She took a moment before saying, "I already have a job."

"Managing your father? You were great at that, but it can't be anything more than a part-time job since he retired."

"So? Why would I want to start working for you?"

"I'll let you run the place however you want. You consult with me on major decisions, but it'll be your show for the most part. And you'll still be able to take care of Sam's business.

What do you say?"

"Get me another beer," Grace said. "Then we'll talk about it. That doesn't mean I'm saying yes. Just that I'm curious."

Joey went to the kitchen. He popped the top off a bottle of Amstel Light and dumped the rest of his soda down the sink. Watching it fizz in the drain, he realized just how much he hated cola. It wouldn't hurt if he drank a little now and then, kept it under control.

When he got back to the living room, Grace was standing at the window. She looked at Joey and said, "This better not be a bunch of bullshit."

"You and Sam have done a lot for me. I'll always stand by you."

Lies, lies, lies.

Even though Joey had meant every word when he said them, he knew they all amounted to lies in the end. How could a guy like him make long-term commitments to anyone? Instead of trying to build a new life in Chicago, he should've kept running from the old one.

But here he was.

Lightning slashed the sky to the west. The rain fell in fat drops that hit so hard and fast the windshield wipers could barely keep up, even set on high. Joey listened to the water pounding on the roof, the tires rolling over the wet road.

13

Most summer days, Wanda drove her Jeep with the top off. She liked feeling the wind in her hair after having it up under the campaign hat all day. Wanda and her estranged husband, Jim, had a bungalow six miles north of town. This afternoon, she took her time going home, smelling the hay fields that had just been cut and watching small boats cruise Wesserunsett Lake. The sky was clear for now; the forecast had warned of thunder showers on the way. June was shaping up to be a wet month, and Wanda hoped the farmers could get their mowing done in time.

The house sat on three acres at the end of Fire Road Nine, with the lake just visible through the trees. Jim had bought it before they met. Wanda moved in a few months prior to the wedding. That was two years ago. Neither of them spent much time there anymore. When he wasn't filling prescriptions at the Walmart pharmacy over in Skowhegan, Jim usually stayed with his new girlfriend, Laurie. Wanda spent three or four nights each week with Evan Barker. On those rare times when Wanda and Jim were home together, there was a strained cordiality.

Jim's truck was in the driveway now. Wanda parked next to it and sat there a moment. This was the night he usually took Laurie bowling. Maybe the little skank had kicked him out. Wanda stepped up on the porch and called through the screen door. "Hey, Jim? You mind helping me put the top on the Jeep?"

Jim came to the door, a can of Pringles in his hand. He was still dressed for work: loafers, black socks, tan Dockers, white short-sleeved dress shirt with a red-and-blue striped tie. Jim said, "Can it wait a minute? I want to talk to you about something."

"That's never good."

Wanda tugged the screen door open. Jim moved aside to let her in the house. She smelled booze on his breath as she passed, went into the kitchen and saw four empty beer bottles on the table, a fifth one well on its way to joining them. The scent of alcohol reminded her that there was still half a bottle of Allen's coffee brandy in the cupboard. Wanda could use a drink herself. She said, "So, what's wrong?"

Jim snorted. He leaned back against the counter, his hands braced on either side of the sink. "You assume 'cause I've had a couple beers and want to talk that there's automatically a problem." His hair was mussed. A few potato chip crumbs clung to his tie.

"Come on, Jim. We never talk anymore and, last I knew, you hardly ever drank this much in an entire week." Wanda reached out to brush the crumbs off him.

Jim grinned, showing off his perfect teeth. "I still care about you, Wanda. You know that, right?"

Him and his damn grin. She couldn't help smiling back when she saw him like that, even though she knew he was about to drop something heavy on her. Wanda tossed her keys on the table. She stepped back. He was only an inch shorter than her. She had loved being able to look him in the eye. Jim would be forty-seven in a few weeks; Wanda was thirty-two. The differences in their ages had never bothered her. For a while they'd been happy together.

But then Wanda got pregnant.

Cynthia June Philbrick died two days after they brought her home. SIDS. Crib death. People said it was just one of those things. Even the doctors said that. None of it made the loss any easier. Jim started staying out later each evening, spending weekends with "a friend." That friend turned out to be Laurie Marcoux, one of Jim's coworkers. Jim didn't care that Wanda knew about his girlfriend, and Wanda surprised herself by not caring either. Then she started seeing Evan Barker because she figured, hey, fair's fair.

Jim opened his mouth like he was about to speak, turned away quickly and belched. He said, "Sorry. Didn't want to burp in your face."

Wanda wrinkled her nose, fanned the air between them. "Noted and appreciated."

"I think it's time we got divorced," Jim said.

So there it was, out in the open after months of dancing around the subject, of having half the people in town gossiping about it. Wanda blew out a breath, sat down at the table. No wonder Jim had needed to drink those beers. He hated confrontations of any kind and probably assumed she'd go ballistic on him.

Jim said, "I mean, there's no point in us still going through the motions, right?"

"Okay." Not that Wanda could see living separate lives as *going through the motions.*

Jim still looked worried. He opened another beer and took a big swallow. "It's for the best, I think."

"I said it was okay, Jim. You don't have to keep trying to justify it to me."

"Thing is, I want the house."

Wanda sighed. "It's your house. I'm not going to try screwing you out of it, if that's what you think. Hell, I offered to move out weeks ago so you and Laurie wouldn't have to stay in her dinky apartment."

Jim pounded down the last of the beer, burped again. He said, "Always so damn agreeable, aren't you? It's a wonder you manage to arrest anybody."

"What? Where the fuck is this coming from?"

"All I'm saying is you're pretty damn quick to go along with this whole thing. It's like you want to get divorced."

"Jesus Christ, Jim. We both just said we wanted it. I'm not in the mood for head games right now. Just have your lawyer call me when the papers are ready, and I'll sign."

Jim dropped his empty bottle on the floor. "Maybe if you'd made a goddamn effort, we wouldn't even be discussing this."

"Me? What the fuck, Jim? You're the one who started running around with that dumb cunt Laurie." Wanda saw the slap coming—Jim was that drunk, that slow—but she didn't duck or try blocking the blow because it took her brain too long process what she saw. Jim had never before laid a hand on her in anger. She'd assumed he knew better. Wanda's head snapped back and she felt a trickle of blood on her lip.

Jim stepped away, looked at Wanda's bloody mouth and then down at his hand as if he were trying to figure what had just happened. When he looked up again, Wanda punched him in the nose. It was a solid shot. Wanda felt the cartilage mash under her knuckles. Jim's blood ran hot down the backs of her fingers.

"Goddamn it." Jim bent over, covering his face with both hands. "You broke my fucking nose."

"No I didn't," Wanda said. She had heard noses break before, and there hadn't been that telltale crunching sound. Taking an ice cube tray out of the fridge, Wanda emptied it into a dish towel. She handed it to Jim. "Here. Now take a seat before you fall down."

Jim pulled out a chair, dropped into it. He took the ice pack and held it to his face, looked up at Wanda. "I'm sorry. I didn't mean to..."

"Yeah, you did," she said. "You just don't know why. Neither do I, but it better not happen again. And as much as I can't stand the bitch, if I ever find out you hit Laurie, I'll kick your ass."

"Laurie," Jim said, pushing himself upright again. "Shit. I told her I'd be home an hour ago."

He stumbled against the kitchen table. Wanda had to steady him with both hands. She said, "Wait until I get the top on the Jeep. I'll give you a ride."

"I'm good," Jim said. He pulled away and headed for the door.

"Jim, you just polished off most of a six-pack. You aren't driving anywhere."

He dropped the bloody towel on the floor, went outside.

Wanda followed while the screen door was still hissing back into place. She said, "James Arthur Philbrick, you'd better park your ass in that Jeep and wait for me."

Jim walked around to the driver's side of his GMC and got in. His upper lip and chin were covered in blood. Some of it dripped onto his shirt. Jim turned the key, yanked the stick into reverse. Before backing into the road, he leaned out the window, said, "Arrest me, why don't you?" He drove off toward the main road.

Wanda's purse was still in the Jeep. She fished out her keys and stood there holding them, watching her soon-to-be-ex-husband speed away. Dropping the keys back into the bag, she grabbed her cell phone to speed dial Ed Gauthier.

14

Joey checked into a motel in Skowhegan, a small town on the banks of the Kennebec River. It would have been better to stay in Wesserunsett. That's where Evans/Barker was. However, Wesserunsett didn't have any motels. But it was only ten miles from Skowhegan to Wesserunsett. No big deal.

The Riverside Motel had two wings stretching east to west from a central office that also housed a game room and laundry area. An in-ground pool with a diving board and slide lay in front of the east wing. Joey had driven out of the thunder storm, but the dark clouds were heading this way. Even so, a family of six was splashing around and shouting when Joey parked in front of the office.

Joey went into the office. The place was close and stifling, all the windows shut tight. The desk clerk was a tall, hunched old guy who smelled like pipe smoke and scented soap. He switched off a TV behind the counter, looked at Joey. "Hot enough for you?"

"It's only about eighty," Joey said. "That's nothing. But if you're too warm, why don't you turn on the AC?"

"Oh, the heat don't bother me none," the old man said.

Joey asked for a room at the far end of the west wing. Fewer people to observe his comings and goings there.

"Yeah, it can get a little noisy near the pool sometimes," the clerk said. "But this is normally a pretty quiet place. I can put you in 210. That's the last room at the far end."

Joey paid cash for three nights in advance, signing in under the name Joe Carmichael. He had a phony New York State driver's license, a Social Security card and two credit cards to back up that identity. The documents and plastic had been in Joey's apartment safe for two years. The credit cards were fakes. The Corolla was "rented" under the Carmichael name, too. When choosing an alias, Joey liked to stick with his real first name. It eliminated any chance of forgetting. He picked surnames that began with a "C" for the same reason. Simple was always best.

The clerk handed Joey a room key. He said, "You got family in the area, or you here on business?"

"Business," Joey said.

"What do you do?"

Jesus, the questions. Joey said, "Sales. Boring stuff, really. I'm meeting clients here and in Wesserunsett, so I'll be out a lot."

The old man nodded. He said, "Well, enjoy your stay, Mr. Carmichael."

Joey walked out to the car, moved it down to the space in front of his room. Room 210 had a queen-sized bed, a nightstand with a clock radio, a small round table with two chairs, a TV set, a three-drawer bureau, a narrow closet and a bathroom. Joey flicked on the lights and the air conditioning, left the curtains closed; the room was not hot, just stuffy like the office. Everything in the place was some shade of brown, from the paneling on the walls to the beige bedspread and the tan phone. Probably hadn't been redecorated since about 1974.

Joey set his laptop on the table, tossed his bag on the bed. He went into the bathroom to take a leak. The smell of Pine-Sol hung heavy in the air. At least the room was clean. Looking in the mirror, he said, "Yeah, it's a dump, but don't be so fucking fussy. You've stayed in worse places."

The worst place he'd ever lived was the Meredith Hotel in Lawndale, on Chicago's West Side. Joey had wanted to stay below the radar for a while after getting to Chicago, just in case Carl had guys out looking for him. A transient hotel that rented rooms by the week or month, the Meredith was not just *under* the radar. It was so far off that it might as well have been non-existent.

At the time, the plan had been to stay there for a month or so. Joey passed the days getting shitfaced on vodka and listening to the blues. He bought himself a book of harmonica lessons: something like *Harmonica for Pinheads.* Most of the songs had been hoary old chestnuts. Joey sat in his room trying to learn "Red River Valley," "The Streets of Laredo" and how to make his harp sound like a train. He figured a start, even a lame one, was better than nothing at all.

Early on the morning of Joey's tenth day there, an old man came into his room. The guy didn't knock, didn't announce himself. He just opened the door and walked right in. Joey was sitting on the bed, fumbling through "Oh! Susannah" while the bottle of Ketel One on his window sill got emptier. He looked up to see this old black man standing there in the doorway, the dim light from the hallway shining off his smooth scalp. Joey had never seen such a dark-skinned black person. Some contemporary of Howlin' Wolf had once described the great blues singer's skin as being so dark it was almost purple. Looking at this stranger in his room, Joey remembered that description.

Joey set his harp on the bed, said, "Thought I locked that door." He kept a loaded .38 beneath his pillow but didn't go for it. If this man had wanted him dead, Joey would already be bleeding out. Still, he ought to kick himself. Getting a little drunk was okay. Drunk enough to forget basic precautions was too much.

"I doubt you could think of much at all over that racket you been making," the stranger said. "Some of the dudes that live here don't hear so good, but you're liable to make the others poke out their own eardrums if you keep blowing like that."

"You the day manager?" Maybe someone had complained and this guy came up to warn him about the noise.

"No, I don't work here," the man said. He leaned back to look at something further along the hallway before returning his attention to Joey. "An old friend of mine was living here. He passed away yesterday and I came with my daughter to collect his things. My name's Sam Turner."

"Joe Collins."

"So tell me, Joe. What did that poor harp ever do to you that you got to mistreat it so?"

Joey squinted, looked him up and down. Sam was a little under six feet tall with an average build. His knuckles were swollen. Arthritis? Lines showed around his eyes, his mouth. The hairs of his soul patch were white.

Sam.

Sam Turner.

The name rang a bell.

Then a gong.

"Jesus Christ, you're Slammin' Sam Turner." Joey stood up to shake the man's hand, fell backward onto the mattress.

"Don't blaspheme, boy," Sam said. "Now, I don't know what business a young man like you has living at the Meredith, but I hate to see it. You want to blow harp for real or is it just some kind of self-torture while you drink yourself to death?"

"I want to learn the blues."

Sam crossed the room, picked up the book and flipped through it. He said, "You ain't going to learn them from this thing. Hanging out in a flophouse won't help, either."

"Man, I'd give anything to play like you. I've got all your stuff on CD."

"That right?"

"Yeah."

Sam grabbed the vodka bottle, tossed it and the harmonica

book in the trash can. "My girl's going to run me on home now. Get yourself together and come see me tonight, little place called Juke over on Wabash. We'll talk after my set, but you better make sure you're sober. I got no time for drunks."

"I thought you said you had a friend here," Joey said. "You have to be a drunk to stay here. Or a junkie. It's in the fine print."

"My friend passed away, like I said. I didn't speak to him the last year of his life. That don't mean I can't take care of his things, make sure he gets a decent funeral. He didn't have no family left." Sam walked out to the hall. "Get your head on right."

Joey sat there a long while with the door still open, trying to decide whether he had just met a blues legend or if it was only the booze. Then he puked in the wastebasket.

The air conditioner rattled, drowning out the noise of the kids in the pool. Joey sat on the bed, picked up his cell phone. He should call Sam. Grace was in the habit of talking to her father every day and Sam would be worried about her by now. Sam would be wondering about Joey, too, wondering why Whitey's Blues was closed. Maybe he'd already called the cops.

Joey held the phone, flipped it open. What was he supposed to say, anyway? Could he give Sam the truth, or would he come up with more lies to cover the four years' worth already hanging over their friendship? He stared at the buttons, said, "Fuck."

It was getting late. Joey still needed to drive over to Wesserunsett, take a look around. He stuffed the phone back in his pocket. He could call Sam later.

15

Jim got pulled over on Tuttle Road, four miles south of the bungalow. People watched from steps, lawns and windows. It looked like a big bust: Jim's truck, two police cruisers with their lights flashing, and Wanda's Jeep all parked at the curb. Jim blew a point-eleven on the Breathalyzer. Bill McKinney handcuffed him, guided him into the backseat of a cruiser.

Ed Gauthier stood next to Wanda, his right cheek distended by the massive wad of nicotine gum he chewed. He was still in his uniform. "This is a clusterfuck," he said.

"What was I supposed to do, let him drive drunk? Maybe get wrapped around a telephone pole or plow into some kids?"

Ed cut his eyes at her. "Wanda, you know me better than that. What I mean is, you're going to take a ration of shit for it. Bill and the part-time boys'll tease you a little, but it ain't them that should worry you. You'd best be prepared for nasty comments when you pull somebody over, maybe some whispers and dirty looks when you're shopping at the IGA. It'll pass soon enough, but when a cop's personal shit goes public, it makes a lot of people talk."

"They can mind their own business."

"Yeah, that'll happen. Look, people like you and they like Jim, too. But they love gossip. I'm just saying don't be surprised by it, and don't let it get to you."

The breeze stirred Wanda's hair, and she pulled it back away from her face. "You know what really sucks? It didn't have to get so public. I could've stopped him back at the house, but I didn't. I just stood there staring while he left."

"So the whole thing's your fault." Ed spat out his gum, pulled another piece from his pants pocket. "That's a load of crap, and I don't want to hear anything like it again. Jim was drunk when you got home. You had a fight. He got in his truck and you told him not to drive. He did it anyway. End of story, Wanda. People make stupid decisions every day and they want us to believe someone else is at fault. You've seen it a thousand times. I wouldn't let Jim blame you for this. I'll be double-god-damned if you're going to do it to yourself."

Big Bill McKinney's cruiser pulled away from the curb, its flashers off now. The town didn't have a jail of its own, not even a holding cell at the police station. Jim would be booked and held overnight at the new Somerset County Jail in East Madison. In an hour or two, Kenny Poissonnier would come along with his wrecker to haul Jim's truck away.

Ed said, "You going to be all right to work tomorrow?"

"Yeah."

"That's what I wanted to hear." He patted her on the shoulder, got into his cruiser and drove off. Most of the gawkers had drifted back to whatever they'd been doing before the excitement. Eleanor Davis, who knew Wanda's parents through church, stood at the end of her driveway, watching with her arms folded across her skinny chest. Wanda gave Mrs. Davis a hesitant wave, said hello as she walked by on her way back to the Jeep.

The old lady scowled. "It's awful, the things that happen when women cheat on their husbands. Maybe somebody's learned her lesson, hmm?" Mrs. Davis turned away and scuttled to her house before Wanda could recover enough to reply.

Wanda backed her Jeep into Mrs. Davis' driveway, idling there while she put her hair into a ponytail. Before she pointed the Jeep toward home, Wanda saw Mrs. Davis in the rearview mirror, watching through the curtained window in her door. The old bitch could kiss Wanda's ass. Sooner or later, something else would come along for her to get all high-and-mighty about.

Dusk was making its lazy crawl across the sky by the time Wanda got home. The clouds predicted by the radio weatherman had moved in. Wanda wrestled the top onto her Jeep. It flapped around in the growing wind, but she got it snapped into place without much trouble. When she finished, she took off her gun belt and sat on the porch, waiting for the rain. One of the most peaceful sounds in the world was fat summer raindrops breaking against the porch's shingled roof. It wasn't long in coming.

Her neighbors across the way had been having a barbecue. Now they scrambled to get their food off the picnic table and into the house before it got drenched. Once his dinner and his kids were inside, Gary Meader came across the road, hunching against the rain even though he was already soaked. There was a white Chevy Caprice Wanda didn't recognize parked at an angle on their lawn, just where the road ended. Gary walked in a wide arc around the car.

"Get on up here before you drown," Wanda said as the man climbed her steps.

"A little warm rain don't bother me." Gary blew water off the tip of his nose. He said, "I got a problem. You see that car over there, the Chevy?"

"Yeah."

"Well, the guy who parked it there, I told him he couldn't. I said it's my lawn and not some public parking lot. You know what he told me?"

"No idea, Gary." All she wanted was to sit here and relax for a little while. Was that too much to ask?

"Well, I can't repeat it, but it was pretty bad." The Meaders were Seventh Day Adventists. Gary wouldn't say shit if he had a mouthful.

Wanda stood up. "Do you know this guy? Ever see him before?"

Gary shrugged. "I've seen him around town some, but I don't know his name. He's real big, Wanda, and I think he's been drinking. He took a bunch of fishing gear out of his trunk and went through the woods there to the lake."

"That's what I need, one more drunk to round out my day."

Gary glanced down at his soggy clothes. Bits of mown grass clung to his sandals, to the tops of his feet. He started back down the steps. "I didn't want to call nine-one-one or anything over a few swears and some tire tracks in my grass. But I thought, you know, maybe you could go talk to him? Get him to move his car off my lawn?"

"I'm off duty, Gary, and I've had a long hard day. Just call the station directly instead of nine-one-one and they'll send someone out."

He looked her up and down. She was still in her uniform. "I hate to bug you like this, but I figured since you're right here anyway..."

Wanda sighed. All she wanted to do was sit on her porch—which would not be hers to enjoy much longer—with a tumbler full of coffee brandy and chill, so of course it would work out like this. Margie had gone home for the day. The chief was either home by now or on his way there. McKinney and the part-timer, Harris, were out on patrol. Anyone calling the station would get a message telling them to dial nine-one-one, which Meader didn't want to do. Wanda buckled on her belt, slid the nightstick into its ring. She followed Gary across the lawn.

The Chevy had dealer plates from Lakeside Auto. The inside was immaculate, not even a candy wrapper in sight. So it belonged to Stony Bouchard or one of his salesmen. Probably the latter, since Stony had a pond stocked with trout on his own property. Also, Stony was slightly built and no one had ever heard him use profanity.

"Go on in the house," she said. Gary nodded and jogged across his yard. Wanda almost called it in on her cell phone to let McKinney handle it. But she didn't need the hassle that dealing with Big Bill would bring. She'd just go tell the trespasser he had to find some other place to fish.

The road ended at the edge of Gary's lawn, where a band of trees and underbrush stood between the homes and the shore. Wanda squinted, trying to see any trace of movement. The rain and the thick cloud cover threw everything beneath the trees into gray-green shadow.

Her hair and clothes were already plastered to her skin, so Wanda slogged through waist-high ferns, burdock and pigweed, trying not to think about deer ticks burrowing their heads into her skin. She had only gone a few yards when a man came huffing up the bank. He grabbed a leaning cedar sapling with his left hand to haul himself up, swinging his right hand, which clutched a broken-down fly rod, for balance. Wanda stood right above him, too close. She had to back away so he wouldn't jab her in the eye with the end of the fly rod as he came up.

The guy stooped over to catch his breath, squinted at Wanda through the rain. He was big, not quite as tall as Wanda, but his shoulders were broad and his biceps stretched the sleeves of his T-shirt. He also carried a good-sized roll of fat around his middle, which explained why he was panting from the short climb up the steep bank. The rain had soaked him. Some of that wetness had to be from sweat as well; Wanda felt the heat coming off him, pulsating in time with his heavy breaths. A Red Sox cap kept the worst of the rain out of his eyes.

"A guy could break his fucking neck in here," he said. "You people ought to post a warning sign or something, keep from getting sued."

"That's funny, because I was just about to give you a warning."

He looked at Wanda, seeming to notice the uniform and badge for the first time. "You pulling double duty as a game warden or something? Go ahead and check my creel if you want. I ain't caught nothing, barely even started casting when the rain hit."

Wanda said, "What's your name, sport?"

"Willard. Willard Bailey."

"Let's see some ID, Mr. Bailey."

Willard's tennis shorts were stretched tight across his wide hips. He reached into the front pocket for his wallet, handed it over to Wanda. "What's this all about?"

Wanda looked at his driver's license. *Bailey, Willard L.* The license gave Bailey's address as 118 Katahdin Road, Millinockett. It also said he was forty-three years old, two hundred and fifty pounds. The license had been renewed in March, so the weight was clearly a lie. Willard looked a lot closer to three hundred, though there was a lot of hard muscle under the fat. Wanda handed back the wallet. "Millinockett, huh? That's a long way to come just to fish, especially when you've got a great big lake right there in your own backyard."

"I live here now."

"Where?"

"Right in town, over on Chestnut Street. Got a nice little house. Want to come see it?"

"How long have you been in Wesserunsett?"

Willard blew out his cheeks. "What does that matter?"

"How long have you been in Wesserunsett?"

"I don't know, a couple-three months. I just ain't had time to get the address changed on my license. Is that okay with you? I want to get out of the rain now."

"You work for Stony Bouchard? What do you do?"

"What the fuck you think? I sell cars."

Wanda smiled. "I'll bet customers just love your way with

people, too. Is that your company car back there, Mr. Bailey? The white Caprice?"

He nodded slowly, looking disgusted.

"Well, you can't park there. This is all private property and the landowner asked you to leave. I doubt if Stony would appreciate having one of his vehicles towed because of you."

"It wasn't posted. I didn't see any *No Trespassing* signs anywhere."

Wanda held up her hand. "That doesn't matter. The owner told you not to park there and you did it anyway, and you were verbally abusive. You're going to have to find someplace else to fish. There's a public landing not four miles from here."

"Like I'm going to go there. Would you eat a fish caught where some moron spills gas and oil from his outboard into the water, or little kids go wading in their pissy diapers?"

"That's really not my problem, Mr. Bailey. Maybe you aren't hearing me clearly, but you can't stay here."

Willard shook his head and grinned. "I was leaving anyway. Or didn't you notice I'm going *away* from the water, Dickless Tracy?"

Wanda took the handcuffs from her belt. "How'd you like to go for a ride with me?" She stood with her legs apart, ready to move fast if Willard decided to try her. It looked like he was thinking about it. Then his shoulders relaxed and he shook his head. Wanda stepped aside, waited while he walked past her with his fly rod held above the undergrowth. It got snagged among low branches instead. Wanda put away the cuffs and followed a few feet behind him, her right hand resting on the butt of her Beretta.

Gary Meader stood on his porch, watching as Wanda and Willard emerged from the woods. Willard stopped next to the car. He pointed his rod at Gary.

"That's enough of that," Wanda said.

Willard put his fishing gear in the back seat. He straightened up, gave Wanda an innocent look. "What now?"

"Don't threaten that man again."

"Pointing at him's a threat?"

"From what little I know about you, I choose to read it that way. If Mr. Meader wanted, he could press charges against you, but he just wants you to stay off his property. Don't even drive down this road again, Mr. Bailey. Because if I find out you did, you're going to jail."

Willard chuckled and shook his hands, pretending to be scared. He slid down behind the steering wheel, tossed his hat onto the passenger's seat. The engine turned over and the window came down with an electric whine. "You need to lighten up, lady," Willard said. "Maybe get somebody to throw a good fuck into you. Or are you really a tongue-and-groover like everybody says?"

He was just trying to provoke her, get her to hit him so he could holler about unnecessary force. She should shrug it off and let him drive away. People had said worse things to her over the years. Much worse. So why was this crap eating at her today? All Wanda had to do was let him leave, now that he'd gotten in the last word. But his smirk got her, that stupid smirk, the same kind she'd seen on the faces of the people who watched while Jim was hustled into a cruiser. It would be so nice to punch this smartass Willard Bailey right in the mouth, to feel his lips rupture against his teeth. Hell, some of Jim's blood was still on her knuckles.

Wanda bent down, close enough to see the hairs sprouting from Willard's nostrils. The bastard grinned like he expected her to lean in and give him a kiss, but he yelped when she laid her baton across his forehead. It wasn't even a blow. She held it by the side handle with the shaft along the outside of her forearm, using just enough pressure to force him back against the headrest. Wanda yanked the keys from the ignition and dropped them on the grass. She took a couple steps back, keeping the same grip on the baton and holding it at an angle across her chest. "Get out of the vehicle, Mr. Bailey."

"Stupid cunt." Willard pushed open the door, rocking the car as he heaved himself up and out. He came at Wanda with his head lowered and his big hands reaching for her. She raised the nightstick, ready to bring it down on his shoulder. But Willard slipped in the wet grass and went down before she could take a swing at him. The breath came out of him all at once when he hit the ground. He lay there on his belly, gulping at the air. Wanda planted a knee in the small of Willard's back, grinding it against his kidney until he yelped. She cuffed his hands behind him.

Wanda clicked on her radio to call for a cruiser. She squatted next to Willard, said, "Now we'll go someplace dry and have a nice little talk. You stupid cunt."

16

Joey pulled into the dirt parking lot of an abandoned factory on the hill above town. A sign over the building's front door read *Wesserunsett Shoe.* A smaller sign, hanging askew, proclaimed Wesserunsett shoes to be *The World's Most Comfortable Work Shoes.* All but a few of the factory's windows were broken. Weeds poked up through gaps in the steps.

Getting out of the car to stretch, Joey left the door open. John Lee Hooker and Van Morrison sang "Serves Me Right to Suffer" on the car stereo, slow, steady bass notes rattling the cheap door-mounted speakers. A headache was building, a knot at the base of Joey's skull that he knew would soon spread out until it squeezed the back of his head. He needed a drink and some sleep. First he had to get the lay of the land.

Wesserunsett looked like a hick town on the maps. It looked smaller in real life. Two church steeples stood above the trees at the east end of town. What passed for downtown was only three blocks. The residential streets stretched out and seemed to disappear, with only house lights showing through the trees to indicate there was any kind of civilization there.

The rain had come and gone, leaving the air dense with humidity. Joey breathed in the smell of wet leaves. It could have been worse; he'd expected to be gagging on the stink of cow shit by now. He retrieved the MapQuest pages from the car and looked them over with a penlight. Barker's house was represented by a little red star on the eastern side of the lake, about six miles north of downtown. 538 Sirois Road. Not on the water, but within a mile of it.

He noticed his songwriting journal lying on the backseat of the car. It was a slim notebook, bought at a stationer's in Winnetka. Joey had been carrying it around for almost four years and it was still blank. But he'd been too damn busy with getting Whitey's up and running, with his harmonica lessons. Maybe once this crap with Barker and Carl was over, he'd have time to sit down and write some songs.

Joey got back into the Corolla, drove down the hill. He stopped at the Cumberland Farms for a small bottle of ibuprofen. Back in the car, he dry-swallowed four of them. He turned onto Main Street, taking note of the police station, a small brick building. There were a lot of empty storefronts. Joey turned around at the strip mall on the far end of town and made another pass down the street.

The only place still open was a bar called The Vault. It had obviously been a bank in a past life. A Budweiser sign glowed in the window above the old night-deposit drop. The parking lot was packed with pickups, cheap cars like Cavaliers and Neons, a few motorcycles. Joey parked across the street. He got out and locked the car.

As he stepped up onto the sidewalk, Joey heard some kind of hard rock music on the jukebox and the clack of billiard balls hitting each other. A couple of biker-looking guys smoked cigarettes next to the open door, but they moved out of his way.

On the inside, the place looked like any other bar, except for the high, stamped-tin ceiling and the big old bank vault.

Joey found an empty stool at the bar, between a girl who looked too young to be there and a tall, skinny guy who should have killed his barber. The bartender was a perky little thing who reminded Joey of a much younger Katie Couric. When Joey ordered a draft, she pulled him one in a Mason jar, smiling while she did it. Just one beer, maybe something to eat, and then he would take a drive past Barker's house before heading back to the motel. He needed to make an early start tomorrow, find out if this Evan Barker character really was Todd Evans. He had to be sure. Bad enough he'd gotten Grace pulled into this shit, but he wasn't about to kill the wrong guy.

"Hey, can I get a burger and some onion rings?" Joey asked the bartender.

"How do you like it?" She grinned just enough to let him know she didn't mean the hamburger.

Joey was too damn tired to flirt. He said, "Medium rare with ketchup, mustard, relish and onions."

"Cheese?" She didn't smile this time. Maybe Joey had put her off. Maybe it was too hard to turn cheese into a sexual innuendo.

"No."

The Couric-clone nodded, wrote it down and went to the far end of the bar to give a waitress the slip. She stayed there.

The guy with the messed-up haircut swiveled around on his stool to lean in close to Joey. He said, "The food here sucks moose cocks. And it's fucking expensive. You're better off getting a couple of those dried-out red hots and a bag of chips over to Cumby's."

Joey sipped his beer. "What's a red hot?"

"A hot dog. They got that red skin, kinda snaps when you bite 'em." The guy looked Joey up and down. "Where you from, anyway?"

"New York."

"New York City?"

"New York City."

The guy shook his head. "What're you, a fucking parrot?"

Joey snickered into his Mason jar. He swallowed and said, "Just forget it."

"I look like a fucking retard to you? Huh? Big man from the big city."

The last thing Joey needed was to get into a fight with some shitfaced redneck, maybe end up in jail. Joey had never gone down for anything serious, but there was a sheet on him. Awkward questions would be asked if the cops had to run Joe Collins' fingerprints and came up with Joey Connolly's record. He set down his beer, turned so he was facing the guy. There was a look in his eye that Joey had seen before, a crazy kind of light that meant you would have to either kill this guy or mess him up real bad if you got into it with him. Joey said, "Hey, we had a misunderstanding, is all. I've been on the road all day and I'm half asleep already. I never called you retarded."

"You bet your ass I ain't no retard." The guy looked over Joey's shoulder and grinned. "You want to see a real retard, check out this fat bastard coming through the door right there."

Joey didn't turn around, in case the guy was trying to sucker punch him. A big fat man came over to stand next to them. He probably weighed around four hundred pounds, almost enough to make Carl Petucci look slim. His face was flushed. Beads of sweat hung from the ends of his hair. He said, "Hey, Hag."

The one called Hag kept grinning, said, "Jesus, Earl, you look like you're going to drop dead right here."

"Them bikers kept blocking the door so I couldn't get in. Didn't you see?"

"I wasn't looking for you. I figured it'd take you at least another hour to talk any money out of your mother."

Earl said, "She let me borrow sixty bucks 'cause I told her I needed it to pay the phone bill. If she knew you were back in town, she wouldn't give me nothing."

Hag grabbed his beer, slid his skinny ass off the stool. He jabbed Joey's arm. "Hey, you ought to come sit at a table with us and shoot the shit."

Joey shook his head. "Thanks, but I'm going to eat my burger, go back to my motel and get some sleep."

"You too good to drink with us? Being from New York City means your shit don't stink? Huh?"

This guy was just begging to be shot. Too bad Joey's pistol was back at the motel. "Walk away," Joey said.

"Tough motherfucker, huh?" Hag tried to hard-eye him.

"Tough as I need to be," Joey said, holding the stare. "But that doesn't matter right now because you guys're going to find yourselves a table and leave me alone."

Earl shifted his weight from foot to foot, said, "Come on, Hag."

"You're lucky I got better things to do," Hag said. They made their way across the room to an empty table.

The waitress brought Joey's order. He took a bite of the hamburger. Hag might have been an asshole, but he was right about The Vault's food. Joey finished it anyway, wiped his mouth and dropped the napkin on the table. He drank his beer, signaled for the bartender to bring his check. Things looked a little better now with food in his belly. Even lousy food made a difference. The short confrontation with Hag had gotten some adrenaline flowing. He paid his tab, left a five-buck tip and left.

Joey looked at the police station again as he drove by it on his way through town. No way did this place have more than half a dozen cops. That was all to the good, but Joey would also have to worry about the sheriff's department, maybe some state troopers if things got nasty. He slid *The Best of Sonny Boy Williamson* into the CD player. His headache was gone.

17
FRIDAY, JUNE 11

Joey rolled out of bed and crouched on the floor, the .38 in his hand, its hammer cocked. Sunlight crept in around the edges of the drawn curtains. What the hell had made that noise? It was a blast of some kind, loud enough to bring Joey out of a sound sleep. He looked at the clock. 6:30 a.m. *Christ.*

He got up and walked slowly across the room. Using the barrel of the revolver, he pushed the curtain just far enough aside to peek out the window. An eighteen-wheeler loaded with logs was heading down the hill into town. The driver let off another blast from its air brakes. Joey shook his head, dropped the curtain back into place. It had been a long time since he'd felt so jumpy, not since the first three or four months after leaving Brooklyn. Grace used to say he was nervous as a whore in church.

Tossing the pistol on the bed, Joey staggered into the bathroom and ran cold water in the sink. He splashed some on his face, filled a drinking glass. He drank, emptied the glass and refilled it, drank again.

After a quick shower, he wrapped a towel around his waist and sat on the bed. Joey picked up his cell phone, stared at it the same as he had the previous evening. He had to call Sam, should have called him right after stashing Weasel Face's body in a Dumpster back in Chicago. Joey dropped the phone on the bed and stood up.

Maybe he'd call after breakfast. Yeah, that was a better idea. Get a few cups of coffee inside him, maybe some pancakes made with those Maine blueberries Carl Petucci's wife so coveted. The clothes he had worn yesterday hung over the back of a chair. Joey grabbed them, slipped them on. He checked on the .38 buried under the clothes in his duffel bag, and put the bag in the closet. He picked up his wallet and car keys from the nightstand, his phone from the bed. Went back to staring at the phone.

Fuck it. There was no way he'd be able to eat until he made the damn call. Joey punched in the number from memory. It only rang twice, despite the fact that it wasn't yet 6:00 a.m. in Chicago.

"Hello?" Slammin' Sam Turner didn't sound like someone who'd just been jolted out of bed by a ringing phone. He had probably been up for hours.

Joey cleared his throat, said, "Sam, it's me."

"The hell's going on, boy? Whitey's is all locked up with a sign on the door, says *closed until further notice.* I can't get hold of Grace. She don't answer her phone. She don't reply to e-mails, don't answer her door. You seen her?"

"I saw her yesterday, Sam. She's okay for now."

Sam said, "What the hell do you mean, *for now?* Where's my girl? Where are you?"

Joey's stomach did a little hitch. "Grace is in New York."

"New York? What the fuck is she doing in New York? I talked to that bartender, what's her name, the one with eyebrow rings. Sherry. She doesn't know what's going on, told me nobody's seen you or Grace since Monday night. You in New York, too?"

"No, I'm not," Joey said.

"Well, where in God's name are you, boy?"

"Sam. Listen to me, Sam. Grace's been kidnapped."

"Say what?"

"Kidnapped," Joey said. "A couple of guys came to the club Tuesday morning. Guys with guns. They took Grace."

"Took her." Sam's voice was soft, controlled.

Joey's throat went dry. He said, "I'm going to get her back, Sam. I'm working on it right now."

"Why?"

"Why what? Why am I working on it? 'Cause I can't go to the cops. And you can't either, Sam. Call the cops and they'll kill her."

"No. Why did they want my girl? Who are these people, Joe?"

How much should he tell Sam? Fuck. "There's a guy in New York, a mob guy. He's been looking for me a few years."

"You steal money from him? You see something you shouldn't have?"

"No."

"Then what does he want with you?"

"I used to do things for him."

Joey's hair had dried in no time at all after the shower, but now it was damp again. He felt sweat creeping down his forehead. The room wasn't even warm.

"*Things.*"

"Yeah, things," Joey said. "But I quit all that, Sam. I walked away from it in '05 and came to Chicago to start over. I went straight. But my old boss, he's not a guy to let you just walk away."

"What'd you do for this man? What kind of things?"

"Bad things."

"You sell drugs? Kill people for him?"

"Sam, I'll get Grace back. She'll be okay."

Sam laughed. "How you gonna get my girl back? What you gonna do?"

"He had Grace brought to New York so he could make me do one more job for him. Once that's done, he'll let her go."

"That's what he told you?"

"Yeah."

"And you believe him? A man like that? Shit."

"I have to take him at his word, Sam. It's me he's pissed at. Soon as I finish this job, Grace will be cut loose." Joey rubbed his chin. Thank God he didn't have to look Sam in the eye right now.

Sam didn't reply for a moment. Joey heard his slow, controlled breaths. Then Sam said, "You might take this son of a bitch at his word, boy, but I sure don't. You do your little *job* for him, do his *things*. Then Mr. Gangster's gonna have you and Grace both killed. A man like that ain't got nothing to gain by turning either one of you loose."

Joey grinned. He couldn't help it. There was no fooling Sam Turner. "Sam, you have to let me handle this. Don't even think about getting involved. I know these people. I know how to deal with them."

"You done a great job so far," Sam said.

"Jesus, Sam. I never thought they'd take Grace. When they came in, I figured they were there to kill me. I knew they were pros, but I thought I could delay them long enough to give Grace a chance at getting out through the back. It didn't occur to me that they wanted to use her as leverage so I'd work for them again."

"What kinda job they want you to do?"

"Does it matter? I'll do what I have to for Grace."

"You're really something. You been lying to Grace and me ever since we met you. I bet your name ain't even Joe Collins, is it?"

"I've got to go, Sam. I'll call you as soon as I have Grace back."

"Damn it all, boy. I ain't done talking to you yet."

Joey turned off the phone. No doubt Sam was trying to call him back right now, but pieces of the phone which had used that old number were scattered among several trash cans at

O'Hare International. The new phone was clean. Disposable. Joey would replace it with another track phone this morning.

He sat there on the bed, shaking, his damp shirt plastered to his back. Time for another shower. His appetite was gone any-way.

18

Hag stood in Earl's backyard, pissing against the storage shed. Whizzing outside was better because the trailer's bathroom had that funky Earl-smell: part jizz and sweaty armpits, part Fritos and Old Spice. Truth be told, the whole trailer smelled the same way. Still, it was a hell of a lot worse in the shitter. Hag shook off, zipped up his cutoff jeans.

He walked out front just as a police cruiser turned into the driveway and parked behind Earl's truck. Hag sat down on the top step, picked up his beer can. There was a bit of damp bark clinging to his pinky toe. He scraped it off against the lower step.

Wanda Philbrick got out of the car, slid her nightstick through the ring on her belt and straightened her hat. As she crossed the lawn, Hag said, "Hey, Sarge. How's Wesserunsett's *finest* today?"

Wanda didn't smile back. "Charlie, I've told you before not to call me Sarge. I'm not a sergeant and Sargent was my maiden name."

"And I've told you not to call me Charlie, so I guess we're even."

Wanda scowled. There was a scabbed-over cut on her lower lip.

"What happened to your mouth? Cat fight?"

"Not your concern."

92

Hag said, "Whoa, sorry. I really hope this is a personal visit, because seeing you strap on that big stick gives me all kinds of ideas."

"I would've thought you got enough of that kind of action in jail, Charlie."

He leaned back and laughed, scratching a mosquito bite in his happy trail. "That's funny. How come you're the only cop in this whole frigging town with a sense of humor?"

"It probably goes along with being the only woman in the department."

Hag raised his beer in a toast, took a long swallow.

Wanda said, "I'm here because some of your neighbors complained you're playing music too loud and drinking liquor out in the street."

"Well, you can see I'm having a beer." He cocked his head to one side like he was trying to hear some faint sound. "But you know what's funny? I don't hear any music at all. You?"

"The caller said you had heavy metal music cranked up full blast with your stereo speakers set up in your windows." Wanda folded her arms below her breasts.

Hag gave her a smile. He said, "Oh, that. Yeah. See, I'm not going to lie to you, Sarge. I did have some loud music on a while ago. I've been locked up in a foreign country for a while and I just got back late last night. I felt like celebrating my freedom a little this morning. I put on some Van Halen and let it rip. I didn't think it'd bother anybody. Bob Rowell came hopping over on crutches to complain, but I turned it down. Hell, it's all the way off now."

"You're just Mr. Agreeable, aren't you? I remember a time when you'd slash somebody's tires for looking at you wrong."

He shrugged, still smiling. "Hey, people change."

Wanda said, "Some people do. So you're a Van Halen fan, huh? You like Sammy, Gary or Diamond Dave?"

"Sammy Hagar sucks moose cocks. And Gary Cherone? Don't even talk to me about that fag." Dumb bitch. Everybody knew David Lee Roth was the motherfucking man. It didn't matter to Hag that he'd only been about six years old when Roth left the band.

"Sounds like you're not so much into change after all." Wanda took out her notebook and flipped through it. "The neighbor who called said you told him, quote: *Why the fuck don't you go fuck yourself you fucking stupid-ass fuck.* I wrote that down because I want to send it in to the *Reader's Digest.*"

Hag drank some more beer. "It was Larry Nichols, wasn't it? I had to listen to his whiny ass a few minutes before Rowell came out. Larry's putting words in my mouth, Sarge. That ain't being good neighbors."

Pocketing her notebook, Wanda moved close. She stood six-foot-two, and she loomed over Hag, looking down, obviously trying to make him lean backwards and feel awkward. She said, "It's nice and quiet here right now, Charlie. Let's make sure it stays that way. I don't want to hear about you retaliating against anybody. And no more drinking beer out here, either. You know all about the open container law. Do it inside the house or in the backyard."

But Hag didn't lean back, didn't try to look up. He sat there staring straight ahead, his face only inches from Wanda's crotch. He breathed deeply through his nose to make it sound like he was snuffling around in her pussy. He smelled her lotion, imagined her rubbing it up and down those long legs. Then he sat back, said, "I'd better go in now. It's almost lunch time and I got a sudden craving for tuna. That ever happen to you?"

Wanda took another step forward, her belt creaking as she moved. Hag scooted backward on his ass far enough to stand up. He saw his own shit-eating grin reflected in the cop's sunglasses. Her mouth was set tight, her hands balled into fists.

Hag said, "I do something wrong? I got a history of that. *Incorrigible,* a juvie court judge called me this one time. Thanks for coming by, though. I get the message. You have a nice day, Officer Philbrick, ma'am." He stepped inside. The screen door, caked with so much crud that no air could pass through its mesh, banged shut behind him.

But Hag didn't fix anything for lunch. He hardly ever felt hungry anymore. Instead of eating, Hag knelt on Earl's couch and pulled back the dusty old sheet covering the window. He watched Wanda walk slowly back to her car. When she drove away, Hag said, "Now there goes one thing I *would* like to eat."

The toilet flushed. Earl came shuffling down the hall to the living room. He said, "Talking to yourself?"

Hag let the sheet fall back into place, squirmed around to sit on the couch where he had spent the night. He picked at some of the exposed foam fill coming out of the arm. "I have to talk to myself," he said. "It's the only way I can get any kind of intelligent conversation around here. Unless you got some deep fucking subject to discuss?"

"Ever sneeze and cut a fart at the same time?"

"That's impossible," Hag said. "You can't do it."

Earl headed for the kitchen, yawning. "I just did it a few minutes ago. Felt like I ripped out a new hole. I'm serious. Every time it happens I check my undies for blood."

Hag laughed, said, "I don't want to talk about your ass no more, Earl. We got to make plans."

Earl pawed through a pile of junk mail on the counter, knocking most of it onto the floor. "Where'd I leave the stupid remote?" It turned up under an empty microwave popcorn bag. Earl wiped some congealed grease off the remote, clicked on the Cartoon Network before pouring himself a bowl of cocoa cereal and sloshing chocolate milk over it. Earl shook the carton at Hag before putting it back in the fridge. "I hear they got satellite TV down to that new state prison in Warren, but I'm pretty sure you can't get chocolate milk in there."

Hag lit up a cigarette. "First it's your ass, now it's food. Fuck, dude. Think about something besides your gut for a change. It's half-past eleven and you're just now drag-assing out of bed. Don't you ever feel bad about being so goddamned lazy?"

Earl shrugged. He piled a TV tray with the cereal bowl, a six-pack of Country Kitchen cinnamon donuts and a Pepsi Big Slam, plopped his ass down in his broken recliner. "What were you looking at out the window?"

"That fucking queer-ass Larry Nichols called the cops on me because of the loud music. You believe that shit?"

"What music?" Bits of cereal fell out of Earl's mouth when he spoke. "I didn't hear nothing."

Hag blew smoke out his nostrils, settled back to watch TV. It was some weird Japanese cartoon he had never heard of, but he didn't care. He was busy wondering if Earl could still be counted on after all these years, the big dumb bastard. Over the cartoon noise, Hag heard tires rolling over gravel.

A car door slammed.

Then another.

Earl looked over at him. "Somebody here?"

Hag turned and moved the sheet a couple of inches. He said, "Stony."

"He alone?" Earl dropped his spoon. "I bet he ain't alone."

Hag slid the sheet back down and shook his head. "He's got some big caveman-looking fuck with him, a guy I never seen before. Must be Stony's idea of muscle."

"Oh God." Earl jumped up from the chair, knocking over the TV tray. Milk, cereal and soda splattered across half the living room carpet. Earl stepped on the donuts. "We're dead meat. Oh my God."

"Would you shut the fuck up?" Hag took his time rising. Somebody gave the screen door a couple of good hard bangs. Stony's pet mongoloid, by the sound of it. Hag stood there like he hadn't heard anything. Earl looked at him wide-eyed, tried shooing him toward the door.

Hag took another long drag on his cigarette. The guy outside pounded the door again, harder this time. Earl started moving down the hall until Hag brought him up short with a raised finger. The next barrage rocked the whole trailer. Hag dropped his cigarette into an ashtray, yanked opened the door. "Stony! How the fuck you doing? Come on in, man."

The big guy walked in, shoved past Hag and forced him to lean backwards over the arm of the couch. Stony followed the muscle into the house without even glancing at Hag or Earl. He stood on the line between the kitchen and the living room, one foot on brown shag, the other on dingy yellow vinyl.

Stony looked around, scowling at the mess. He turned to the big guy, said, "Willard, you see this place? These boys give trailer trash a bad name. You want to be like them, Willard?"

Willard said, "Nuh-uh. I wouldn't let a dog live in this dump."

Stony's real name was Peter Bouchard, but everyone called him Stony. Hag didn't know why. Couldn't have cared less. It was just one of those things. Stony was about fifty years old, a little guy who was half-French and half-some-kind-of-Indian. He called himself an "entrepreneur," owned a bunch of businesses: a car dealership, the Wesserunsett House of Pizza, an automated car wash and The Vault.

Now that Hag got a better look at Willard, he saw the guy was not just big. Willard was big and fat. Not all flabby and squishy like Earl, though. Willard's arms and shoulders were huge, his broad hands horned with calluses. He carried at least twenty or thirty extra pounds in his gut. Willard glared down at Hag, still bent back over the couch.

Earl sidled toward the hall, cellophane donut wrappers crinkling as he moved. Stony looked at the spilled food on the floor, then up at Earl's scared expression. Stony said, "If I didn't know better, I'd say you boys aren't real happy to see me."

Hag eased around to the front of the couch and stood there. "It ain't that, Stony. Earl's on some medication, pills for his bad back, and they make him jumpy, that's all. Willard scared the shit out of him with all that racket.”

“Is that right, Earl?” Stony said.

Earl swallowed and nodded.

Stony shook his head again. “Funny, you’d think a side-effect like that would keep doctors from prescribing it. Last thing you want is to have a patient with a bad back making those kinds of sudden movements. Exercise is the thing for a guy like you, Earl. Why don’t you get out of here while Charlie and I talk over a few things?”

Earl headed for his bedroom.

“Not there,” Stony said. “Take a walk down the street. God knows you could use the fresh air after being in here.”

“I got to put my sneakers on.”

“Go barefoot. I don’t have the time or patience to stand here listening to a fat man wheeze while he tries to tie his shoes. Going barefoot won’t kill you.”

“Go on,” Willard said. “Get the fuck outta here.”

Stony smiled, said. “Willard spent last night as a guest of the county and he’s in an ugly mood this morning. It got a lot worse when he saw Wanda Philbrick pulling out of your door-yard just now. I wonder what she was doing here. Hmm?”

Hag said, “Polishing my knob.”

Willard snorted. “Yeah, right. That girl’d bite your dick off and shove it straight up your ass.”

Stony said, “Why are you still here, Earl?”

Earl started for the door.

Hag placed a hand flat against Earl’s chest to stop him. “No,” he said.

“Pardon?” Stony looked like he had just found a hair in his soup.

Hag said, “This is Earl’s house. More important, him and me are business partners. He can hear whatever you got to say to me.”

Stony said, “Business partners? Whatever. The sooner I get out of here the better, so let’s get right down to it. I want my money.”

"What fucking money?"

Stony kicked an empty pizza box. "Don't try that with me, Charlie. You were supposed to come back from Quebec with eighty thousand dollars. I'm wondering where it is. You've been back in town since last night. A conscientious employee would have made sure I had the cash in my hands before he went on a drinking binge. You had money for beers at The Vault, but now there's nothing for me, huh?"

Willard moved so that he was between Stony and Hag, but a little off to the side so as not to block the boss' view.

"I owe you eighty grand?" Hag said. "Shit, you'd think I'd remember something like that. Wouldn't you, Willard?"

Willard chuckled and grinned, looked over at Stony. Hag kicked Willard in the balls, felt the guy's bag squish against the bones at the top of his bare foot. Willard fell to his knees hard enough to rock the whole trailer.

Earl backed away, said, "Oh Jesus."

Hag grabbed a handful of Willard's hair, pulled him forward so he was on all fours. Hag looked up at Stony, who hadn't moved. "He carrying?"

Stony said, "What do you think?"

Willard cupped his crotch with his left hand and wheezed as he tried to breathe.

"Where's it at?"

"Shoulder holster," Stony said.

Keeping hold of Willard's hair, Hag pulled out the gun. He pointed it at Stony. "Now how much money did you say I owe you?"

"Eighty thousand dollars. Your waving a gun around doesn't change that one cent's worth. You went to Canada with one of my Arctic Cats and a large amount of merchandise. You made the drop and got a gym bag full of money. You counted it out in front of Severin's boys. Then you hit the bars and three hours later you hit a police car while driving my snowmobile down the middle of a street in St. George. Now I don't care about the snow machine. It wasn't registered in my name and can't be traced to me. But I still expect my money."

Hag laughed. "You're one cool son-of-a-whore, Stony. I'll give you that, but nothing else. The cops confiscated the money because I wouldn't tell them where I got it. I told them I brung it from home but I couldn't prove it because I entered their fucked-up country illegally. The cash wasn't declared at customs. You want your money? Shit. I just spent six months trying to keep my asshole from getting stuffed full of Canadian bacon and not once, not one fucking time, did I say anything to anybody about who I was working for. And that was after the Canadian *and* American cops took turns at me, tried getting me to roll over. You want your money? You better write it off as a business expense or whatever you do because there is no fucking way you'll ever see it again. I ain't paying you a dime. More I think about, the more I figure you owe me."

"You got arrested because of your own stupidity," Stony said. "The money was your responsibility and you lost it to the police. So you will pay me back."

Hag cocked the revolver. "Is your life worth more than eighty grand to you?"

Earl said, "Hag, don't."

Stony smiled. "He won't shoot me, Earl. Not here."

"No? You owe me, you little fuck. We're going to settle up real soon."

Part of the talk about Stony was that he had never said a swear word in his life. He looked like he was about to spoil his record. Stony stepped forward, said, "Willard, do you want to end up a nothing like these two?"

Willard was still gasping. He managed to shake his head.

"Then get up off that filthy floor," Stony said. "We're leaving."

Hag let go of Willard's hair and stepped back, keeping the gun aimed at Stony. Willard got up slowly, his eyes watering. He still held onto his nuts, but he managed to open the door for

Stony with his free hand.

Stony paused in the doorway, his back to Hag and Earl. He said, "You have two days to come up with my money. After that, I'll burn this dump to the ground with both of you in it. If I'm in a good mood, I'll have Willard shoot you first."

Willard glared at Hag through tearing eyes. "I hope you don't pay," he said and then limped off down the steps behind his boss.

Hag stood in the doorway, waving and smiling at them as Willard backed Stony's Cadillac out of the driveway. When they rounded the corner at the end of Heron Lane, Hag turned to Earl, said, "Why don't you clean that shit off the floor? I'm getting tired of living in a pigsty."

19

The offices of Wesserunsett Realty occupied a Cape-style house with weathered gray shingles on Main Street. Joey parked in the gravel lot between an old Saab and a Ford Expedition. He got out of the car, leaving the windows rolled down. After his second shower, Joey had changed into Dockers, deck shoes and a maroon polo shirt. If he was going to pretend to be a tourist interested in buying property, he might as well look the part. He carried the classified section of the morning paper, folded over to a half-page ad for Wesserunsett Realty.

A bell chimed as he opened the front door and stepped inside. The receptionist, a conservatively dressed brunette in her late fifties, looked up and smiled.

"Good morning," she said. "I'm Bonnie. May I help you?"

"I hope so, Bonnie. I'm in the area for a few days and I noticed your ad while I was having breakfast this morning." Joey held out the paper and pointed. "I'm interested in this house on the lake."

The woman glanced at the paper. "Oh, yes. The Federal on the lake. It's a beautiful property. Would you like me to schedule a viewing for you? Evan is showing it to someone this morning, but I think I could get him to squeeze you in this afternoon." She gestured to a chair in front of her desk.

Joey sat down, said, "Evan?"

"Yes. Evan Barker. You'll like him."

Joey smiled. "No doubt, Bonnie, no doubt. That house really caught my eye, but I'd be willing to look at other properties as well. Are a lot of these listings Evan's?"

Bonnie leaned back in her chair, cranked her smile up a notch. She said, "Quite a few of them are his, but all of our agents are awesome at what they do. Any of them could help you find a place that's just right."

"That's great," Joey said, nodding. "But I've found it's easier to deal with just one person on this sort of thing. That way no wires get crossed, we're all on the same page. You know what I mean?"

"I sure do. Even if a listing is in the hands of another agent, Evan could act as your representative." Bonnie sat up straight and opened one of her desk drawers. After shuffling through it a moment, she handed Joey a business card with Barker's name, office extension and cell phone number.

Joey took the card. He said, "Great. Has Evan been with you long?"

"Three years. No, no. It's two years, sorry. Two years this August."

"So he must know the area pretty well by now. Great." Joey stood. He took out his wallet, slid the card inside.

Bonnie rose also, holding out her hand. Still smiling, she said, "I'm sorry, but I don't think I caught your name."

Joey took her hand and gave it a light squeeze. "Don't apologize. It's my fault for not introducing myself. Joe Carmichael."

"Would you like to leave your number, Mr. Carmichael? I can have Evan call you about the appointment."

"No, my cell phone has been acting up. I'll give him a call when I get back to my motel tonight."

Bonnie's smile slipped a little. Maybe she'd had more than business in mind when she asked for the number. "Oh, all right. Well, thank you for stopping in. It was nice to meet you, Mr. Carmichael."

"I'm glad I came in, Bonnie. And, please, call me Joe."

Joey walked outside. So Barker had been in town almost two years. That made sense if he really had run away from Witness Protection. Carl was convinced that Barker was out on his own, but Joey couldn't see how the guy got a real estate job without some kind of help. Researching Maine's requirements for real estate agents last night, Joey learned the state regulating agency did background checks on every applicant. Either the feds had set up this gig for Barker—which would be stupid even by their standards—or Barker paid for a new identity by himself.

If the latter were true, it meant the ex-pornographer might have some money stashed away. Money that, when added to what Joey already had, could help buy Grace a new life in a safe place.

20

Summer Weissman said, "I'm glad it's on a lake. Living on the coast, we've grown accustomed to being near the water." They lived in Rockport, she said, so close to the water you could step off their porch, walk a dozen steps across the street and be standing knee-deep in Penobscot Bay.

Evan Barker gestured toward where the backyard sloped down to Wesserunsett Lake. He said, "You have three hundred feet along the lake here. That floating dock comes with the property. You take it out before the water freezes."

"Wesserunsett. I assume it's a Native American name of some kind. Does it mean anything?"

Evan looked out over the water. "It's an Abenaki word. Funny thing. Beautiful lake like this, and the Indians called it *Bitter Water Place.* Nobody's really sure why."

Joel Weissman came up out of the basement through the bulkhead doors. He was maybe ten or fifteen years older than his wife, who looked to be about thirty-five. Both Weissmans were tanned. Their clothes were studiously casual. Trust fund babies trying to look like Mr. and Mrs. Average and fit into this blue-collar town. Most people Evan knew didn't iron their T-shirts, though.

"This is the third time we've looked at it, and I still love it," Joel said.

Evan said, "Are you prepared to make an offer, then?"

"What was the asking price again?" Summer said, as if she honestly couldn't remember. The kind of woman who wants you to think she's smart, but still tries to play dumb when it suits her.

It was a huge house, built in 1819 just as the Federal style was going out. The current owners lived in Massachusetts but had hired a caretaker to look after the place the past twenty years. The man had done a good job. Down on the coast, a house like this—even with a lot less acreage—would go for more than a million dollars.

A bead of sweat rolled down Evan's back. He loosened his tie, undid the top button of his short-sleeved Oxford shirt. All the information on the property was in the folder he carried, but he knew it by heart. He said, "Well, there's the house and six acres on this side of the road, the three hundred feet of lake frontage, like I said. Plus you have the barn and fifty-eight acres of fields and woods on the other side. The woods haven't been cut since the 1950s, so you have some prime lumber in there. You check around for a reputable logging contractor, get him to do selective cutting, and you could almost get back what you paid for the place. The owners are asking four-fifty."

Sucking his teeth, Joel Weissman glanced at his wife. She nodded at him, as if the teeth sucking were some kind of secret code and she agreed with his message. Joel turned to Evan, said, "We'll offer three-eighty."

Evan knew that was too low, but it was a good place to start. The house had been on the market seven years already. Evan had shown the place a dozen times over the past year and come away with nothing for all his time and effort. The owners would not sell to anyone who wanted to subdivide the land across the road, and no one who lived in the area could afford to make a reasonable offer otherwise. Evan wanted to unload this albatross. He was confident the Weissmans, after some dickering, would be willing to meet the owners at least halfway.

"Do you have the paperwork with you?" Joel asked.

"Right on the seat of my truck," Evan said. "We can go on inside and use the kitchen table. I'll walk you through the papers and the fine print, go over the details on the septic tank, well, taxes, things like that again."

The Weissmans went inside ahead of him. Evan grabbed the papers and followed, checking out Mrs. Weissman from behind. She was tall and thin. Willowy, his father would have called her. Even so, Summer can looked nice in those khaki shorts and she clearly knew it. In his past life, only ten years ago even though it sometimes seemed like decades, he would have cast her as a soccer mom in one of his movies. The kind of woman who seemed to live only for her kids but turned into animal in bed. A real MILF. He saw the title of the movie, splashed across a video box in his mind: *Sexy Soccer Moms.* No, make that *Slutty Soccer Moms.* Or *Soccer Mom Sluts.* Yeah, that was better. She didn't have the body to be a porn superstar, but there was always a demand for that fresh, amateur, neighborhood-mom look.

Then Carl Petucci's fat, sweating face blocked out images of Summer Weissman in front of Evan's camera. Nothing dampened his libido and creative spark like remembering the Petucci brothers. Besides, he had to keep his mind on the here and now. Once he and the Weissmans agreed on a figure, Evan could go to the credit union and put their earnest money into an escrow account; a thousand-dollar check was nothing to a guy like Joel. Filing the papers at the office never took long, so there'd be time to show two or three more listings before having drinks with Wanda Philbrick at five-thirty.

With her husband out on bail for that OUI charge and wanting the house back, Wanda would be looking for a place to stay. Evan hoped she wouldn't ask to move in with him. It was too much of a pain in the ass, having a woman around all the time. Still, Wanda might let him take some more pictures of her naked. No one else would see the pics, he'd promised Wanda that, but Evan liked to stay in practice. He might get back into porn someday if Carl Petucci and his brothers would oblige him by dropping dead or getting whacked. Real estate paid well, but the easiest money had always been in sex.

21

"I can't wait to get my hands on that shotgun again. I mean, look at this friggin' thing," Hag said. "What kind of pussy uses a gun like this?" He held up the.38 he'd taken from Willard.

Earl checked the rearview, said, "I think that was a cop back there at the Rite Aid." He was driving his beater south along Madison Avenue and hadn't shut up about the police since they pulled into Skowhegan.

Hag said, "You think a cop's flak vest would stop a .38 slug?"

"Don't even think about it, Hag."

"Would you just frigging chill out?" Hag grinned and cocked back the hammer.

"Would you just stop waving that gun around?"

Hag eased the hammer down and set the revolver on the seat between them. They passed Bloomfield's Tavern. Hag wanted to stop off for a couple cold ones, maybe go upstairs to shoot some pool. Later. It was best to stay straight when dealing with his wife. Christ, the things a man had to do to get his property back.

He looked over at Earl, said, "This one time I was in Bloomfield's, a guy came up to me, drunk as a cunt. I could tell he wanted to pick a fight, but I wasn't in the mood. He gets in my face and says, 'I know you.' I look right back at him and say, 'Whooptie shit for you.' The guy grins and tells me he knows my wife's fucked every colored guy in Somerset County. I say, 'That ain't so bad. There can't be no more than fifteen or twenty of them.' The stupid prick laughed so hard he about pissed himself."

"So did you fight him?" Earl said.

Hag shook his head, looked out the window. "The guy was still laughing when I left half an hour later."

They crossed the two Margaret Chase Smith bridges and turned onto West Front Street. They drove up the hill past expensive houses that stood alongside apartment buildings packed full of welfare families. Earl missed the turnoff for Indian Ridge. He swung into the parking lot outside the Troop C State Police barracks. While Earl waited for an opening in traffic, Hag fidgeted with the gun and looked back at the low white building.

"Wish I had a grenade to chuck through their window," he said. "Wouldn't they shit if I just walked in there and started shooting?"

Earl started shaking. He stomped on the gas. The truck lurched back into the road, where it stalled. Hag laughed all the way to McClellan Street.

Indian Ridge was one of two low-income housing developments in that part of town. The buildings were dark brown with yellow trim, four units to a building. Roxanne Hagopian and her five children lived in apartment 27. All the parking spots were full, so Earl pulled up on the grass. He stayed in the truck while Hag went across the lawn.

Hag's son Dakota was playing whiffle ball in the yard with some neighbor kids. Dakota was at bat and didn't notice his father getting out of the truck. Hag walked up behind him, started chattering: "Swing-batter-batter-batter-swing. Swing you little son of a whore."

Dakota swung at a pitch and missed, threw the fat red bat at Hag. Missed again. "Fuck," the little boy said. "I thought you were in jail."

Hag picked up the bat, flung it across the road. He walked past Dakota without looking at him. "I busted out. Killed twenty Mounties doing it, too. Where's your mother at?"

"What's a Mountie?"

Hag said, "The other kids around?" He and Roxanne had been married eleven years. His oldest son, Tucker, was almost eleven. Then there were nine year-old Dakota and their sister, Makayla, who was eight. The other two girls, Cheyenne and Keisha, weren't Hag's even though they had his last name. Cheyenne's real father, a burnout named Roland Dennis, had fallen off the walking bridge over the Kennebec six years earlier. The dipshit smoked a couple of fatties and decided to climb up on top of the bridge railing like some kind of gymnast. They found his body washed up on a little island a mile downriver. Keisha was the baby, not even two years old yet, cute as hell even if she was a mulatto. Her father was a mystery to Hag. Not even the Rock herself could say for sure who the guy was.

Dakota didn't answer.

Hag turned around and glared at him. "Are you deaf, boy? I asked you a question. Who's in the friggin' house?"

"Nobody."

"Door locked?"

The kid only shrugged.

Hag walked over and cuffed him upside the head. Dakota's friends stood there with their mouths hanging open. Hag said, "Is the door locked?"

"No." Dakota's face turned red. Tears lurked at the corners of his eyes, but he didn't cry.

Hag dug into his pocket, came out with a handful of crumpled bills and some lint. He gave Dakota five dollars. "Get lost before I kick your scrawny ass."

Roxanne's apartment had two floors. There was a small entryway cluttered with jackets, sneakers and kids' toys. Hag stood there listening for the Rock, just in case that little shit Dakota had lied to him. Nothing. He opened another door, walked into a hallway. The kitchen/dining area was on the right, spotless and smelling of lemons. Straight ahead were the living room and bathroom. Without even looking, Hag knew they would be just as clean as the kitchen. The Rock couldn't stand dirt, said poverty was no excuse for being filthy.

Hag climbed the stairs. Two bedrooms there: one for the girls, one for the boys. The Rock must have been spending her nights on the couch, though her clothes hung in the girls' closet. He went back downstairs and into the living room. Sure enough, the couch was a foldout. Hag moved from room to room, looking under furniture, into closets and cupboards, any place that was large enough to hide the Mossberg twelve-gauge his father had left him. Nothing. At first Hag was careful to make sure he put everything back where he'd found it. As his search went on with no success, he started throwing things. Fuck her. He left everything lying on the floor. He felt like getting his .38 out of the truck and doing an Elvis on her TV, changed his mind. The Rock might come looking for him if he did that.

When he went outside, the whiffle ball game had broken up and the kids were gone. Hag climbed into the truck and slammed the door.

"You get it?" Earl asked.

"Yeah, I got it. I hid it up my poop chute so nobody'd notice. Jesus H. Christ, Earl, does it look like I got it? Do you see a twelve-gauge shotgun in my fucking hands?"

Earl turned the key in the ignition and the old Ford belched to life. He pawed through a mess of tapes on the dashboard until he found his Skynyrd. "Was Roxanne in there?"

Hag shook his head. "Where'd Dakota go?"

"Him and that bunch of kids went off down the street a minute ago. They can't be far." Earl slid the tape into the player. "Tuesday's Gone" poured out of the speakers. Hag hated that Southern-fried bullshit, it being just a two-step away from country-and-western. At least the tape didn't drag like most of the others Earl kept in the truck.

They drove down McClellan and turned onto West Front again. There were the kids, just walking across the parking lot outside West Front Market. Hag pointed. Earl pulled into the lot, drove past the kids and parked near the door. When the kids got close, Hag leaned out the truck window to wave his son over.

Dakota stopped just out of Hag's reach. He said, "Yeah?"

His friends went inside.

Hag lit a smoke, said, "What'd your mother do with my shotgun?"

"What shotgun?"

"*What shotgun?*" Hag said, mimicking his son's voice. "Don't play stupid me, fuckhead. Where's it at?"

Dakota shrugged.

"Do that again and I'll fix it so you'll have to come live with me," Hag said.

"Five bucks."

"What?"

"I'll tell you about it for five bucks."

Hag got out of the truck. "I just gave you five dollars, you little shit."

Dakota stepped closer to the store. "Touch me and I'll scream. That lady in there'll call the cops. Five bucks." He held out his hand.

Hag gave his son the money. "Now, where is it?"

"Mom sold it last month. She put an ad in the *Swap & Sell.*"

"So who has it now?"

The boy shrugged. He darted into the store before Hag could grab him.

Hag didn't say anything as they left the parking lot. While they were waiting for the light by the bridge to change, he looked over at Earl. "You believe that shit, man? The Rock put an ad in the *Swap & Sell*, sold my shotgun. Only thing my father ever gave me besides bruises, and she frigging goes and sells it."

Earl said, "We going home now?" When the light changed, he turned down the hill onto the first bridge.

Hag ejected Lynyrd Skynyrd and threw the tape out the window. It spun through the air a few feet before falling into the river. "Yeah, Tuesday's gone all right," he said. "Stop someplace they carry the *Swap & Sell.* I got an idea."

Dakota had taken all of Hag's cash, so Earl bought a copy of *Swap & Sell* at Cumberland Farms. He came out of the store flipping through the pages and gnawing on a giant Slim Jim. "It's the new one," he said as he slid behind the steering wheel. "Just came out yesterday."

"Give me that," Hag said. He grabbed the magazine. "We ain't got time for you to see if anybody's selling their old porno tapes." He turned to the section marked *Firearms* while Earl drove him back to the trailer.

22

Muddy Waters played low on the car stereo. Joey had parked in a gravel lot out front of a Pentecostal church that looked more like a double-wide trailer with a big plastic cross tacked onto the roof. The church stood across the road from Barker's house, but about fifty yards closer to town.

Evan Barker lived in a neat little Cape set well back from the road, two miles east of downtown Wesserunsett. Except for the church, his closest neighbors were more than half a mile away. The land on either side of his lot was taken up with tall grass. Forest bordered the fields a couple of hundred yards back. Barker's front door and porch were almost completely screened from the road by massive lilacs to either side of the walk. An old sag-roofed barn stood behind the house. Barker probably chose the place for its privacy. Joey liked it for the same reason.

Two vehicles occupied the gravel driveway, both nicer than Joey's Corolla. One was Barker's silver Toyota Tundra pickup. The other one, a soft-top Jeep belonged to his girlfriend. She was late-twenties or early-thirties, brunette and built like a brick shithouse. Married, too. Joey had seen her wedding band and diamond through his binoculars while she was kissing Barker just before they went inside. The police uniform she carried on a hangar caught Joey's eye, too. Maybe the outfit was for some kind of sexy role-play they'd planned. No, Joey knew that would be asking too much.

115

Joey lowered the binoculars and laughed quietly. Even hiding out from the mob and the feds, that idiot Barker couldn't avoid trouble. Here he was, screwing around with a married woman—a cop, no less—when he should be keeping as low a profile as possible. But a marked man who let his picture go up on the internet couldn't be all that bright to begin with. Joey had been married for a short time, fifteen years earlier, and he would have killed any guy he caught messing with his wife. In fact, that was why he'd divorced Michelle; she fooled around on him a lot and he didn't want to kill any of her lovers because even the dumbest homicide cop could solve a crime of passion. Joey assumed that up here in Maine, with plenty of forests and bogs that were perfect for dumping bodies, husbands didn't put up with assholes like Evan Barker for very long.

He reached for a potato chip from the open bag on the passenger's seat. His stomach rumbled, but the chips were all he had.

What Joey wanted to do was hide the car, then walk through the woods around to the back of Barker's house. He could wait until the woman left. Then he would go inside, make Barker give him the tape, cap him and retrace his steps to the vehicle. Joey had gotten a good enough look to be sure that the little turd really was his man.

Problem was, there was no good place to hide the car out here. Joey would have to cross those open fields, walk along the side of the road or go traipsing through the woods. No matter what, he'd be too far from the car if a fast getaway became necessary. The other problem was, now that he was so close to doing the job, Joey didn't want to kill Barker. Sure, the guy was a sleaze, but he hadn't done anything to Joey. Maybe there was a way to get the tape and let Barker walk. It was the tape Carl wanted anyway; without that, even if Joey did whack Barker, Grace was dead.

A car door slammed. Joey raised his binoculars. The girlfriend had come out wearing the cop uniform and gotten into the Jeep. Joey checked his watch. It was twelve-twenty-three. No way was this just a kinky quickie. The lady cop backed her vehicle out of the driveway and headed into town. Maybe she was about to start her shift. Joey needed to find out more about her routine. The last thing he needed was for her to walk in on him.

Joey slid down in the seat as she drove by. When she was about four telephone poles away, Joey sat up and threw the rest of his potato chips out the window. He hit the road, staying well behind the Jeep.

23

June Sargent pulled leaves from a head of romaine lettuce, tore them into small pieces before dropping them into a colander. She looked over at her daughter, chopping cucumber on a small wooden cutting board, and said, "A great big man like that? You could have been killed."

Wanda rolled her eyes, wishing she'd never let her mother prod her into talking about work. It was showing up announced for supper, in uniform, that set her off. Wanda said, "Mom, it wasn't that bad. I could have called for help if things got out of hand. Bailey wasn't armed."

"But you couldn't know that when you went into the woods."

"True, but I get to carry a gun, remember? That gives me a slight advantage over a perp with a fly rod," Wanda said. She pointed to the gear on her belt. "Look, I also have pepper spray, a Taser, my nightstick, all kinds of fun toys."

"Well, I hope you didn't pull your gun on poor Jim. I imagine he was humiliated enough as it was, getting beaten up and arrested by his own wife."

"Jesus Christ, Mom. He was driving drunk and he dared me to arrest him. He got what he deserved. Besides, the chief arrested him, not me."

"But you punched him," June said.

"Yeah, after he slapped me. What am I supposed to do, stand there and take that kind of shit?"

June wouldn't look at Wanda. She ran the lettuce under the water, stirring it with her hand. She shut off the tap, shook the colander up and down to get rid of the excess water. When she was satisfied it was dry enough, June said, "I wish they'd wrap these heads in plastic like they do the iceberg kind. You never know who has touched them or sneezed on them, never mind the pesticides they spray all over them in the fields."

At least she was changing the subject and backing off. It was too hard to switch out of argument mode, though. Wanda said, "I read somewhere that rinsing vegetables in water doesn't even come close to getting off the chemicals. The farms have to use pesticides that will stay on even when it rains, so running veggies under your kitchen tap doesn't do a thing. All it does is make you feel more secure. You're still eating the same chemicals."

"Well," June said, dumping the lettuce into a big stoneware bowl. "This sure is your day for making me feel better about everything. I'd buy organic foods, but you know how much your father hates 'hippies.' He thinks only commies worry about food safety. I tell him there aren't any more communists, but then he starts in about Castro, Chavez, Putin and Kim Jong what's-his-name, and I can't get a word in."

Wanda laughed and some of the tension went out of her with the sound. Her mother was a retired junior high social studies teacher who had long ago given up trying to argue history or politics with anyone. Wanda leaned out into the hallway, said, "Dad, Putin's not a communist anymore."

Walter Sargent shouted from the living room. "He was a KGB spook. Once a commie, always a commie. It ain't like changing a shirt, you know. That jackass Bush couldn't stand up to him and Obama won't, either."

Wanda's father lost his left foot and part of the shin to a grenade explosion during the fight for Dak To in the winter of 1967. He believed deeply in the rightness of the Vietnam War but was angered by the way the politicians ran it, by what he saw as the lies the media had spread about it. He had worked at Wesserunsett Shoe from 1975 until the company shipped all its jobs to India in 1998. Now Walter ran a furniture repair business out of his garage and worked part-time as a hospital janitor.

Wanda grabbed a bottle of Rolling Rock from the fridge, took it into the living room. She found her father sitting in his recliner.

Wanda handed him the beer. She sat on the edge of the couch, sipped her beer. She pointed to a book lying on the coffee table. "You read Walt's new one yet?" *Old Growth* was her brother's fourth poetry collection, published just two weeks. Walt's work had earned him a couple of Pushcart Prizes and a James Laughlin Award, but damn little real money. He taught English at a Boston high school and his wife, Abby, worked for the Massachusetts Arts Council. They were always trying to get Wanda to move down there.

Walter said, "You know I love your brother, but a lot of his poems depress the bejeezus out of me."

"So you haven't finished it yet?"

He grinned. "I'm almost to the end. I have to read the poems in groups of four or five at a time. Otherwise, it's just too much."

"Mom once asked me why Walt couldn't write novels, something that would sell a million copies," Wanda said. "Thrillers."

Walter finished his beer. "Yeah? She asks me why you have to be a cop, why you can't find a safer way to make a living. She read that thing in the police log this morning, about the guy that tried to beat you up, and it took me an hour to calm her down. Now there's this other thing, too."

"I know. We were just talking about it."

"She kept hoping you and Jim would try again. She wants to be a grandma. Me? I was only hoping Jim would get me cheap meds."

Wanda grinned. "You going to give me a hard time about it,

too?"

"Nope. Not about that or your job. I keep telling your mother she should worry more about what you'll do to the bad guys than what they'll do to you. What I don't get is why you want to waste your time being a small-town cop. If you'd gone into the state police, you could have made detective by now. No more pulling over speeders or hoping the drunks won't puke all over your cruiser."

Wanda slid back on the couch, leaned into the thick cushions. "Dad, I like what I do. That's all there is to it. I like being a small-town cop. I like working in the town where I grew up. If I were a state trooper, I'd have to go where they told me, and they rarely assign you to your hometown. I'm happy. Really."

"Don't try bullshitting a bullshitter. You're bored in Wesserunsett. I can see it all over your face. Walt's the one who went to college, but you were always the smart one. Do something smart now, Wanda. Get out of this town while you're still young enough to make a break."

"You sound like Ed Gauthier."

"Well, if we both see it, why can't you?"

Wanda held up her hands. "Can we talk about this some other time, Dad?"

"Fine. But don't think I'll forget about it. There's no way I'm going to sit by and let you dry up from boredom."

"Mom worries about me too much now," Wanda said. "Just imagine how she'd freak out if I took a job somewhere else."

Walter frowned and shook his head. "You can't live your life around your mother's fears. She'd have you off the force and producing little Jims for her."

June came in, wiping her hands on a dish towel. "Did I hear you talking about me? Dinner's ready if you're interested."

"I've always been interested in food," Walter said. "You still have enough time to eat with us, Wanda?"

"I'm good for another twenty minutes or so unless I get a

call." Wanda followed her parents into the dining room. There was a poem Walt had e-mailed her a couple of weeks earlier. It was an early draft, something new he was working on. The last few lines stuck with her:

A shiver snaps
your trance, renders
the evening's warmth a lie
as the sun slides
down behind the walls
of this tired valley.

Wanda felt that same shiver as she dished herself a mound of mashed potatoes. She hated most poetry and shared her mother's wish that Walt could write bestsellers. Walt had moved out of Wesserunsett years before, but his writings showed he had not escaped at all. As busy as he was with his family and work and friends, Walt could never put the place out of his mind. Wanda wanted out, too. Everyone knew it, even if she wouldn't admit it publicly. But how could she leave? Her parents were here. She didn't want to leave them alone. Despite what her father had said, they both needed her. Didn't they?

24

If the whole thing was trap set by the feds, Joey wasn't able to see it. He had followed Barker around town for a few hours, watching him show houses and make stops at the realty office. Barker didn't act nervous, like a guy taking part in an operation. He spent a lot of time going to places where help would be too long in coming, houses out in the country, a camp that was for sale miles out of town. Joey had almost braced him at the camp. Decided to wait and do it in Barker's house that night.

Barker's girlfriend served on the Wesserunsett police department. Her life seemed only a little less boring than Barker's. Joey watched her pull over speeders, ticket an old lady whose car had a broken taillight. The woman had probably never pointed her gun at a live target. She wouldn't be much of a problem.

Joey drove to the public boat landing, parked looking out over the lake. A couple of guys fished from a canoe just offshore. Joey rolled down the windows, killed the engine.

Someone had a car radio blasting at the far end of the lot, making Ozzy Osbourne's voice echo around the landing. It was "Flying High Again," a song Joey remembered from high school. He'd been into guitar then, but while his buddies tried to shred like Randy Rhoads or Yngwie Malmsteen, Joey was spinning old blues records. He would rather study Hound Dog Taylor's licks than learn two-handed tapping. All because of a record he'd found in his dad's collection: *Muddy Waters at Newport.*

Maybe he should've stuck with music instead of signing up for the Marine Corps. At the time, though, Joey didn't see much of a future in playing old music. College held no appeal for him; he didn't have the money anyway. So Joey had joined the Marines after high school. He fought in Panama and Kuwait, killed when he had to and never felt bad about it. When his second enlistment ended in '92, Joey got out.

The blues was growing in popularity again as a new generation of white people discovered it. Joey considered buying a guitar, getting back into music. He ended up working as a bouncer at a Brooklyn tittie bar. After putting a couple of drunks in the hospital one night, Joey got a visit from a guy named John Florio. John worked as an enforcer for the Petucci crime family, but he didn't tell Joey that right away. Instead, Florio eased Joey in, having him back up shylocks and making calls on businesses that paid for protection. Less than a year after meeting Florio, Joey got paid twelve grand to kill the leader of a crew that had started cutting into Petucci territory. It didn't seem like a big deal by then. He was still a few months away from meeting Carl Petucci and getting stuck with the name Joey Kotex.

Damn that fat bastard Carl anyway. Joey got out of the Corolla, walked along the shore. He took off his shoes and socks, stood on the little gravel beach while slow waves washed over his feet. Jesus! The water was like ice.

Joey stepped back, got out the track phone he had picked up at the Cumberland Farms that morning. He keyed in a number Carl gave him.

A woman answered after three rings, said, "Yes?"

"Tell him to call me."

"Who's this?"

"Frank," Joey said, going through the script he and Carl had worked out. Then he hung up, waited for Carl to leave the office and find a pay phone far enough away that there wouldn't be any reason for the cops to have it tapped.

The call came fifteen minutes later. Joey said, "It's him."

"I told you it was," Carl said. "I can't believe you doubted me. Is it done yet?"

"No."

"Why the fuck not?"

Joey said, "For one thing, I had to be sure."

"So now you're sure. What's the problem?"

"He's involved with a woman. A cop."

"Oh."

"*Oh* is right."

"She shouldn't make that much of a difference. Keep her out of it if you can, but do the fucking job on schedule."

"That's my plan," Joey said.

Carl burped through the phone. "Then why're you wasting my time, making my driver haul me all over the fucking city?"

"You told me to check in. I did. How's my friend?"

"She's having a great time," Carl said. His voice faded after that, as if he had put the phone down. Joey couldn't make out the words. He only heard Carl and someone else laughing. Probably that asshole, Nick. Carl came back on the line, said, "Don't worry about her right now. Just keep your mind on business and I'll see you tomorrow night."

Joey said, "If your guys lay so much as another finger on her, I swear..."

But Carl had already hung up.

25

Hag wore a Levi's jacket even though the night was warm. Sweat dribbled down his sides. He needed a pocket to hide the .38 until he got inside the guy's house, so the jacket stayed on. "Beats me why I didn't think of this before," Hag said as they pulled into the guy's driveway. "This is a work of fucking genius."

Earl slammed the truck into park, kept the engine running. He looked like he didn't know whether to shit or wind his watch. "You sure we need to do this, Hag?"

Hag knocked on Earl's forehead, just hard enough to snap him out of his mood without hurting him. Much. "Hello? Earth to Earl. We can't just buy our guns at the Walmart. That leaves a paper trail. This is perfect, and it ain't like you got to do anything anyway. You sit here and chill. Let me do all the work."

It had taken them all morning and half the afternoon to find the kind of guns Hag wanted, along with just the right sort of seller. Hag had circled a dozen ads in the *Swap & Sell,* made some calls. The first few were a waste of time. Two were not home and Hag wouldn't leave a message with his name or phone number. He hit *67 before every call. They said that was a way to block *69 and caller ID, but who knew for sure? It didn't hurt to try, even if it seemed kind of dumb. A man picked up the third call, a bunch of kids shouting in the background. Hag said, "Sorry. Wrong number." No good going someplace where there might be lots of people around. Numbers without answering machines, he called back every few minutes if no one picked up. It went on like that for a while, Earl whining the whole time about racking up his phone bill.

A little after two in the afternoon, Hag punched in one of the numbers he had already tried four times. The listing said the place was in St. Albans, about twenty miles away. A guy with a heavy smoker's voice picked up at the other end. "Hello?"

Hag said, "Yeah, I'm calling about your ad in the *Swap & Sell*. The twelve-gauge pump and the Ruger .44?"

"I still got them," the man said. "You interested in both of them?"

Hag said he was, added, "You willing to dicker a little on the price?"

The guy waited a second, said, "I've had a bunch of calls already. What I put in the ad was two hundred dollars for the shotgun, that's a Remington, and three-twenty-five for the other. I paid almost five hundred dollars for that .44 all by itself. The guns are like new and them are good prices."

Hag hemmed and hawed a little, like the cost was too high for him.

"Look," the seller said. "I can't knock anything off the price, but if you buy both of them I'll throw in a couple boxes of ammo."

"Okay," Hag said. "What's a good time to come by then? I don't want to interrupt your dinner or get your wife mad by stopping in too late."

"Don't worry about it. My wife took off three years ago, so she ain't going to get all bent out of shape about nothing."

"Sounds good." Hag got directions and agreed to meet the guy at nine.

So now they were parked in the guy's driveway. The night was good and dark, with clouds hiding the waning moon, only a few lights on in the house and no streetlights for miles. The nearest neighbors were at least a mile down the road. It couldn't fail, so long as Earl just stayed with the program. "You hear what I said, Earl?"

"Look, there's a bike on the porch," Earl said. "And a basketball hoop over the barn door. There's a kid living here, Hag."

Hag got out of the truck. "Relax. The dude's divorced. His kid probably visits him sometimes. But he didn't mention a kid being around, so chill the fuck out. All you gotta do is stay here and keep the truck running. Be ready to burn rubber."

Earl nodded. The fat slob was sweating, and he was in short sleeves. Hag slammed the door and walked across the yard. The porch light came on, one of those motion-sensing things. A guy opened the front door, stood there looking out. He was a couple of inches shorter than Hag but heavier by about thirty pounds. Mostly muscle, by the look of him.

"You the guy called about the guns?"

Hag said, "Yeah. I'm Dave." He stepped up and held out his hand. The guy shook it, a pretty light grip for such big hands.

"Art. Art Brochu. Come on in, man."

They went into the kitchen. Old car magazines and a pair of bowling shoes sat on top of a big iron cook stove.

"Bet you don't use that stove much," Hag said, smiling.

Art rubbed his bristly chin. "Just in the winter, for extra heat. Even then you can't keep it going too long without having to crack a couple of windows. Makes it hot enough in here to knock up a goat."

Hag laughed. He heard squealing tires and gunshots from the living room, figured Art was watching a cop show on TV. Then he saw shadowed movement and realized there was a woman in there on the couch, playing some video game. She held a controller and swayed to one side or the other in time with whatever the video game character was doing.

Art noticed Hag looking into the living room. He said, "That's my girlfriend Carrie. My son stays with us on the weekends, and he got her hooked on that damn PlayStation."

Hag pointed to the kitchen table. "So these are the ones?" An old blanket was spread over the chrome-and-Formica antique. A Remington twelve-gauge pump shotgun and a Ruger Super Blackhawk .44 Magnum lay on top of it. The Ruger was blinding chrome, with a barrel that looked to be nearly a foot long. Hag licked his lips.

"Yeah," Art said. "That's them. Check them over. You'll see they're nice and clean, hardly ever been fired."

Hag picked up the Magnum, whistled as he turned it over in his hands. Heavy. "It's a beauty. How come you want to get rid of it?"

"I bought it to go bear hunting with. Ever hunt bear, man? You tree him with your dogs, and then bring him down with the .44. But I can barely get time to go deer hunting anymore, let alone chase after bears. Sold my dogs a while back. The bullets cost too much to use for target shooting and it kicks like a son of a bitch, though it ain't nearly as much of a thumb-buster as the older models."

Hag pointed the .44 at the window. He scrunched up his left eye, sighting down the barrel. "You said you'd throw in a couple of boxes of bullets if I bought both?"

"You got cash, man? I'd rather not take a check if I don't gotta. No offense."

Hag said, "A check's nothing but a fancy IOU. I only use cash." He laid the Ruger on the blanket.

Art nodded his approval. Carrie hollered something, lost in the middle of a video massacre.

Hag said, "Well, go on and get them bullets, 'cause I think we've got a deal here."

"All right. I'll make out a bill of sale, too. Piece of notebook paper, nothing fancy. But we'll both sign it to make everything all legal." Art clapped him on the shoulder and left the room.

Hag slid the .38 out of his pocket, held it down close to his hip. He stepped near the door. Art came back a moment later with two boxes of Remington cartridges and a gray box of shotgun shells.

"These shells are only birdshot," Art said. "I thought I had some buckshot for you, too, but I couldn't find it when I looked this afternoon. The box is full, though."

Hag reached out, put his .38 up to Art's temple and jerked the trigger. He wasn't prepared for the little revolver to make so much noise. The top of Art's head blew apart, spattering the wall and ceiling with gore. It splashed hot against Hag's face. It soaked his shirt, his jacket, made the pistol grips slick in his hand. Art gave out a kind of hollow sigh. His legs folded up beneath him. Blood trickled down the wall, fell in fat drops through the smoky haze.

Where did all that blood come from? Hag swallowed hard to keep from puking. Brochu's body still twitched. Blood pumped from the hole in his head and spread across the old linoleum. Next time don't stand so fucking close. That was tonight's lesson. Next time, Hag would know better.

The sound of the shot still lancing through his ears, Hag heard screaming from the living room. It was the girlfriend, Carrie. She dropped her game controller, scrambled back to the far end of the couch, huddling there with her back against the wall. Standing in the kitchen doorway, Hag aimed the .38 and fired. The bullet missed, drilled a hole in a family portrait about three feet above the bitch's head. Hag lowered the revolver a little to take another shot. Missed again.

"Fuck this," Hag said. He walked into the living room and put two rounds into Carrie's face from less than a foot away. No point in worrying about getting splashed now. He was already soaked in blood.

Five shots to kill two people. Pathetic. He stuck Willard's gun into his jacket pocket. The ammo boxes had burst when Art dropped them. The .44s were fine because the bullets were mounted into some kind of plastic rack inside the box anyway, but the shotgun shells were scattered all over the kitchen floor. Hag grabbed a bunch of them, stuffed his pockets, but ended up leaving about half the box behind. He wrapped the guns in the old blanket. Hauled ass out of there.

Earl was just about hopping up and down inside the truck by the time Hag left the house. Hag made Earl lean forward so he could stuff the guns behind the seat. Then he climbed in. "Get this piece of shit in gear, Earl."

When they'd gone a mile or so west along Route 43, Earl said, "What happened back there? Is that your blood or the guy's?"

"Relax. It went down just like I said it would." Hag's heartbeat was just starting to settle down. His face felt flushed. His balls tingled.

"I heard a bunch of shots," Earl said. "How come so many?"

Hag leaned back in the seat and rested his trembling arm on the open window. "Oh, yeah. The guy shot first. I think the fucker was planning on robbing *me*. You know, keeping the five hundred bucks and leaving me holding my dick. So yeah, it took a couple shots."

"You killed him?"

"Duh. I said I was gonna, didn't I?"

"What about his kid?"

"I told you, there wasn't no kid," Hag said. "Just the guy and his girlfriend."

"Girlfriend?"

"Shut the fuck up."

26

Wanda piled boxes of books and CDs into the back of the Jeep, she threw dresses, jackets and blouses—hangers and all—on top of those, weighed them down with suitcases full of clothes from her bureau. She dumped an armload of shoes onto the passenger side floor. One box was full of Cynthia's infant clothes, three pastel-colored photo albums, a rattle and a plush bunny that she never got to hold.

Laurie Marcoux watched Wanda from the porch, arms folded across her nonexistent tits. Not for the first time, Wanda wondered if Jim was gay and in some kind of weird denial; the woman had the figure of a ten-year-old boy, for Christ's sake. Wanda dropped a Croc on the ground, swore and bent down to pick it up.

"I told Jim he ought to press charges against you," Laurie said. "It's police brutality."

"I wasn't on duty, Laurie, and he hit me first."

"That's what you say."

Wanda turned around and walked to the porch. Even standing on the walk, with Laurie three steps up, Wanda could almost look her straight in the eye. "Yeah, that is what I say. I don't know what your problem is, skank. Jim asked me to move out. Fine, I'm going without any fuss except for the one you're making. This whole thing would be a lot easier if you would just get off my ass."

Laurie went inside. Wanda heard her through the screen: "I can't deal with her. The woman's a psycho."

Jim stepped out onto the porch, came down the steps. He said, "I'm sorry. She gets wound up sometimes." He looked over his shoulder to see if Laurie was listening at the window, but she was somewhere deeper inside the house now.

Wanda chuckled. "I don't get it. I mean, why her?"

"Is it a blow to your ego?"

"Hell, yeah it is," Wanda said. "I don't mean that I think I'm a total hottie or anything, and I know I'm no genius. But you're divorcing me for Laurie Marcoux? She's dumb as a rock, Jim. Not much to look at, either."

"I'm not divorcing you for her. I'm divorcing you for me."

"How Zen of you."

"I'm serious. Right now, this is what I need. I need Laurie, too."

Wanda waved away the explanation. "Whatever. I have Monday off. I'll come by for the rest of my stuff then." She got in the Jeep.

Jim walked around to her side. He reached out, hesitated, and then touched her arm. "I'm sorry about yesterday," he said. "You know...the whole thing. It shouldn't have been that way."

"Apology not accepted, and don't expect me to say I'm sorry for punching you. You had it coming. Just promise me you're not going to marry that little bitch. Because in a couple of years, it'll be you lugging your stuff out in boxes while Laurie keeps the house."

Jim said, "You can go to Hell."

Wanda drove across the lawn, tearing muddy furrows through the grass. Childish maybe, but it felt good.

27

They went straight to the trailer because Hag wanted a shower. He wrapped his bloody clothes in the old blanket he'd taken along with Brochu's guns, dropped the whole mess off the back steps. He stood naked in the hall. "I'll burn those tomorrow. You still got a grill in the shed, Earl?"

"Yeah, but I lost the rack part." Earl sat in his recliner, eating a bag of chips. His hand shook so much that most of the chips broke in his grip and fell to the floor. On the way home, they had almost gone off the road twice because he was so goddamned jumpy.

Hag said, "I ain't planning a cookout, you know. I don't need the fucking rack. Call up Linda while I'm in the shower and tell her to come on over here. Make sure you shove my guns under the couch first."

Hag went into the bathroom and slipped on the flip-flops he kept under the sink. Nobody with half a brain would ever step barefoot into Earl's tub. There was no soap. Hag had to wash his whole body with shampoo. He scrubbed extra hard at the blood on his arm and face with a threadbare washcloth.

The thrill of the kill faded, left Hag jittery, tired. He closed his eyes and stuck his head under the spray, seeing Art Brochu's brains running down the wall of that old house. Hag heard the woman scream. He started laughing, couldn't help it. Couldn't stop. He hadn't been ready for the killing; Hag knew that now.

But he got a taste of killing and it tasted pretty fucking sweet. The next time would go off like a dream.

He rinsed the last of the last of the shampoo out of his hair, turned off the water. There were no clean towels, so Hag walked dripping and naked into the living room. "How the fuck am I supposed to dry off?"

Earl shrugged. He was still in his chair.

Hag grabbed a roll of paper towels and made do with that, then picked bits of soggy paper off his body. He put on his other pair of jeans, found a T-shirt that didn't smell too bad. Sitting on the couch, he said, "You get hold of Linda?"

"She'll be here in a while. You got to pay her up front this time."

Hag said, "Shit. How much money you got on you?"

"Not enough to get you laid. Roxanne called too, said she's been trying to reach you all night."

"She pissed 'cause I made a mess at her place?"

Earl said, "She thinks Stony did it. I guess Dakota didn't rat you out."

"Huh?"

"Roxanne told me Stony and Willard were at her place when she got home from work. They were inside, looking around."

"The Rock lay into them?"

"I don't know. She's wicked mad, though. They told her you owe a lot of money and they're gonna keep going to her house until you pay."

Hag pulled a hangnail from his left thumb while he looked around the room. The phone sat on the floor next to Earl's chair. Hag pointed at it, said, "Kick that thing over here."

Earl did, said, "You calling Roxanne?"

Hag punched in Stony's home phone number.

Stony's wife, Arlene, answered.

Hag said, "Hi, may I speak with Mr. Bouchard please?"

Earl heaved himself out of the chair and started pacing the

room. "Hang up," he said. "I don't want to mess with Stony no more."

Hag flipped him the bird. When Stony came to the phone, Hag said, "Hey, Stony. Where's my fucking money?"

"Who is this?"

"You know good and goddamn well who it is, you little pig fucker. Threatening my wife was a waste of your time. I don't give a goddamn about her or the kids."

Silence.

Hag said, "So you're better off getting my eighty grand together."

Stony hung up.

"What a prick." Hag tossed the phone to Earl. He went into the kitchen to rifle through the cupboards. All he found was a bottle of tequila with about three fingers left in the bottom. He sloshed it, watched the worm drift back and forth.

There was a knock on the screen door. A woman said, "It's Linda."

Earl let her in without saying a word, then went shuffling down the hall to his bedroom. He closed the door behind him. Hag heard the TV in Earl's room come on a couple seconds later. The volume went up.

Linda sat on the arm of the couch. She fished a pack of cigarettes out of her purse, lit one up. Smoke curled up around her head.

Hag closed the cupboard and carried the booze into the living room. He said, "How you been, Linda?"

She shrugged. Linda Turcotte was still in her early forties. Her face was crossed with deep lines that not even thick layers of makeup could hide. Hag had seen her naked enough to know that her body was still in decent shape so long as a guy didn't mind a little bit of a belly and droopy tits. She did okay with the skidder boys from up to Solon or Athens, even better with the old farts around town whose wives wouldn't put out anymore.

Linda said, "You got money?"

Hag grinned and held out the bottle of booze. "I got this," he said.

Linda blew smoke through her nostrils. She stood up. "I wouldn't even give you a peek at my snatch for that."

Hag pointed at the entertainment center on the other side of the room. "You like that TV?"

She turned and looked at Earl's thirty-two-inch set. "It's not bad. HD?"

"Yeah."

"You gonna deliver it? Set it up for me?"

"Yeah."

"Okay." Linda put her purse on the couch, unzipped her faded denim miniskirt and let it fall. She didn't wear panties. There was a blue and yellow butterfly tattooed over her shaved pubic area.

"That's new," Hag said.

"You like my little butterfly?" Linda touched his cock through his jeans, giggled when she discovered he was already hard. "I guess you do."

Hag grabbed a fistful of her hair and yanked her around so that her back was to him. He said, "Bend over."

She reached for her purse.

Hag knocked it out of her hand.

Linda said, "My lube's in there. Rubbers, too. I ain't doing anal without them."

Hag undid his pants with his free hand, let them drop. Grunting, he pushed himself inside Linda's ass. She'd been butt-fucked a lot; even though he was doing her dry, Hag didn't meet much resistance. Linda groaned and tried to squirm away. Hag yanked back on her hair until she held still.

After a dozen thrusts, Hag felt his orgasm building. He let go of Linda's hair and grabbed her ass cheeks with both hands, started pumping her faster. When he came, he pushed her so far forward that she ended up with her belly flat on the couch, her face jammed into the stained cushions. Hag pulled out and squatted there, watching her. How pale she was. Hag slapped her on the right buttock, just as hard as he could. She yelped and he hit her again. Her white flesh turned a hot red.

Linda rolled onto her back, panting and sweaty. Mascara ran down her cheeks. When Hag wiped his dick on her skirt, she sat up and tried to scratch him. Hag backhanded her. She slumped down against the front of the couch, crying.

Hag spotted Linda's purse on the floor. He dumped it out on the kitchen table and pawed through the contents: lipstick, a compact, a small bottle of Astroglide, breath mints, three rubbers, some baby wipes in a zip-lock sandwich bag, pepper spray, half a pack of GPC smokes, a pink disposable lighter, a scratch ticket and eighty-two bucks cash. Hag set aside the money, lottery ticket, cigarettes and pepper spray, shoved everything else back into the purse. Throwing it at Linda, he said, "Get out."

She stepped into the filthy skirt without bothering to tuck in her blouse, and picked up her purse. Linda wiped her nose with the back of her hand, said, "When you bringing the TV over?"

Hag lit one of her cigarettes, sucked in the smoke, held it there before letting it out. He crossed the room in two steps, took the butt out of his mouth and ground the cherry end into Linda's cheek. She screamed, tried to rake him with her nails again. Some bitches just never learned.

28

Wanda slapped at a blackfly that had been chowing down just below her ear lobe. The little bastards were always worse at Evan's place because of the boggy woods out back. There was no breeze tonight to blow them away. At least the blackfly died happy. Wanda had stopped off at The Vault for a couple of drinks before coming here. She heard the screen door creak open, then bang shut.

Evan came down the steps. He said, "What's going on?"

Wanda grunted and lifted out her suitcases, shoved one at Evan. "You're always saying how great it would be if we lived together. Well, here I am."

Evan took the suitcase, looked at it as though it were a cow turd. He said, "I thought Jim was giving you a couple of weeks to find a place."

"Yeah, but that was before I got him arrested," Wanda said. "Oh, wipe that look off your face. I know you don't really want me here. I just thought you wouldn't mind if it was only for a few days."

"It's not that I don't want you…"

Wanda shouldered past him and headed for the house. "I'm not in the mood for bullshit, sweetie. I know what we have isn't love and I sure didn't have dreams of us growing old together. We had some fun. That was enough for both of us."

She heard Evan scrambling to catch up with her, already

breathing hard from carrying one lousy suitcase. One suitcase with nothing in it but her underwear, cosmetics and toiletries, a couple of pairs of jeans and a few T-shirts. What in the world had she ever seen in this guy?

He said, "So you're moving in, but breaking up with me?"

"I guess so."

"You guess so? Jesus, Wanda."

Still holding a suitcase, Wanda stretched out her fingers to catch the doorknob. She pulled the door open a few inches, shoved her foot in the crack and toed it the rest of the way open. "Come on, Evan. Tell me you ever thought of me as anything more than a fuck buddy? Besides, I'm not really moving in. I just need a place to crash for a few days."

Not wanting to hear Evan grunting and whining anymore, Wanda went inside. She dumped her stuff on the living room couch. It would do until one of the spare bedrooms upstairs could be made ready. If Evan thought Wanda would pay for her room and board by letting him fuck her again, he could forget about it.

29

Joey was crouched in the woods across the road from Barker's house, watching the place through binoculars while blackflies and mosquitoes feasted on his blood.

It looked like the lady cop—Joey had learned her name was Wanda Philbrick—planned on spending the night with Barker. Since her Jeep was loaded with boxes, suitcases and loose clothes, maybe she was moving in for good. That was the last thing Joey needed. Damn. He should have broken into the house this afternoon instead of tailing Barker across half of Somerset County.

Barker stood on the lawn while Wanda started lugging her things inside. He looked around like he was lost, then shook his head and carried a suitcase inside. When they'd taken everything into the house and turned off the porch light, Joey crossed the road. Every room on the ground floor was lit up. Joey walked around the house, peering in each window until he found Barker and the woman in the living room.

Her stuff was heaped near the couch. She and Barker stood facing each other, arguing about something. The windows were all closed and an air conditioner hummed, muffling their voices. Maybe Wanda would get pissed off and leave. Joey didn't figure he could be that lucky. No, best to wait until morning and hope that the girlfriend had an early shift.

Crouching beneath the level of the windows, Joey loped

across the grass toward the driveway. His car was parked down the road, behind the Pentecostal church. Just as he passed the far end of Barker's house, something hard and blunt jabbed against Joey's lower back.

Joey froze.

A man leaned close, whispered, "Hello, asshole."

That accent was what, Russian? So who was this clown? Even if Joey could've turned around, the night was too dark for a decent look. Not a very big guy, though. Definitely a few inches shorter than him; when the guy spoke, his breath gusted hot between Joey's shoulder blades. The gun barrel poking Joey's right kidney made up for the size difference.

"There's a cop in the house. Shoot me and you're history."

The stranger giggled, said, "I do not think so. I kill you then go inside. No one hears a thing."

So Yakov had a suppressor on his pistol.

Good.

"Yeah? How come I'm I still breathing?"

"Orders," the Maybe-Russian said. "Turn around slow and get on your knees."

Joey did as he was told, keeping his hands at his sides. Just another shadow in the lee of Barker's house, the hitman took a step back. His arm came up and Joey smelled gun oil. The pistol was right there in front of his face.

Joey lashed out, reaching for Yakov's gun hand. He missed his mark and grabbed the guy above the wrist. That left the stranger free to swivel his hand and shoot at Joey anyway. Two bullets ripped past Joey's head. He saw the muzzle flashes, heard the faint, hollow sounds made by the pistol's suppressor. The slugs passed so close that his ear and cheek felt singed.

To hell with this. Tightening his grip on Yakov's arm, Joey launched himself up and forward. He made a fist of his free hand and drove it deep into his opponent's belly. Joey's would-be killer doubled over, breathless. Disarming him was easy after that. Joey beat the guy unconscious with the butt of his own pistol.

Joey knelt on the grass with the gun in his hand, listening for signs that Barker or Wanda Philbrick had heard the fight. No other lights came on in the house. Nobody stepped outside. Joey ran his hand over the pistol. It felt like a Glock.

Thumbing the safety on, Joey slid the Glock into the waistband of his jeans. He lifted Yakov in a fireman's carry—the guy couldn't have weighed more than one-fifty, one-sixty—and returned to his hiding spot in the woods across the road. It was harder getting him to the car that way, but there was no telling when somebody might drive down the road.

The night was muggy. Joey was sweat-sheathed by the time he stepped out of the woods at the parking lot's edge. Yakov groaned and Joey dropped him on the ground next to the Corolla. Popping the trunk, Joey searched for anything that could be used to tie up his new friend. There was a set of jumper cables and a small tool kit. Joey snapped the catches on the plastic box. Each of the contents sat snug in a little niche: cheap socket wrenches, some fuses, a screwdriver with interchangeable heads, a folded sign that read EMERGENCY CALL 911 and could be spread out inside the windshield, a pair of needle-nose pliers and a roll of electrical tape.

Joey rolled Yakov onto his stomach, taped his wrists together behind his back. The bright light over the church's back door made the job easier. Joey took a good look at the guy. He was about five-eight and wiry, with long black hair pulled back into a ponytail and a nose that had once been broken and indifferently set. His mouth hung open, showing stained teeth—all but the gold incisor. Joey had never seen this guy before.

The wallet was more helpful. It held just over twelve hundred dollars in cash. According to the New York State driver's license, Yakov's name was Vassily Fedoseev. He was twenty-six years old and lived on Ocean View Avenue in Brooklyn. That was Brighton Beach. Little Odessa. Why the fuck was a Russian trying to whack him?

Fedoseev's front pockets yielded three keys on a ring with the Mercedes logo and a cell phone. There was a gravity knife hidden in his right boot. Joey flicked it open and thumbed the four-inch blade before closing the knife and slipping it into his own pocket. Undoing the guy's pants, Joey yanked the jeans and red briefs down to his boot tops.

The Russian groaned again, started coming around. Joey sat him up and propped him against the rear bumper. Fedoseev's eyes fluttered before opening wide. He took in the parking lot, looked at Joey squatting next to him and tried to get up, pulling at the tape that bound his wrists. It was only then that his brain appeared to register the gravel beneath his bare buttocks.

Joey laid a hand on his shoulder, pushed him back down. "Let's talk, Vassily."

Fedoseev cocked his head back and spat at Joey. His saliva dribbled down Joey's cheek. Wiping it off with the back of his hand, Joey sighed. Why did everybody have to play at being a badass?

Joey reached for the toolbox, found the pair of needle-nose pliers. He grabbed Fedoseev by the nose, pinching the Russian's nostrils shut and forcing him to breathe through his mouth. When Fedoseev opened up, Joey used the pliers on one of his front teeth. He didn't yank it out, just tugged enough to let his new friend know he meant business.

"Can we talk now, Vassily?"

Fedoseev gurgled something. The defiant look in his eyes made the translation.

Joey took the pliers out of his mouth, said, "The hard way it is, then." To emphasize his point, he laid the business end of the pliers against the Russian's scrotum. Both men looked down as Fedoseev's genitals shriveled up along with his courage.

Licking his lips, Fedoseev said, "We can talk."

"First things first, then. Who sent you?"

"Carl Petucci."

"Bullshit," Joey said. "Carl could've had me whacked back in the city."

"Look, I get call from Nick the Brick, saying Carl wants to hire me for job. He gives me address and description of you and the real estate man, Evans. Says to kill you both, but make sure you get it in the face. Very particular. Is why I made you turn around. He wanted photos, too."

"I'm not buying this, Vassily. Who the fuck is Nick the Brick?"

Fedoseev raised one eyebrow, said, "Nick Bennato."

"Still doesn't tell me anything," Joey said. He pinched the Russian's foreskin with the pliers. Fedoseev squirmed and kicked, the heels of his cowboy boots digging furrows in the gravel.

When Joey took away the pliers, Fedoseev shook his head and said, "Nick the Brick is body builder. Injects steroids for fun and looks like King Kong dressed up in fancy suit."

"Goddamn it." Joey stood up. He said, "You're talking about Carl Petucci's bodyguard, *that* Nick?"

Fedoseev nodded. "Yes. Nick says Petucci will pay me fifty large to do you and Evans."

Jesus. Why would Carl do that? And why would he farm out the job to a fucking *Russian*? Word would spread that the Petuccis couldn't handle their own affairs anymore. That was weakness; it was like blood in the water. Joey paced back and forth in front of his captive. The simple answer was that Carl wouldn't do it. But maybe Nick wanted to get even for what Joey had done to his brother-in-law-to-be. Joey squatted again, said, "And you didn't think it was weird that the greaseballs would hire you for a hit instead of keeping it in-house?"

"I do it once before," Fedoseev said. "Was five, maybe six months ago. A man they needed removed."

"Your regular crew know you're doing piecework for Petucci?"

"No. I am discreet. A little extra money on the side, you

know? There is no harm in it."

"Just as long as you don't fuck up." Joey chewed at the inside of his lip. *Six months.* Carl had said John Florio was murdered six months ago. "Look at me, Vassily. Was the guy you killed named Florio?"

Fedoseev nodded again.

What was going on? Maybe Florio had also done something to piss off Nick. Hiring Fedoseev had been smart; neither he nor Nick would ever tell anyone in his own camp that he'd worked with the competition. The only other possibility was that Nick wanted to take over Carl's operation, but Joey dismissed the notion right away. The pumped-up freak was a follower, not a leader. Flipping open Fedoseev's cell phone, Joey said, "Let's give Nick a call. You got his number programmed in here?"

Fedoseev didn't, but he'd memorized Nick's phone number. Joey made the call.

Nick picked up after five rings, said, "Yeah, what?"

"Is this Nick?"

"Who wants to know?"

"How're you doin', Nick?"

"I said who the fuck is this?"

Joey winked at Fedoseev. "Take a guess. Vassily and I were just talking about you."

Nick breathed into the phone. It was a sound a trapped animal might make.

Joey said, "See you soon, buddy. Don't try fucking with me again." He broke the connection before Nick could say anything else. Joey hadn't told Nick that he knew the truth about Florio. Let the bastard wonder just how much Fedoseev said. Let him wonder and sweat. John Florio had been a made man. If word ever got back to Carl Petucci, Nick's death would be slow and painful. Besides, the information might come in handy before this was over.

"So now you kill me, eh?" Fedoseev said. He looked Joey in

the eye, probably bracing himself for the bullet, ready to go out like a man.

Waving the phone at him, Joey said, "Now you say *cheese.*"

Fedoseev had parked his silver Mercedes about a hundred yards up the road from Barker's house. Leaving the Russian in the trunk of the Corolla, Joey unlocked the other car and checked it for weapons. There was nothing hidden under the seats; nothing in Fedoseev's overnight bag except for a change of clothes, toiletries, a PSP and a few games, along with a baggie of what looked to be a quarter ounce of pot. Joey popped the Mercedes' trunk and looked there, checking the spare tire well, too. The car was clean. He slammed the trunk closed.

When he'd gotten the Russian out onto the road, Joey marched him over to the Mercedes. They stood there in glare of the Toyota's headlights, Joey now holding his .38 revolver and Fedoseev with his hands still taped behind his back. Joey tossed his would-be killer's wallet through the open window. The keys followed the wallet.

Joey used the gravity knife to cut Fedoseev's bonds. He said, "You'll have to charge your way home. I took all your cash."

The Russian started to protest.

"Better get going, Vassily. You want to make it home before your cousin wakes up and checks his inbox." While they were still in the church parking lot, Joey had taken three pictures of him lying there with his pants bunched up around his boots. One photo showed the Russian's own Glock, suppressor still in place, stuck in the crack of his ass. Joey then flipped through Fedoseev's e-mail address book. Only first names were listed. When Joey had asked which ones were relatives, Fedoseev told him to eat shit and die. Only the threat of having the photos e-mailed to everyone in his address book got him to cough up the name Sergei. His older cousin, he'd told Joey, and the head of his crew. After sending the e-mail, Joey had smashed the phone.

Fedoseev slid behind the wheel and started the car without saying anything else. Joey stood on the roadside, watching the taillights of the Mercedes get smaller and smaller. There went one less thing to worry about. He could've shot Fedoseev, but the problem was where to hide the body and the car. Joey didn't know the area well enough. If some local came across them and called the cops, they'd run fingerprints, trace the registration. Since Fedoseev most likely had a record, too many red flags would pop up. Maybe the feds would get interested and start poking around. Joey wanted to be hell and gone away from there before anyone in law enforcement caught a whiff of him.

But that didn't mean the Russian was getting away clean.

"You poor dumb bastard," Joey said. It didn't matter how fast Fedoseev drove. When he got back to Brighton Beach, he'd learn that Joey had forwarded the pictures to every person in his address book.

All fifty-four of them, including Nick Bennato.

Joey got in his car, turned on the stereo. Without thinking, he slipped in one of his favorite CDs: *Hubert Sumlin and Slammin' Sam Turner Live in '95.* Joey rested his head on the steering wheel. Sam and Sumlin played Howlin' Wolf's "Sitting on Top of the World."

Goddamn Carl Petucci.

Goddamn Barker and Nick and Angie.

Goddamn the whole worthless fucking lot of them.

Joey did a three-point turn and headed for his motel. He planned to hit Barker's place early in the morning and get that damn tape. If Wanda Philbrick was still hanging around then, it was her own tough shit.

30

SATURDAY, JUNE 12

Grace woke to the sound of a key being turned in the lock. She raised herself up on one elbow and waited. No need to dress because she slept in her clothes, the same clothes she'd been wearing for days. The closet's mothball smell was long gone, supplanted by the stink of her unwashed body.

"Get up," Nick said after opening the door. He stood back, giving Grace enough room to stand and step out of the closet. "You're eating breakfast with Mr. Petucci."

"Lucky me."

"Shut the fuck up."

Was it Grace's imagination, or did he seem like even more of an asshole this morning?

Nick shoved her down the hall to the bathroom. It was a half-bath, really: just a toilet and sink with a bare light bulb hanging from the damp-stained ceiling. No window, of course. When she opened the door, Grace saw the most beautiful sight her eyes had beheld all week.

The toilet lid was down, and on top of it were piled a pair of clean jeans, three T-shirts, clean underwear and three pairs of socks. Four fluffy towels and a couple of washcloths sat folded on the top of the toilet tank. The sink was lined with a fresh bar of soap, a ladies' shaver, shampoo, and a hairbrush, a set of

149

nail clippers, an emery board, St. Ives moisturizer, a deodorant stick, a new toothbrush and tube of toothpaste. Grace crouched next to the toilet and picked up one of the shirts, held it to her face. She took a deep breath. Not only was it new, but it had been laundered. The perfume of fabric softener brought tears to her eyes.

"It'll have to be a sponge bath," Nick said. "We got showers here, but they're all in bathrooms with windows. I figure you can make do with what we brought. And don't take too long. Mr. Petucci's hungry."

Nick closed the door. Grace heard him talking to someone else out there, but couldn't catch the words. To hell with them. For the next twenty minutes, Grace Turner did her best to forget her problems and just enjoy getting clean.

No handcuffs or duct tape this time. No elevator ride, either. Grace went up five flights of windowless stairs ahead of Nick, past a receptionist who pretended not to see her and into that same office. The drapes were still drawn. The fat man was behind the desk again. He was the biggest man Grace had ever seen; that was saying something, since she'd known B.B. King all her life. But where B.B. carried his weight with dignity and style, this other guy was a full-blown tub of lard, a fat slob. He probably blamed it on his glands or told himself he was just big-boned.

Grace snickered.

Nick said, "Shut up."

Grace burst out laughing.

"I said shut up."

That only made it worse. Grace let herself fall back onto that big couch. The cushions made a whooshing sound when she hit them. Hell of a time to get the giggles.

Nick said, "You fuckin' deaf or what?"

Grace doubled up, biting her lip and trying to stop laughing.

"You can go, Nick," the fat man said.

"But Mr. Petucci…"

"Don't start that shit again."

Nick went out.

When Grace looked up, the fat guy was staring at her. She got herself under control and sat up. Her stomach muscles ached. She said, "I'm okay."

"Good. Come sit over here." He pointed at a chair in front of the big desk, opposite his own.

Grace did as he said, noticing for the first time a buffet cart parked at the end of the desk closest to tubby's right hand. It held half a dozen covered dishes, a pitcher of orange juice and carafe that Grace hoped to Christ held hot coffee.

"We haven't been formally introduced," the fat man said. "I'm Carl Petucci." Without waiting for Grace to say anything, he lifted the lid from one platter after another. Grace salivated at the aroma. Carl grabbed a plate, loaded it with scrambled eggs, bacon, buttered wheat toast, slices of cantaloupe and a small mountain of fresh strawberries. He passed the plate to Grace before pouring her a glass of OJ and a cup of coffee.

Grace dug into her breakfast. She had a thousand questions but was content to let them wait a few minutes. This was the first real meal she'd had in days and she would damn well enjoy it without any distractions. For his part, Carl seemed willing to play along.

When she had wiped up the last fleck of egg with her toast, Grace held out her coffee cup. Carl took it and gave her a refill. Blowing on the steamy surface, Grace looked him in the eyes. She said, "Why am I here?"

"Insurance."

"That sounds like a polite way of saying I'm a hostage."

Now it was Carl's turn to laugh. His enormous belly shook. He loosened his tie. "I like you, Miss Turner," he said. "You're tough and you cut right through the bullshit. Yes, you're my hostage."

"Again, why?"

Carl popped a strawberry into his mouth. "I sent your friend Joey Kotex to do a little job for me. Keeping you here is my way of making sure he doesn't try to fuck me over."

"I don't know what you're talking about. You mean Joe, right? Joe Collins?"

Carl nodded.

"What did you call him? Joey Kotex? What the hell's that all about?"

"Before he ran away to Chicago, Joe Collins worked for me," Carl said. "His real name is Joey Connolly, but people in our, uh profession, knew him as Joey Kotex."

Grace took a sip of coffee. She set the mug on the desk. "Right. So you're, what, in the maxi-pad business?"

"You ain't stupid or naive, Miss Turner. So cut the fucking act. I'm going to tell you something about Joey, just so you'll understand the kind of trouble he's brought down on your head. Then you're going to do something for me."

Grace didn't reply. She picked up her coffee and sat back in the chair, waiting.

"This happened back when Joey was just starting out," Carl said, "He'd only been working for me a year or so, but I sent him to whack this Puerto Rican who ran a little *bodega* in Brooklyn. It was supposed to be easy, just walk in and pop the guy. Anyway, somebody tipped off the Puerto Rican, even told him when Joey was coming. So when Joey walked in, the 'Rican grabbed an old .45 he had stashed under the counter. Just opened up on our boy: *bang, bang, bang.* You know?

"Lucky for Joey, this guy wasn't such a good shot. Probably never even fired the gun before. Joey ducks down the candy aisle, pulls his piece. They start shooting back and forth. The way they were going at it, somebody was sure to call the cops. Then the 'Rican got in a lucky one, grazed Joey's left arm. Joey's right-handed, so that wasn't too bad, but he was bleeding all over the fucking place. Joey said fuck it, jumped up and put his last three bullets right through the guy's chest."

Grace watched Carl, waiting for the rest of the story to come out. She'd listen to almost anything if it kept her out of that closet a while longer.

Carl said, "So the job was done, but Joey still had to get out of there before the cops showed up. He was bleeding like crazy, so he tried to find some bandages. The store was out of them. Only thing he could find was a box of maxi pads and some duct tape. He slapped one of those pads on his arm, taped it down and got the fuck out of there."

Grace downed the rest of her coffee. She said, "That's quite a story. So Joe's a hitman. That's what you're saying, right?"

"He was. Then he had a change of heart and decided to walk out on the life. I trusted him, even though he's a mick, and he pulled that shit on me?" Carl's face reddened. He pounded the desktop with his pudgy fists.

"So you're like the Godfather, huh?"

Carl took a deep breath, sat there a moment. His color returned to normal. He said, "Not really. But if it helps you to think of me that way, go right ahead."

Grace said, "You mind if I stand up? Being locked in that closet's made me kind of antsy." When Carl nodded, she stood and stretched. She paced the length of the room and back again. "So you started calling him Joey Kotex? I can't see Joe liking that."

"It was supposed to be a joke," Carl said. "Some guys in this business end up with colorful names. I mean, you gotta picture my face when Joey comes back to tell me what happened. I laughed so hard I almost gave myself a hernia. You know? Yeah, I knew it pissed off Joey. But he didn't say anything, didn't even make a fucking face. All the boys called him Joey Kotex after that and he took it.

"After a while, I think it became a point of pride with him. See, a lot of the guys used to laugh about the name. I mean, who wouldn't? But even while they were laughing, these fuckers remembered that Joey Kotex blew that Puerto Rican clean out of his sneakers. It was the only time he fucked up until he left me."

Grace kept pacing. "Well, that's a heartwarming success story, Carl. But why don't you get to the point of this whole thing?"

"You got a mouth on you, lady. A woman in your situation ought to be more careful about how she says things. Here's the point: Joey's off doing one last job for me. He doesn't want to, which is why you have to stay here until he finishes. When I have proof the job's done, you'll be let go."

Yeah, like she believed that. There was no way Petucci could afford to release her. Grace walked back to the desk. Pouring herself another cup of coffee, she said, "You mentioned wanting me to do something for you."

"I worry about Joey," Carl said. "I worry he'll lose focus, maybe forget what's at stake here. He's run from me before. Joey's due back today and he'll call to tell me what time his plane's coming in. When he does, I'm gonna have you chat with him. You tell him you're okay and being treated well."

Grace snorted.

Scowling, Carl went on. "You say you're being treated well, but that you need him to stick to the plan. Remind him that if he fucks with me, you die. Slow and ugly."

"You'll kill me anyway, after Joe does what you want."

Carl didn't say anything for a moment. Then he held up his hands and said, "You don't want to cooperate? Fine. I guess Nick will have to go back to Chicago, say hi to your father."

Grace's guts went watery and cold. "Leave Dad out of this."

Carl chuckled, said, "Then help me out here, Grace. Nobody wants to hurt your old pappy, so don't force me to. Deal?"

Grace flicked her wrist, splashing hot coffee across Carl Petucci's fat, sweaty, grinning face. The mob boss kicked back away from the desk, screaming in Italian. Nick came running in with a big gun in his hand.

Picking up a fork, Grace climbed over the desk. Carl still had his hands on his face, trying to rub away the steaming liquid. No way to get at his throat. Grace stabbed him with the fork, skewering one of his man boobs. Carl howled.

Nick grabbed Grace by the ankle, hauled her backwards off the desk. She hit the floor, banging her elbows and knees. When she rolled over, she found herself staring into the barrel of Nick's gun.

"You okay, Mr. Petucci?" Nick asked.

"Do I look okay to you?" Carl's chair squeaked as he pushed himself upright. He said, "Take this fucking bitch downstairs and teach her how to behave."

"Sounds like fun." Nick slid his gun into a shoulder holster. He adjusted his sport coat and grabbed Grace by the wrist, squeezing so hard it made her fingers go numb.

Carl said. "Just a beating, Nick. Bust her up good, but keep her alive."

31

Earl hadn't slept all night. While Linda was taking care of Hag, Earl watched *Talladega Nights* on the TV/VCR/DVD combo he kept on top of his bureau. When that was over he switched on his computer to watch some of the porn clips he had downloaded. The samples only ran about ten seconds each, but if you strung enough of them together it was almost like watching a real porno movie.

He opened his video files, put on a pair of headphones and turned the sound way up. A little redhead with pigtails was taking on two guys at once. Earl had a total of forty-five seconds from the movie, set to repeat in a loop. He watched it a few times, rubbing himself through his sweatpants. Nothing. He was still limp.

Leaving the headphones on, Earl clicked off the video application. Maybe he would play *Grand Theft Auto IV* a while. No, he didn't want think about shooting right now. He settled for *Minesweeper*.

Earl shut off the computer a little after one in the morning. The trailer was quiet, Linda most likely long gone. Earl climbed into bed with his clothes still on. He lay there hearing the gunshots, imagining Brochu's screams over and over. When he closed his eyes, he saw Hag running out of that house covered in blood from head to toe. It was better to keep his eyes open, to stare at the dark ceiling.

At 5 a.m. Earl turned on the TV and flipped to the Channel 5 news. It was a Bangor station that also covered central Maine. And what was bigger news than a murder and robbery? Earl usually missed the early reports because he didn't like to get up until noon.

The lead story was a double homicide in St. Albans, a man and a woman. Instead of a live camera feed, there was a graphic of a chalk outline in the shape of a human body and a diagonal strip of yellow crime scene tape. The cops weren't releasing any names yet because relatives still needed to be notified, but Earl knew it was the guy with the guns. Had to be. How many murders were committed a year in St. Albans? It was a dinky little town that made Wesserunsett look like Boston.

At least there hadn't been a kid there. That counted for something. Didn't it?

The anchorwoman said, "Department of Public Safety Spokesman Steve McCausland told WABI News that robbery may have been a motive in the shooting deaths. Apparently, there were several bullets scattered on the kitchen floor that did not match any of the guns in the house. TV Five will have more on this shocking story as it develops."

Earl clicked off the TV. *More as the story develops.* Either the cops didn't know anything yet or they knew it all and were just keeping quiet. Earl rolled out of bed. He needed to talk to Hag.

The hall carpet was gritty under his bare feet and he promised himself to vacuum it this week. He saw Hag sleeping on the couch in nothing but a pair of briefs. There was a streak of dried blood on Hag's chin that hadn't been there after he'd showered last night. Was the blood his or Linda's? She was gone, but a crumpled pack of menthols sat on the arm of the couch next to a canister of pepper spray.

A gleam caught Earl's eye. The barrel of the big chrome revolver stuck out an inch or two from underneath the couch. Earl pushed the gun out of sight with his foot. He didn't want to look at it now. He sure as hell didn't want anything to do with killing people. Right up until he'd heard the shots, Earl believed Hag would change his mind, that the whole thing was some kind of bad joke. He should have driven away and left Hag there to wait for the cops, but Earl knew Hag would get back at him somehow. Was it normal to be afraid of the guy who had been your best friend since eighth grade?

Earl looked at Hag lying there on the couch. The need to talk to him about the shooting was replaced by something else. "I knew what he was going to do and I took him there anyway," Earl said. He went to the cupboard and got out an unopened box of Little Debbie snack cakes. He had hidden them there a week ago.

Earl sat at the table and peeled off the cellophane wrappers one by one. Then he ate all the cakes , stuffed them into his mouth just as fast as he could chew and swallow. When he finished, Earl wiped his hands on his pants and went outside.

He looked at his truck. As he'd expected, there was a long smear of dried blood on the passenger's side door where Hag's arm had rested on the way home last night. The back of the seat was a mess, too. Earl went around the other side and got in the truck. The engine turned over on the second try. Earl slammed an Aerosmith tape into the player before backing out of the driveway. He didn't have any money for the car wash, but he would drive around until ten. That was when his mother went to the Pentecostal church with some other ladies to make cookies and cake for the next morning's after-service fellowship hour. She always had lots of cleaning things at her house. If anybody asked about the blood before then, Earl would say he hit a deer.

32

Joey pulled into the parking lot of the Pentecostal church at 5 a.m. and parked behind the building again. It was starting to feel like his spot. He locked the car and, taking along a plastic grocery bag, trudged through the woods until he was in the same place where he'd crouched the previous night.

A cup of coffee would have been nice, but then he'd have to take a leak before too long. The last thing Joey wanted was to dangle his junk out here where mosquitoes, blackflies and Christ only knew what else could bite it.

The plastic bag held Vassily Fedoseev's knife and pistol, as well as all the pieces of his cell phone. Joey cleared away some leaves with his foot and used a flat rock to gouge a shallow hole in the ground. It was a good thing he didn't need a deeper one, with all the roots and stones he hit. He set the bagful of evidence—each thing already wiped clean—in the depression and covered it over with dirt and rocks.

Then Joey squatted in the underbrush to watch Barker's house and wait.

The lady cop left for work at 6:30 a.m. Barker didn't come out to see her off. From his hiding place, Joey gave her a wave. That was one less worry. He wouldn't have to whack her just to get at Barker now.

Joey stood, eased out onto the shoulder of the road. No traffic coming either way. Even Wanda Philbrick's Jeep was out of sight. He crossed the road, pulling on a pair of latex gloves as he walked right up to Barker's front door. Joey slowed down on the steps, worried about the boards creaking under his feet. He already knew there was no security system. Hell, from what he had learned talking to locals at the diner where he ate breakfast, most people around here didn't even lock their doors at night.

Barker was apparently an exception. Maybe he wasn't as dumb as Joey thought. Or maybe it was his cop girlfriend who insisted on locking up. Either way, Joey had to spend a couple of minutes picking the lock. He was out of practice, had never been much of a house creep anyway.

He opened the door slowly, cringing as he waited for the old hinges to squeal. They didn't. As soon as he was inside, Joey eased the door shut, locked it. He stood there in the entryway, listening. Joey spared a glance at the clothes heaped on top of overloaded cardboard boxes—the girlfriend's stuff. Dead ahead stood a set of stairs next to a short hall that led to Barker's bedroom.

Joey drew the .38 from the back of his waistband and moved toward the snoring. He stopped at the door, peeked around the corner. Barker was sprawled face down across a king-sized bed beneath a rumpled leopard-print sheet. A matching pillow lay at the foot of the bed, with two more on the floor.

What, no waterbed?

"It's time to rise and shine, stud." Joey grabbed Evan Barker's ankles, hauled him off the bed, tacky sheets and all. Barker hit the floor before he was even awake. He rolled around, trying to untangle himself. Joey squatted next to Barker and jammed the muzzle of his revolver against his nose. Barker's eyes opened wide. The weapon's front sight was inside his left nostril.

Joey said, "You know who I am?"

Barker swallowed. He tried to speak, but his mouth was too dry. He swallowed again and licked his lips.

Joey said, "Well?"

"No."

"Good. You know, you shouldn't fuck around with other men's wives. Didn't your father ever teach you that?"

Barker seemed to recover a little, even with a gun halfway up his nose. He took a deep breath, said, "This is bullshit, man. You can tell Jim Philbrick to..."

Joey laughed. "Your girlfriend's husband doesn't have anything to do with this. I don't even know the guy. I'm just saying you shouldn't bang married women. It's not cool, Todd."

Barker's eyes went wide at the mention of his real name, probably the first time he had heard it spoken aloud in years. He said, "Petucci sent you?"

"You got it, Einstein."

"Oh fuck."

"Oh fuck is right. So here's the big question, genius: Why haven't I killed you already?"

"I don't know."

"Yeah, you do." Joey slapped him.

Barker squirmed, started whimpering.

Joey gave him another slap before taking the .38 away from his face. He slid it along Barker's chest, down his belly, let it rest against his package. Barker rewarded him with a yelp.

"Scary, huh? Don't worry, Todd. I'm sure you won't make me go that far." Joey stood, tucked the gun back into the waistband of his jeans. He offered his hand.

Barker hesitated, but accepted the help. Sitting on the edge of the bed and rubbing his nose, he said, "You're not going to kill me?"

"You misunderstand me. What I said was that I won't shoot your balls off unless you make me. Now, then. Where's the tape?"

"What tape?"

Joey grabbed him by the throat, squeezed. Barker tried to kick, but Joey stood too close. He tried to break Joey's grip.

That didn't work either. Barker's face turned red, then purple. The reek of urine clawed at Joey's nostrils. After a few seconds, Joey let go.

Barker laid there panting in his own piss until he got his breath back. He said, "You want the tape I made of Mikey P's daughter."

"Yeah, so where is it?"

"It's in a safe-deposit box, down at the credit union."

Joey said, "Go take a shower and throw these sheets in the laundry. I can't stand smelling you. And leave the bathroom door open. If I even think you're making a run for it, I'll shoot you."

The bathroom was right off the bedroom. Barker hurried to do as he was told after Joey checked the medicine cabinet and toilet tank for hidden weapons. While the little rat showered, Joey went through the house. Barker didn't have any video-cassettes, only DVDs. Joey popped each of the fourteen discs into the player for a few seconds just to make sure Barker hadn't transferred his porn tape onto DVD and disguised the disc with a fake label. Nothing. Just regular movies, the discs all matched the names on the boxes.

There was nothing on the second floor but a sparsely furnished guest bedroom, a small office with a computer and camera gear, and a half-bath. The house did not have an attic. If there was a trapdoor leading up into the crawlspace, Joey couldn't find it.

Joey went down into the cellar, too. Nothing there but the oil furnace, hot water heater and the smells of dust and mildew.

Joey went back into the bedroom. He shoved the mattress off the bed, flipped over the box spring. Nothing. He rifled through the closet. Along with three joints and half a bottle of OxyContin, he found two bundles of nudie pictures, secured with rubber bands and stashed in a shoebox on a high shelf. The pics starred Wanda the cop. They were all pretty soft-core, considering the kind of stuff Barker used to do. How the hell a loser like Barker got an attractive and seemingly intelligent woman to get naked in front of a camera was beyond Joey's understanding. He put the photos back and grabbed a digital camera he found next to a printer on Barker's nightstand.

Steam filled the bathroom, drifted out into the bedroom. When Joey walked in and rattled on the glass shower door, Barker squealed like a girl. "You're clean enough," Joey said. "Get out of there and get dressed. We're going to be at that bank when it opens."

Barker turned off the water but didn't slide back the door. He said, "I have money. We can work something out."

Joey hurled the camera through the door at the rear of the tub. Long shards of glass fell inward. Barker yelped, huddling beneath the dripping showerhead. Joey said, "You don't have anything to bargain with, so don't waste my time. All I want is the tape, along with any copies you made."

"I didn't make any copies. I swear I didn't. But I just remembered. Today's Saturday, right? The credit union closes at noon, but they only have the drive-thru open anyway. We can't get to the safe-deposit box until Monday morning."

Two more days. Jesus Christ, Grace could be dead by then. Yanking the top off the toilet tank, Joey swung it against the remaining sheet of glass, the one right next to Barker. He pulled back his swing at the last second, kept it from hitting hard enough to shatter the door. Tapping the heavy porcelain against the frosted glass, he said, "I need it now."

He hit the glass again, a little harder this time.

"Fuck, man. What do you want me to say?"

"That's just it, Todd. I don't want you to say another goddamned word. Don't try to weasel your way out of this. I want you to realize there's only one way for you to live through the weekend, which is to do exactly as I tell you. Don't make me any offers. Don't try to bargain with me. You say we can't get the tape until Monday. Fine. I'm going to call them to check their hours."

"It's not a lie. I swear."

"You lie like normal people draw breath. If you're telling me the truth right now, then I'm going to be your houseguest for the rest of the weekend." Joey slid back the shower door. He dropped the tank lid on the floor, said, "Now get out of there and get dressed. Watch out for that broken glass. You wouldn't want to get cut, Todd."

Barker tiptoed his way out of the shower and wrapped a towel around his waist. He stood there, water dripping off the ends of his hair, staring at Joey.

"The fuck are you looking at?"

Barker shook himself out of it and looked down at the floor as he edged around Joey and left the room. "It's just...I haven't heard anyone call me by my real name in a long time."

Joey shoved past him. He said, "Am I supposed to feel sorry for you now?"

"No."

"That's good because I don't want to be here, but I am. That's your fault. And I'm all done calling you Todd now. To keep things safe and simple, you're still Evan Barker. Got it?"

Barker nodded. "What do I call you?"

"Joe. Just Joe. Now shut the fuck up and get dressed."

"But what about work? I have appointments today."

"You call the office, tell Bonnie you're sick. Have her reschedule."

Barker pulled on a pair of clean skivvies, Dockers and a pale pink Oxford shirt. He said, "What about Wanda?"

"What about her?"

"She moved in last night."

Joey had to laugh. This just kept getting better and better.

33

Wanda parked her Jeep behind the station. She checked herself out in the sun visor mirror. Not too bad except for the bloodshot eyes. She'd had a couple of mudslides at The Vault before going to Evan's place last night. He gave her a hard time about moving in, but then acted hurt when she told him she would no longer sleep with him. All of a sudden, it was *we have a good thing going, Wanda, let's keep seeing each other, but take it slow.* Blah, blah, blah. Take it slow? They'd been having an affair for months. It was too late to take it slow now. When Wanda pointed that out, Evan's only answer was to sulk in his bedroom. So she got into his liquor cabinet and hit the vodka. She crashed on the couch and overslept because she forgot to unpack her alarm clock.

Giving her hair another going-over with a brush, Wanda got out of the Jeep and headed inside. The smell of coffee made her mouth water. Margie had a fresh pot going and it was just about full. Coffee reminded her of bagels. Wanda's stomach rumbled. There hadn't been time for breakfast this morning.

Margie sat at her desk with the newspaper spread out, working on the Jumble. She had a pencil in her left hand, another tucked behind her ear. Margie gave Wanda a smile that held more apology than happiness. "Ed wants to see you right away, honey," she said.

Great. Wanda stopped by the coffee maker and pushed the

pause 'n' pour button. "I have time to grab a cup?"

Margie nodded. "Take one of the mugs off the bottom shelf."

That shelf was reserved for Margie's *Far Side* mugs. Anyone who even thought about touching them risked life and limb. Margie never offered to let anyone in the department drink out of one. Taking one down now, Wanda felt like a death row inmate accepting her last meal. Whatever was going on this morning, it was bound to suck. Best to get it over with quickly. The sooner she did that, the sooner she could get out on patrol. Wanda filled the cup, dumped in three packets of Splenda.

Ed Gauthier's door opened and the chief poked his head out into the lobby. He nodded at Wanda, said, "I thought I heard your voice. Bring your coffee on in here."

Wanda followed.

"Close the door, please." Ed sat behind his desk and gestured for Wanda to take a seat across from him. He said, "Margie let you use one of her mugs? Did the end times come and nobody told me?"

Wanda chuckled. She said, "Surprised me too. She probably figures I owe her a kidney now. Maybe a lung."

"What do you figure?"

"I figure there's bad news about to come my way."

Ed opened his mouth to say something, but stopped himself. He pulled a stack of papers from his "in" tray, shuffled them a little before putting them back. Leaning back in his squeaky chair, he said, "This whole situation is lousy. I want you to know that right now. It's a bunch of bullshit, but we're going to have to go along with it. For a little while, anyway. I know it will get cleared up soon."

Wanda blew on her coffee before taking a sip. "I must've missed something somewhere, Boss, because I have no idea what you're talking about."

"Jim is pressing charges against you."

Wanda laughed, sloshing coffee out of the mug and over the

back of her hand. She set the cup on the floor, sucked at her hand until the pain dimmed. "Jesus, that's hot. So just what is my husband accusing me of?"

"His lawyer called me last night, that little shitbird Allman from over to Norridgewock. According to Jim, the two of you got into an argument about the house. You threatened to kill Laurie Marcoux unless Jim signed it over to you. He said no and you told him he was under arrest."

"This is fucked up," Wanda said. "So what am I supposed to have arrested him for?"

Ed scowled. "Allman says you told Jim that you'd think of something on the way to the jail. Anyway, after you 'arrested' him, you slugged him."

Wanda reached for her coffee. "But I didn't arrest the son of a bitch. I only punched him after he slapped me. Then he ran out of the house and drove away after I warned him not to."

"His version of it is that he only drove drunk out of fear for his own life."

"What?"

Ed spread his arms. He said, "Jim claims you pulled your piece and pointed it at him."

Wanda got up, walked around the chair a couple times. She sat down.

"I told you it was bullshit," Ed said. "They can't do anything until Monday morning, but they'll get Judge Perkins to take out a restraining order against you—they want you to stay away from Jim and the Marcoux woman. To top it off, Allman told me he'll file a formal complaint against you: excessive force, misuse of authority, criminal threatening. I'm sure he'll think up a few more charges."

"It's Laurie," Wanda said, picking up her coffee.

"What?"

"She was at the house last night while I was getting some of my stuff. They were both there. Laurie must have been listening when I said some things to Jim about her, how she was a no-good skanky whore who will take him for what little he has. Laurie wouldn't have liked that. She must have put Jim up to all this. No way he'd ever do it on his own."

Ed rubbed his belly through his uniform shirt. "Well, whether she did or she didn't, we're going to have to deal with this. Allman will be on the phone to the newspaper right after he gets what he wants from the judge. I imagine you'll make the front page of Tuesday's *Morning Sentinel.* The whole thing stinks, but we have to play it by the book all the way."

Wanda nodded. Her stomach churned, the coffee going sour. She set it down again so Ed would not see her hands shaking.

"Until we can clear you of the charges, I'm going to have to put you on paid suspension. I'll need your shield and your weapon."

"I haven't been charged with anything yet," Wanda said.

"Don't make this harder than it has to be. We're on the same side. Think of it as a vacation. I want you to try and relax so we can get this straightened out." Ed held out his hand, waiting for the pistol and badge.

Wanda handed them across the desk. Ed started to say something else as she got up to leave, but Wanda didn't wait to hear it. She walked past Margie, slammed the front door behind her. Squinting against the sunlight, Wanda wiped a tear from the corner of her eye. That was it, just the one.

"I'll be goddamned if I ever shed another," Wanda said.

34

Hag drank his first beer of the morning standing under the shower. Even though he'd showered last night, he still found flecks of dried blood in his hair. It took two more shampooings before Hag was convinced he had gotten rid of it all. He dressed in the living room, the same clothes he wore after getting back. All his underwear was dirty, so Hag went commando.

The clock on the DVD player read 11:15 a.m. Hag grabbed another beer from the fridge. There were only three cans of Schaefer left. As the money ran low, the beer got cheaper. He checked his wallet. Just the eighty-two he had taken from Linda. Earl lived on food stamps and whatever cash his mother felt like giving him after paying his rent. He was probably just as broke as Hag.

"Get your fat ass out of bed, Earl. We got to make some money." When Earl didn't answer, Hag shouted again. Earl still wasn't up by the time Hag finished his beer. He went down the hall, banged on the bedroom door. It swung open. The place was a pigsty as usual, the bed unmade. Clothes, magazines and food containers lay strewn all over. No sign of the pig.

"What the fuck?" Hag crushed his empty beer can, tossed it onto the bed. He went back to the living room. Earl never got up much before noon, so where was he? A glance out the living room window showed that his truck was gone, too. Had Earl freaked out and gone to the cops?

Hag sat at the kitchen table, sipped at a third beer. "No friggin' way. Earl ain't a rat. His fat ass is on the line, too. He just went out for donuts or something." He couldn't quite convince himself, but there was time to worry about Earl later. First thing Hag had to do was get rid of Willard's gun. The .38 was a murder weapon. Hag didn't want to be left holding it, especially if Earl did come back with the police.

The guns were under the couch. Hag got down on his knees and pulled them out. The bullets and shotgun shells rattled around loose. Hag had only managed to scoop up a couple of handfuls in the rush to get away from Brochu's house last night. There were red spots on some of the brass. The .38's muzzle and grip were covered with dried blood. The shotgun's stock had a crimson streak along one side. Hag shoved the shotgun, the .44 and the heap of ammo back under the couch. He could swipe one of Earl's blankets to wrap them in later.

Using a wet dishcloth, Hag got most of the mess off the .38's grips. He wasn't worried about the blood on the stubby barrel. The more he thought about it, he wanted it there, since it was further proof that the little revolver was used to kill Art Brochu. What Hag needed to get rid of were his fingerprints. He wiped down the cylinder too. Then he wrapped the gun in a piece of newspaper, stashed it in a Walmart bag. The bag went onto the top shelf of a cupboard above the counter.

Hag went out to the backyard, found the blanket full of his bloody clothes. He hated to burn them, especially the jean jacket, but just washing them might not get out all the blood. The cops could get all kinds of microscopic evidence these days. Best to play it safe and torch the whole bundle.

Larry Nichols was on his hands and knees gardening in his small plot next door. Hag couldn't wait for the old queer's tomatoes to get ripe so he could steal some. Larry looked up at Hag, gave him one of his typical pissy looks before getting back to weeding.

An old charcoal grill stood next to Earl's shed. Like Earl had said, the rack was long gone. The lid was rusted through and speckled with bird shit. Useless, but Earl was too lazy to get rid of it. Hag didn't want to cook burgers anyway. He put the blanket in the grill, doused it with half a bottle of lighter fluid he found in the shed.

"Hey, Nichols," Hag said. "You got any matches so I can light this thing? All I got's a cigarette lighter a whore gave me."

Larry didn't even look up from his carrots or whatever they were. "I don't smoke."

"You're a pole smoker, though." Hag went into the trailer, still couldn't find any matches. He ended up rolling some newspaper into a tube, lighting it with Linda's Bic before throwing the burning paper onto the blanket. The *whoosh* of the igniting fluid got Larry's attention. He stood, brushing dirt from his kneepads.

"You aren't supposed to have any fires without a burn permit," Larry said. "You know that, don't you?"

"It's just a charcoal grill."

"I can see that. But what're you going to cook over a burning blanket?"

"None of your fucking business."

"I'll bet you got drunk, passed out and wet the bed. You don't want your buddy to find out, so you're burning the mess while he's gone."

Hag said, "I like your kneepads. You wear them when you're on glory hole patrol out at the rest area?"

"Seems like you know where all the queers go cruising, Charlie. Finally coming out of the closet?"

Hag scooped up a chunk of broken brick and went into a pitcher's wind-up. The old man dropped his garden trowel, hoofed it on into his trailer. Probably calling the cops right now. Hag tossed the brick into the shed, went back to check the grill. The fire was mostly out, the blanket just a black ball that smelled like melted plastic. He poked it with a stick, pried it open a little. The clothes inside were still untouched by fire.

"Fuck."

So much for disposing of the evidence. He went back inside to wait for Earl. Where the hell was he? Out to his mother's? Maybe. But today was Saturday and Earl's mom usually spent Saturdays dubbing around the church with the other old bitches.

Hag lit a smoke and stretched out on the couch. If Earl was visiting his mother, it could mean trouble. She was always trying to get him away from Hag's "bad influence." Earl's resolve was shaky at the best of times, but Hag knew last night had freaked him out. That was all right, though. Hag would toughen him up. He saw now that he had been going too easy on Earl lately. What he needed was to get some blood on his hands.

Failing that, it might be a good time for Mama Coro to have a little accident.

35

The woman who answered the phone at the Wesserunsett Federal Credit Union had confirmed what Barker told Joey. The lobby was closed on Saturdays, the drive-thru window open until noon. Joey was stuck out here in the boondocks until Monday morning. He had to call Carl, so he walked around the house and sat at the picnic table by the back door. Barker was watching TV in the living room; Joey had already confiscated his cell phone and truck keys.

Joey thumbed in Carl's number, went through the rigmarole of the call script again. Bunch of bullshit. When Carl finally came on the line, Joey said, "I can't get it until Monday."

"What the fuck are you talking about? You trying to pull some shit on me?"

Joey said, "Our boy has the thing locked up in a safe deposit box at the bank. We can't go get it until Monday morning."

"And you believe that?"

"I had the guy pissing himself. Yeah, I believe him."

"I got somebody here wants to talk to you."

There was a pause, then Joey heard Grace say, "Joe?"

Joey smiled, couldn't help himself. "Are you okay?"

"What do you think?" Grace's voice sounded thick, the way someone talks when her lips are swollen and split. She said, "They want me to say you know better than to fuck things up."

"Did they beat you up?"

But Carl was back, saying, "Monday then. And no more dicking around. Get the thing, do the second part of the job and then get your ass on a plane. I want you in my office before midnight. Call me with your arrival time."

"Fine." Joey hung up, headed back inside.

Barker was still in his recliner, watching *Firefly* reruns. Joey sat on one end of the couch, leaned back and put his feet up on the coffee table. They'd moved Wanda's things into the dining room so there would be enough room to relax in here. Barker looked over at Joey, said, "Are we just going to sit here all day?"

"Maybe."

"Bonnie was pissed that I canceled all my appointments."

"She'll get over it."

Barker was quiet for a while.

Joey took a harmonica out of his shirt pocket. It was an A minor, one of the harps he'd taken from Deke's Music four years earlier. He blew out the lint, moistened his lips.

Barker said, "You're kidding me. A fucking harmonica?"

Joey ignored him, went into the opening riff from "One Way Out." Got through it twice with no mistakes. Not bad. Not Sonny Boy either, but not bad. He wiped the harp on his shirttail, said, "The Allman Brothers do that one in the key of E, but Sonny Boy Williamson and Elmore James wrote it in A."

Barker did a little golf clap.

"You don't like blues?"

"I don't like being entertained by a killer while trapped in my own house. I'm weird like that," Barker said.

"That was for my entertainment, not yours."

"Whatever." Barker folded his arms across his chest. He said, "You know, I made a pretty good life for myself here. It's not fair for you to come along and fuck it all up."

"Don't talk to me about fair, asshole. If it weren't for you, I wouldn't be here. Think I like this any more than you?" Joey started playing again, hoping Barker would take the hint and shut up.

Barker sat up straighter. "What's going to happen to me? I mean, once I give you the tape."

"What do you think will happen?"

Barker looked like he needed to puke. He said, "Maybe I won't cooperate. I know Petucci wants that tape bad. Maybe I won't give it to you unless you agree to let me go."

Joey said, "Carl's not my favorite guy in the world. Maybe I'll shoot you right now and tell him you didn't have the tape. Like that idea?"

"You can't just kill a federal witness. They'll come after you."

"The feds don't know where you are," Joey said. "They could probably find you if they wanted to, but I doubt they care enough to make a fuss. The only real information you had was on Mikey. He's in prison, so you've got nothing new for them. What's another dead scumbag? It won't even be their fault, since you ditched them. Why'd you do that, anyway?"

"Shitty jobs in shitty towns. A decade of them. My handlers thought it was funny. I got sick of it."

Joey laughed, said, "So you came here? I don't see it as a step up."

"There's nothing wrong with Wesserunsett. I like it here. When I was a kid, I had an uncle who lived in southern Maine, a little town called Buxton. We used to visit him for a week every summer. I had some money stashed away, used it to set up a new life here. I didn't think anyone would find me."

"Want to know who found you?"

"Some fucking rat, I imagine."

"No. It was Carl. He found your picture on the Wesserunsett Realty website. Smart move, by the way. It was almost as smart as trying to blackmail a mob boss."

Barker rubbed his eyes, slouched in his chair. "I don't believe this is happening."

"So play along and you get to enjoy this paradise a couple

more days." Joey saw no point in telling Barker that he'd rather not have to kill him. That knowledge might make him harder to manage. Joey said, "I'm getting hungry. What's in the fridge?"

36

It took Hag a while to locate Earl's phone book in all the mess. He flipped through the yellow pages, found the number for Stoney's car dealership.

A woman answered the phone. "Lakeside Auto Sales."

"Hi, how you doing? I was hoping you could help me out. A guy named Willard told me he worked for you. He said he could get me a good deal on a new truck. Is Willard there right now? He told me his last name, but I forgot it. I'm lousy at names."

"You don't mean Willard Bailey, do you?"

"Big guy, right? Yeah, that's him. Is he there? I want to come down and look around the lot." Hag leaned back against the couch.

The woman said, "Um, I'm sorry sir, but Willard isn't one of our salesmen, so he doesn't really have the authority to offer you any kind of deal. We have an awesome sales team here, though. If you'd like to drop by, any one of them could put you into a nice, clean vehicle."

"You mean Willard was just jerking my chain? He don't sell cars. What's he do there, sweep the floors and stuff like that? Man, don't that just figure." Hag switched off the handset and grabbed the phone book again. There was no listing for a Willard Bailey. Hag hadn't seen him around before, so maybe the guy only started working for Stony after Hag got busted.

Or he had an unpublished phone number. Why did killing a guy and blaming him for a pair of homicides have to be so complicated? The only thing left to do was get hold of Earl so they could drive around looking for Willard.

Hag finished the last can of Schaefer, said, "Coming to get you, Willie."

"I don't want to do this," Earl said, carrying the shotgun with his finger outside the trigger guard. He'd never held a real gun before.

Hag said, "Don't be a pussy."

They were on a narrow dirt road north of the lake. Scrubby trees crowded both sides of the road, growing so close together that the ground was cast into dense green shade. Wild raspberry bushes had shot up in the few patches of direct sunlight. Earl's stomach growled, but the berries were a long way from ripe. He raised the shotgun, waved it around to drive off the mosquitoes that swarmed him. They ate better than he did. Earl hadn't gotten to finish his lunch.

Hag stood next to him, checking the loads in the .38 revolver. He said, "This thing's only got one bullet left, so I got to make it count. All I need you to do is cover the son of a whore. You don't have to shoot, but you better look like you're ready to."

Earl had been eating a big plate of baked beans and red hots at his mother's house when Hag walked in and dragged him out. Then they'd driven around in the truck searching for Willard Bailey—with Hag complaining the whole time that the cab smelled like Lysol and was giving him a headache. They spotted Willard coming out of the video store with a handful of DVDs, followed him to a house on Chestnut Street.

They had parked down the block, sat there almost an hour until Willard came out again. He loaded fishing gear in the trunk of his car and drove off. They followed him out here.

Hag insisted on staying so far behind that they almost missed seeing him turn off onto this old logging road. After a couple of miles bouncing over old ruts, they found Willard's Chevy Caprice parked at a dead end. There was no sign of Willard himself, but a trail led away through the woods. Earl heard rushing water.

"I still don't see why you have to kill him."

"It's him or us," Hag said. "Somebody's got to take the rap for Brochu and his fucking girlfriend. It ain't going to be us. I don't imagine old Willard'll just walk into the cops and confess to a murder he didn't do."

"Us? In case you forgot, I didn't kill nobody."

Hag gave him a backhand slap him in the chest. "You ever hear of being an accessory to a crime? That means you knew about it and helped out. Accessory to murder is what the court calls it. Who drove me out there last night? Who's letting me keep stolen guns in his house? Who washed the dead guy's blood off his truck this morning? Don't be a fucking retard, man. If I go down, so do you. But we ain't going down."

They walked along the overgrown trail, Hag in the lead and taking care not to snap branches or trip over the uneven ground. The sound of the water grew louder with each step. Earl doubted anyone would hear a stick break over the river's noise.

"What's he doing out here?" Earl said.

Hag shushed him. "He brought a fishing pole, retard. What do you think he's doing?"

Earl carried the twelve-gauge in his right hand, swatted mosquitoes with his left. The bugs didn't seem interested in Hag. Earl stepped in a hole, turning his ankle. Trying to keep from falling, he ended up poking Hag in the back with the shotgun.

Hag turned around, glaring. "We want to take this cocksucker by surprise. Watch what the fuck you're doing."

The trail ended at the river. The noise of it muffled all other sounds. So much for all of Hag's sneaking. At this spot, the

Wesserunsett River was a hundred yards or so across. The bottom was a shallow jumble of rocks and boulders. Water raced over them on its way to the dam at the north end of Wesserunsett Lake.

Willard Bailey stood with his back to the shore a little ways out there, up to his knees in the water and whipping a fly rod around. He wore hip waders, and a wide-brimmed hat festooned with flies. For a second, Earl didn't think it was the same guy who had come to his trailer with Stony.

Earl tapped Hag on the shoulder and pointed across the river. A small camp stood on the opposite bank, but there were no vehicles parked near it, no sign of anyone moving around. Hag shrugged. He stepped aside so Earl could stand next to him.

Hag called out to Willard.

Willard didn't turn around, just kept fishing. Even Earl had barely heard Hag over the river's noise.

"Willard."

Nothing.

"Willard!"

The guy still didn't make any sign that he'd heard Hag.

Earl leaned over, spoke into Hag's ear. "Now what, professor?"

Hag pointed at the water.

"I ain't going in there," Earl said. The rocks looked slippery, and all he had on his feet were sneakers.

Hag jerked his head toward the river. He said, "If I fall down and lose this gun, we can't pin the St. Albans thing on Willard. If you fall and lose yours, we can just get another. Now get moving. Bring him back here."

Earl stared down at the water. He stepped in, gasping as the cold water drenched his sneakers and the legs of his sweatpants. Twice he lost his footing and almost went down. The fact that the water was only up to Willard's knees was deceptive, because he was a good three or four inches taller than Earl. The cold water came well up to Earl's thighs. Every few seconds, it splashed his crotch. There were shallow holes peppered along the bottom, too, gouged out by the force of spring floods. So he found himself belly-deep a couple of times.

Finally, Earl made it just behind where Willard stood casting. What was he supposed to do now? Jam the gun in Willard's back to get his attention? Say something cool? It was hard to act tough when your pants were soaked, your bag all shriveled from the icy water.

Willard turned around while Earl was still thinking about his next move. He saw the shotgun right away, but didn't seem to recognize Earl. Willard lowered his fly rod, the line draping out along the current. Earl cocked a thumb over his shoulder. Willard looked over at the bank, saw Hag standing there with the .38 in his hand.

Willard said, "Shit."

Earl stepped back, pointed the shotgun at Willard. "He wants you to go over there."

Willard reeled in his line.

Hag yelled something neither of them could hear.

"He don't like to wait," Earl said. "I don't either." Something bumped against Earl's leg, probably just a stick getting swept downstream. He hoped to God it wasn't a snapping turtle.

Willard hawked up a loogie. He kept on reeling. "I ain't in any hurry to get shot."

Hag paced the narrow clearing on the bank, waving his pistol around.

Earl said, "We better go."

"Fuck you."

Earl racked the pump on the shotgun. Willard stopped reeling and headed for shore, a few feet of line floating along behind him. Hag quit pacing when they climbed out of the river. He grabbed Willard's fly rod, tossed it back in the woods.

Willard said, "This is really stupid."

"Down on your knees," Hag said.

Willard looked at Earl, maybe figuring he was the only one who could listen to reason. He said, "I can talk to Stony, you know. Get him to leave you guys alone."

Hag laughed. "Give me a break. Stony don't give a fuck what you say. You're just one of his peons, like we used to be. Besides, this is nothing to do with Stony. I ain't worried about him."

"Well, what the fuck you want with me?"

"You deaf, or what? Get down on your knees."

Willard looked at Earl again. Earl shrugged, trying to show this wasn't his idea. His sweatpants hung heavy off his hips. Because he needed to hold them up, he only had one hand free to steady the shotgun. He propped it against his thigh, keeping it trained on Willard.

Willard shifted his weight. His waders squeaked. He said, "I ain't getting down on my knees for you or anybody else."

Hag stepped up next to Willard, put the .38 against his temple. "Tough guy. Hey, Earl. You might want to back off a little. This gets really fucking messy."

Earl didn't know what to say. If Willard got scared, maybe Hag would call it off and let him live. But his best friend's eyes were glassy, like he was drunk or high. It wasn't just the money. Hag got off on this. Earl closed his eyes, turning away just before Hag squeezed the trigger. Even this close, the shot was not all that loud compared to the flowing water. No one would hear it.

"Whoa, baby," Hag said. "You smell that, Earl? I think he shit himself."

For a second, Earl believed that Hag had fired into the air just to scare Willard. But then he saw Willard lying on his side in the mud with his mouth working like there was something stuck in his throat. Blood pumped in bright red gouts from a hole in his head. Earl bent over and puked. Some of it splashed onto his sneakers, but most of the vomit mingled with the dark puddle behind Willard's head.

Hag rolled his eyes and snatched the shotgun from Earl's hand.

He's going to shoot me now.

But Hag knelt beside the body. He picked up Willard's right hand, worked the index finger into the shotgun's trigger guard and fired a blast into the air. "They have these tests to see if you've shot a gun," he said.

Then he wiped down the pistol with a Kleenex and put it in Willard's hand, squeezed the dead man's fingers tight around the grip. Hag tossed the wadded-up tissue into the water, squatted on the bank to wash the blood from his hands in the cold current. He stood up, grinning. "You gonna make it, Earl?"

Earl wiped his mouth with the back of his hand, said, "I never seen nothing like that before."

Hag handed him the shotgun and started back along the trail. "Let's go get cleaned up. Then we can see about making us some money."

Walking out, Earl saw Willard's fly rod hanging in the branches of a poplar. Hag had forgotten to wipe his finger-prints off it. They ought to get it down and make sure it was clean.

"Hey, Hag?"

"Now what?"

Earl hitched up his pants, started walking faster. "Never mind."

37

If Wanda was going to have an unexpected Saturday off, she might as well try to enjoy it. After making her stoic exit from the station, she'd had to go back in and clean out her locker. There were dirty clothes in there. Wanda was damned if she'd leave them behind to stink up the place. For some reason she no longer remembered, her bathing suit had been in the locker, too. So after driving around all morning, Wanda decided it was as good a time as any to go for a swim at the public beach.

Wesserunsett was a deep lake, left behind by a retreating glacier. Even at the height of summer its water would be cold. June had been much rainier than usual and today, almost three weeks after Memorial Day, stepping into the lake sent a chill shock up Wanda's bare legs.

Wanda took a deep breath to steel herself, waded out beyond the shallows. When the water was up to her chest, she dove in. Surfaced a few yards away, gasping. She did a breast-stroke, evened out her breathing.

Richmond's Island was a small dab of land studded with a lot of rocks and one scrubby pine tree, half a mile straight out from the gravel beach. Wanda climbed onto the biggest rock to rest a few minutes. She wrung water from her hair, let the sun ease some of the goose bumps from her shoulders and arms.

Boats motored around the lake and the occasional squeal of a kid or the shout of a parent carried across the water, but the day was quiet. And what was wrong with a quiet life? There had been a pair of killings last night in St. Albans. Wanda heard the man and woman had both been shot in the head at close range. She wanted more out of her job—assuming that a judge saw Jim and Laurie's allegation for the crock of shit it was and she got to keep on being a cop. She wanted to be a detective and work real cases like that murder.

She had stayed up late thinking about what her father and Ed Gauthier said about being bored in Wesserunsett. Even though they were right, it didn't necessarily follow that she'd take their advice. Not that there was much to keep her here now. Her parents didn't need her, not really. The divorce would go through before long, but people would keep gossiping about her. The relationship with Evan was over, had been over for some time. He'd made it clear that he didn't want her living there, which came as a relief. Wanda just needed a place to crash for a day or two until she figured out what to do next. Maybe she'd stay in Wesserunsett a while longer, then apply to the state police once the trouble with Jim got cleared up. It would give her mother some time to get used to the fact that the marriage really was over before Wanda dropped another bomb on her.

There was no chance of making detective in a small-town PD, where there was no budget—or even a need—for the position. State police detectives investigated major crimes like murder, except in Bangor, Lewiston and Portland. They worked undercover operations on narcotics, kiddie porn, you name it. At thirty-two years of age, it was finally time for Wanda to decide where her life would take her. There were too many people trying to push her toward their idea of who she should be.

Her stomach growled. Time to swim back to shore and get something to eat.

Wanda dove off her rock and sliced through the water in an Australian crawl, letting the rhythm of the strokes take over.

The beach was a lot more crowded than it had been when she first arrived. Her towel and backpack lay on the picnic table where she'd left them, though a chubby woman and her three little boys had come along while Wanda was swimming. Now their lunch took up most of the table.

"Looks good," Wanda said after she toweled off. She put her hair in a ponytail.

The woman dished macaroni salad and slices of bologna and American cheese onto a paper plate, handed it to the youngest boy. She looked up and chuckled, said, "Help yourself if you want. These little monsters'll only eat half their lunches before running back to the water anyway."

The oldest boy stared at Wanda over the lip of his plastic cup. Disappointment showed on his face when she pulled on a pair of jean shorts and a big Patriots T-shirt. Wanda shoved the damp towel into her backpack. "Thanks, but I've been starving myself all week just so I can get away with eating a ham Italian at Sandy's."

"After three kids, you kinda stop worrying about that," the woman said.

Wanda scuffed her feet in the grass to get rid of most of the sand, slipped them into her favorite pair of old sandals before heading across the road to Sandy's. As she stepped onto the warped wooden porch, Evan came outside carrying a pizza box. He was with another man, a big guy with short blond hair and rough Irish features who carried a paper grocery bag. Bottles rattled against each other inside the bag.

Evan stopped, did a double take. He said, "Aren't you supposed to be at work?"

"I'll tell you about it later. Kind of surprising the news isn't all over town yet."

"Well, what happened?"

"Don't worry about it, Evan. Who's your buddy?"

The big guy said, "Joe Carmichael."

Evan said, "Joe, this is Wanda Philbrick." Then to Wanda,

"Joe's an old friend of mine from New York and he's thinking about moving here. Hey, if you're not working, you might as well come out to the house for lunch. We got plenty."

"I don't know. I need some time to myself right now. Things to think about, you know."

"Oh, come on," Evan said. "I could use your help convincing Joe to buy a house."

"I'm really just here to go fishing," Joe said. He looked Wanda up and down once, then glared at Evan. "I guess Evan thinks he's going to get something out of it."

Wanda grinned. "That's Evan for you."

"We'd better get going. It was nice meeting you, Wanda." They stepped off the porch and crossed the small parking lot.

Wanda watched them get into Evan's truck. As they pulled out of the lot, Joe waved to her and smiled. Evan looked like he was driving to his own funeral.

Sandy Pomelow came outside, wiping her hands on her apron. She was a tiny woman in her early fifties, a transplant from a Georgia town even smaller than Wesserunsett. She wore a red bandana on her head, a small pink breast cancer ribbon pinned to her T-shirt. Sandy said, "Hey, Wanda. You keep holding that door for people, I'm gonna have to put you on the payroll. I appreciate the help, but you're letting the flies in, too."

"Sorry. I forgot it was open." Wanda closed the door.

"It's all right, darlin'. I saw your mom and dad the other day. Just to say hey, not to stop and talk. How's things with you and Jim?"

Wanda grinned. "How can you be the only one in town who doesn't know we're getting divorced?"

"Oh, God, I'm sorry to hear that. I was down in Portland the last few days."

There was nothing like a friend in chemo to remind you that you were not the center of everyone's universe. Wanda bent at the waist, gave Sandy a little hug. "Don't worry about it. You just work on getting better. I bet you'll have your hair back by the end of summer."

Chuckling, Sandy wiped a tear from her eye. "I'll do my best, darlin'."

"Did you wait on Evan Barker a minute ago? Was it my imagination, or was he acting kind of weird?"

"Yeah. Don't he look a mess? He's usually all smiles and handshakes, but today he acted fidgety. You ask me, I think he was scared of that fella with him."

"Joe Carmichael," Wanda said. "You ever see him before?"

Sandy shook her head. "I have to get back inside. It's only Brenda in there. She'll stand at the counter, watching kids shove candy in their pockets without saying a word. I'd fire her if she wasn't my sister-in-law. You coming in for your usual?"

Wanda stepped off the porch, pulled her car keys out of her backpack. She said, "I was going to, but there's something I need to check out."

38

Joey didn't say anything as they drove up the hill away from the store. Barker's hands shook on the steering wheel. Good, let the little prick sweat. After a mile, Joey told him to pull over. Barker stopped next to an old gray barn that leaned so badly it looked like a strong breeze might tip it over. If he was of a mind to do it, Joey could dump his body in there, and years might pass before anyone found it.

"That was stupid," Joey said. He looked straight ahead. "That whole thing at the store. You thought she could save you. Well, forget about it. I would've had to deal with her this afternoon, one way or the other. You better believe I'm going to get what I came here for, and no fucking cop'll stop me."

Barker started crying. *Jesus.* Any second now, he'd make another try at bargaining his way out of this. Joey turned away, glanced at the side mirror. Wanda's Jeep Renegade crested the hill behind them and was coming on fast. Its top was off. Joey saw Wanda at the wheel.

"She's following us," Joey said. "Drive normally. Get moving. We get to the house, you play it cool. She asks why we pulled over, it's because we saw a deer. City boys like me get fascinated by that shit. I don't like killing cops, but sometimes it can't be helped. Look at me."

Evan did.

Joey said, "We get through this weekend without any more

fuck-ups on your part, and I won't kill you. There's no reason why you have to die. All I really want is the tape. I'll take it Monday morning and disappear. You can do the same, but only if you do what I say. Got me? Carl doesn't need to know I let you walk."

Barker nodded. Whether or not he believed Joey was another story. He shifted into first, swung the truck back onto the road.

Checking the side mirror, Joey saw Wanda's brake lights come on as she slowed enough to stay a couple of lengths behind them. He reached around, slid the .38 from the clip-on holster at the back of his belt. There hadn't seemed to be any reason to bring it along beyond a hunch it might be necessary. He picked up the grocery bag and punched a hole in the bottom, worked the pistol inside and held it there next to the beer and potato chips. All this trouble because you couldn't get pizza delivery in a hick town like Wesserunsett.

They pulled into Barker's driveway, parked near the barn. Wanda stopped right behind them. She slid out of the Jeep, gave Joey's Corolla the once-over. Joey watched to see if she wrote down the plate numbers, but she only adjusted her ponytail and walked over. She carried a purse: probably a cell phone in there, maybe a gun too. Joey had never heard of a cop who didn't carry a piece off-duty. Why should things be that different out in the sticks?

"Change your mind?" Joey said. He held the bag with both hands, his right index finger resting comfortably on the .38's trigger. Barker carried the pizza; his hands shook a little, and he looked like he might drop it. Joey watched him. *Come on, you little shit. Don't screw this up. None of us has to die today.*

Wanda smiled. Damn. She was the kind of woman who smiled with her whole face. All his life, Joey had been a sucker for girls like that.

"It's hard to turn down a free lunch," Wanda said.

Barker propped the pizza carton against his hip so he could

unlock the front door. He went inside without waiting for the others, letting the screen door bang shut behind him.

Wanda looked up at Joey on the top step. She said, "The way Evan was hustling, I guess we ought to get in there before he eats it all himself. He might be skinny, but he eats like a horse."

Joey stepped aside, held the door for her. Barker was already in the dining room. He had set the pizza on the big oak table and went into the kitchen, saying, "We need plates and napkins."

"I'm going to put some of these beers in the fridge," Joey said. "You want me to leave one with you, Wanda?"

Wanda shook her head, looked at her things piled in the near corner of the dining room. Joey hit the kitchen, pulling his .38 out of the bag. The chrome was slick with moisture from the beer bottles. Joey wiped it down with a clean dish towel, jammed it back into the holster, making sure his shirttail covered it.

Barker got out plates, napkins, forks and a shaker full of crushed red pepper, laid them all out on a tray. He carried the tray into the dining room. After putting four beers in the fridge, Joey joined him.

When everyone was seated, Barker gestured to the pizza carton. "It's self-serve at lunch time," he said. His hands still shook a little, though his voice had stopped quavering.

"So Evan said you're from New York, Joe?"

Joey nodded. He took a bite of pizza, chewed and swallowed. The pizza wasn't great, but it wasn't bad either. He said, "Originally, yeah. But I've been in Chicago the last few years. I own a club there." Whoa. Why the hell did he tell her that?

"Yeah? What kind of club?"

"Blues. You like blues music, Wanda?"

She shrugged. "It's okay. I'm more of a classic rock girl."

"Nothing wrong with that. A lot of the sixties and seventies bands took their sound from the blues. They all got famous playing songs these old black guys wrote twenty, thirty year earlier. If it hadn't been for Robert Johnson and Willie Dixon, there'd be no Rolling Stones or Led Zeppelin."

Wanda said, "You left out Eric Clapton."

Joey laughed. "You know your music."

"Well, my older brother played bass in a garage band when he was in high school. I used to hang out and listen to them jam on stuff by The Who, The Allman Brothers, Dylan, you name it."

"I'm surprised there isn't a blues scene around here," Joey said. "From what I've seen it's a down-and-out place. Closed factories, empty storefronts, every other house up for sale."

Wanda swallowed, wiped her mouth with a napkin. She said, "Yeah, we're pretty hardscrabble. One of the poorest towns in Maine's poorest county. But country music's king around here. I guess that's depressing enough for us."

Barker ate slowly without joining the conversation.

Wanda finished her first slice, helped herself to a second.

"I like a woman who isn't afraid to let you see she likes food," Joey said. God, what a body. And she was confident without a chip on her shoulder like you saw with a lot of female cops. She was...what was the right term for it? *Self-possessed.* Yeah.

"Oh, I do love food," Wanda said. "But I starved myself all week so I could indulge like this. I'm doing my part to keep the department's combined cholesterol level under three thousand."

"Cops are cops, no matter where you go." Joey chuckled, but Wanda didn't.

She arched her left eyebrow and said, "You have a lot of experience dealing with the police, Joe?"

Oh, fuck. He had let himself get too relaxed. Trying to recover, he shrugged it off. "I run a bar, so you know. The usual."

Wanda's expression didn't change.

"Plus a few speeding tickets," Joey said.

Barker looked up, grinning. "That sounds more like Joe from the old days in Brooklyn," he said. "A foot made of lead and shit for his brains."

39

On the way home, Hag bought six forty-ounce bottles of Milwaukee's Best, a pack of smokes and a couple Slim Jims for Earl, who claimed to be broke. "How come you ain't hit your mother up for any money?" Hag said as they turned onto Heron Lane.

"I did, but they're taking her gallbladder out next week. She's afraid to spend a penny more than she has to for anything right now."

"Who said there's anything wrong with her gallbladder?"

"The doctor."

"How come you didn't tell me before?"

"I didn't figure you'd give a care."

"Good fucking guess." They stopped in Earl's driveway. Earl took the bag full of beers, headed for the house. Hag tipped the seat forward to get the .44 and shotgun. With the blanket from Art Brochu's house half-melted/half-burned, the guns were now wrapped in one of Earl's spare sheets.

Larry Nichols was mowing his little front yard with an electric mower. He gave them a dirty look, but turned away when Hag stopped halfway up the porch steps and flipped him the bird. Hag stood there watching him a minute. Larry looked down and kept his attention on the grass. Hag went inside.

The place was trashed. Not the normal everyday dirt and messiness. Earl's recliner lay on its side. The couch had been pulled away from the wall, its cushions scattered on the floor along with DVDs and overturned ashtrays. The TV was smashed, a broken chunk of cinder block sticking out of the screen.

Earl stood in the kitchen, cramming both of the giant Slim Jims into his mouth at once. The doors of the refrigerator and freezer stood open. What little food Earl had kept in them was spread out on the floor.

Empty cupboards.

Broken dishes.

Broken glasses.

Hag opened one of the beers and chugged, savored the coldness in his mouth, the warmth in his throat as the beer went down. When he came up for air, he said, "I feel like going out to The Vault tonight."

Earl almost choked on the last of his Slim Jim. "What?"

"You heard me."

"Look at this place," Earl said. "God knows what they did in the bathroom and my bedroom. We can't go out."

"This? This is just Stony fucking with our heads, man. It's nothing."

"They trashed my house."

"Jesus, Earl. Get some perspective. Stony's scared of us. This is all he can think of doing. It means he's gonna pay us our money."

Earl shuffled down the hall. It sounded like he was crying. After a few minutes, Earl came back, said, "They slashed my mattress and broke the computer. The other TV's in the bathtub. In pieces."

Hag said, "You can hang around here and moan if you want. I'm going to The Vault tonight."

"But all this stuff's smashed. We ain't got no money to replace it."

"We can always get money."

"This ain't working, Hag. Let's just forget about this hitman stuff and find something else. We can still talk to Stony, get things straightened out."

"Fuck that."

Earl righted his recliner, sat down. He said, "Maybe I'll stay at Ma's for a while."

"No. I can't stand your mother's house. All those angels everywhere: the figures and the pictures. Even when you sit on the crapper, you got the damn things staring at you. We're staying right here."

Earl said, "You can stay here. It's fine by me."

"We don't split up. You're with me or against me, Earl. Make up your fucking mind right now."

Earl didn't answer. Outside, Larry Nichols' lawn mower stopped buzzing along.

Hag said, "You know who's always got money? Faggots. Think about it. They got money because they don't have women or kids to spend it on. Queers always drive decent cars, wear jewelry and shit, live in nice houses. Even Nichols, man. He's like sixty and lives in a trailer, yeah, but it's the nicest trailer on the fucking street. He drives that Saturn. I'm telling you, that cocksucker's got some cash squirreled away."

"Leave Larry alone."

"You'll drive me out to kill some guy, but you ain't got the balls to rob an old queer? The fuck's up with that?"

Earl leaned to the right, farted. He said, "It's stupid, that's what's up with it. You know what this street is like. People home all day, sitting on their steps or looking out their windows, seeing what everybody else is doing. There's going to be a dozen witnesses swear they saw you go in Larry's house."

"It's funny how none of those concerned citizens called the cops when your house was getting trashed, Earl." Hag stood over Earl, staring down on him like Wanda had tried the day before.

It didn't work. Earl's eyes were still closed.

"Fine," Hag said. "Be a fucking pussy, see if I care." He

went down the hall and out the back door. Standing on the step, he looked around. There were no fences on Heron Lane. The backyards all stood open to each other, facing the back of the strip mall. Sheds, clotheslines hung with laundry and someone's above-ground swimming pool would give Hag a small amount of cover.

He shut the door behind him, stood there a little longer. Maybe Earl was right. Maybe doing this in the afternoon was a bad idea. Maybe he should just go back inside and finish his beer, help lardass clean up some of the mess. But that would mean admitting Earl was right. No way in hell would Hag let that fat retard get one up on him.

Hag walked over to Larry's yard. Three steps led up to the back deck. The stairs creaked, but it wasn't much of a noise. Larry would never hear it over his air conditioner. Hag stuck his hand up under his T-shirt, took hold of the knob. It slipped a little. Gloves would've been better. Hag squeezed harder, got a good grip. The knob still didn't turn. Larry kept his back door locked.

Hag knocked on the door, not much more than a tapping with his knuckles. No answer. This time he gave it a couple of good bangs with the meat of his fist.

The door opened a crack. Larry looked out at him. "What do you want, Charlie?"

"I was wondering if you saw anybody go into Earl's place this morning," Hag said.

"No. I was in Waterville most of the morning." Larry started to close the door.

"Look, man. I want to say I'm sorry about what I said before, when I was trying to light that grill." Hag's stomach gave a hitch. This sucked. Nichols was never going to buy this whole apology thing. He should have brought the .44 with him and parked a couple of slugs in the old queer's face. His skin tingled just thinking about it.

Larry opened the door wider. He leaned out, looking Hag in

the eye. "You've been drinking. I can smell beer on your breath, big surprise. I'm getting ready to go out to the lake, but I guess you can come on in for a minute." Without waiting to see what Hag would do, Larry turned around and walked along the hall to his kitchen.

Hag followed, shutting the door.

"You had the wrong kind of dog. Should've got a Chihuahua." Hag moved so that he stood between Larry and the front door.

Larry leaned back against the sink, his hands in his pockets, said "I guess it didn't look like this the last time you were here, did it? What was that, twelve or thirteen years ago?"

Hag snorted. "I was twenty, so it was almost ten years ago. I was way too fucking young for that shit."

"I didn't hear you making any complaints back then. You were a grown man and seemed happy to be here."

"I was just a kid. I didn't know no better."

"If I remember right, you came to me on your own. I never chased after you." Larry straightened, reached for the keys. "I hope that's not why you're here now. You aren't my type any more, Charlie. Besides, a lot of people think you and the chub next door have a thing going. I wouldn't want to be a homewrecker."

Hag stepped up close, punched him in the kidney. Larry gasped, twisted away and went down on one knee. Hag planted his foot right between Larry's shoulder blades, gave him a shove. Larry's face banged off the fridge. He dropped the keys. Cradling his head with both hands, he tried to stand up.

"Where's your money?" Hag said. He grabbed a fistful of thin white hair to keep Larry from turning around.

Larry stomped on Hag's foot. He dug at Hag's hand. His nails scratched pink-white furrows in the flesh but Hag held on. Larry let go. He doubled up his fists, swinging backwards, hitting Hag's legs, his stomach and once—just a glancing blow—his balls.

Hag saw a paring knife on the drain board. He picked it up and pressed the tip against Larry's cheek. "Tell me where your money is, or I'll cut your faggot head off."

Larry stopped clawing. He clamped his hands tight around Hag's wrist to ease some of the strain on his scalp. "It's in the bank. I don't keep much here."

The bank. Fuck. It was easy to forget that normal people with normal jobs had bank accounts. Hag was too used to keeping all his money in his wallet and a coffee can. "How much you got here?"

"There's forty or fifty in my billfold, maybe three hundred in the strongbox where I keep my papers. In the bedroom closet."

Hag poked him with the knife, enough to draw out a thick bead of blood. "Let's go open it." He let go of Larry's hair and lowered the knife.

Panting, Larry turned around. Blood dribbled from his nose. He said, "I need a drink of water first."

"Yeah, whatever. Don't want you having a heart attack before I get my goddamn money." Hag glanced back down the hall toward Larry's bedroom. He swung around on Larry, said, "Hurry the fuck up."

Larry grabbed a glass pitcher that had been upside-down on the drain board and made a backhanded swing, lashed the pitcher across Hag's face. The glass shattered. Hag stumbled back against the table. He tried to grab it, tried steadying himself, but it slid away. Landing on his ass, he banged the back of his head against the wall.

Blood dripped from a gash above Hag's right eye, half-blinding him. He dropped the paring knife and yanked up the bottom of his shirt to dab at the wound. It stung like a bastard, felt like it ran right through his eyebrow.

Larry held onto the broken handle. He picked up his cell phone. "They'll send you to prison for this, Charlie."

Sitting there bleeding, with broken glass all around him, Hag grinned. He said, "You called them on me for playing loud music the other day, but not this morning when I threatened you. I bet you won't do it now, either. How come?"

Larry put his phone on the counter. "God, you're pathetic."

"That's funny. I think you've still got a crush on me. Is that what it is? You want to suck me off right now?"

"Charlie, you need help."

"Fuck that. All I need is money."

Larry said, "You won't get any here."

Hag held a hand over the cut on his forehead. He said, "Give me that three hundred you've got stashed away or I'll tell the cops you ass-raped me when I was a kid and it messed up my head. Repressed memories made me come over here to kick your ass. I'd get maybe thirty days and probation for hitting you, but everybody in the county'd know you like to screw little boys. How're you gonna like being on the sex offender registry, Larry?"

"I never molested you or any other children, you lying bastard," Larry said. His hands shook.

"My word against yours," Hag said. "You know how these things work. All it takes is an accusation for half the dumb shits in this town to believe you did it."

"Get up."

"Gonna get me that cash?"

"Get up."

Hag braced his hands against the floor, careful to avoid any shards of glass, got his feet under himself and stood. He wiped his eye again. The bleeding had slowed to a trickle.

Larry dropped the handle in the sink. Raising his fists, he shifted to a boxing stance.

Hag laughed, said, "Oh, for Christ's sake, Larry. Don't be retarded."

Larry stepped in, landed a hard right jab on Hag's mouth.

Hag felt his lip split. *Motherfucker.* He swung at Larry, hoping to knock the old queer back against the sink and trap him there. Larry blocked the punch with his left forearm and followed up with another shot to Hag's mouth. Hag back-pedaled. He needed room to get under Larry's fists so he could charge, but Larry kept coming. He slugged Hag in the gut, hit him so hard that Hag dropped to one knee and stayed there trying to get back his breath.

Larry threw a right hook into his good eye. Hag fell over on his side. He lay there a moment before Larry grabbed him by the shirt and dragged him across the room. Glass dug into his knees and his left hand. When they got to the front door, Larry released Hag.

Hag said, "This ain't over."

"Don't even think about that pedophile crap. Your word against mine? That's rich, Charlie. Just look at yourself. You've been in and out of jail since you were a kid. You're a drunk and deadbeat dad. Oh, and you just got your ass kicked by a faggot."

Hag felt heat in his face and his own pulse thundering in his head. The sunlight made him wince when he went outside. He left the door open behind him and limped across the lawn.

<h1 style="text-align:center">40</h1>

Joey wiped his mouth with his napkin, dropping it on the floor. He leaned over as if to pick it up, ready to pull out the .38 if he had to. Goddamn that little son of a bitch Barker. If his *shit-for-brains* crack was just a warm-up before spilling everything to Wanda, he was in for a serious letdown. Barker had no idea what was at stake here. If Joey had to, he'd shoot both of them without thinking twice. Nothing was going to keep him from getting Grace out of Carl Petucci's hands.

But Wanda snickered. The snicker turned into full-blown laughter. Barker laughed too, and Joey found himself joining in. He grabbed the napkin, sat up.

"That's how we met," Barker said. He pointed at Joey. "Joe was the toughest kid in school and I was in the photography club. So we're in like, tenth grade, and I'm taking random shots of kids in the hall for yearbook filler, you know? Then this brick wall slams into me. It's Joe. He says something clever like, 'Watch where you're goin', wimp.' So I tell him if he didn't have shit for brains, he'd have seen me standing there with a camera in front of my face instead of plowing into me."

Joey rolled with it. He said, "I didn't know what to think at first. You think he's skinny now, you should've seen him in high school. If he stood sideways he disappeared. I figured he must have some giant balls to stand up to me like that. Instead of kicking his ass, which was my first instinct, I let him hang out with me."

Barker rolled his eyes, still grinning.

"Sometimes I think I should have beaten the shit out of him anyway," Joey said.

Wanda finished her second slice of pizza, crust and all. She wiped her mouth, slouched a little in her chair, said, "It's cool you guys stayed in touch over the years. Even though I grew up right here, I hardly ever see the people I graduated with. There's still a few that didn't move away, but we don't have much in common."

"Their loss," Joey said.

Barker shook his head, said he was going to get another beer. Joey nodded. No doubt he'd need it after taking the chance he took. It worked, though. Wanda had relaxed. Joey couldn't fault the little shit for thinking quickly like that. Barker fixed the problem he had caused.

Joey waited until Barker was gone and said to Wanda, "So you and Evan are, what, going out?"

"We were, sort of, but it didn't work out. I'm just staying here a couple days."

Barker came back. Half of his fresh beer was gone already. He said, "I thought you were supposed to be on duty until five today, Wanda."

"Things change. I've been on administrative leave since this morning."

"What the hell does that mean?" Barker sat down.

"She got suspended," Joey said.

Wanda toyed with her napkin. "That's exactly what it means. My soon-to-be-ex-husband and his girlfriend claim I beat him up. They said he was so afraid of me that he drove drunk to get away."

Joey whistled. "No shit," he said.

"No shit."

Barker tipped his head back and chugged the rest of his beer, the muscles in his scrawny neck flexing up and down. He burped as soon as he came up for air, then looked at both of his house-guests. "What are you going to do now?"

At first, Joey could not tell if the question was addressed to him or Wanda.

Wanda said, "Right now, I'm going to take a shower if you don't mind. I smell like the lake. After that? I have no idea." She grabbed some clothes and a small vanity case from among the boxes.

Joey watched her walk down the hall to the Barker's bedroom. He got up to make sure she didn't come right back. Satisfied, he leaned close to Barker. "That was pretty cool, the way you played that, but try to give me some kind of warning next time. I almost popped the both of you. She's got to go. Think up some excuse to get rid of her."

He stood up just as Wanda returned to the dining room. She had taken off her T-shirt and shorts and stood there in a one-piece bathing suit. Joey stared. He couldn't help it. Jesus Christ, was he getting a hard-on for this girl?

Wanda looked Joey in the eyes. Her half-smile made it hard to guess whether she was flattered or amused. She said, "Hey Evan, how'd you break your shower door?"

41

After cleaning up most of the mess and piling the broken electronics in Earl's shed, Hag and Earl drove into Skowhegan to get ice cream at Gifford's. It would help take Earl's mind off the trouble with Stony. The ice cream might feel good on Hag's fat lip, too.

Gifford's made the best hard-serve in the state. Hag ordered two scoops of chocolate on a sugar cone. It started melting almost as soon as the teenaged girl handed it to him. He stood aside, licking at the drips and ignoring the stares his face invited while they waited for the girls to take care of Earl's order. The Gifford's Special was five scoops of ice cream, a whole banana sliced lengthwise, pineapple, hot fudge and strawberry toppings, whipped cream, chopped nuts and a cherry. It came in a giant waxed-paper cup. Earl got one with all coffee ice cream and extra cherries.

"You're only getting one this time?" Hag had once seen Earl devour a pair of these monsters, along with an entire two-liter bottle of Pepsi.

Earl jabbed his long-handled plastic spoon deep into the mound of whipped cream. He said, "Don't want to spoil my dinner."

Hag laughed. "We're going to The Vault tonight, man. If I was you, I'd spoil my appetite now so I wouldn't have to eat the shit they serve." It didn't matter, though, because Earl always ate The Vault's food without complaint. But money was tight right now, so it was good that Earl could settle for one ice cream. They had taken all of Earl's DVDs—the ones Stony's fuckheads didn't break—and pawned them in Norridgewock. The guy only gave them fifty bucks. Between that and what was left of the money Hag took from Linda Turcotte, they had about a hundred bucks.

Now they sat at a picnic table in the shade of a maple tree at the rear of the Gifford's parking lot. A narrow stream ran through a ravine next to the parking lot. Where the bottom widened out, the owners had put in a miniature golf course. Hag watched groups of players move slowly along from trap to trap. "You ever play that mini golf?"

Earl nodded, grunting through a mouthful of ice cream. A piece of peanut clung to his upper lip.

"Is it as fucking stupid as it looks?"

Another nod.

Hag looked around some more. Bunch of dorks, chasing colored golf balls around. Hey, hey. Who was that down there? Hag grinned, said, "Earl, you see what I see?"

Earl was too busy trying to keep a piece of banana on his spoon to look up. "I don't know. What do you see?"

"Stony."

"Where?" Earl dropped his spoon. The banana chunk hit his shirt, rolled down his belly, leaving a trail of hot fudge. He looked around the parking lot and at the other picnic tables. "I don't see him."

"Chill out, will you? He's down there playing a round with his kids."

Earl looked like he was going to have a heart attack. He said, "We got to get out of here. What if he knows about Willard?"

"Jesus H. Christ, Earl. Willard ain't been dead more than a few hours. I doubt anybody's even started missing the stupid fuck. If Stony was looking for the guy, you think he'd be dicking around with miniature golf?" Hag got up and tossed his ice cream in a trash can. He started down the hill toward the little mock clubhouse where customers paid for their game.

"Where you going?"

"Gonna play some golf. What do you think?"

A zit-faced teenaged boy took Hag's money in exchange for a putter, a yellow ball, a scorecard and pencil stub. "It's more fun if you have someone else to play with," the boy said.

"Kinda like sex, huh?"

The kid blushed, making his acne flare brighter.

Hag said, "Guess you don't know about that. Never mind. I'm going to join my friend over there." He left the scorecard and pencil on the counter. Cutting across the course, Hag skipped the first four holes, collected some ugly stares along the way.

Stony Bouchard stood with his back to Hag, holding his club loosely and lining up a shot that had to go through rotating windmill blades.

His daughter was about twelve or thirteen years old. She chewed the nail of her pinky finger while she watched her father.

The boy was younger, maybe eight, but he already had the same dark and cocky look as his old man. He chewed gum with his mouth open and glared like he owned the place at a four-some that was waiting for Stony to finish so they could take their turns at the windmill.

Hag loped up behind Stony and goosed him with the putter. Stony jumped and swung his own club, sending the ball off the fake green onto the walking path. He whipped around, jaw clenched.

"Can I play through, Stony? Looks like you're having a good time here. Mr. Family Man." Hag poked at Stony again.

Stony blocked with his putter and said, "Go away."

"That's okay. I'll do all the talking. You think you're pretty big fuckin' shit, don't you? Telling me I owe you all that money, wrecking Earl's house, trying to scare my wife. How do you even fit balls that big into your pants, man?"

The girl said, "Daddy."

Stony shushed her with a wave. "You watch your language around my kids, Charlie. I won't put up with that."

Hag tossed up his golf ball and caught it. He stepped close to Stony, said, "Fuck you. And fuck your kids, too. Things are changing around here. You don't run me anymore, you little half-breed douche bag."

"Get away from us or I'll have you thrown out of here." Stony tried to turn away but Hag wouldn't let him.

"Who's going to make me leave? I don't see Willard around anywhere. Must be his day off, huh? You're going to need a new bodyguard. Or whatever the fuck it was Willard did for you. Now listen up because I'm tired of playing around. *You* pay *me* eighty grand for the shit you put me through. I told you this already, but it didn't seem to sink in."

"No."

Hag threw up his arms, said, "Okay, be that way. But I'm going to have to kill you and your whole worthless fucking family."

"You're out of your mind." Stony pushed his kids back, swung his putter at Hag.

Hag jumped away, felt the breeze made by the club's passing. *Jesus.* If he hadn't moved when he did, he'd be rolling around on the grass and spitting out teeth. That goddamn Stony never did have a sense of humor.

Someone in the group waiting for this hole let out a little scream. Hag couldn't tell if it was a man or a woman. His grin returned. He said, "You sure you want to do this here, a respectable motherfucker like you? I bet some of these people have even seen your shitty-ass TV commercials." He nodded at the rubberneckers. "Hey, any of you assholes got a camera phone?"

"Dad," the boy said. He had his hand on Stony's wrist. The girl was crying. Stony dropped the putter and led the kids across the course and up the hill.

Hag watched them go. He returned his putter to the clubhouse. "This game's more fun that I thought," he told the attendant.

$$42$$

Wanda showered, staying right under the head as best she could so the water wouldn't spatter through the empty doorframe at the back. Evan told her he'd slammed it too hard and the glass shattered. He didn't get cut, but he was bitching to Joe about the cost of replacing the sheet when she left the dining room.

She washed as fast as she could, shaved her legs and armpits. She had noticed Joe checking her out in the kitchen. Great. Perfect. It had been a couple of days since she'd last shaved. The guy probably got an eyeful of stubble when he'd looked at her legs. That always made a good impression.

She turned off the water and dried herself slowly, wrapped her wet hair up in a towel. Makeup? Just a little blush and some eyeliner, nothing heavy. If Joe really did like women who enjoyed food, then he probably didn't go for the ones who plastered themselves in makeup. Good. Wanda slipped into clean panties, dressed in faded denim shortalls and a Red Sox T-shirt. She pulled off the towel and plugged in her hair dryer.

When she finished, Wanda heard faint music coming from the living room. What was that, a harmonica? Wanda couldn't place the song, if it even was a song. It sounded more like a long, drawn-out wailing. Like a lonesome train whistle. Maybe Joe had put a blues CD on the stereo.

Wanda found Joe and Evan sitting at opposite ends of the

living room sofa. Evan was staring out the window while Joe played a harmonica. When Joe noticed Wanda standing in the doorway, he stopped playing and shoved the harmonica into his pocket.

"That was nice," Wanda said. "But sad."

Joe shrugged off the praise. He said, "I'm still just learning how to make it talk. I've got a good teacher, though."

Evan stood up. Still staring out the window, he said, "We need to talk about your housing problem, Wanda."

"I was hoping to stay one more night, but if it's going to be a problem…"

"I'm going to have company tonight," Evan said.

Joe picked up one of Evan's old science fiction paperbacks off the end table, started reading. Or pretending to read.

Wanda said, "Well, if it bothers Joe, I can get a motel room. It's just that it'll cut into what little I have saved up, and I need every penny to get an apartment."

"It doesn't bother me," Joe said. "But Evan's talking about female company."

"Oh." It shouldn't bother her, so why did it? Maybe it was just because he had found someone else so quickly. Or maybe there had been another woman all along. *Come on girl, you knew the score when you started fooling around with him. It's not like you were going to get married.* "Okay. No problem."

"It's just that it would be awkward, you know?" Evan still wouldn't look at her. Apparently the view out the window was more interesting. The lilac bushes seemed to hold his attention.

"Hey, like I told you, it's not a problem."

Joe laid the book open and face down on the couch. He said, "You could always share the guest room with me, Wanda."

"Excuse me?" Not that it was an idea without appeal, but talk about forward.

Leaning back on the couch, Joe said, "Evan showed me those pictures he took of you. I liked what I saw. The real thing is always better."

What the fuck? Who did this asshole think he was? Wanda crossed the room, grabbed Evan by the arm and yanked him around to face her. "You bastard. Those pictures were private. Just for us, you said."

Evan tried to pull away. Wanda was stronger and would not let go. She swung on him with her left, slapped him upside the head. He leaned away from her with all his weight. Wanda released the stupid prick, watched him go staggering sideways against the wall. He sat down hard on his recliner, holding the side of his face.

Joe hadn't moved. He just stayed there on the couch, a grin on his face. He said, "You've already got one assault charge hanging over your head. Want another? Besides, it's not like he put the pics on the internet or anything. Or maybe he did. I don't know."

Wanda kicked the bottom of Evan's chair, stubbing her toes. She had forgotten she was still barefoot. Damn, that hurt. "Did you?" she asked Evan. "Did you post them on some website?"

"No."

"Give them to me."

"Now?"

"Yeah, now. You think I'm going to leave them here for you to show anyone else?"

Evan got up and left the room. Wanda turned on Joe, clenching her fists. He would be a lot harder to fight than Evan, but she had rage on her side. Joe looked up at her with that goddamn grin still plastered across his face.

"Something you want to say to me, Joe?"

He shook his head, picked up the book.

Evan came back with the bundle of pictures wrapped in a pair of wide rubber bands and a CD in a paper sleeve. He handed them to Wanda, said, "That's all of them."

"Better be, or your ass is in trouble. I hope your new girlfriend is smarter than I was."

"Evan always did like them dumb," Joe said.

Wanda reached for the can of pepper spray she always carried clipped to her belt, remembered she was not wearing a belt. She had a can in her purse, though. No, Joe wasn't worth wasting it. "I'm leaving now because the temptation to shoot both of you is too much," Wanda said. She picked up her purse, vanity case and one of the suitcases. "I'll come back for the rest of my stuff tomorrow. Don't fuck with it."

She kicked open the screen door, stubbing her toes again. The pain was good. It helped fuel her anger. It kept her from crying. After the door banged shut behind her, Wanda tried to remember if she had any extra shoes in the Jeep.

43

Stony walked along the edge of his pool, cell phone pressed against his ear. Brian and Tina were in the house with Arlene. Even out here, Stony could hear Tina crying. He paused, watched the automatic vacuum scuttling along the bottom of the pool.

After six rings, someone picked up on the other end, said, "Hello?"

"Gerry?"

"Yeah."

Stony said, "It's me. Have you seen Willard around today?"

"No, why?"

"Forget it. I have a proposition for you. I financed your new truck, right? How would you like me to write it off?"

Gerry snorted. "Man, who do I gotta kill?"

Stony described Charlie Hagopian and Earl Coro, where they lived and the old wreck that Earl drove. He said, "I want it done tonight. Hagopian and the fat one, I want them both gone by morning. It would be best not to do it at the trailer. Too many eyes and ears around there. Do we have a deal?"

"Hell, yes."

"Good. Anything goes wrong, you just keep your mouth shut and I'll take care of you. Understand me?"

"Yeah."

Stony broke the call, thumbed through the phone's memory until he got the number for The Vault. Dean Campbell picked up right away. He was the main bartender and managed the place for Stony.

Dean said, "You're in The Vault."

"Cute. Listen up, Dean. I need you to do something for me."

"Sure, man."

"You know Charlie Hagopian?"

Dean snorted. "That friggin' loser? Yeah, I know Hag."

"You call me if he comes in tonight."

"Want me to throw his ass out?"

"No. Just give me a call. And Dean? You don't mention this to anyone else. Get what I'm saying? No matter what time it is, I want to know if he comes in. Call my cell, not the house."

There was a pause before Dean said, "Yeah, man. Okay. I got it."

Stony switched off the phone, headed toward the patio.

Arlene came outside and waited for him by the gas grill. Her face was drawn. She said, "How could you let some lowlife say those things in front of our kids?"

Stony took her in his arms, pulled her close and toyed with her blonde hair. He said, "The guy's out of control. I couldn't do anything to him at Gifford's, and certainly not in front of the kids."

"But where was Willard?"

"I didn't need him for anything, so I gave him the day off. That was a mistake."

Arlene sniffed and pressed her face against Stony's chest. "Yeah, no kidding."

"No, I'm serious. I think Willard's dead."

"What?"

Stony stepped back. Taking Arlene by the hand, he walked her to the far end of the pool. He said, "Hagopian's face was a mess, like he'd been a fight with someone. He told me I need to replace Willard. Nobody knows where Willard is, and I've called all the guys. It looks like maybe Charlie killed him."

"Oh, God."

He hugged her again, said, "It's never as bad as you think. I already sent Tom Moody over to Willard's. Maybe I'm wrong about him being dead. Maybe he's only hurt somewhere. Maybe he went fishing. I don't know. In any case, Tom's going into Willard's house to make sure there's nothing to incriminate us. We'll be fine, baby. We'll be fine."

"But what if Hagopian comes here?"

Stony laughed. "Even Charlie's not that stupid."

Arlene broke the embrace and leaned back, gave him the eye.

"All right, he might be dumb enough to do that," Stony said. "Take the kids and go spend the night at your mother's."

"What about you?"

"I'll be fine."

"Don't lie to me, Peter."

Stony watched his wife, how she stood there with her arms folded across her chest and that cold fire in her eyes. It was the same look she'd given him fifteen years before, when she caught him in his one and only affair. She'd had a gun in her hand then.

Arlene unclipped her cell, punched a few buttons. She held it to her ear, said, "Hi, Ma. It's me. Oh, not bad. You doing anything tonight? Yeah? Any chance Brian and Tina could spend the night at your place? Oh, not much. We just thought it would be nice to have some time to ourselves. Okay, you're awesome. Thanks." She ended the call.

Stony said, "I notice you only asked about the kids staying there."

"You need me for this."

"No. You go to your mother's, too. Make up some excuse. If you're worried about me, I'll call Gerry back, have him and another guy come out. Hagopian goes to The Vault almost every Saturday night, but just in case he doesn't, I'll have backup. Dean will call if he shows up at the bar, and I'll send Gerry after him. Once Tom Moody clears Willard's house I can use him, too. How's that sound?"

Arlene pressed herself against Stony. She kissed him, open-mouthed and hungry. When she pulled back, she said, "I like this plan, Mr. Bouchard. Think we've got time for a quickie while the kids pack their bags?"

Stony grinned. He was halfway hard already, just from the kiss.

44

Earl slammed the refrigerator door. He pressed his head against the cool metal. "You told him about Willard? Why? What if he calls the cops?"

Hag was parked on the couch, playing with a lighter. He said, "Drug dealers don't call the cops on people, dumbass. Besides, I scared him bad, and that's just what I want. The little fucker needs to be afraid when I kill him."

"I thought you told him you wouldn't kill him if he gave us that money."

"Us? No, Earl. I said he had to give *me* that money. Me. I'm the senior partner in this business. I'll handle the money. You'll get your share, don't worry. By the time we're done you'll be able to buy your own Little Debbie factory."

Earl's head hurt. He sat down in a kitchen chair, tried to focus. "So you ain't really gonna kill Stony, then."

Hag jumped up and came out to the kitchen. He said, "You bet your ass I'm gonna kill him. Ain't you been listening? Stony pays me eighty thousand not to kill his whole fucking family. Then I go ahead and blow his brains out anyway. It's him or us, Earl. Just like it was with Willard. But this time, we get to make a lot of money out of it."

"You're not gonna kill the kids, though. Right?" Earl looked at Hag standing there next to him with that smirk on his face. It was that *I-know-something-you-don't* look, the same one

Earl had seen on him hundreds of times over the years. "Just promise me you won't do nothing to the kids."

Instead of giving a straight answer, Hag asked, "What've Stony's kids ever done to me? You worry too much, Earl. I'm gonna take a nap, then we'll go out to The Vault later." He lay down on the couch.

From where Earl sat, he had a clear view of Hag's guns under the couch: the butt of the shotgun and a glint of chrome from the .44 Magnum. How hard would it be to go over there, get down on his knees and slide one of them out? The pistol was probably the easiest to use. Earl had never fired a gun before, but he'd seen plenty of movies and played a lot of video games. Never mind watching Hag shoot Willard Bailey out by the river. It looked easy. That was the problem. Hag acted like it was all no big deal, like it was normal.

What Earl ought to do right now was grab one of those guns and point it at Hag while he called the cops. Yeah, right. Beat up as he was, Hag ought to be a lot slower than usual. But Hag was so crazy he might not sit still while all that went on. No, Earl couldn't see Hag letting him get away with calling the cops.

So what if I just shoot him? Earl could wait until Hag fell asleep, do it then. The cops would believe his story. Everybody knew Hag was nuts. Earl sat there, staring at the guns while the afternoon wore on.

45

A car full of teenagers whipped past them, heading south toward Skowhegan. Joey looked over as they went by, watched their faces, how they were all so caught up in their little world. The oldest looked to be about eighteen. Joey said, "I wasn't much older than that the first time I killed a man."

Barker, in the passenger seat, grunted and looked straight ahead.

"I can hardly remember what it was like, being a kid. You know?"

"Not really," Barker said. Then he glanced over at Joey. "Didn't you ever feel guilty about it? Beating the shit out of some guy who couldn't pay the vig, smashing his knees or whatever it is you did. That never bothered you?"

"The United States Marines taught me how to kill. They had me doing it in Kuwait way before I hooked up with Carl Petucci."

"That's not the same," Barker said. "That was in defense of your country."

Joey relaxed his foot on the gas pedal as they came up behind a truck full of wood chips. He said, "Soldier and hitman are just jobs. Saddam had to know what he was getting into when he started fucking with us. Look how he ended up. The people that go to shylocks know the score too, or they should. How about you?"

"What about me?"

"The porno thing," Joey said. "What you did to Angie Petucci. Blackmail. I mean, that's the cause of all this bullshit we're going through right now."

Barker snorted.

"What?" Joey asked. "I say something funny?"

"You act like you're being inconvenienced here, and that's fucked up, man. I'm the one riding around with a guy who's been paid to whack him. I'm *just a job* to you, remember? So spare me your goddamn sob story."

Joey hit his blinker and yanked the wheel to the right, stepping on the brake. The Toyota's right-side tires dug into the gravel shoulder. The car slewed, its rear end sliding toward the ditch.

A helmetless woman on a Harley rode by, her braided hair streaming out behind her. "Asshole!"

Barker had grabbed the dashboard with both hands. He still held it tight. Joey was out of the car and around to the passenger's side before the prick could even let go. He opened the door, grabbed Barker by the front of his shirt, pulled at him. Barker hardly moved.

Joey said, "Unbuckle that fucking seat belt before I strangle you with it."

Cars and trucks kept going by. A few slowed, but none of the drivers stopped to ask if there was a problem. Joey dragged Barker across the shallow ditch, through burdock and milkweed, then up the other side into a scraggly stand of alders. The trees shielded them from the road. The next house was at least a hundred yards further up the road. Joey kicked Barker's legs out from under him. He had the .38 in his hand, the hammer cocked.

Barker said, "You said you wouldn't kill me if I cooperated."

"So this whole thing is inconvenient for you, huh? I'll tell you something. I could shoot right here, right now. No one would pay any attention to the noise. Yeah, maybe somebody would remember seeing two men get out of a rented car, but by the time anyone found you I'd be long gone. Carl wants that tape and he wants you dead. All I really have to do is cap you, go on back to Brooklyn. *Oh, sorry Mr. P. He didn't have the tape anymore, said he threw it away a couple years ago. What's that? Yeah, I worked him over real good and he wasn't lying.* That's it. I could do it now. The tape would just sit in the safe-deposit box until the feds finally got around to seeing what you had there. Who knows how long that would be?"

Barker started shaking.

Joey hoped he would not piss his pants this time. "Want to know why I haven't done that?"

"Why?"

"If I don't get my hands on that video, a good friend of mine, an innocent woman, is going to die. I didn't want this job. I ain't getting paid for it. I'm not even in the life anymore. The only reason I'm here is because Carl grabbed this person who's important to me and he's holding her until I do what he wants. You with me so far?"

Barker nodded.

Joey said, "There's no reason why you have to die. I don't feel guilty about the killing I've done, and I'll do it again if I have to, but I'd rather not. Far as I'm concerned, you're free to take off once I get that tape. Start over somewhere else."

Barker didn't say anything

Joey stepped back and eased down the revolver's hammer. He holstered it, said, "Come on. Get up. These mosquitoes are killing me."

When they left the woods, Barker's shirt was plastered to his skin, the ends of his hair dark with perspiration. It wasn't because the day was warm. His sweat stank of fear, of desperation.

A Wesserunsett police cruiser sat behind Joey's car, its light bar flashing. The cop saw them, waited while they crossed the ditch. His gut pushed out over the top of his gun belt. The nametag on his uniform read *McKinney*. "There a problem here? That you, Barker?"

Joey said, "No trouble, officer. Evan just had to throw up." This was it. This was the moment. Barker would either follow Joey's lead or scream for help and fuck the whole deal.

The cop took another look at Barker, a long one. "Any chance you guys have been drinking this afternoon?"

Barker shook his head. "No, Bill. I had some shrimp for lunch. I think they were bad."

The cop grimaced. He said, "Better get home then, or maybe the ER. Food poisoning ain't nothing to screw around with." He turned back to Joey. "This your rental?"

"Yeah."

"I don't know how they do things in New *Yawk*," McKinney said, pointing at the tag. "But up here in the boonies we turn on our hazard lights when we have to make an emergency stop."

"I wasn't thinking, officer. I just wanted to get Evan out of the car before he puked all over the front seat."

McKinney watched Barker drag himself back into the car. He nodded toward Joey and said, "You mind waiting right here a second, sir? I want to have a quick word with Mr. Barker."

Joey waited while the cop leaned down and stuck his head inside the open door. After a moment, he walked back to his cruiser. "You can go now, sir," he said as he passed Joey.

The cop car was still parked on the shoulder when Joey went around a long, slow curve and lost sight of it in the rearview mirror. He looked over at Barker. "What'd that cop say to you?"

"Nothing to worry about."

"What was it?"

Barker wiped sweat from his eyes with the bottom of his shirt. It didn't help much; his skin still looked pale and clammy. He said, "His name's Bill McKinney, everybody around here calls him Big Bill. He told me he knows I'm the reason Wanda's marriage went to hell, said I was about due for a good ass-kicking."

Joey snorted.

Barker started laughing, too. "Like I'm worried about that, right?"

Joey turned down the air conditioner and slid a Rory Block CD into the player. Sweet. He said, "That was a shitty thing we did to Wanda. That friend of mine who's in trouble? Her father's seventy-three years old. He'd come after me with his fists up if he ever heard I'd been part of something like that. And I'd stand there and take it from him because he'd be right. Does it bother you?"

"Yeah." Barker looked surprised by his own admission. "It does."

"So you actually do care about her?"

"It's not like that. I didn't want her for anything but a fuck buddy. She knew it. Shit, man, she obviously wanted that, too. I didn't force her into anything. But I feel bad about humiliateing her like that, with the pictures."

"You made a career out of degrading women," Joey said.

Barker held up his hands. "No, no, no. I don't regret taking those pictures of Wanda. I'd have done a lot more if she'd let me. It's only what we did today that bugs me. I wish we'd found some other to make her leave."

"You're fucked in the head, you know that?"

"At least I never killed anybody."

Joey said, "Don't start that shit again. We get to the motel, pick up my bag, then we head back to your place and you can avoid me until Monday morning. I don't care." He turned up the CD player to drown out whatever else Barker had to say.

46

Wanda leaned on the bar at The Vault, grinding her hips to Def Leppard's "Pour Some Sugar on Me." She'd been drinking mudslides steadily since about two o'clock, but was slowing down now, sipping at each glass to make it last.

Dean the bartender brought her mudslide. He was a couple of years older, a rugged guy with a dark crewcut and neat beard. Wanda liked the way his beard looked, but it tickled. It tickled so much that she'd been unable to relax when Dean went down on her those couple of times they went to bed together, back before she married Jim.

"You okay?" Dean asked. "You look a little wobbly. I haven't seen you like this in a long time."

Wanda nodded slowly. "I've never been better."

"How about a cup of coffee instead?"

"You cutting me off?"

Dean smiled and shrugged. "You know I gotta."

"Fuck."

Dean took away the cocktail glass, reached under the bar for a coffee mug. He said, "You want me to call you a cab?"

Wanda waved her cell phone at him while he poured the coffee, loading it with cream and sugar, just the way she liked. Watching him, she thought maybe she should give him one more chance. But then Wanda remembered Terry's bristly facial hair scraping against her inner thighs, against her labia. Why

225

was she so damned horny tonight, anyway? Every guy she'd spoken to in the past week had given her nothing but grief. She said, "Be better off buying a vibrator."

Dean slid the coffee across the bar. "What's that?"

"I just noticed I forgot to put my phone on vibrate." She turned away from the bar, headed back to her table with the coffee. Two men had taken her spot, though: a skinny one and a shorter, fat guy. Oh Christ, it was Charlie Hagopian and Earl Coro. Hag poured draft beer from a pitcher into a Mason jar. His hair stuck up all over the place and he needed a shave. Not that it would help him much, not when his face looked like he'd gone a few rounds with Mike Tyson.

Earl held a beer in his right hand, a big dripping cheese-burger in his left. There were spatters of grease and ketchup down the front of his T-shirt. Yeah, they were both living up to their usual high standards.

Wanda almost went to look for another seat, but she stopped herself. Why should she let a couple of morons chase her away? She walked over to them, said, "Hey, that's my table."

Hag said, "Give me a lap dance and you can sit here."

"Screw you." She swayed, sloshing coffee onto the floor.

Earl giggled, but Hag said, "You're pretty fucked up, lady. You better sit down before you fall down. It wouldn't look good to have Wesserunsett's finest passed out on the floor."

The Def Leppard song ended. George Thorogood came on doing "I Drink Alone." Wanda didn't want to be alone just then. Jesus, how sad was that? At least there was never any chance she would get drunk enough to go home with Hag. Once she sobered up a little, she'd leave. No big deal. Wanda pulled out a chair and sat down, dabbing her scalded hand with a napkin.

"You know Earl already," Hag said.

Wanda nodded. She said, "You pay that fine yet, Earl?"

Blushing, Earl mumbled something and slurped his beer.

Wanda said, "So what happened to your face, Charlie? The missus come looking for child support?"

Hag leaned toward her. If she hadn't already been drunk, Wanda could have gotten hammered off his breath. "What're you drinking, Wanda? Irish coffee?"

"No, just plain old black coffee."

"Trying to sober up, huh?"

Wanda picked up the mug, blew away some of the steam. "It wasn't my idea."

Hag laughed and elbowed Earl in the side. "Fucking Dean cut her off," he said. "Cut off a cop. That'd be a bitch if it wasn't so damn funny."

Earl chugged his beer, let out a burp that would have done Godzilla proud. He giggled, belly shaking the whole table. "'Scuse me." He reached for the pitcher.

Hag slapped his hand away.

Earl said, "What's the problem?"

"There's only enough for one more in there. We ought to offer it to the lady."

Wow, manners. Wanda shook her head. "I'm good, thanks."

The way Hag's eyes narrowed and his face reddened when he stopped Earl from taking the last of the beer, it looked like he was ready to knock the table over and start swinging. The last thing Wanda needed was to be in the middle of a bar fight. Ed Gauthier would never let her go back to work. She looked around for some other place to sit. No luck.

Hag backed down. "So what were you drinking before dick-less over there said you had to stop?"

"Mudslides."

"What the fuck's a mudslide? Sounds like something Earl leaves in the toilet after he eats those microwave burritos."

Wanda said, "Kahlua, vodka, Baileys and a little cream."

"I'll give you a little cream," Hag said. Before Wanda could tell him off, he leaned back and pulled a wad of money from his jeans pocket, thumbed out a few bills that he gave to Earl. "Go on up and get us another pitcher. I don't feel like waiting for that fucking waitress to come back around again. And a mudslide for Wanda."

"But Dean said she can't..."

"Like I give a flying fuck what Dean says. The place is packed. You think he's got nothing better to do than watch us?"

Earl got up to make his swaying, shuffling way to the bar. Wanda sipped her coffee, stared off at disco ball above the tiny dance floor. Maybe she should call Evan and let him come get her. No, she was done with Evan. There was no way she would ask any more favors of that little prick. Maybe Joe? He was good-looking, and it would be a way to rub Evan's nose in it. Joe bragged about seeing those pictures, though. That was an asshole thing to do, almost as bad as Evan showing them to him in the first place. What the hell was wrong with her, any-way? She'd wanted to kill both of them this afternoon. Now with a few drinks in her, she was thinking about forgiving them? Sleeping with Joe? God. So maybe it was better to sit here next to this pair of losers a little while longer. Soon as the floor stopped rippling, she would get up and walk away.

Hag waved his hand in front of Wanda's face. "Hey, you gonna pass out on me, or what?" He grinned at her. Either he did not know how to use a toothbrush, or he just didn't own one because his teeth looked even worse than his breath smelled.

The jukebox switched to Dwight Yoakam. "Fast as You." Wanda nodded her head, pretended to play the organ parts on the tabletop. She said, "I love this song."

Hag snorted. "I hate country. It's music for pig-fucking inbred shitkickers."

Wanda sat up straight. "So you're saying I'm inbred? My parents are related? I fuck pigs? You know, you're one hell of a smooth-talking ladies' man, Charlie."

He stopped smiling and pointed at Wanda's left hand. "Your

hubby know you're out drinking by yourself?"

Wanda folded her arms across her chest. "Do I look like I care what my husband thinks?"

"You got a boyfriend, then? Something on the side?"

"None of your fucking business."

"You had a fight with him, huh? With your husband."

"I said it was none of your business."

Earl came back with a pitcher. He placed it on the table with the exaggerated care of the intoxicated. Hag looked at the pitcher and then at Earl's now empty hands. He said, "Hey, retard. Where the fuck's Wanda's mudslide?"

Earl sat down, wiped sweat from his forehead with the back of his hand. "Dean knows she's sitting with us. He says all she can have is coffee or a cab ride."

Wanda said, "He's a prick."

Hag poured a beer. "I'll kill him for you if you pay me."

"What?"

Earl squirmed in his seat, looking like he had to use the bathroom.

Hag guzzled his beer, still holding onto the pitcher. When the glass was empty he poured himself another. He shoved the pitcher toward Earl and rested his elbows on the table. "That's what I do for a living now, Wanda," he said. "I'm a fucking hitman. How do you like that?"

Wanda laughed. Christ, this guy was something else. Sitting here, telling a *cop* that he was a professional killer. Maybe he thought it would get him laid. "No shit? How many people have you killed?"

"None," Earl said. The sweat was rolling down his cheeks now. He grabbed a handful of napkins from the waitress's tray as she walked past.

"What Earl means is that he ain't killed nobody. Not personally, because he's not a hit man. Mostly, he's just retarded, but I let him drive for me. Slow in the driveway on Sundays. He's an excellent driver."

Wanda raised her eyebrows. "And you're confessing to me. Real smart, killer. So what's your body count or whatever the hell you call it?"

"Ten."

"Ten?" Earl and Wanda said at the same time. Earl looked scared Wanda might believe Hag, while she filled the word with scorn and disbelief. What she really felt like doing was laughing in the loser's face and walking out. She got out her cell, flipped it open.

"You don't believe me," Hag said.

"Caught on to that, did you?"

"I've got two guns out in the truck."

"Big fucking deal," Wanda said. "We live in Maine, moron. Half the pickups on the road have a gun hanging in the back window."

"You pay the price and I'll kill any motherfucker you want me to."

Earl said, "He's just kidding."

Wanda shoved her phone back in her purse. "All right, tough guy. Get rid of my husband. Whack him. Rub him out, pop a cap in him. Whatever the fuck it is you do."

Hag nodded. "But how much is it worth to you?"

"Five thousand."

"Fifteen."

"Come on, Hag," Earl said, grabbing him by the arm.

"Ten," Wanda said.

Still looking at Wanda, Hag pushed Earl away. He shrugged, said, "I'll do it."

Wanda laughed. "Okay, but you have to do it right away," she said.

"When?"

"Tomorrow morning. Five o'clock when he goes out to the mailbox for the newspaper."

"Give me your address."

Wanda took out a pen, wrote a made up address on a cocktail

napkin. There wasn't even a Mill Road in Wesserunsett. If she knew Charlie Hagopian at all, he would waste a couple of hours tomorrow morning trying to find the place before going home to drink himself into a coma. Or maybe the whole hitman thing was a dumbass attempt at getting into her pants. Either way, it would be a good laugh. She handed him the napkin and pen.

"No problem. What about my money?" Hag laid the napkin on the table without looking at it.

"What about it?"

"Half up front," Hag said. "Right now."

"Are you stupid? Do you think I have five thousand dollars in my purse?"

Hag held up his hands. "All right, all right. Calm down. Fuck."

"I'll pay you when you do the job," Wanda said. "Don't screw it up."

"I'm a fucking pro."

An AC/DC tune came on next. Their songs all sounded the same to Wanda, but Mr. Hitman seemed happy with it. He nodded his head in time with the music.

"Hey, I fucking love this one," Hag said. "'Dirty Deeds Done Dirt Cheap.' It ought to be my special theme song." He drummed on the table with Wanda's pen.

Christ, what a loser. Wanda couldn't take sitting there any longer, so she got up and headed for the door, leaving Dumb and Dumber behind.

Dean moved to cut her off. He said, "You're still too drunk to drive. Come sit at the bar for a minute while I call you a cab."

She waved her cell phone in the bartender's face. "I've already got a ride coming. I just need to go outside and get some air."

Dean stared at her.

"Hey, it's me," Wanda said.

"Gimme your keys." Dean held out his hand.

Wanda nodded toward Hag and Earl. "I left them with those guys."

"Not a bright idea. Hag's the kind of guy who'd drive your Jeep into the lake just for shits and giggles," Dean said.

"I told him I'd shoot him if he so much as touched the door handles."

Dean shrugged, went back behind the bar.

"Moron." Wanda opened the door and stepped outside, fishing her keys out of her purse. Now she just needed to remember where she'd parked the Jeep.

47

Hag got up to use the men's room. After shaking off and zipping up, he used Wanda's pen to write *Larry Nichols gives good head* on the wall above the hand dryer. The faggot had gotten lucky with those cheap shots, but his day was coming. Soon.

By the time Hag returned to the table, Earl had ordered another pitcher. The jukebox played "Girls, Girls, Girls." Mötley Crüe. Fuckin' A, but it sounded good. Some nights Hag came in here and all anybody punched up was country or some Top Forty crap. Hag's interest in new music had ended when Pearl Jam and Nirvana came out. What good was rock and roll if it depressed the shit out of you?

But Earl wasn't into the Crüe tonight. He sat there sweating and scowling.

"What the fuck are you giving me that look for?" Hag said when he sat down.

"Why do you think? You told a cop we're hitmen and agreed to kill her husband. Remember? She was probably wired or something, like on TV."

Hag tossed the pen on the table next to the napkin with the address. "If she was, then it's entrapment. Any judge in the state would laugh the case right out of court. Wanda can't do anything. No cop is ever gonna touch us, so just fucking relax. I got us a job, didn't I? Ten grand, Earl. Think about that shit for a minute. Neither one of us has ever seen that much money at one time. Not unless it belonged to Stony, and he wouldn't even let us sniff it. That ten, plus what I'm getting from Stony. We're gonna be rich, just exactly like I promised you."

Earl's frown hung even lower.

"There ain't no pleasing some people," Hag said. He slumped in his chair. "I don't see why you're getting wound up over this shit. You don't know Wanda's old man, so what do you care if we kill him? Fuck, I don't even know the guy's name and I'm happy as a pig in shit to do the job."

Earl still didn't say anything.

"Pour me another beer if all you're gonna do is sit there and pout."

Earl picked up the pitcher and Hag's Mason jar. Three girls walked by, hooting and hollering on their way to the can. One of them bumped Earl's elbow. Earl jerked, banged the lip of the pitcher off the glass, sloshed beer all over the table. The napkin with Wanda's address sat there in the middle of the puddle, soaking it up. Hag grabbed it, tried to wring it out.

"Stupid bitches!" But the girls didn't hear him over the music. Hag opened the napkin, squinted at the blurry blue lines. "Can't even read the fucking thing now," he said and threw the wet mess at Earl, who was still holding the pitcher and glass.

Earl put down the pitcher. He peeled the napkin off his chest, sat there in his chair while beer dribbled over the edge of the table onto his gut. "What do we do now? Quit?"

Hag said, "Shut up. She only left a couple minutes ago. Let's haul ass out to the parking lot and follow her home. Then we find a good place to park the truck and wait for the hubby to come out in the morning for the paper."

Earl pushed back from the table, brushing at the huge wet spot down the front of his clothes. "Why don't we just tell her what happened and ask her for the address again? Then we can go home and get a little sleep."

"You want her to think we're a couple of fuck-ups?" Hag

took him by the arm and started dragging him toward the door. "Jesus, you're retarded sometimes, Earl."

Earl's old pickup rattled like it was going to fly apart. The faster they went, the worse it got, but Hag could barely see the taillights of Wanda Philbrick's vehicle. It looked like she was heading out of town, north along the Sirois Road.

They'd almost missed Wanda when they left The Vault, but then Hag spotted her behind the wheel of a Jeep Renegade. The reason he had seen her was that Wanda honked her horn at a couple of women she'd almost run over on her way out of the parking lot. Once she hit the street, Wanda stomped on the gas pedal and took off. Hag and Earl had had to run for the truck. Running not being one of Earl's specialties, he needed to sit there catching his breath—with Hag screaming at him to hurry the fuck up—before turning the key in the ignition.

Was the address on the napkin for a place on the Sirois Road? Hag wished he'd thought to read the thing before Earl spilled beer all over it. Fuck it. His head felt warm and light, a fine goddamn feeling. No need to blow a decent buzz worrying about every little dumbass thing Earl did.

But wait a second. Was it Hag's imagination, or did Wanda's taillights seem to be getting smaller? Hag said, "Are you fucking retarded? Get up there on her ass." He waved his hand, banged his fingers on the dashboard. "Jesus Christ." He sucked on a knuckle.

Earl grinned that big goofy drunk-ass grin of his and shook his head. "I'm already doing seventy-five. I don't need to get pulled over for no OUI."

"I'm gonna pull you over and beat the shit out of you if you don't put the fucking hammer down on this heap."

Earl finally got with the program and sped up. Hag sat back, relaxing a little. Once this job was done, they could afford to do some serious partying. Hag figured to stash a couple of thousand, start a sort of retirement account by putting in a little from every hit. Maybe he would buy a new truck for Earl, too. Well, a newer truck anyway, something he could get for three grand, tops. Hag knew how to drive, but the state had taken away his license six years earlier, after his ninth OUI conviction

"I think that's a cop back there," Earl said.

Hag shifted around on his end of the seat until he could see out the passenger-side mirror. He saw the headlights a long way back, at least a quarter mile behind them. Hag said, "Cop, my ass. He ain't even trying to catch up with us."

"It's a cop."

"Just shut up and keep that bitch in sight. I ain't losing out on ten thousand bucks just because you got no balls." He leaned out the window to clear his nose, then pulled his head back inside. "I hope she lives a little further out. There's too many houses around here for my taste. Too many nosy fucks that might hear the shots or see us driving away."

After another couple miles, Wanda's brake lights came on. She had just passed a church. There was a house coming up on the right. Earl slowed down, too. Hag backhanded him on the arm.

"What's your problem now?" Earl asked.

"Don't fucking slow down, retard. I don't want her to know she's being followed. Just keep on going like you were."

Wanda had parked in the driveway of a Cape-style house with big lilac bushes in the front yard. The lights were on downstairs and there were two vehicles already in the dooryard: a car and a small pickup. Hag just caught a glimpse of Wanda walking up to the front door before he and Earl went past the house.

Earl said, "That other cop's still back there."

Hag switched on the radio, turned it up loud enough so he couldn't Earl whining anymore. Once past Wanda's place, Hag was pleased to see the houses thinned out and the woods grew thicker. Except for the church, Wanda's nearest neighbor was close to a mile away.

"What we'll do is park in front of that church in the morning," Hag said. "When our man comes outside to get the paper, we drive by and *bang*! Ten thousand bucks, just like that." Maybe Wanda would give him some pussy to seal the deal.

"That's my mother's church."

"So what?"

Earl said something Hag didn't hear. The truck weaved back and forth across the road as Earl concentrated on the rearview mirror. Hag snapped off the music, said, "You trying to kill us or what?"

"That cop's coming right up on us."

Hag didn't bother to look back this time. "Probably just some dickhead in a hurry and he's getting ready to pass us. A cop would have put his flashers on by now, the way you're driving."

Then Earl's truck lurched forward. Hag was thrown against the windshield and bounced back. He felt blood on his forehead. Earl yanked on the steering wheel to keep the old Ford on the road.

When Hag turned around, he saw headlights right behind Earl's tailgate. The other vehicle was a truck, probably a four-by-four with jacked up wheels because it sat higher than Earl's. The truck backed off a little. Hag heard its engine race as it surged forward and rammed them again.

This time Hag held onto the seat, but he still got bounced around. "Pull over," he said.

"No!"

"Do it!" Hag knew there was no way they could outrun the assholes in that four-by-four. It would only be a matter of seconds before he and Earl were upside down in the gully or wrapped around a tree. Earl braked hard as the other truck hit them again. The old Ford's rear end slewed over toward the ditch and the right wheel dug for purchase in the soft shoulder.

Earl fought the steering wheel. Hag tried to buckle up. Where was the fucking seat belt? The big truck rammed them again and all Hag saw in front of him was a stand of scrawny birches, their bark so white it glowed in the headlights.

48

"These guys fucking dead or what?"

Hag heard the man's voice, couldn't tell where it came from. There was a bright light in his eyes. It was all he saw, burning into his skull. Somewhere close by, Earl was crying big wet blubbery sobs.

A different man said, "That fat one's crying, and I saw the other one move his head a second ago."

There was something digging into Hag's shoulders and upper back. His legs were pushed up against his chest, but he couldn't feel anything beneath his rump. Where the fuck was he?

The first man spoke again. "So how do you want to do 'em? Stony didn't specify."

"They're pretty fucked up, dude." The other guy laughed. "That skinny prick looks just about folded in half there. He's Hagopian?"

"That's him."

"Don't look like he'd have balls enough to pull what he did."

Both of them laughed this time.

The dashboard. That was what his back was jammed against. Hag felt the stick shift against his right elbow. He was jammed down between the dashboard and the edge of the seat, folded up like a jackknife, with his head just high enough so he could look over the back of the seat. The other truck's headlights shone right in his eyes. Turning away and looking down, he saw the floor of the truck beneath him.

"I say we smash their heads in," the second guy said. "Just another drunk-driving accident." Twigs snapped under their feet as they came closer.

Hag spotted something shiny on the floor to his left. A couple of inches of the .44's barrel stuck out from under the seat. He reached for it, his fingers brushing the metal. Working it back and forth between his index and middle fingers, Hag managed to get it out far enough to grab the barrel.

"Hag," Earl said. His voice was thick and gurgling, like he had something in his throat. "I think my nose is broken."

The big revolver was in Hag's hand now. He had never fired it before, couldn't even remember if the damn thing was loaded. He switched it from his left hand to his right, clutched it to his chest. Maybe Stony's boys wouldn't notice the motion.

"You shitbirds fucked up big-time," the second guy said. He was over by Earl's side. The whole truck rocked as they tried yanking open both doors. "Damn, the fucking doors are jammed."

Hag saw a big guy silhouetted in the passenger-side window. This guy, the one who had spoken first, said, "Let's jam some broken glass in their necks."

"Easy for you to say. This fucking blimp's neck is too fat. Use your shotgun."

The man on Hag's side of the truck said, "It ain't rocket science, Scott." He reached in and grabbed Hag by the shirt, pulled him toward the window. Hag jabbed the Ruger against the bastard's chest.

He squeezed the trigger.

If the little .38 had seemed loud to Hag back in Art Brochu's house, the .44 Magnum sounded like a cannon going off. He wasn't ready for the kick, either, even though Brochu had warned him about it. The revolver bucked out of his hand, fell to the floor.

The guy Hag shot staggered backwards, arms flailing and disappeared from Hag's limited field of vision. The other asshole, the one called Scott, cried out and started running back toward his own truck.

Earl held his face and said, "Oh shit, oh shit, oh shit…"

Hag squirmed as fast as he could, ignoring the pain in his back for now. He managed to get over onto his belly. He scooped up his gun and pointed it out the window, but the man he had shot was sprawled between a pair of birch trees. A double-barrel shotgun lay a couple of feet away.

"Get it together, Earl," Hag said. "We're in big fucking trouble here." He banged on the door, but it still wouldn't open.

Scott ran into the other truck's headlight beam. Hag grabbed the sides of the window, pulled himself most of the way out. Sitting on the door frame with his feet still on the seat, Hag aimed at Scott's back. The angle was bad and he knew he'd never make the shot. "Better stop right there or you're fucking dead, Scott!"

Weird thing was, Scott actually did stop. Why not, though? The guy didn't know Hag had just fired that gun for the first time ever. "All right," Hag said. "Now get your ass back here."

Scott did as he was told. He never even looked at his dead partner, kept his eyes on the gun. "We wasn't really gonna kill you, dude," he said. "It was just for a scare. That's all."

It took Hag a few awkward moments to climb down off the truck's door and onto his feet again while keeping the pistol aimed at Scott. This guy was easily as big as Willard had been, only without the gut. Hag said, "Christ. Stony's kinda running through help these days, ain't he?"

"You ain't gotta kill me. Let's work something out."

"Whatever." Hag took a peek inside the truck. "You gonna make it, Earl?"

"My nose is broken."

"I heard it the first time you said it. Now get the fuck out of there."

Earl tried opening his door, had no more luck than Scott. Hag waved Scott over to Earl's side. Between Earl shoving on the door and Scott pulling at it, they managed to get it open. It hung there like a broken wing. Earl slid out, one hand cupped over his nose again. Blood covered his mouth and chin, his neck and the front of his shirt.

Hag retrieved his shotgun from behind the truck's seat. "Get all the ammo out of the glovebox, Earl. Scott, drag your buddy's carcass over to that other truck and throw it in the back. Whose truck is it anyway, yours or Stony's?"

"Gerry's." Scott pointed at the dead man.

Hag shrugged. "Mine now. Get your ass in gear and don't even think about trying for that double-barrel." He switched off the Ford's headlights and followed Scott. Earl's truck had come to rest twenty or more yards off the road, leaving behind a trail of broken birch saplings.

The dead guy's truck was a big black Dodge with oversized tires and a Hemi. Hag wasn't exactly sure what a Hemi was or did; he just knew it meant the truck had some balls. The front end was all stove up, but of course Stony would've had his mechanics fix it up for free as part of whatever deal he'd made with Gerry and Scott. It was parked almost perpendicular to the road, the headlights shining directly on the rear of the old Ford. The tires were big enough so that backing across the ditch should be no problem at all.

Gerry was damn near as big as Scott, and Earl had to help get him up on the tailgate and shoved into the bed. Once that was done, Earl found some rags in Gerry's toolbox, wiped the worst of the blood off his face.

"Give Earl your shirt."

Scott said, "What?"

"Earl's shirt's covered in blood and it's your fault. Give him yours."

Scott pulled his shirt over his head and tossed it to Earl, who missed. Earl bent down to pick it up, huffing and puffing from the effort. He turned his back on Scott and Hag to take off his ruined T-shirt, giving his chest and belly a wipe-down with the rags before putting on the clean shirt. When he turned around again, he held up the bloody clothes. "What should I do with these?" His gut hung out the bottom of Scott's shirt like he was wearing an apron made of fat.

"Toss them in the back," Hag said. "And get in the truck, 'cause we're leaving in a minute."

Scott looked worried about the *in a minute* part. He said, "Look, dude. I won't give you no trouble and I won't say nothing to nobody about any of this. Okay?"

"You got a cell phone on you?"

Scott nodded.

"Call Stony and tell him me and Earl are dead."

Scott shifted his weight from foot to foot, said, "Whatever you want." He made the call. "Stony? It's done. Yeah, both of them. Okay." Scott hung up.

Hag gestured for Scott to drop the phone. "I thought you were only supposed to scare us. So what'd Stony say?"

"Me and Gerry are supposed to go out to the house now."

"Stay right there," Hag told Scott. He walked backwards to the cab, set the shotgun inside, leaning it against the seat.

"Hey, this thing has air conditioning and a CD player," Earl said. He started the truck and fiddled with a bunch of buttons. "Check this out, Hag. It's got a compass, too."

"Who gives a flying fuck? We ain't keeping it. Be ready to drive when I tell you, but not before." Hag moved slowly along the side of the truck, watching Scott watch him. Jesus, but his back still hurt like a bastard. This whole thing had killed his buzz. Using the rear wheel as a step, Hag climbed over the side and into the bed. "Get on up here, Scotty, and pull the tailgate up behind you."

Scott climbed in.

Hag said, "Get down on your knees and turn around so your gut's against the tailgate."

Scott did it. He kept his hands on the top of the tailgate. "It's all cool, dude. I'm doing it just like you say. I don't want to end up like Gerry."

Hag spread his legs, braced his back against the back of the cab. Taking aim with both hands, he put the front sight on a line with the base of Scott's skull.

"Hag? We cool?"

Hag cocked the .44's hammer. He eased it back down. "That ain't gonna fucking work," he said.

Scott stiffened. "What ain't gonna work, Hag? We can make this work, I'm telling you. Don't say it won't work, dude."

The easiest thing would've been to kill Scott back by the Ford and leave both bodies right there. But not long after sunrise, someone would be bound to notice the heavy skid marks in the road, the trail broken through the trees. They'd find Earl's truck and the dead men. They'd call the cops. Hag didn't want to leave corpses lying around where they could be connected to him and Earl. He knew without even trying that the old Ford would never get back out of the woods without a wrecker and a winch. That truck was fucking *done.*

When the cops finally did find it and came looking for Earl, he could just say they had swerved to keep from hitting a deer and crashed into the woods. Everybody knew Earl didn't have a pot to piss in. It would be perfectly believable that he couldn't afford to call in a tow truck and had just walked home. The cops would assume Earl was OUI, but they'd never be able to prove anything. Worst thing that could happen, they might charge Earl with failure to report an accident. That meant a fine of a few hundred bucks and his insurance premium would go up. Whooptie-shit.

But Gerry's nice new Dodge would get them to Stony's house. Then a nice ride home to get cleaned up and be ready to waste Wanda's husband in the morning. So the only remaining problem was what to do with Gerry and Scott. Hag's first inclination was to dump their bodies on Stony's lawn. "I'm trying to figure something out," Hag said to Scott. "I need your help on it."

Scott's shoulders sagged as he relaxed a bit. "You name it, dude. I'm with you all the way."

"Killing people is messy fucking work, Scotty. You'd think it would be so easy, but it ain't." Hag walked back and forth across the truck bed, watching Scott. "You shoot a guy in the head, and it's like a geyser coming out of the hole. I don't like having to take a shower just to get some asshole's blood out of my hair. Plus, the way you're kneeling there, if I put one in your head, you might fall over the side of the truck. Then I've got to give myself a fucking hernia trying to get you back in."

Scott's voice cracked like he'd just been hit in the nuts. "Me? You ain't gotta shoot me."

"I could make you lie down here and shoot you like that, but I'm worried these big-ass bullets will go right through you and fuck up something important. It would suck to blow the transmission out of this thing and have to walk all the way to Stony's. Or imagine if I shot you and the gas tank at the same time. Holy shit, man!"

Scott started to get up. He moved slowly, probably getting ready to jump over the tailgate and make a run for the trees.

"You better get back down your knees or I'll kill you for sure, Scotty."

"You're gonna do it anyway," Scott said. "Just cut the fucking bullshit!"

"Okay." Hag braced himself again, aimed at Scott's back.

The truck lurched.

Scott fell backwards onto the bed-liner, next to Gerry.

Earl shouted from the cab. "Sorry, my foot slipped off the brake."

The big guy squirmed around, grabbing at Hag's ankles. Hag swung the gun down, but Scott batted it away. It banged off the back of the cab, fell over the side. Scott stood up and punched Hag in the mouth before jumping out of the truck bed.

By the time Hag found the pistol, Scott had vanished into the trees.

49

Joey heard Wanda's key in the lock. He'd seen the distinctive Jeep headlights turn into the driveway from the living room.

A bottle of Ketel One he had picked up at the Wesserunsett IGA stood half-empty on the end table beside his chair. No glass. Shifted himself around in the chair so he could reach his .38 if necessary.

She stood in the doorway, swaying more than a little. "Where's your buddy?"

"He's asleep upstairs."

Wanda raised an eyebrow. She said, "Huh. He gave you his bedroom. What a generous asshole. I came for my stuff."

"I was hoping you would."

"Yeah? Thought I might let you look at those pictures again? Tough shit. I cut up all the prints and smashed the disc."

Joey said, "You've been drinking. You ought to sit down."

"I've been drinking? Looks like you've been pounding down the vodka pretty good. No, I'm getting my shit and getting out of here. Fuck you, fuck Evan, fuck Jim, fuck his little skank, fuck this whole town." Wanda looked around the room. "What did you assholes do with all my stuff?"

Joey got up, nodded the hall. "It's in the dining room, remember? Look," he said. "I'll help you load up, but not tonight. You're lucky you made it here from wherever."

Wanda glared.

"I get that you've had a lousy week. Believe me, I understand." He reached out to take her by the elbow, but she jerked away. Joey shrugged, said, "I'm going to make coffee. You want some?"

Wanda moved aside to let Joey go into the hall, followed him through the dining room and into the kitchen. She said, "I'm trying to figure out what your deal is."

Joey turned on the cold water, let it run while he put a clean filter into the machine and scooped in coffee. "My deal?"

"Why are you here? This old high school buddy I never once heard Evan mention the whole time I was with him, and you just show up out of the blue." Wanda sat on a stool beside the kitchen island.

"He invited me up for the fishing."

Wanda snorted. "Cut the bullshit. Evan's not exactly the outdoors type. I doubt he could bait a hook if you held a gun to his head."

"How do you know I didn't?" Joey filled the pot and dumped the water into the machine. He switched it on, parked himself on the other stool. They sat kitty-corner across from each other. Wanda was tall enough so each could look into the other's eyes. Hers were bloodshot but intent on Joey's face. He shook his head. "Just let it go."

"I could beat it out of you," Wanda said. "Maybe I'll pistol-whip you. I've already been accused of police brutality. Might as well live up to the rep."

Joey sat up straight, arms folded across his chest. He said, "Sounds like fun, but I don't see a gun."

"It's around here somewhere." Wanda waved toward the dining room. "Don't have any cuffs, though. There might be a cable tie somewhere in all that mess."

"Kinky."

Wanda leaned forward, said, "Keep dreaming, stud. You aren't bad looking, but I've had it up to here with men lately."

Damn, she must have been hitting the booze hard. Her breath

was a good eighty-proof. Joey had a nice mild buzz going because he'd been sipping at his bottle all night. He said, "Look, I'm trying to apologize about this afternoon. It's just not coming out right. I wish I never brought up the pictures."

"So why did you?"

How much to tell her? Yeah, Wanda was drunk and in trouble, but she was still a cop. What better way to get herself out of her own mess than by nailing a professional killer on the job? This was fucked up. He should be helping her load her stuff into the Jeep right then. Get her the hell out of there, out of the way. Make some more remarks about the nudie pictures just to be sure she stayed gone. She'd be better off. So why was he keeping her here? Why the half-assed apology? The old Joey, the one he was before meeting Sam and Grace, would've capped Wanda so he could go on about his business. But that Joey was dead, wasn't he?

Joey felt the weight of the .38 at his lower back. How easy it would be to pull it now and drill one through Wanda's forehead. No answers for Wanda. No risk of her poking around more after she sobered up. Barker would freak, but he'd help Joey bury Wanda in the cellar, dump the Jeep and her possessions somewhere.

No. If Wanda disappeared now, the other cops would start asking questions. The encounter with that McKinney guy proved that Barker's affair with the woman was common knowledge. Besides, the only people Joey wanted to kill were in Brooklyn.

Joey shrugged, said, "You know how guys are."

"That's one hell of an apology."

"Sorry."

"Hmm…that's not much better." Wanda propped her elbows on the counter, rested her chin in her hands. "Were you raised by wolves or what?"

"My mother died in a car crash when I was just a little kid. Dad did his best to bring me up right. I guess it didn't take."

"So what's he like?"

Joey got up to check on the coffee. The pot was almost full. He said, "Dad died in '97. Heart attack. What does that matter?"

"I'm trying to figure you out."

"Thought you were fed up with men."

Wanda said, "For now. You might be worth a second look down the road."

"Down the road is where I'm heading. I have to get back to New York by Monday."

The coffee maker gurgled and hissed.

"Chicago," Wanda said.

"Huh?"

"You told me you live in Chicago."

Jesus. Even hammered she was sharp. And Joey was slipping up with only a buzz on. How stupid could he get? Joey said, "Yeah, I do. But I'm originally from Brooklyn. Gonna visit the old neighborhood. Didn't the accent clue you in?"

"Flatlanders all sound the same to me."

"What the hell's a flatlander?"

"Anybody who isn't a Mainer. How about pouring me some of that coffee?"

A rack of mugs stood on the counter near the coffee maker. Joey grabbed two, filled them both. He opened the fridge. "I don't see any creamer."

"Milk's fine," Wanda said. "And two sugars. I like it sweet."

Joey poured and stirred, handed Wanda her mug. He drank his own coffee black and bitter. They sat there looking at each other, not saying anything for a few minutes.

Wanda broke the silence. "Want to hear something funny?"

"I could use a laugh," Joey said.

Wanda raked her teeth across her upper lip. She said, "There's this guy named Charlie Hagopian, a real loser, in and out of jail for nickel-and-dime stuff. He just got out of lockup in Canada; hit a cop car with a snowmobile up there last winter after sneaking across the border. They figure he was running drugs for somebody, had a bag full of cash on him, but he wouldn't flip. Anyway, I ran into Charlie at The Vault tonight and he bragged about how he was this big-time hitman now, tried to get me to hire him. I gave him a fake address and told him to go shoot my husband."

"Does this guy know you're a cop?" *Hagopian. Hag?* That same idiot Joey had met at The Vault his first night in Wesserunsett?

Wanda said, "Hell yeah, he does. He was only two or three years behind me in high school." With her thumb and forefinger, she made an L against her head and grinned. "That just shows you how stupid the guy is."

"You bust him?"

"I'm on suspension. Besides, if Charlie lives up to his usual standards, he'll pick a fight with somebody at the bar and get his ass kicked."

Joey laughed, said, "Sounds like a real bad guy."

"Compared to whom? There aren't any good guys left." Wanda stood up and walked around the island. She stopped next to Joey. "Hey."

Joey turned to face her. "Yeah?"

Wanda leaned forward, kissed him hard. Her tongue darted into Joey's mouth, tasting of coffee and alcohol. She touched his face, stroked his neck. Joey slid his hands down to her waist. Wanda stiffened, broke off the kiss and backed away a step. She said, "That's enough for now."

Licking his lips, Joey said, "What the hell was that all about?"

"I just felt like it. Any complaints?"

Joey shook his head.

Wanda said, "I'm going to bed now."

"Good idea." Joey stood up, switched off the coffee maker. This was the last thing he had expected to happen tonight.

"I mean on the couch."

"Oh."

"Alone."

Joey said, "Yeah. I figured that. You can take the bedroom, though. I don't mind sleeping on the couch."

Wanda placed her hands against the flat of her back, stretched and yawned. She said, "No thanks. I'd rather wake up with a backache than climb into Evan Barker's bed again, even without him in it."

When Wanda was gone, Joey turned out the lights. He sat there in the darkened kitchen, still tasting that kiss.

50

If there'd ever been a time when Earl sobered up this fast, he couldn't remember it. He white-knuckled the steering wheel of that big Dodge Ram pickup, felt the power vibrating straight through him when he stepped down harder on the gas. The high beams on this thing lit up the road like noon. That was the best part. One of the headlights on his old Ford had been skewed off to one side like a lazy eye, leaving a shadowy area at night. Earl had always expected to see a deer come leaping at him out of that blind spot.

Next to him, Hag said, "Couple more miles to Stony's place. You clear on the plan?"

"Yeah, I'm clear, but it don't make no sense to me. I mean, how are you gonna get the money you want out of him if you kill him?"

Hag flipped through a CD wallet he found in the storage compartment. He took out a disc and slid it into the player. There was the sound of a crowd cheering and then, *You wanted the best, you got the best. The hottest band in the world...Kiss!* "Detroit Rock City" came barreling out of the speakers, the bass making the back window rattle. "*Alive II*," Hag said. "Gerry was an asshole, but he had good taste."

He did that kind of crap to Earl all the time, ignored questions. Not this time. Earl had to shout above the music. "How's Stony gonna pay you if he's dead?"

Hag sang along with Paul Stanley.

Earl reached over, turned off the CD. "Guess you didn't hear me, Hag. I asked how Stony's gonna pay you if you kill him."

"Jesus, Earl. I'm gonna make him cough up the money first. You think I'm an idiot?"

"Nobody keeps eighty grand just lying around the house," Earl said. "Not even a guy like Stony. So then what? If he says he doesn't have it there, what do you do?"

Hag turned the music back on but kept it low. He turned sideways in his seat to give Earl that look. Earl felt it, even in the dim green glow from the dashboard. It was the look that screamed *retard* instead of saying it out loud for thousandth time this week. "You ain't even gonna be inside. So what the fuck do you care?"

"I'm done with all this killing, Hag. I ain't gonna go along with it no more. We're either gonna spend the rest of our lives in jail or somebody's gonna shoot us. No more. No way."

"I don't believe this fucking shit," Hag said. "You don't tell me what we do. I make the plans, I do the real work. You're the fucking wheelman. There ain't no quitting. You got that?"

Earl stared out at the road.

"I said you got that, you fat bag of shit?"

Earl bit his lip, kept driving.

"We've been best friends since the eighth grade. That don't mean nothin' to you? Huh? If you think I'm letting you bail on our friendship now, you're out of your fuckin' mind."

Earl's face burned, the blush and the tears hidden—he hoped—by the darkness. His nose throbbed, broken for sure.

"Now," Hag said. "You clear on the plan?"

"Yeah."

By the time "Detroit Rock City" crashed into "King of the Night Time World," they were coming up on Stony's house. Earl slowed for the turn into the long driveway. It led past a stand of dwarf apple trees, their blossoms shining white in the Dodge's headlights.

Stony's house was a sprawling log home. The inside lights were off with only a spotlight burning above the garage.

Earl drove across the lawn, flattening Arlene Bouchard's rose bushes. He stopped just feet from the huge bay window at the front of the house, leaving the high beams on and the engine running.

Hag jumped out. He shoved the .44 down the front of his jeans, picked up the shotgun. "Wait here," he said. Then he ran in a half crouch around the far end of the house. Earl remembered there was deck out there by the pool, with a sliding glass door that opened from the kitchen. Hag's plan was to have Earl draw the family's attention to the living room with the truck while Hag snuck in through the back and cornered them there.

A small bright light flashed in one of the downstairs windows. There was a pop. Something hit the truck's fender. Another flash and pop. A bee buzzed past Earl's ear just as a spiderweb of cracks spread out across the windshield. Was Stony shooting at him? This was Hag's brilliant idea? Earl was not a distraction. He was a big fat target, same as always. Stony, or whoever it was, fired again.

Earl's window shattered, throwing glass across his face. Pain lashed through the left side of his chest. A heart attack? No. Earl rubbed the spot where it hurt the most, felt a hot, sticky wetness beneath his hand. *Oh, God. Not this, please.* He had to get out of there fast.

Hag's twelve-gauge boomed from somewhere inside Stony's house.

Again.

Again.

Earl yanked the truck into reverse, spun around on what was left of the flowerbed and tore out of there. He bottomed out at the end of the driveway. Something thumped behind him. It was Gerry, still rolling around in the bed of the pickup. Earl turned onto the road, headed back toward town with the gas pedal floored. If he made it home and called nine-one-one, they could save him. Let the cops ask all the questions they wanted when he was safe in a hospital bed. This was all Hag's fault anyway. Earl never wanted to hurt anyone. Breath coming in shallow, ragged gasps, Earl stared straight ahead and tried to see through the ruined windshield.

He could make it home.

Please, God.

He had to make it.

51

Joey stayed in the darkened kitchen. He could hear Wanda moving around in Barker's bathroom, running water, brushing her teeth, probably removing her makeup—not that she needed or wore much. She finished up and Joey heard her walk down the hall to the living room. Waiting for her to get herself situated in there, Joey sipped his coffee.

After a few more minutes, Joey stood up and made his way around the house. All the lights were out now, but he'd memorized the layout and reached the front door with ease. Wanda was already snoring lightly on the sofa when Joey stepped outside.

He went down the steps and stood on the lawn, breathing the cool night air. It was so quiet here, except for the wind soughing through the treetops, and the occasional passing car. The breeze was good; it kept the mosquitoes away.

Taking out his cell phone, Joey walked to the far side of the old barn. He called a number in New York. It rang six times before a voice came on the line, said, "Yeah?"

"Nick the Brick. How'd you like those pictures I e-mailed you the other night?"

A pause at Nick's end. Then, "What do you want, asshole?"

"Your help."

Nick laughed.

Joey said, "I know all about Florio, Nicky."

The laughter stopped. "You got no proof I had anything to

do with that," Nick said.

"No? I have what Vassily Fedoseev told me. Just the fact that you hired a *Russian* to off me would be reason enough for Carl to kill you. After that, all I'd have to do is tell him what our mutual friend said about Florio's death. Carl won't need any kind of physical evidence. Jesus Christ, Nick, did you expect to get away with having a guy like that whacked? John Florio made his bones with the Petuccis when you were still giving your junior high gym teacher blowjobs in the locker room."

"Fuck you. If you were gonna rat me out, you'd have done it by now. You want something from me."

Joey grinned, said, "You're smarter than I thought. Let me lay this out for you, then. You're going to get Grace the hell out of there and onto a plane back to Chicago tonight. In exchange, I'll keep what I know about Florio to myself."

"Mr. Petucci'll notice she's gone. Who you think's gonna catch the blame for that, huh?"

"Sally."

"What?"

"Sal Manfredo's on the door, right?" The breeze died down, and Joey shifted the phone from one hand to the other as he slapped at some bugs that had found his bare arms. He said, "Say Sally nodded off on the job, something like that."

"The nigger'll run to the cops," Nick said. "We'll all be fucked."

"Use that word again and I'll hang up just long enough to give Carl a ring."

"So what's in this deal for me?"

Joey sighed. "You get to live, stupid."

There were a few moments of silence. Joey was beginning to think he'd somehow lost the signal when finally Nick spoke again. "Okay," he said. "I'll do it."

In the darkness, Joey grinned. "Good. I'll call Grace at home in the morning. She'd better be there to answer the phone."

"She will."

"Oh, and there's just one more thing, Nick."

"What the fuck *now*?"

"No way could you afford to pay for two hits," Joey said. "Not on the kind of salary I know Carl gives his bodyguards. So you're skimming from him somewhere. If I were you, I'd leave right behind Grace."

Joey hung up and walked back to the house. He sat on the steps for a while, putting off going inside until he was tired enough for sleep to come quickly.

52

Hag heard the first shot as he reached the patio door. He hadn't expected Stony to open fire right away. Shit! Scott's phone. Hag forgot to pick it up and the son of a whore must've gone back for it. Well, Earl ought to be smart enough to duck.

The sliding door was locked. The lights from the pool shone bright enough that Hag could see the latch on the inside. He frigged around with the handle for a couple of seconds.

"Fuck it." He stepped back, blasted a load of birdshot through the glass. It goddamn *exploded.* Unable to help himself, Hag started giggling and kept it up while he went inside. Tried to get his bearings. He was in the kitchen as planned, but it had been a long time since Stony last had him out here…and that was in the daytime. *Get your shit together, be a pro.* All the fucking lights were off now. The truck lights shining into the living room did not help him at all back here.

Nope, hold on. There was a light on in a room down the hall, on the back side of the house. Hag racked the pump and held the shotgun low against his side as he went that way, passing a closed door on the left. He heard pistol shots from behind that door. It was Stony's home office, if Hag remembered right. That little bastard must have been hiding in there and was now firing at Earl. Hag heard two more shots from the office.

Hag stood in front of the door. Should he try kicking it in or just start shooting through the wood? The kick would give Stony too much of a warning. Hag raised the shotgun, pulled the butt tight against his shoulder. He was about to fire when he caught movement from the corner of his eye.

Stony Bouchard stepped out of the lighted room at the far end of the hall. The sneaky bastard wasn't in the office at all. So who was? The wife? Stony had a gun in his hand. Hag swung toward him, squeezed the trigger.

Thrown back through the doorway, Stony screamed. The gun flew out of his hand, bounced off the wall. Hag pumped another shell into the chamber.

"Boss!" The office door swung inward. Tom Moody ran out, almost slammed into Hag. Moody was tall and thin, a big-nosed motherfucker who did all kinds of dirty jobs for Stony. Right now he was bringing a big semi-automatic pistol to bear on Hag.

Hag didn't have enough time or room to pivot and aim the shotgun. Instead, he stomped on one of Moody's feet. The guy howled, raised his gun and fired.

The muzzle flash left Hag half-blind. For a moment he thought Moody had shot him in the face. No pain, though. There was only the bright spot wobbling in front of his eyes and that ringing in his left ear. Hag said, "Jesus fucking Christ." He cut loose with the twelve-gauge, backed a couple of steps toward the kitchen and fired again.

Maybe the shots cut Moody in half. If not, the son of a bitch would have to retreat to the office. Hag needed time to think. His vision was returning to normal. Now, instead of one big purple spot, he saw a lot of small ones. But the shotgun going off in such a tight space had fucked up his ears. He could hear a little, but both were ringing something wicked. The hallway reeked from the burnt gunpowder hanging there like a fog.

Hag knelt to present a smaller target just in case Moody decided to start shooting again. No problem there. Moody sat with his back against the doorjamb, arms limp at his sides, his face and upper chest a glistening red ruin. The pistol in his dead hand looked big enough to put down a moose.

Okay, that left the wife and kids, maybe Stony. If he was still alive, Hag could get some money off him. Whatever they had in the house wouldn't even come close to eighty grand. So what? The money didn't matter much. A greater principle was at stake, the one that said *you don't ever fuck with Charlie Hagopian.* If Stony happened to have a few thousand stashed in a house safe, that was just gravy.

Hag rose and moved down the hall. He picked up Stony's automatic, held it and the shotgun in front of him as he stepped into the lighted room. *Jesus.* Stony's master bedroom was almost as big as Earl's whole trailer.

Stony lay on his back at Hag's feet. His head lolled from side to side and he kept licking his lips. Hag's shot had taken him just above the right hip. Stony had both of his hands pressed over the biggest wound. The shot pattern had spread because of the distance; small red spots on his chest and thighs showed where he'd been hit by stray pellets.

Hag crouched beside his old boss and poked Stony's face with the pistol. "All right, asshole. Where's my money?"

Stony looked up at Hag. He didn't answer.

"Don't want to tell me? That's all right," Hag said. "I'd rather talk to your wife and kids anyway."

Stony went into a coughing fit that wracked his whole body. When it stopped, he said, "Not here."

Hag stood up, said, "You always thought you were better than everybody, didn't you? Walking around like your shit don't stink. Look at you now. Tell you what, I'm gonna take a walk upstairs.

"So stupid," Stony said.

Then Hag noticed the cell phone in his hand. He said, "There's no way you had time to call nine-one-one."

Stony's answer was a grin.

Hag ran out of the room. If Stony had really made the call, he had to nail the rest of them before the cops showed up. This whole fucking family was going to die. Hag had promised Stony that. He paused long enough to kick Moody on his way past. It made a squishy noise he liked, so he did it again. *Better focus, mister man. Time's wastin'.* He picked up Moody's gun, tossed it and Stony's into the office.

The kids' bedrooms had to be upstairs. Rich little shits like that probably had phones in their rooms or cell phones next to their pretty beds. So even if Stony didn't call nine-one-one, the kids could. Hag took the stairs two at a time, the twelve-gauge held tight against his chest. He kicked the first door he came to at the top of the landing and it swung open: a bathroom.

Hag made his way along the hall. None of the doors had light showing beneath them. Hag tried the next door. It opened. No movement inside. The ringing in Hag's ears was fading, but he still couldn't hear any noise in this part of the house. He felt for the light switch, found it. The bedroom walls were covered with baseball posters. A shelf above the bed held a row of trophies. Hag used the shotgun to lift the Batman bedspread. There was nothing under there but board games and some little cars. The closet door was closed. Hag put two loads of birdshot through it. Pulling away the broken bits of louver, he checked the closet: clothes and more toys.

All right, maybe they were hiding in the daughter's room or one of the guest bedrooms. Hag checked them all. No sign of Arlene or the goddamn kids. Maybe they were up in the attic. Maybe the basement. Maybe they had climbed out a fucking window as soon as the shooting started.

The ringing in Hag's ears got worse again.

No, wait a minute.

Sirens.

Hag said, "You better be ready to haul ass, Earl." He stepped out into the hall, saw Stony standing just a few feet away. The guy panted like an animal and one leg was sheathed in his own blood. The button down shirt he'd been wearing when Hag shot him was now tied around his waist. Stony had found an aluminum baseball bat somewhere. Like that was going to do the dumbass any good. Hag raised the shotgun, squeezed the trigger.

Nothing happened.

Fuck! Hag had forgotten to reload after shooting up the boy's closet. He stood there for a moment, trying to work out his next move.

Stony came at Hag, swinging the bat. Hag raised the shotgun just to keep his skull from getting smashed. His right hand got caught between the bat and the twelve-gauge's stock. Hag screamed as his knuckles shattered under the blow. He dropped the shotgun, tried to draw the .44 out of his pants with his left hand. No good.

Stony went upside Hag's head with the bat. There was a *tink* sound when it hit his skull. Hag yanked on the .44 again, but the hammer was caught on one of his belt loops. The crazy bastard stepped back and hit Hag in the mouth. Something snapped on the left side his face; he heard it and felt it at the same time. Stony was going to beat Hag to death if he didn't get out of there. Christ, why didn't the guy just lay down and die? That shirt was the only thing keeping Stony's guts from slopping out onto the floor.

Hag watched Stony raise the bat again. *Think, motherfucker, think.* He shoved his good hand deep in his pocket, pulled out the canister of pepper spray he'd stolen from Linda Turcotte. Gave Stony a face full of the shit. Hag shouldered him aside, ran down the stairs and out the front door.

The sirens sounded closer.

Hag looked around. The truck. Hag started puking before he even realized he was doing it. The truck was gone.

That fucking Earl.

53

Larry Nichols switched off the TV, laid the remote on the stand beside his chair. He stood and stretched, telling himself he should've gone to bed hours ago. The Motrin helped quite a bit, but he still ached from his fight with Charlie. Too many years had gone by since he'd last boxed. Sleep would do him a world of good. What if Charlie came back while he was sleeping, though? Larry could take him in a fair fight. That much had already been proven. But what if the sleaze got in here with a weapon? Maybe a big knife or even a gun.

Yawning, Larry had to admit he was too tired to put up much of a fight just then anyway. He turned off the lamp before checking to make sure the front door was bolted and chained.

The only illumination came from the streetlight outside, but Larry didn't even need that. He'd bought this trailer brand new almost twenty years ago and lived in it ever since. Even with all the times he had rearranged the furniture, Larry could still find his way from one end to the other in the dark.

There was a roar outside. What the hell? The kitchen and living room lit up as though someone were shining a spotlight into Larry's windows. No, it was a pickup truck. Charlie and Earl. It just had to be. The truck came bouncing across Earl's yard toward Larry's house.

This was the end. If Charlie Hagopian wanted to keep playing his nasty games, Larry was calling the police. He grabbed

263

his cell phone off the counter.

Outside, the engine raced. What was Earl trying to do, anyway?

Larry looked up from his phone, said, "Oh my God."

The truck plowed into the right front corner of Larry's trailer, knocking that end of the place off its cinderblocks. The floor tilted down toward the backyard. Cupboard doors swung open, spilling glasses and plates. The microwave hit the floor and its door shattered. The entertainment center fell over. Larry dropped his phone, made a grab for the edge of the counter. He got a quick glimpse of the pickup as it went by. It was too new to belong to Earl Coro.

Larry held his breath, waiting for the house to roll over. How many seconds had passed? Nothing else happened. The trailer had tipped, though not at as steep an angle as Larry had feared. Barefoot, he picked his way through the expanse of broken glass to the front door. Lights came on all along Heron Lane and Maple Street—except for Earl's place. The whole neighborhood would've heard a crash like that.

The grass was damp and cool beneath Larry's feet. He hurried to the back of the trailer to see where the truck had gone. After hitting Larry's house, the strange truck had veered slightly and scraped along the siding before going through the backyard. It had crossed the pavement behind the shopping center and slammed against the rear of the building. The driver's side door hung open. Larry squinted. It looked like the driver was still inside.

Bob Rowell hobbled over on crutches, wearing only a pair of pajama bottoms. He said, "Jesus, but that was a hell of a thing. You okay, Nichols? I thought somebody must be dead for sure when I heard that crash."

"Who said they aren't?" Larry popped the trunk of his car to find the first-aid kit he kept there. There was an old pair of sneakers, too. The treads were worn nearly smooth. Larry had meant to throw them in the trash, but they were a welcome sight now. It took just a few seconds to slip them on. Then he jogged through his yard with Bob Rowell huffing and gasping along behind him.

"Joyce's calling nine-one-one," Bob said when they were close to the truck. "Nice Dodge. I don't recognize it. You?"

Larry shook his head. Slivers of glass and plastic crunched under his feet. He walked up to the door, said, "Better stay back, unless you want your good foot cut up."

The truck's front end was all stove in, the hood buckled almost in half and the windshield a jumble of cracks. Larry heard crying. The driver was weeping softly. Well, that was a good sign. At least the fool was still alive.

"You hang tight there," Larry said. He got up close to make a visual assessment of the man's injuries. Even through the mask of blood, Larry recognized Earl.

"Sorry," Earl said. "I just wanted...home." His whole body shook when he spoke, each word punctuated by a wheeze. Pink bubbles frothed from a small hole in the left side of his chest.

Larry opened the kit, pulled on a pair of latex-free gloves. He felt the area around the hole. Good God, it looked like a gunshot. Larry had never even seen that kind of wound before, could barely remember what the first-aid instructor told his class all those years ago. Opening a gauze bandage and pressing it against the hole, Larry said, "The ambulance is on its way, Earl. Try to breathe slowly, okay."

Still sobbing, Earl nodded.

"Were you shot?"

No answer.

Larry heard the sirens now. He said, "Stay awake, Earl. Did someone shoot you?"

"I was...Hag."

"Charlie shot you?" Larry's hand shook. What the hell had he done? Was this his fault? If only Larry had called the police on Charlie when he should have, Earl might not be dying right in front of him.

Earl said, "Hag." He stopped crying.

Larry couldn't feel or hear Earl breathing. He checked for a pulse at the carotid artery. Nothing. Still, he had to wait for EMS to get here and take over.

A crowd gathered around Bob Rowell. Larry hadn't even noticed them until that moment. A teenaged girl Larry recognized as part of the hard-partying crowd from Maple Street walked over to the truck. The vehicle rocked as she climbed up on the rear bumper.

"Get down from there," Larry said.

The girl sneered at him. "Um, just so you know? There's a dead guy in the bed."

Larry craned his neck but couldn't see the other body. If there was any justice in the world, it would be Charlie Hagopian back there.

54
SUNDAY, JUNE 13

Hag's right hand looked like a catcher's mitt. He could barely move his jaw. Stretched out across the backseat of Tom Moody's Forester, he'd slept in jerks and starts, dozing off and jumping awake at every noise. He sat up to look around. The sky was that pre-dawn gray, something Hag hadn't seen in a long time. His revolver lay on the floor in a puddle of congealed vomit. The stink of blood, puke and booze filled his nostrils.

The SUV sat behind a double-wide trailer with white siding, at the edge of a gravel parking lot bordered by trees. But where the fuck was he? Hag's head throbbed. He probed the left side of his mouth with his tongue. At least three teeth were missing, a couple others broken. He didn't remember spitting them out. Had he swallowed them?

That fucking Stony with his ball bat. If he were still alive, he could identify Hag. Never mind that his prints were all over the shotgun he'd had to leave behind. The whole thing was fucked up. Yeah, he'd nailed Moody good, but he didn't know about Stony. And Arlene and the kids? No way to get them now. Hag had barely had time to go back inside the house and rifle Moody's pockets for the car keys.

Hag dragged himself out of the car, taking the barf-caked .44 along. He walked around the building to see where the fuck he was. Oh, yeah. It was the Pentecostal church on the Sirois Road. Hag had parked behind it last night. It was the closest building to the house where he was going to kill Wanda's hubby. Plus it was a good place to hide from the cops who'd been tear-assing all over town trying to find him. Pretty fucking funny, really…carloads of cops beating the bushes for him while he waited around to kill another cop's husband.

Shit. Breathing hurt. The air passing over his broken teeth sent lances of pain through Hag's skull. Jesus, Stony had messed him up badly. Hag should've killed him right there in the master bedroom, made sure it got done right. If he had known the wife and kids were gone, he would've taken more time. Too bad about Arlene, she would've been fun. Damn. Even with all the pain, Hag's dick twitched, stiffened when he thought about Arlene. A need overtook him, something stronger than simple horniness or the thirst for booze: the need to destroy.

Hag went to the back door of the church, smashed out a pane of glass with the pistol butt and reached in to turn the knob. There was a short flight of carpeted stairs going up, another leading down to the basement. He went down, felt around for the light switch. Fluorescent tubes flickered on. The floor was bare cement, the walls hung with framed Bible verses and pictures of angels that little kids had drawn in crayon. A pair of long tables surrounded by folding metal chairs filled the center of the room. The far end was kitchen space. An open door led to a small restroom.

First thing to do was clean the gun. Hag found a roll of paper towels and wiped off the biggest chunks of puke before laying the .44 on a table. Now what? His fingers twitched. Time to have some fun.

He tore the kids' drawings off the walls, took them into the restroom and crammed them into the toilet. He unzipped and tried to piss on them, couldn't do it with his dick still hard. Nothing happening in here, so he tucked his junk away. Zipping up was tougher with his left hand. He caught a look at himself in the mirror on the way out. His hair stood up and out, stiff and crusty and dark with blood. The whole left side of his face was swollen, the skin above his cheekbone stretched tight and shiny over a reddish-purple bump. His lips were fat. Dried patches of blood mottled his neck, too. It was on his arms, his good hand, under his fingernails. The fluorescent light made him look a Hollywood zombie.

Hag tried to say, "It came from beyond the grave." His mouth wouldn't open all the way, so he *sounded* like a zombie, too. A zombie in church. Pretty funny.

He hit the kitchen. No booze in the fridge, of course, just some half-and-half and a pitcher of what looked like grape juice. Wine, maybe? No, that was the Catholics. What the hell did Hag know about religion? Goddamn Bible-thumpers were all the same when you got right down to it. Standing there in the church kitchen, Hag felt their condescension pressing down on him. Who the fuck did they think they were, anyway? Earl had said his mother went to this church.

Earl. Where the hell was Earl? *Oh shit, that's right.* The fat retard had taken off and left him at Stony's house last night. If Hag hadn't found Tom Moody's keys, he'd be in jail right now, or maybe shot dead. What was up with that? Earl was the getaway driver, the wheelman. Your wheelman wasn't supposed to take off and leave your ass hanging in the wind. What Hag ought to do, after he blew away Wanda's husband, was to go back to the trailer and teach Earl a thing or two about loyalty. Old lardass needed a good beating to remind him Hag was his best friend.

Hag took out the pitcher, sniffed it. Grape juice. He threw it across the room. The pitcher skittered along one of the tables, hit the floor and shattered. He dumped the carton of half-and-half all over the stovetop.

That was lame. So he kicked at the open refrigerator door until it came off its bottom hinge. Every kick made his jaw hurt even worse and the increased pain made him kick harder. One-handed, Hag rocked the whole unit away from the wall, tipped it over onto the floor. He emptied all the cupboards, smashed glasses, flung plastic plates and bowls everywhere, opened boxes of crackers and cookies, dumped them on the floor and stomped them into crumbs. He stuck knives and forks into the foam ceiling tiles, then grabbed his gun before heading upstairs.

He didn't dare turn on the lights in the sanctuary, but enough of the early sunlight came through the windows to let him see. The windows were plain glass, not stained. The place didn't even have any pews, just rows of folding metal chairs. A lectern with a microphone stood at the far end. Behind that a tiny stage with a five-piece drum kit, guitar stands and a couple of amplifiers. What kind of church was this? If they had bands, they ought to have a bar, too. Hag unplugged the amps, rolled them to the top of the stairs, sent them tumbling down. They didn't break, so he went back to kick holes in the drum heads.

A table near the stairs held stacks of hymnals. Hag swept the books onto the floor with the barrel of the Ruger. He sat on the table, panting and sweating. A hot wetness trickled along his inner thigh; it took Hag a moment to realize he'd creamed his jeans. Holy fucking shit. That hadn't happened since he was a horndog teenager. Sweat ran down the back of his neck. Then the pain flared again. He wanted to drink a twelve-pack and pass out.

Hag looked around the room, would've grinned if he could. Those stupid churchy bastards would see something to pray about when they came in later that morning.

That morning. Goddamn, what time was it now? No clock hung on any of the walls in this part of the church. The preacher probably didn't want his flock paying more attention to the minute hand than to the sermon. Hag went back down the steps, kicking the amps the rest of the way down to the basement so he could get through the backdoor.

He slid behind the wheel of the Subaru, turned the key. The stereo came on, WBLM blasting out "Blinded by the Light."

The Manfred Mann version, with the synths and distorted guitars, not Springsteen's original. Fuckin' A. It wasn't the Boss, but it would do.

The LED readout flashed from the radio tuner to the clock. 6:03 a.m. Wanda had told him to kill her husband at five. What was wrong with his brain this morning? It was unprofessional to let fun get in the way of business like that. Hag slammed the car into drive, floored the gas pedal. The SUV threw up a wake of gravel as it whipped around the church and onto the road. The climbing sun stabbed at Hag's eyes.

55

Evan slept in fits and starts all night, finally giving up a little after five o'clock. Between the police cars tearing up and down the road with their sirens blaring and the worries about Monday morning nagging him, there was no rest for Evan. He lay there on his back, scratching his nuts and staring at the ceiling. He knew Wanda was downstairs, probably in bed with Joe. He'd heard her come in last night, heard them talking in the kitchen. She didn't leave. Did they screw? He hadn't heard any sounds; no creaking of bedsprings, no moans, groans or screams... and Wanda usually made a hell of a racket in the sack.

That was the weird thing. Wanda had never been more than a good lay to Evan. He wasn't interested in getting her to leave Jim and move in with him or take that walk down the aisle. Evan had been looking for ways to cut her loose without pissing her off too much anyway when Mr. Killer came along to fuck up everything. Yeah, she was a good lay, but she never wanted to do the wilder things that Evan was into. He needed a little kink. So why did it bother him then, the thought that Joe might have put the boots to her?

Maybe because it meant the Petuccis had taken one more thing away from him. First it had been his dreams, getting him to make their porn movies instead of finishing film school and becoming a legitimate director. Mikey P.—that fucking psycho— exploited Barker's gambling debts and obsession with raunchy sex to keep him in line. Then, when he'd turned state's evidence against Mikey and had to go into witness protection, they took the life he had known. It wasn't much of a life, but it was his.

He tried making the best of things here in Maine. Once he finally got away from feds, things had started working out for him. Then Joe showed up and ruined it all. Sure, Joe claimed he wouldn't kill Evan as long as he turned over the tape. Of course the guy would say that. It made things easier for him if Evan went to the gallows with a smile on his face.

But that tape was worth a lot of money. If Carl Petucci still wanted the thing badly enough to send a hitman after him, then the mob boss would sure as hell be willing to pay for it when the killer failed. Evan's original demand had been three hundred thousand. The presence of that asshole downstairs meant that the price would now go up to a nice, even million. With that kind of cash, Evan could start over again somewhere else, maybe even on a Caribbean island. No more Petucci brothers. No more hitmen.

So let Joe fuck Wanda's brains out. Who cared? Evan got out of bed, padded across the room. He opened the door slowly, ready for the creak of the hinges. The noise was soft, but Evan stood there listening anyway. Nothing. He stepped into a pair of sweatpants and his Crocs, pulled on a T-shirt.

The easy part was done. Now he had to get downstairs and outside. He had to get into the barn to grab the videotape. Angie Petucci's finest performance was wrapped in three layers of plastic sheeting locked inside a metal strongbox along with nine grand in cash, the whole thing buried under some old rotten hay in a long-unused stall.

The lie about the safe-deposit box at the credit union had bought Evan some time, but that was all. Joe expected him to produce the tape tomorrow morning. Joe didn't seem like the kind of guy to be amused if Evan told him the truth. No, Evan would get the tape, hop in his truck and hit the road right now. In just a couple of hours, he could be sitting in a hotel room in

Portland, calling up Carl Petucci to arrange the trade.

The stairs creaked—every goddamn step! The floorboards in the downstairs hall creaked. Jesus H. Christ, Evan had never noticed how much noise this old house made. Evan's keys sat in a bowl on a table by the front door.

"The fuck are you going?"

Evan froze. The skin along his spine prickled and his scrotum tightened up. He turned around. Joe stood in the doorway to the spare bedroom, wearing a pair of boxer shorts. He held a gun casually, like it was no more dangerous or unusual a thing to carry around the house than, say, a towel or a spatula.

"I couldn't sleep," Evan said with a smile. He tried not to look at the gun. "I'm just going down the driveway to grab the paper. You staying up? I'll put on the coffee and fry some eggs. There might be some bacon in the fridge, too."

Joe exhaled, a long breath through his nose. He stepped forward, fished Evan's keys out of the bowl. Then he turned around, went back into the bedroom and closed the door.

Motherfucker.

Evan stood by the front door. He looked out through the transom windows. The sun was almost above the trees across the road. What was he supposed to do now? It was useless to retrieve the video if he didn't have a way to get out of here. Evan went into the kitchen, switched on the lights. He might as well start the coffee and go get the paper, like he'd told Joe. He could sit and think over breakfast.

The morning was cool. Dew-speckled webs of ground spiders dotted the lawn. The grass needed cutting, but someone else could worry about that. Evan walked down the path. He grabbed the *Morning Sentinel* from the delivery tube and started back.

An SUV came down the road and pulled over close to the end of Evan's driveway. It was a new Subaru, but the guy who climbed out looked like he'd been living under a bridge for years: clothes all twisted around, hair sticking up. Evan smelled the booze and vomit on him from ten feet away. Only in Maine would you ever see a bum driving around in a Forester—or a welfare family packed into an old Cadillac. What was all over this guy's arms and face? When the man got closer, Evan saw his face was busted up and bloody. The guy mumbled something Evan couldn't make out.

Evan said, "You okay, man? Looks like you need an ambulance."

"Mmmfffrrr." The guy raised his hand, pointed something shiny at Evan. Jesus, it was a gun. Evan dropped the paper, put up his hands. The bum smiled, his swollen lips split open and raw. He stepped right up and shoved the muzzle under Evan's nose.

56

In the dream, Joey saved Grace. He killed Nick the Brick and Weasel Face Paul with ice-cold moves that nobody could do outside a John Woo flick. Then he was in Brooklyn, walking through the coffee shop with a gun in each hand. The customers were all wiseguys. Joey shot them down. He went upstairs, killed Carl and Mikey, and even old Jimmy Petucci.

They all deserved death.

They all got it.

He awakened in Evan Barker's guest bedroom, with his head throbbing from too much vodka. Joey lay there under the sheet, watching the shadows diminish as the early rays of sunlight made their slow way across the room. He lay there, saw Grace as Nick dragged her out of Whitey's and into the waiting van, saw confusion and betrayal in her eyes. Grace had seemed to know that, whatever was happening, it was all because of Joey.

And it was his fault, wasn't it? There was always somebody willing to make a buck by dropping a dime and it didn't matter who else got hurt. Joey knew that better than anyone. How many times had informants led him to some poor dumb fuck the Petuccis wanted whacked? The informant called a guy who knew a guy; that guy called a guy who knew a guy high up in the Petucci organization; *that* guy talked to Carl or Mikey; they called Joey, and the poor dumb fuck in question was as good as dead. So Joey should've known better than to try and settle down, to get comfortable, to make friends.

What was the last thing he and Grace talked about? His drinking? Hiring new wait staff? Jesus, the trivial shit that makes up so much of our daily lives. Joey stared at the ceiling. He saw himself cleaning up the scene at Whitey's: locking the door, rolling Weasel Face into a couple of black trash bags he'd duct-taped together; mopping up the blood, brains and little shards of bone; picking up the shells ejected from Paul's pistol, shoving them in another bag with the bloody cleaning rags; putting a CLOSED UNTIL FURTHER NOTICE sign in the window; bringing his car around through the alley; carrying out the body and putting it in the trunk. Then Joey drove to an abandoned factory out by the rail yard, where Petucci's man went into a Dumpster. The bag with the rags, the clean-wiped gun and shell casings went into a trash can outside a Pizza Hut a few miles away.

This business with Barker should've been over and done with by now. All Joey had to do was get the tape, kill Barker and get Grace. That was the plan. It should have worked. But here he was, spending the weekend as Barker's "guest," having already promised to let Barker live and help him go on the run. And last night, he'd been ready to jump in the sack with a cop. Christ.

First thing tomorrow morning, he'd take Barker to the credit union to get the video. Then he could call Carl, tell him he had it, that Barker was dead. They'd set up an exchange. Of course, Carl would probably try fucking him over. Joey's knowledge of the tape meant he had to die. One way or another, Carl needed to have him killed. The best Joey hoped for now was to make sure Grace was released and on her way to someplace safe. Maybe he could take out Nick and Carl before they finished him off.

Floorboards creaked in the hall. It sounded like Barker coming down the stairs and trying to do it quietly. What the fuck was he doing up so early on a Sunday? Joey sat up, took his .38 from the drawer in the bedside table. Then he eased out of bed and crossed the room. He opened the door a crack, peered out.

Barker stood by the front door with his back to Joey. He pulled a set of keys out of the bowl that stood on a table next to the front door.

"The fuck are you going?"

Barker stopped, said, "I couldn't sleep. I'm just going down the driveway to grab the paper. You staying up? I'll put on some coffee and fry some eggs. There might be some bacon in the fridge, too." He looked at Joey's gun like he was trying too hard not to look at it.

Joey took the car keys away from him and went back to the bedroom. Whatever Barker had been up to, it was nothing to do with breakfast. He was still a sneaky little bastard, even after Joey promised not to kill him. Joey slipped the gun into the drawer, got into bed.

He thought about Wanda again, wished all the lies he'd told were true. There was something in the way she looked at him, like she knew it was all bullshit. She was interested in him, too. It might be good to stay in Wesserunsett a while, get to know the lady better. But that was fantasy. It could never happen, not unless Joey wanted Wanda to get murdered by the next scumbag to come after him.

Joey jumped out of bed, scrabbling for his gun again. He was halfway to the front door, moving on instinct alone, before his mind registered the noise from the front yard as a gunshot.

57

Wanda lay on the couch, thinking about getting up to pee. She had to go badly, but she was finally comfortable after a long night. The sirens had kept her awake, made her wonder what was going on. It wasn't her problem or her business, though. Ed had suspended her. Her cell phone never rang, so Ed didn't seem to need her for this emergency, whatever it might be.

She finally decided to get up and use the bathroom when she heard the shot. It sounded like a big handgun. Wanda sat there in her T-shirt and panties, unsure of her own ears for a moment. Then Joe ran past the living room door in his boxers, a gun in his hand. Wanda heard the front door open. Standing made her head ache. The screen door banged shut as Wanda crossed the hall to search through one of her suitcases. There it was, her Glock. She checked the magazine, thumbed off the safety.

Crouching, Wanda looked out the window at the front yard. Joe stood barefoot in the damp grass, holding his pistol on someone Wanda couldn't see because that damn lilac bush blocked her view. An SUV she didn't recognize was parked near the end of the driveway.

"Shit." Wanda ran through to the kitchen and out the back door, digging her underwear out of her crack. She made her away around the north end of the house only to fall down in the slick grass, nearly smashing her head against the oil barrel. When she got up, her butt and left side were soaked. The fall didn't do much for her headache, either. Wanda went a little further and knelt down so that she was in a good shooting position well behind Joe, off to his right. From this angle, she saw a fucked-up looking man standing next to the passenger side of the strange vehicle. The guy had a huge gun pointed at Joe. A body lay at his feet. Evan?

She heard Joe say, "I'm not telling you again."

The other guy grunted something.

Wanda squinted. Was that Charlie Hagopian? Jesus, he was a mess: covered in blood, face looking like a smashed pumpkin. So who did the red Subaru belong to, and where was Earl Coro? Charlie never went anywhere without him.

Hag kicked the body. He said, "Hmbnnd."

Husband? Was he trying to say husband?

"Oh my fucking God," Wanda said. She flashed back to last night at The Vault and her mouth went dry. It took her a moment to work up enough saliva to shout Charlie's name.

He turned his head just enough to see her there while keeping Joe in sight. He said, "Mnnee."

Money? How the hell did Charlie find her here anyway? She'd given him a made-up address, for Christ's sake. Wanda said, "Put down the gun and let's talk."

Hag fired at Joe, swung the gun around toward Wanda.

Wanda squeezed off four quick shots, slamming Hag back against the Forester's front fender. He rolled over and half-slid, half-fell off the hood.

Arms locked, pistol held out in front of her, Wanda approached Hag. She kicked his gun away. It was even bigger than those hand cannons Dirty Harry used to carry in the movies. Hag lay still, but Wanda squatted to check his pulse. Nothing. He'd taken all four rounds in the chest. Evan was dead, too. Hag had shot him in the face and blown away the whole back of his head.

"Don't worry about me or anything," Joey said. He was on the grass, trying to sit up while holding his right side. Wanda saw blood between his fingers. She ran to him, forced his hand away from the wound. A red furrow ran across his ribcage.

Wanda said, "Either your reflexes are good, or Charlie was a lousy shot."

"I don't think he was a lefty. He held the gun all wrong, but his right hand's broken."

"It's just a graze," Wanda said. "They'll clean it up in the ER and give you something for the pain. Smile, painkillers are fun."

Joey stood, said, "I gotta get out of here."

"Uh-uh. You can't leave a murder scene. I have to call this in." Wanda walked over the SUV, took a look inside. No sign of Coro. Weird. She wanted to open the glove compartment and check the registration. Without gloves, she'd only risk contaminating the evidence. Wanda turned back to Joe, said, "Come on, let's get you inside and I'll call Ed Gauthier."

Joe was already on his feet, though. He pointed his gun at Wanda.

Wanda held her own weapon at her side. Could she raise it before Joe fired? She said, "What's this about?"

"Drop the gun."

"Or what? You'll shoot me?" Wanda kept a tight grip on the Glock. It helped her focus and keep her voice from sounding shaky.

"Yeah."

Wanda said, "We're standing next to the road, Joe. A car could come by any minute, and you've got two bodies lying here. Gonna make me the third? Whatever you have planned, it's already fucked."

"Oh, you have no idea how far beyond fucked I am."

"So tell me, then."

Joe scowled. He looked at Evan, then at Hag. "You knew that guy. Who was he?"

"Charlie Hagopian," Wanda said. "The loser I told you about last night, the one who tried to get me to hire him as a hit man? That's him right there."

"You hired him to kill Barker."

Wanda laughed.

Joe said, "Was it because of the pictures or something else?"

God, this guy was nuts. As if Wanda would want Evan murdered over some beaver shots. She said, "I wouldn't pay Charlie to mow my lawn, let alone kill anyone. You need to put the gun down and step back."

Joe glanced up the road. He said, "We're wasting time. Drop your weapon and get these assholes into the vehicle. We'll hide it in the barn."

Enough of this crazy shit. Wanda squatted, laying her Glock on the driveway gravel. She stood slowly. If she played along with Joe, made a grab for Hag's gun while she was moving the bodies, maybe she could take him down that way.

Joe approached, holding his revolver at waist level. It looked like a .38 special. Wanda backed away. Keeping the .38 pointed at her, Joe crouched to pick up Wanda's Glock. Just when Wanda thought the situation couldn't get any weirder, Joe walked over to Evan and started kicking the corpse.

"You fuck, you stupid fuck." Joe kicked and cursed until he stubbed his toe on a rock. He limped around in a circle. Fuckfuckfuckfuckfuckfuck."

It couldn't be this easy, could it? Wanda stuck out her foot. Joe stumbled, his arms pinwheeling with the pistol still in his hands, and fell. Wanda scooped up Hag's hand cannon. Christ, what was that sticky stuff all over the butt? Joe rolled onto his side, scrambling to get his weapons up. Before he got the chance, Wanda lunged on him. She drove her knee into his kidney, snuggled the barrel of the .44 right up behind his earlobe. "You know what to do now, Joe."

Joe let go of the pistols, and Wanda tossed them aside with her free hand. She sat there on his hip, waiting for her heartbeat to even out. At least the adrenaline rush had gotten rid of her hangover. Wanda looked down at the graze along Joe's rib. It had stopped bleeding, but he'd have a scar to show for it. She noticed a scar from what must have been a similar wound across the outside his left bicep.

"How many times have you been shot at, Joe?"

Joe spat out gravel, said, "A few. You?"

"This was my first," Wanda said. "Not sure it counts, though. Neither one of you got a chance to squeeze the trigger." She picked wet grass off her thigh, realized she was still only half-dressed. McKinney would have a field day with that: Wanda wearing her lacy panties, sitting on a perp in boxers.

"Listen, Wanda. You're making a big mistake. If I don't get the hell out of here, an innocent woman is going to be murdered."

"Nice try."

Joe raised his head, craned around to look Wanda in the eye. He said, "I'm serious. That's the reason I came up here. Barker and I weren't old high school buddies. I never even met him before yesterday morning."

"So why are you here?"

"I was supposed to kill him."

"Oh yeah?"

Joey glanced down the road. "Of course, you could keep me here until your boss shows up, but I'd have to tell him about you hiring that dipshit to whack your husband. Even if it was only a joke, how's it going to look?"

Wanda said, "You've got my attention. Just make it quick."

58

Joey told Wanda everything, the short version anyway. He had to. There hadn't been time to call Grace's apartment and make sure Nick kept up his end of the deal—and it might still be too early for that anyway, depending on flight times out of JFK. Besides, for all Joey knew, Grace could still be in Carl's basement. Joey needed proof. To get that proof, he needed time.

So he had to confide in Wanda. Joey left out most of his past involvement with the Petucci family, especially how they called him Joey Kotex. Much of the talk was about how Grace and Sam had saved Joey from himself, given him a purpose and people to care about for the first time in years. He told her about the porn movie that had been the key to Barker's blackmail scheme, how the little shit testified against Mikey P. and went into witness protection when that failed. When he mentioned the videotape in Barker's safe-deposit box, Wanda started laughing. She stood up then.

"What's so funny?" Joey rose, brushing bits of gravel and dirt off his chest.

Wanda said, "Evan fucked you over. The Wesserunsett Credit Union doesn't have any safe-deposit boxes. It's just a dinky little place."

Joey felt like he'd just been kicked in the balls. "Oh, Jesus."

"Let's get my boss out here. Tell him what's going on, and he can get in touch with the FBI. They'll take down Petucci.

Kidnapping, solicitation to murder? He's going away for a long time."

Was she nuts or naïve? Joey said, "It doesn't work that way. They need a warrant, but they'll waste a lot of time questioning me first. By then, Carl will know the deal went south and he'll get rid of Grace. If I can make him think I have the tape, I'll have a chance to save Grace."

"The only thing you'll manage to do is get yourself killed."

"So?"

Wanda looked up and down the road. She said, "Get your stuff and get out of here. We never saw each other. Hear me? Never."

Joey nodded and started toward the house.

Wanda grabbed him by the arm, pointed at the .38 lying in the driveway. "You might need that."

Joey pulled on an Alligator Records T-shirt and a pair of jeans, stepped into his sneakers, grabbed his duffel bag. What he needed was time to clean the place, wipe away his fingerprints, erase as many traces of his presence in Barker's house as possible. That wasn't going to happen. He knew Wanda would make the call to her boss right away. She had to cover own ass, too. While he was wiping down the kitchen, Joey saw a small corkboard on the wall above the phone. Wanda's cell number was there with some others on an index card. Joey committed it to memory.

He heard the screen door bang shut. When Joey walked out of the bedroom, Wanda was standing in the hall with a cell phone held to her ear. She raised her eyebrows at Joey and nodded toward the door. Joey touched Wanda's arm lightly as he passed. *Thank you* would've sounded lame. She smiled at Joey, then he was outside and running to the Corolla.

The thing he needed most was a place to clean up and wait until it was time to call Carl. Joey hadn't checked out of his room at the Riverside Motel, just in case. He'd even mussed up the bed when he and Barker went there to pick up Joey's bag yesterday. The housekeeping staff would think he'd spent the night in the room. Joey drove along the road toward Wesserunsett, keeping to the speed limit. He was just another tourist out for a Sunday drive.

After he'd gone a couple of miles, he saw flashing blue lights up ahead. A pair of Wesserunsett police cruisers whipped by, doing about ninety. The cops didn't even glance at Joey.

59

"If this ain't a clusterfuck of biblical proportions," Ed Gauthier said. "I don't what is."

Wanda handed him a cup of coffee, passed the sugar bowl. They sat across from each other at the work island in Evan Barker's kitchen. It was ten-forty in the morning, and Ed's uniform looked like he'd slept in it. Wanda knew he hadn't gotten any sleep, what with the manhunt for Charlie Hagopian. That was what all the sirens had been about last night. She got all the gory details not long after Ed and Big Bill showed up.

The state police detectives had questioned Wanda for over two hours. She kept the story simple: She'd run into Hagopian at The Vault last night and he'd hit on her; she turned him down, went back to her boyfriend's house; she didn't wake up until she heard the gunshot that killed Evan; then she used her Glock—her personal handgun, not department issue—to shoot Hagopian, but only after he fired on her. So what it boiled down to was that Wanda had spurned Hagopian's advances and he came here to punish her as part of his bloody rampage. The mobile crime lab guys did their thing, too. Wanda's Glock was tagged, bagged and on its way to Augusta. Everyone seemed satisfied.

For the time being, anyway.

Wanda sipped her coffee. "Long night," she said.

"I could've used you, Wanda. You wouldn't believe what the

Bouchard house looks like. Stony and one of his employees both gunned down. Arlene and the kids spent the night at her mother's place, but they're in a .hell of a state now. Thank Christ they weren't home when that fuckin' psycho showed up."

"Why the Bouchards?"

Ed shrugged, said, "I don't know. The state boys are looking for some kind of connection. We'll have to wait and see what they dig up. It also looks like Hagopian vandalized the Pentecostal church this morning, though nobody can figure why. We lifted some prints. No doubt they'll match the ones he left in Stony's house and Tom Moody's vehicle."

Wanda blew on her coffee. "And Earl Coro's dead, too?" That news was almost enough to make Wanda start going to church again. With Coro out of the picture, there was no one left to say that Wanda had agreed to pay Charlie for killing her husband. She doubted Ed or anybody else would believe the whole thing had been a joke.

"Shot through a lung, no idea yet who did it. He was driving a truck that belonged to a guy named Gerry Taylor, who just happened to be lying in the back of that same truck with a great big bullet hole in him. Want to hear something funny?"

"Sure," Wanda said. "It's been a day filled with laughs so far."

"It seems the late Mr. Taylor worked as a mechanic at Lakeside Auto. Stony's car dealership."

"Oh my God."

"What now?"

Wanda said, "I just thought of something. You remember on Friday morning, I went to check out that noise complaint on Heron Lane?"

"I guess so."

"Well, the complainant was Larry Nichols, the guy whose trailer Coro plowed into. That's not the good part, though. As I was driving away, I saw Stony Bouchard's Caddy turn onto Heron Lane. He was in the passenger seat. The driver was

Willard Bailey—you remember, the fly fisherman who tried to swing on me—and they stopped at Earl Coro's trailer. Hagopian was married, but he lived with Coro."

"Jesus God." Gauthier slid off the stool and stretched. He crammed a piece of nicotine gum into his mouth. Chewed it for a few seconds and said, "So there's a strong possible connection. I'll tell the staties."

"You should pick up Willard Bailey, too."

"We've tried. Can't seem to find him just yet."

"I'd offer to help, but I'm suspended."

Ed gave her a sharp look. He said, "Don't start on me."

Wanda walked him to the door. Ed's cruiser was parked on the side of the road. A rectangle of crime scene tape strung from stakes blocked the end of the driveway and the area where Evan had been murdered.

Ed paused on the bottom step. Without looking at Wanda, he said, "I shouldn't have told you as much as I did just now, in case you're mixed up in it somehow. Which I doubt, or I wouldn't have said a goddamn thing. But this conversation was just between you and me."

As soon as he left, Wanda took a long, hot shower. She told herself she wouldn't cry for Evan. The tears came anyway, but Wanda didn't know if they were for Evan or Joe's friend or even herself. The water washed them away regardless.

60

Before going to the motel, Joey stopped at the Walmart in Skowhegan. He bought a first-aid kit, a package of safety razor blades and a new track phone. His stomach rumbled as he paid for them. A quick trip through the McDonald's drive-thru took care of that. He made it back to the motel a little after 9 a.m.

Joey let himself into the room. He hung the DO NOT DISTURB tag on the doorknob and locked himself in.

The bathroom fluorescents made the wound look worse than it felt. The bleeding had already stopped. The skin burned, but Wanda had been right. It wasn't too bad. He washed the whole area with soap and water, threw the blood-stained washcloth in the trash. Later on, he would bury it beneath wads of tissue. Joey smeared on antibiotic ointment from a small tube. Two squares of gauze and four strips of surgical tape covered everything. It wasn't exactly duct tape and a maxi pad, but it would do.

His side ached. The bottle of ibuprofen he'd bought when he first arrived in Wesserunsett lay on the bedside table. Joey swallowed four of the caplets with a glassful of Skowhegan's nasty water before activating his new phone and calling Nick Bennato. There was no answer. Joey tried the number three more times before giving up. Was Nick's phone switched off? Was he with Carl and unable to talk right now? Or was he just taking a dump. Joey would try calling him again later.

He called Grace's apartment. Her answering machine picked up. Joey hung up without saying anything. She might be on her way home.

But she might not.

For now, he'd stick to the plan.

Joey plugged in his laptop and booted it up. He started a search for airline tickets to New York. Carl had specified that Joey should fly back. There wasn't enough time to make the trip by car anyway.

The best thing Joey could do was to tell Carl that he'd gotten the tape and whacked Barker. Sooner or later, the authorities would discover that Barker was really a federal witness who'd slipped his leash. The story would make news reports all across the country. Joey needed to get to Carl before those details came out.

He activated the phone and called the number Carl Petucci gave him. He went through the script with the person who answered, a man this time. Joey pictured Carl grinning as he and Nick drove around in search of a pay phone blocks away from the house. What a fucked-up way to live, even if it had all seemed normal to him just a few years ago.

While Joey waited for the callback, he filled out an online reservation for a 5 p.m. flight to Newark out of the Portland Jetport. Car doors slammed outside. Joey left his seat to peek out through a gap in the curtains. Kids ran up and down the sidewalk while their parents yelled; families packing up to get a little further along the road to wherever it was they were headed. How did they do it? Just go about their lives like that? Joey had given it a shot. The days in Chicago had been the best of his life, but he'd always felt like the imposter he was.

The track phone rang. Joey pressed the talk button, said, "Yeah?"

"That you?" Carl sounded surprised.

"Who else would it be?"

Carl chuckled. "I didn't expect to hear from you 'til tomorrow, that's all."

"Yeah, well I finished up early."

"How'd you manage that?"

Joey sat down again. He said, "I found out our boy was lying."

"So it's it done, then?"

"That's what I said."

"And you got the thing?"

"I do."

Carl laughed, said. "Well, I can't wait to see you."

"How's my lady?"

"Fine."

"Yeah?"

"Yeah. We just had brunch together."

"Okay, then. I'm coming in by train at seven-thirty-nine tonight." According to their code, that meant Joey's flight to Newark was scheduled to land at six-thirty-nine. Carl might have made a good spy.

Joey hung up. He had a few more things to do before catching a little rest. He dug the C-major harmonica and his Leatherman tool out of the duffel bag. The Leatherman had a couple of small Phillips screwdriver attachments. The smallest fit the head of the screws fastening the cover plate to his harmonica. Joey loosened one of the screws just enough to ease the cover plate away from the reeds. Then he slid a razor blade between the cover plate and the body of the harmonica. He moved the blade back and forth until there was just a slight edge sticking out over the side of the instrument. Joey screwed the cover plate back on tight.

Holding up the harmonica, he could barely see the edge of the blade. Joey pressed it against the corner of the table. The blade stayed in place, making a small slice in the table's veneer. He got up and found a wrinkled Hawaiian shirt in his bag, slipped it on and dropped the harp in the pocket, blade-end first. Joey tried it three more times. It didn't cut him.

Could he risk trying to get it through airport security? If the TAS guys caught him with it at the gate, the whole deal was fucked. He'd wind up in a holding cell and Grace would go into a landfill somewhere. There was nothing to do but put it with the other harmonicas in his carry-on bag. The only luggage he had was the duffel and the laptop. Once the wiseguys picked him up at the Newark airport, Joey could get out the C-major and blow a few careful notes. The greaseballs would complain and tell him to put it away. No problem. Into his shirt pocket.

The gun and the money were his other main concern. He could dump the .38 before leaving Skowhegan. But there was more than forty large in cash packed in among Joey's clothes. It was the five thousand Carl had paid him plus what Joey had pulled from his bank accounts in the city, along with the twelve hundred he took from Fedoseev. He'd paid Shelly seven grand for the Corolla. That and incidental expenses left him with almost thirty-nine thousand dollars. When he'd still held out a small hope of living through all this, Joey thought of it as his escape money. His and Grace's. But no way would that get through the airport X-ray machines without raising a lot of questions.

Okay. So he needed to check the duffel bag as luggage and get something else for carry-on; a backpack, maybe. Shove in a few clothes, some CDs and the harmonicas. No, that was stupid. Whoever Carl sent to meet Joey would never let him wait around to claim baggage. The money would be there, going round and round on the carousel until somebody stole it or reported it as lost luggage.

Joey picked up one of the bundles of money, snapped the band. He stuffed eight hundred dollars in his wallet. That was more than he'd need to get through the next few hours. He stacked the rest of the bundles on the bureau. Thirty-eight thousand, give or take a few hundred. Joey's first thought was to box it up and ship it UPS to Sam. But even without Joey's name on it, Sam would guess the money's provenance and have nothing to do with it. Besides, Grace had smartly invested the old bluesman's money over the years, and he was well-provided-for in his retirement. And Grace would never touch Joey's money either, not now.

So, what to do with the cash?

Joey called. While it rang, he wondered where she was at that moment. Barker's house? An interrogation room? Getting the hell out of town?

She answered. "Hello?"

"Are you alone?"

"Yeah. I thought you'd be long gone by now."

"I will be, but I want to do something for you."

Wanda snorted. "What's that?"

"You know the Riverside Motel in Skowhegan?"

"Yeah."

"Come to room 210 this afternoon at two. I won't be here, but I'll leave the key in the planter outside the door. There's something I want you to have. I've got no use for it anymore. Maybe it can help you a little."

"How do I know this isn't a set-up?"

"Think about it." Joey ended the call. If she trusted him, Wanda would come and find the money waiting for her. If not, the maid was going to find herself with one hell of a tip the next morning.

Joey napped for an hour, then took a shower and changed his bandage. The wound slowed him down, made him avoid using his left arm. It took him a while to put on jeans, his Doc Martens and the Hawaiian shirt he'd worn that first night in Wesserunsett. Once he was dressed, he sat on the bed to make some more phone calls.

Nick still wasn't answering.

All Joey got when he tried Grace again was her machine.

But when he called Sam's number, the bluesman picked up on the first ring, said, "Grace?"

"No, it's me."

"Where's my girl? You told me you'd get her back."

Joey said, "It's happening tonight, Sam. I promise."

"Your promise ain't worth a damn thing to me anymore, boy. If I don't hear from Grace by midnight, if I don't hear right from her own mouth that she's okay and on her way home, I'm going to the cops."

"Sam…"

"What's this mafia dude's name?"

"You're better off not knowing right now."

"Don't matter if you tell me or not," Sam said. "All I got to do is give the cops your name, and I'll bet they can work backwards from there."

"I'll get her out of there."

"You can go to hell."

"Sam, listen…"

But Sam had already hung up.

Joey's eyes burned. He hadn't cried since his father's funeral a decade earlier. After their first meeting at the Meredith, Sam had become more like a father to him than his real dad. Joey cleared his throat, started packing.

Grace wasn't at her place and Sam hadn't seen or heard from her. Calling her father was the first thing she'd have done upon her release. That meant Nick had either gotten caught or he'd changed his mind about the whole thing. Maybe his hatred of Joey was enough to override his fear of what Joey could tell Carl.

It was almost time to leave. Joey still had to find an old VHS tape somewhere, maybe at a flea market or yard sale on the way to Portland. It seemed like you couldn't go more than half a mile in this state without finding someone trying to sell their old junk on the side of the road.

61

They were waiting for Joey when he left the terminal, three of Carl Petucci's pet assholes. One of them was a little guy, just about five-five and chewing a piece of gum like it had wronged him somehow. The shrimp wore a leather jacket and a Yankees cap pulled low, kept his hands in the jacket pockets. The second guy was closer to Joey's size, decked out in one of those nylon track suits the greaseballs loved. Joey didn't see the telltale bulge of a gun, but there was probably one strapped to the small of his back. And Nick the Brick stood behind the first two, wearing a light blue double-breasted suit, a muted pink shirt with the two top buttons undone, and a shit-eating grin.

Joey looked Nick up and down, said, "What, you couldn't be bothered to put on a tie? I'm hurt."

Nick sneered. He gave the other two a nod. Pee Wee grabbed Joey's backpack and computer bag. With him on the left and Track Suit on the right, they ushered Joey through the crowd into a men's room. Nick followed them.

The men's room was all white tiles and shined chrome. Joey's minders pushed him into a handicapped stall at the far end. Nick stepped inside and closed the door.

"People are gonna get the wrong idea," Joey said.

Track Suit spun Joey around, shoved him face-first against the wall, started frisking him. When he finished, he stepped back and said, "Clean."

Joey straightened his shirt. He turned around, said, "It's hard to get on and off a plane with a weapon these days."

"Checkin' you for a wire, too, smartass," Pee Wee said. He had unzipped Joey's backpack and dumped everything on the floor: clothes, CDs, harmonicas and a VHS tape.

Joey had stopped at four different yard sales between Skowhegan and the I-95 onramp outside Waterville. At the last yard sale, Joey found a box full of old Memorex videotapes on which someone had recorded movies and TV shows. Joey paid fifty cents for a tape marked *Fresh Prince* and peeled off the label before continuing on his way to the airport.

Pee Wee held the bag upside down, shook it. He opened the laptop bag, searched all the pockets and shook the computer. "Nothing else," he said.

Nick stepped on *Muddy Waters at Newport*, crunching the jewel box under a polished loafer. "The boss said to make sure he brought a videotape. Just grab it and leave the rest of that shit here. He ain't gonna need it. Better bring the computer too, so we can check the files."

"I want my harps." Joey bent over to gather up the harmonicas.

Track Suit kneed Joey in the side, nailed him right where Charlie Hagopian's .44 slug had slid along his ribs. Fire flashed across Joey's torso, forced him to take a sharp breath. Track Suit giggled and drew back his foot for a real kick.

Nick grabbed Track Suit's arm. He said, "Not here, Gino."

Joey stood and put the C-major harmonica in his shirt pocket. "I'll just take the one, then. Maybe I can play you guys a song on the ride to Carl's."

Gino said, "Start blowing that thing in the car and you'll need a proctologist next time you wanna play it."

They walked out the same way they had come in, with Nick's buddies clinging to Joey like jealous lovers. Ten minutes later, as they made their way through the parking garage, Nick said, "You guys leave Joey here with me and go make sure everything's clear."

Pee Wee looked back at Nick, said, "Huh?"

"Just fucking do what I tell you."

Gino and the runt walked over to a Lincoln Town Car like the one Joey had ditched in Connecticut.

"I tried to call you, Nick. Several times. How come you never answered?"

Nick stood close enough to whisper in Joey's ear. He said, "I couldn't get anyplace private enough to talk."

"I tried to call Grace, too. She wasn't home and her father hasn't seen her. I warned you not to fuck with me."

"Maybe I should kill you right here. Tell Mr. Petucci you made a run for it."

Joey shook his head. "Carl knows me better than that. You need to work with me if you want to live. It's that simple."

"Yeah? This morning I got word Vassily Fedoseev was found face down under a pier. Somebody worked him over good before giving him two in the hat."

"His cousin Sergei must've done it. Little Vasya made the family look bad."

"No, you made them look bad, asshole."

Joey said, "Only because you broke ranks and sent the prick after me. I'm sure Vassily and Sergei had a lot to talk about. And you can bet all the money you've skimmed off Carl that both our names came up in the conversation. So you gonna help me out, or what? Get Grace away from Carl, put her on a plane to Chicago, I'll keep my mouth shut about you and the Russians and John Florio. Same deal I offered you last night."

"All right."

Pee Wee and Gino came back. "Looks, uh, y'know, clear," Pee Wee said.

Nick gave Joey a shove. "Just get him to the fuckin' car."

They crammed Joey into the backseat of the Lincoln Town

Car. Gino slid in next to him. Pee Wee drove and Nick rode shotgun.

His pants crinkling and hissing, Gino turned sideways just enough to glare at Joey.

Joey let it go for a couple of miles, then said, "Don't try so hard."

"Fuck you."

Pee Wee wheezed halfway to Brooklyn. He only stopped when Nick threatened to shoot him.

The lights were out at Java 'n' Juice. A sign in the window read CLOSED FOR RENNOVATION. Nick unlocked the back door and led Joey and the others through the kitchen and out to the seating area. Sally Manfredo waited for them at the stairwell door. He held it open and followed them through. As the door banged shut behind him, Sal said, "What's the matter, Joey? You run out of smart remarks?"

"No, it's just that your mother sucked me off in the car and now I'm tired."

Gino drove a fist into Joey's right kidney. Joey's legs buckled. He bit back a grunt, forced himself to stay upright.

"Mr. Petucci's waiting," Nick said.

They left Sally Manfredo downstairs and walked up to the secretary's office. Her desk lamp was on, but there was no sign of her. Joey grinned. Considering what Carl no doubt had planned, it was nice of him to let her have the evening off. Or maybe she was just on a smoke break. Nick gave Carl's door a couple of sharp raps.

"Get the fuck in here," Carl said.

They did as they were told. Nick crossed the room, walked around the desk to stand next to Carl. Gino shoved Joey to the middle of the floor. He stood on Joey's right. Pee Wee took the left.

Joey scanned the room. He noticed a nasty-looking burn on

Carl's cheek, decided against mentioning it yet. There was a TV/VCR combo unit on Carl's desk. The five men were the only people in the office. Joey said, "I don't see Grace."

Carl ignored him. He swiveled his chair around, said, "He give you the tape, Nick?"

Joey rolled his eyes. Nick had the fucking tape right there in his hand.

Nick said, "Right here, Mr. Petucci." He gave Carl the cassette.

"Is this the only copy, Joey?"

"Yeah."

"You know that for sure?"

Joey said, "I blew off both of Barker's kneecaps and put a knife to his sack. If he had anything else to bargain with, he'd have used it."

Carl sat back in the chair, holding his belly. He grinned. "That's the old Joey Kotex. It's good to see him one last time."

"Thought you were gonna let Grace and me go," Joey said. "That was the deal."

"You knew I was feeding you a line. I saw it in your eyes at the time, so let's not pretend anymore. Okay?"

Joey shrugged. He said, "You could at least let me see her first. Let me tell her I'm sorry she got caught up in this shit."

Carl pointed at Joey. Even his fingers were fat. He said, "You'll join her soon enough. She's a little worse for wear, but we'll fix that once we get where we're going."

Heat rose up Joey's face and neck. He felt the weight of the razor-fitted harmonica in his shirt pocket. "Just let her go, Carl. You want me to beg, I'll do it."

Nick smiled.

Carl didn't say anything.

Joey pointed to the TV. "Aren't you going to watch that thing, make sure I'm not trying to fuck you over?"

Jowls shaking with laughter, Carl turned the set so its screen was facing only him. He said, "Even your balls ain't that big,

Joey." But he slid the tape anyway, fiddling with a tiny remote.

Joey looked at Carl. The kept pressing buttons on his remote. The VCR clicked and whined as he searched the video-cassette for his niece's big triple-X debut.

Finally, Carl turned the machine so everyone could see the screen, and turned up the volume. Will Smith was trying to talk his nerd of a cousin into going out to some club or concert.

"Aw, I love that show," Gino said.

Nick told him to shut up.

"The real tape's still out there, Carl," Joey said. "It's something to see, sweet little Angie Petucci getting fucked like a crack whore. Let me see you turn Grace loose right now, and I'll take you and Nick to it." He grinned, waiting.

Carl sat up straight, started sputtering.

Nick bent down. "You okay, Mr. Petucci?"

"I will be when you make this fucker sing," Carl said. "Tie him to a chair."

So much for bargaining. Joey lunged to his left, grabbed Pee Wee by the neck and pulled him close. The little guy was reaching inside his jacket. Joey pulled out the harmonica. He pressed the razor blade hard against the left side of Pee Wee's throat and cut as deeply as possible. Giving up on drawing his gun, Pee Wee clamped his hands over his bleeding throat and shrieked. The razor-rigged harp had slashed his jugular vein, but not the artery.

Joey dropped the Lee Oskar, slid his free hand inside Pee Wee's jacket.

Nick drew a big black automatic that he aimed at Joey.

"Don't fuckin' kill him," Carl said. "I need him alive."

Gino pivoted. He reached behind his back, whipped out a snub-nosed revolver. There were now two guns pointed at Joey, with Carl scrabbling for something in his desk drawer. That Beretta he'd pulled the other day, no doubt.

Joey's fingers wrapped around a pistol butt. He kept his grip on the back of Pee Wee's neck and pulled out the gun. It was a

.45 automatic. No time to rack the slide. Joey had to assume there was a round in the chamber. He swung Pee Wee toward the desk. Nick fired two shots, both tearing into the little guy.

Pee Wee screamed and jerked.

Still Joey held on.

Gino wasted half a second cocking the hammer of his revolver. Joey squeezed the .45's trigger three times, blowing the tubby bastard across the room. Gino crashed backwards through the window, pulling the heavy drapes down to the sidewalk with him. Somewhere in all that noise, Joey heard screams. From the street? From the café?

Nick crouched down next to Carl. He steadied his arm across the desk top, fired again. The first slug ripped through Pee Wee's head, plastering Joey with brains and bits of scalp. Something tore into Joey's belly. He felt a terrible burning before everything below his waist went cold and watery.

No. Not yet, goddamn it.

Joey fell to his knees. *Not yet.* He lifted the .45. Christ, it was heavy.

Carl had the Beretta out now. "I fucking told you not to kill him," he said.

Nick stood up, grinning, with his gun pointed at Joey. Before he could squeeze the trigger, Carl turned and shot Nick in the face. Nick went down, screeching and grabbing at his mouth. Joey lost sight of him behind that big desk.

Carl was panting. He swung his arm around to cover Joey. "Drop that gun right now."

The door crashed open behind Joey. Sal Manfredo said, "What the fuck?"

Carl glanced at Sally.

Joey got the .45 up, held it steady as he could while getting off shot after shot without aiming.

Carl took a round in the chest and another in the throat, dropped straight down onto his chair and sat there. He worked his mouth like had something important to say. Only a froth of blood came out.

Joey kept squeezing the trigger until he realized he was dry-firing because the gun was empty.

Somewhere behind him, Sal threw up on the floor. Joey ejected the clip, fidgeted it around a little before jacking it back in. He eased himself around to look at the last man standing.

Sally's cheap suit was spattered with puke. He had a pistol drawn, but he was bent over with both of his hands resting on his knees.

Joey pointed the empty .45 at him, said, "Drop it, Sally."

Dumb as Sal was, he didn't have to be told twice. His gun clattered against the floor.

"Kick it over here."

Sally obeyed.

Joey picked it up, dropped the .45. He smiled at Sal, said, "Thanks."

"Aw, man."

"Who else is here?" Joey coughed, spat out a wad of bloody phlegm.

"Nobody."

"Don't you fuckin' lie to me."

Sally shook his head, said, "I swear, Joey."

"Is Grace still in the basement?"

"Who?"

"My friend. They had her locked away down there."

"I don't know, Joey. They don't tell me shit like that." His hands shook. "They don't tell me nothin'."

"There's a key ring in Carl's pocket. Get it out and unlock the elevator."

Manfredo hustled across the room. When he reached the desk, Joey said, "Just the keys. If your hand so much as brushes a gun, I'll kill you."

Sally found the key ring. Holding it up, he said, "God man, half Nick's face is gone. We gotta do something for him."

"He couldn't keep his word, so fuck him. Let's go."

Sally had to help Joey up and into the elevator—with Joey's gun stuck in his side the whole time. They rode down to the basement.

Before the doors hissed shut behind them, Joey started calling for Grace. His voice cracked and he tasted blood, kept shouting anyway.

She didn't answer.

They moved along the hall, Joey with one arm across Manfredo's shoulders. Manfredo grunted with the effort of supporting most of Joey's weight, but he didn't complain. Even Sally wasn't that dumb.

They found Grace locked in a closet just a little way down the hall. She lay on a dirty cot with her hands bound behind her back. Her right eye was swollen shut, her neck and arms mottled with bruises. Dried blood covered her lips. She licked her lips and opened her mouth. "About damn time," she said.

Joey grinned and slumped against his reluctant helper.

Not strong enough to carry his full weight, Sal let him drop and then took a step back. "I didn't have nothing to do with this, Joey. Swear to God I never saw her before."

"Help her up," Joey said. "Get her hands free."

Sally didn't bother wiping his mouth. He said, "Those are sirens, Joey. Don't you hear 'em? We gotta get the fuck outta here."

"There's time enough," he told Manfredo.

When Grace was sitting up and rubbing her wrists where the rope had chafed them raw, Joey said, "Get lost, Sal."

Sal stared at Joey like he couldn't believe his own ears.

"I said go, shitbird."

Manfredo stood there for a second before turning and running for the stairs.

Now Joey heard the sirens, too.

Sirens.

Cops.

Paramedics.

People who would have questions Joey didn't want to answer.

Sitting propped against the wall, Joey looked down at his belly. It was going to take more than a maxi pad and some duct tape to patch that hole. He tried to laugh. Coughed blood instead.

The elevator door hissed open.

Arms pinwheeling like a character in a cartoon, Sally skidded to a stop. "Jesus," he said, but Joey couldn't see who was coming out of the elevator car. Cops, maybe? A gunshot echoed through the hall and Sally was spun around, bright arterial blood spraying from the side of his neck. The second bullet got him in the back, putting him down on the floor. Nick stood over the corpse.

Grace shrank back against the closet's back wall. Joey winked at her.

Nick's eyes were wild, like the eyes of an animal that knows it's about to die, but has determined to take its slayer with it. Half of Nick's lower jaw was a mess of shredded meat and shattered bone. He pointed his gun at Joey and began walking closer. With each step, blood dribbled down Nick's jacket and shirt.

Joey took careful aim. Why were his hands so steady?

A noise like crying came out of the hole in Nick's face. Maybe he was trying to get in one last *fuck you*. The pistol bucked in his hand and Joey felt the slug punch through his left side, felt all the breath rush out of his body.

"Sweet Jesus," Grace said.

Joey shot Nick through the heart this time, dropped him clean. Then his fingers went numb and he heard the .45 hit the floor.

The hallway stank of blood, of fear and vomit and death. Joey felt comfortable among those smells. They had followed him more than half his life. Carl's voice popped into Joey's head: *It's because you love killing, Joey. Tell me I'm wrong.*

The sirens were right outside. Joey thought he heard shouts on the floor above.

Grace was kneeling beside him, pressing at his wounds with a blanket she'd hauled off the cot. She said something, but Joey couldn't hear her words over the rushing in his ears.

A coughing fit wracked his body and Joey spat up more blood. Even if the paramedics got him to an emergency room and he survived the surgery, then what? Prison, for sure. It didn't matter that Mikey P. was locked up. Jimmy Petucci was still out there. The eldest Petucci brother was retired, but he had more than enough juice to guarantee Joey's stretch inside became a life sentence, a short and painful one. Sergei Fedoseev would want a piece of Joey, too. Why give any of those cocksuckers the satisfaction? Joey wished he still had Sally's pistol in his hand, wished he could press the barrel against his skull, just behind his earlobe. If he'd had the balls to off himself years ago, back in that shithole of a room at the Meredith, none of this would ever have happened.

Now Grace looked away, back toward the elevator and the stairs. Her lips formed words that might have been *hurry* or *hurry up.*

Joey tried to say Grace's name one last time, but he couldn't be sure any sound came out. There was too much blood in his mouth anyway.

EPILOGUE
THURSDAY, JUNE 17

Holding two bottles of Rolling Rock, Wanda leaned against the garage wall and watched her father work. Walter had an armchair up on a pair of padded sawhorses, removing tacks from the worn-out old upholstery with a claw tool and rubber mallet. The garage was Walter's furniture repair shop.

The door was up to let in fresh air and extra light. Even so, the garage smelled of varnish, wood glue and old cloth. Wanda closed her eyes and breathed it in. It was her father's smell.

Walter laid his tools on the bench, pushed his safety goggles up onto his forehead. He held out his hand for one of the beers, said, "I ought to put you to work, get you earning your keep."

"I'm not dressed for it. How about I supervise?" Wanda wore her favorite pair of shortalls over a green tank top. A pair of sandals was her only concession to the stray tacks and splinters along the garage floor.

Wanda heard a car pull into the driveway. Her Jeep and her father's pickup truck kept her from seeing who it was.

Limping toward the door, Walter said, "If it's another one of those goddamn scribblers, I'm gonna kick his ass." In the four days since the shootings, Wanda and her parents had been plagued by reporters. Not just the local TV and newspaper crowd, but *The Boston Globe*, *The New York Times*, CNN,

Fox News and MSNBC. When a man in a small Maine town goes on a killing spree, and one of his victims turns out to be a missing federal witness, the trip out to the middle of nowhere becomes worthwhile.

Wanda refused all interview requests. Some of the stories cast her as a hero cop who stopped a homicidal maniac in spite of being suspended. Still others focused on Jim and Laurie's allegations or raised questions about Wanda's involvement with Evan Barker, *aka* Todd Evans. Did she know the man was a pornographer who had ratted out his bosses in the mob? Was it true she'd just been contacted by *Penthouse* about doing a photo shoot? Was it more than just coincidence, her encounter with Charlie Hagopian less than an hour before he claimed his final victims? Had Wanda known that the man seen by several witnesses—including Officer William McKinney—in Barker's company, was in fact a New York organized crime associate who'd been missing for four years and presumed dead?

Oh, yes, that son of a bitch Joe turned out to have been serious about that whole hitman thing. The FBI spent all day Tuesday grilling Wanda about her encounter with Joe Carmichael, alias Joe Collins, alias Joey Connolly, alias Joey Kotex. Never formally charged with murder, Joe had been a "person of interest" in a dozen New York area homicides from the mid-1990s to 2005.

Wanda told them that she'd had lunch with Joe and Barker, but left because she was depressed about being suspended and wanted some time to herself. She didn't tell them about the photos. She didn't tell them what Joe had said about his friend Grace Turner. In Wanda's version of events, Joe spent Saturday alone in his motel room. The last time she'd seen or spoken to the guy had been Saturday afternoon. The agents seemed skeptical. Well, fuck them. They had no way of proving otherwise. Too bad the hitman had died after taking out Carl Petucci and at least three underlings. The Turner woman was alive and in protective custody. That bothered Wanda the most out of everything the feds told her: The one innocent person in the whole affair had to be locked away somewhere just to keep her safe.

Walter and June disconnected their telephone. They kept the curtains drawn against the reporters who camped out on their front lawn until Tuesday, when much of the national interest flagged. Even most of the local hacks had given up by Wednesday.

Now here it was Thursday, and they had another visitor.

"Morning," Ed Gauthier said as he walked up the drive between the Chevy pickup and the Jeep. He was in uniform. His cruiser sat idling behind the truck.

Wanda stopped just outside the garage.

Walter stood beside her, nodded at the chief. "Ed."

The two men shook hands.

Gauthier squinted, looked up at the late morning sky. "Hot enough for you yet? Weather guy on the TV said it might hit eighty-seven."

Walter said, "That's fine by me. Just so long as it don't turn muggy on us."

"I hear you."

The two men stood there eyeballing each other, Walter with one hand in his pocket, Ed with his hands clamped over the front of his gun belt.

Wanda sipped her beer. She said, "I'd offer you one, but it looks like you're on duty."

Ed cleared his throat. "I got some news for you, Wanda."

"It had better be good news," Walter said. "Like the kind where she gets her badge back plus a formal apology from you for ever believing Jim Philbrick's bullshit story."

"Well, that's more or less it, though I knew the allegations were all a lie. Jim dropped the charges against you, Wanda. Seems a lot of people are pissed at him; it's not good for business when his customers want to know how he could make such claims about a hero."

Wanda snorted, said, "I killed a guy. What's so fucking

heroic about that?"

"Now how about giving her back her badge?"

Ed scratched his belly. "I'm not so sure when you can come back to work, Wanda. Christ knows I need you, though. The AG's office is still looking into the shooting, but I wouldn't worry there. I can't remember the last time the state made a finding against any cop who had to use deadly force in the line of duty."

"Yeah? How about a cop who was way off-duty?"

"You're gonna be fine."

Wanda said, "Everybody still running around, trying to figure out Charlie's motive?"

"Oh, you know it. Got a ballistics report from the staties yesterday. They say Willard Bailey was killed with the same gun used in that double homicide out to St. Albans. Hagopian's prints were on the farmhouse doorknob as well as a fly rod hung up in a tree near Bailey's body. They took a statement this morning from some guy who says he was there when Hagopian shot Gerry Taylor. I haven't heard what that's all about yet. Either Stony or Moody fired the shot that killed Earl Coro. Arlene Bouchard's lawyered up and not saying anything yet. This clusterfuck's gonna get even more clustered, I expect."

Walter pulled a piece of lint from his pocket, flicked it toward the garage. He said, "Know something funny? I haven't heard anything like an apology yet."

Ed flushed.

Wanda said, "Never mind. I'm not coming back."

"No?" Ed stopped chewing his gum.

"My brother's been after me for years to move down to Boston. I guess it's about time I made a change. I'll send you my new address in case there are any more questions about Evan."

Walter patted Wanda on the shoulder. Though she'd been thinking about the move for days, she hadn't yet discussed it with her parents. Her dad's hand felt good on her shoulder and she reached up to hold it there.

Ed started back down the driveway. He stopped in front of his cruiser and looked back. "Nothing I can say to change your mind?"

Wanda shook her head. She waved to Ed as he backed his car out of the drive.

Her dad sipped at his beer. Neither one said anything for a long while. Then Walter let out a burp. He said, "You know your mother's going to have conniptions."

"She'll get over it."

"Yeah, she will."

Wanda watched the girls skipping rope in the neighbor's yard. She'd been like them once. It seemed a hell of a long time ago. Wanda's daughter could've grown up playing and laughing here; even little Cynthia's death felt like an old memory now. Wesserunsett was a good place to live, but it wasn't the only place. Maybe she would make a new life in Boston, maybe somewhere else. Money wasn't an immediate concern. Not anymore.

When Wanda had driven to Joe's motel room Sunday afternoon, she had no idea what to expect. A trap? Maybe Joe wanted to kill Wanda and eliminate any chance she might spill what she knew. She'd parked her Jeep outside his room and sat there a moment, her father's .30-06 rifle lying across the backseat just in case. But she went into the room; the key was right where Joey had said. The room was empty except for a plastic IGA bag on the bureau. Opening it, she found stacks of bundled cash—damn close to forty thousand dollars. The only other thing was a message on a sheet of notebook paper: *Put this to good use.*

And she would.

Wanda led her father back through the garage. She said, "Come on. Let me take you and Mom out to lunch. We can break the news over dessert."

ACKNOWLEDGMENTS

Several people have been crucial in the birth and strange, ongoing life of this book: Kelly Link, Scott Wolven, James Patrick Kelly, David Anthony Durham, Patricia O'Donnell, Jan Elizabeth Watson, and Michaela Roessner. Thanks also to Eric Campbell and Lance Wright at Down & Out Books for all their hard work.

Patrick Shawn Bagley's stories of rural mayhem have appeared in *Crimespree, The Iconoclast, Thrilling Detective, Great Jones Street,* and *Spinetingler Magazine,* as well as the Bleak House Books anthology *Uncage Me.* He was one of the founding editors of *The Lineup: Poems on Crime.* Bagley lives on a dead-end dirt road in a one-stoplight central Maine town, where he is writing a horror novel and a sequel to *Bitter Water Blues.* During the day, he works at a community supports program for adults with intellectual disabilities.

PatrickShawnBagley.blogspot.com

On the following pages are a few
more great titles from the
Down & Out Books publishing family.

For a complete list of books and to
sign up for our newsletter,
go to DownAndOutBooks.com.

Dangerous Boys
Greg F. Gifune

Down & Out Books
March 2018
978-1-946502-52-0

All they had was each other…and nothing to lose…

Part coming-of-age tale, part dark crime thriller, *Dangerous Boys* is the story of a group of young punks with nothing left to lose, fighting to find themselves, their futures, and a way out of the madness and darkness before it's too late.

Down on the Street
Alec Cizak

ABC Group Documentation,
an imprint of Down & Out Books
978-1-943402-88-5

What price can you put on a human life?

Times are tough. Cabbie Lester Banks can't pay his bills. His gorgeous young neighbor, Chelsea, is also one step from the streets. Lester makes a sordid business deal with her. Things turn out worse than he could ever have imagined.

Cleaning Up Finn
Sarah M. Chen

All Due Respect, an imprint of
Down & Out Books
978-1-946502-49-0

Life is a constant party for restaurant manager, Finn Roose. When he seduces an underage woman on one of his booze cruises and loses her—literally, it sets off a massive search involving the police, her parents, and a private investigator. Finn is an expert manipulator but his endless lies only tighten the screws on himself and his unsuspecting best friend. Finn scrambles to make things right which may be too much to ask from a guy who can't resist a hot babe and a stiff drink.

Les Cannibales
DeLeon DeMicoli

Shotgun Honey, an imprint of
Down & Out Books
978-1-943402-96-0

During a robbery, Blinky sees police activity down the street. His crew assumes cops have the art gallery surrounded, unaware of their true presence, which is responding to a car accident that has left one man dead. The thieves shoot at responding officers and take hostages. When Detective Reynolds arrives on the scene, he seeks to hunt down the thieves' true identities and work out a peaceful resolution before S.W.A.T moves in.

But when S.W.A.T teams get the "go-ahead" to overtake the gallery, it's dog-eat-dog as the gunmen plan their escape.